A DOG'S L▮▮▮▮▮S

DOGS OF WAR

EDITED BY DAVID DRAKE

FEATURING WORKS BY

HARRY HARRISON ✳ JOE HALDEMAN
RICHARD MATHESON
AND OTHERS

ASPECT®

WARNER BOOKS

An AOL Time Warner Company

WARNER BOOKS EDITION

Copyright © 2002 by David Drake and Tekno Books
All rights reserved. No part of this book may be reproduced in any form or by any electronic or mechanical means, including information storage and retrieval systems, without permission in writing from the publisher, except by a reviewer who may quote brief passages in a review.

"Or Battle's Sound" by Harry Harrison. Copyright © 1968 by Harry Harrison. First published in *Worlds of If Science Fiction Magazine*, October 1968. Reprinted by permission of the author.

"Liberty Port" by David Drake. Copyright © 1987 by David Drake. First published in *FreeLancers*. Reprinted by permission of the author.

Copyright information continued on page 303.

Aspect® name and logo are registered trademarks of Warner Books, Inc.

Cover design by Don Puckey / Shasti O'Leary
Cover illustration by Donato Giancolo
Book design by H & H Roberts Design

Warner Books, Inc.
1271 Avenue of the Americas
New York, NY 10020

Visit our Web site at www.twbookmark.com.

An AOL Time Warner Company

Printed in the United States of America

First Printing: January 2002

10 9 8 7 6 5 4 3 2

Contents

Introduction

Costs and Benefits

These are stories about wars which haven't happened, can't happen, and generally never could have happened. I've chosen them because they're good stories, and because they explore two questions which I wondered about before I was drafted to Viet Nam and which I've wondered about a great deal more in the years since:

1. How do you make a soldier? And
2. What do wars do to the people who fight them?

There's no single answer to either question, but the first one seems to boil down to two alternatives—you start with a natural soldier, a warrior if you will; or you take an ordinary man (or maybe woman; that wasn't common in the past for reasons involving muscle mass, but that's less a factor today), strip him of all civilized norms, and build him back in the form you want for the new task you've set him: killing other human beings.

Most people writing military SF focus on the first group, the warriors. Many species have certain members specialized for the group's defense. In social insects like ants and termites, the warriors are physically larger than the workers and may have jaws so hypertrophied that they can't even feed themselves. Likewise, male lions are twice the size of females, but don't hunt for themselves when they're living as members of a pack (or pride, if you prefer the collective noun that gained currency at the end of the 19th century). Physical variation isn't as important in the human species, but there's evidence that one or two percent of the male population is psychologically specialized for similar duties.

If all goes well, the warriors spend their entire lives doing nothing but eating the fruits of others' labor. Nice work if you can get it.

But if resources are limited, there's going to come a time when your colony or pack or tribe has something that another colony or pack or tribe wants. This is as true for developed nations of the 21st century as it was sixty millennia ago when humans hunted herds of bison with spears of flaked stone. When that time comes, you'd better hope your group has somebody walking the boundaries, watching the would-be interlopers; and needs must, closing with those interlopers in the willingness to kill or be killed for *your* sake.

Natural warriors are, as I said, a small minority of the population. The military leadership of developed nations has learned how to make passable substitutes by teaching perfectly ordinary men to kill. That's the easy part. The process nonetheless leaves a problem that governments rarely address, at least directly.

Despite most fiction and almost all TV and movies, the only people who can kill without compunction and remorse are sociopaths. It doesn't matter if the soldier kills in a good cause (all causes are good in the minds of those who decree them), if he saved his own life and those of his loved ones by killing, or if he returns to honor and glory among his fellow countrymen as a result of that killing: he's still paid a price, and he'll continue to pay, to a greater or lesser extent, for as long as he lives.

There are ways around the problem. Sometimes killing can be made impersonal, a matter of switches and icons rather than blood and screams. Even so, reality may intrude unexpectedly: the firestorms that devastated Tokyo during WW II lifted the smell of burning flesh up to the B-29s raining incendiary bombs from two miles high above the city.

The soldier at the sharp end doesn't have the option of pretending he's fighting map coordinates or phosphor dots, but he can withdraw into himself. His training has already started his process of desocialization, so it's a natural progression. He's no longer fully human—in fact, he more and more mimics a sociopath—but he can continue carrying out the tasks required of him for much longer than would otherwise be possible.

If the process goes on too long, he'll break nonetheless and become useless to his group, his society. That won't matter much to society. He'll have guarded the boundaries while he lasted, and society will by then have trained somebody else to take his place.

And it won't matter to him: there's no 'him' left, after all, in the sense of a human being with human responses.

Those who were close to him in the days when he was still human may regret what he's become; maybe they'll even be able to help him return to a greater or lesser extent. And the others whom society has sent down the same path and who've managed to come back—they'll care very much about the poor bastards who used to be men but are now locked in their own heads with no reality but their own hellish memories.

We may not be able to help, but we'll care.

—Dave Drake
david-drake.com

DOGS OF
WAR

Or Battle's Sound

★

Harry Harrison

I

Combatman Dom Priego, I shall kill you." Sergeant Toth shouted the words the length of the barracks compartment.

Dom, stretched out on his bunk and reading a book, raised startled eyes just as the Sergeant snapped his arm down, hurling a gleaming combat knife. Trained reflexes raised the book, and the knife thudded into it, penetrating the pages so that the point stopped a scant few inches from Dom's face.

"You stupid Hungarian ape!" he shouted. "Do you know what this book cost me? Do you know how old it is?"

"Do you know that you are still alive?" the Sergeant answered, a trace of a cold smile wrinkling the corners of his cat's eyes. He stalked down the gangway, like a predatory animal, and reached for the handle of the knife.

"No you don't," Dom said, snatching the book away. "You've done enough damage already." He put the book flat on the bunk and worked the knife carefully out of it—then threw it suddenly at the Sergeant's foot.

Sergeant Toth shifted his leg just enough so that the knife missed him and struck the plastic deck covering instead. "Temper, combatman," he said. "You should never lose your temper. That way you make mistakes, get killed." He bent and plucked out the shining blade and held it balanced in his fingertips. As he straightened up, there was a rustle as the other men in the barracks compartment shifted weight, ready to move, all eyes on him. He laughed.

"Now you're expecting it, so it's too easy for you." He slid the knife back into his boot sheath.

"You're a sadistic bowb," Dom said, smoothing down the cut in the book's cover. "Getting a great pleasure out of frightening other people."

"Maybe," Sergeant Toth said, undisturbed. He sat on the bunk across the aisle. "And maybe that's what they call the right man in the right job. And it doesn't matter anyway. I train you, keep you alert, on the jump. This keeps you alive. You should thank me for being such a good sadist."

"You can't sell me with that argument, Sergeant. You're the sort of individual this man wrote about, right here in this book that you did your best to destroy . . ."

"Not me. You put it in front of the knife. Just like I keep telling you pinkies. Save yourself. That's what counts. Use any trick. You only got one life, make it a long one."

"Right in here . . ."

"Pictures of girls?"

"No, Sergeant, words. Great words by a man you never heard of, by the name of Wilde."

"Sure. Plugger. Wyld, fleet heavyweight champion."

"No, Oscar Fingal O'Flahertie Wills Wilde. No relation to your pug—I hope. He writes, 'As long as war is regarded as wicked, it will always have its fascination. When it is looked upon as vulgar, it will cease to be popular.'"

Sergeant Toth's eyes narrowed in thought. "He makes it

sound simple. But it's not that way at all. There are other reasons for war."

"Such as what . . . ?"

The Sergeant opened his mouth to answer, but his voice was drowned in the wave of sound from the scramble alert. The high-pitched hooting blared in every compartment of the spacer and had its instant response. Men moved. Fast.

The ship's crew raced to their action stations. The men who had been asleep just an instant before were still blinking awake as they ran. They ran and stood, and before the alarm was through sounding the great spaceship was ready.

Not so the combatmen. Until ordered and dispatched, they were just cargo. They stood at the ready, a double row of silver-gray uniforms, down the center of the barracks compartment. Sergeant Toth was at the wall, his headset plugged into a phone extension there, listening attentively, nodding at an unheard voice. Every man's eyes were upon him as he spoke agreement, disconnected and turned slowly to face them. He savored the silent moment, then broke into the widest grin that any of them had ever seen on his normally expressionless face.

"This is it," the Sergeant said, and actually rubbed his hands together. "I can tell you now that the Edinburgers were expected and that our whole fleet is up in force. The scouts have detected them breaking out of jump space, and they should be here in about two hours. We're going out to meet them. This, you pinkie combat virgins, is it." A sound, like a low growl, rose from the assembled men, and the Sergeant's grin widened.

"That's the right spirit. Show some of it to the enemy." The grin vanished as quickly as it had come, and, cold-faced as always, he called the ranks to attention.

"Corporal Steres is in sick bay with the fever so we're one NCO short. When that alert sounded we went into combat condition. I may now make temporary field appointments. I do so. Combatman Priego, one pace forward." Dom snapped to attention and stepped out of rank.

"You're now in charge of the bomb squad. Do the right job and the CO will make it permanent. Corporal Priego, one step back and wait here. The rest of you to the ready room, double time—*march*."

Sergeant Toth stepped aside as the combatmen hurried from the compartment. When the last one had gone he pointed his finger sharply at Dom.

"Just one word. You're as good as any man here. Better than most. You're smart. But you think too much about things that don't matter. Stop thinking and start fighting, or you'll never get back to that university. Bowb up, and if the Edinburgers don't get you I will. You come back as a corporal or you don't come back at all. Understood?"

"Understood." Dom's face was as coldly expressionless as the Sergeant's.

"I'm just as good a combatman as you are, Sergeant. I'll do my job."

"Then do it—now *jump*."

Because of the delay, Dom was the last man to be suited up. The others were already doing their pressure checks with the armorers while he was still closing his seals. He did not let it disturb him or make him try to move faster. With slow deliberation, he counted off the check list as he sealed and locked.

Once all the pressure checks were in the green, Dom gave the armorers the thumbs-up okay and walked to the air lock. While the door closed behind him and the lock was pumped out, he checked all the telltales in his helmet. Oxygen, full. Power pack, full charge. Radio, one and one. Then the last of the air was gone, and the inner door opened soundlessly in the vacuum. He entered the armory.

The lights here were dimmer—and soon they would be turned off completely. Dom went to the rack with his equipment and began to buckle on the smaller items. Like all of the others on the bomb squad, his suit was lightly armored and he carried only the most essential weapons. The drillger went on his left thigh, just below his fingers, and the gropener in its holster on the outside of his right leg; this was his favorite weapon. The intelligence reports had stated that some of the Edinburgers still used fabric pressure suits, so lightning prods—usually considered obsolete—had been issued. He slung his well to the rear, since the chance that he might need it was very slim. All of these murderous devices had been stored in the evacuated and insulated compartment for months so that their temperature approached absolute zero. They were free of lubrication and had been designed to operate at this temperature.

A helmet clicked against Dom's, and Wing spoke, his voice carried by conducting transparent ceramic.

"I'm ready for my bomb, Dom—do you want to sling it? And congratulations. Do I have to call you Corporal now?"

"Wait until we get back and it's official. I take Toth's word for absolutely nothing."

He slipped the first atomic bomb from the shelf, checked the telltales to see that they were all in the green, then slid it into the rack that was an integral part of Wing's suit. "All set, now we can sling mine."

They had just finished when a large man in bulky combat armor came up. Dom would have known him by his size even if he had not read HELMUTZ stenciled on the front of his suit.

"What is it, Helm?" he asked when their helmets touched.

"The Sergeant. He said I should report to you, that I'm lifting a bomb on this mission." There was an angry tone behind his words.

"Right. We'll fix you up with a back sling." The big man did not look happy, and Dom thought he knew why.

"And don't worry about missing any of the fighting. There'll be enough for everyone."

"I'm a combatman . . ."

"We're all combatmen. All working for one thing—to deliver the bombs. That's your job now."

Helmutz did not act convinced and stood with stolid immobility while they rigged the harness and bomb onto the back of his suit. Before they were finished, their headphones crackled and a stir went through the company of suited men as a message came over the command frequency.

"Are you suited and armed? Are you ready for illumination adjustment?"

"Combatmen suited and armed." That was Sergeant Toth's voice.

"Bomb squad not ready," Dom said, and they hurried to make the last fastenings, aware that the rest were waiting for them.

"Bomb squad suited and armed."

"Lights."

II

As the command rang out, the bulkhead lights faded out until the darkness was broken only by the dim red lights in the ceiling above. Until their eyes became adjusted, it was almost impossible to see. Dom groped his way to one of the benches, found the oxygen hose with his fingers and plugged it into the side of his helmet; this would conserve his tank oxygen during the wait. Brisk music was being played over the command circuit now as part of morale sustaining. Here in the semidarkness, suited and armed, the waiting could soon become nerve-racking. Everything was done to alleviate the pressure. The music faded, and a voice replaced it.

"This is your executive officer speaking. I'm going to

try and keep you in the picture as to what is happening up here. The Edinburgers are attacking in fleet strength and, soon after they were sighted, their ambassador declared that a state of war exists. He asks that Earth surrender at once or risk the consequences. Well, you all know what the answer to that one was. The Edinburgers have invaded and conquered twelve settled planets already and incorporated them into their Greater Celtic Co-prosperity Sphere. Now they're getting greedy and going for the big one—Earth itself, the planet their ancestors left a hundred generations ago. In doing this . . . Just a moment, I have a battle report here . . . first contact with our scouts."

The officer stopped for a moment, then his voice picked up again.

"Fleet strength, but no larger than we expected and we will be able to handle them. But there is one difference in their tactics, and the combat computer is analyzing this now. They were the ones who originated the MT invasion technique, landing a number of cargo craft on a planet, all of them loaded with matter-transmitter screens. As you know, the invading forces attack through these screens direct from their planet to the one that is to be conquered. Well, they've changed their technique now. This entire fleet is protecting a *single* ship, a Kriger-class scout carrier. What this means . . . Hold on, here is the readout from the combat computer. *Only possibility single ship landing area increase MT screen breakthrough,* that's what it says. Which means that there is a good chance that this ship may be packing a *single* large MT screen, bigger than anything ever built before. If this is so—and they get the thing down to the surface—they can fly heavy bombers right through it, fire pre-aimed ICBMs, send through troop carriers, anything. If this happens the invasion will be successful."

* * *

Around him, in the red-lit darkness, Dom was aware of the other suited figures who stirred silently as they heard the words.

"*If* this happens." There was a ring of authority now in the executive officer's voice. "The Edinburgers have developed the only way to launch an interplanetary invasion. We have found the way to stop it. You combatmen are the answer. They have now put all their eggs in one basket—and you are going to take that basket to pieces. You can get through where attack ships or missiles could not. We're closing fast now, and you will be called to combat stations soon. So—go out there and do your job. The fate of Earth rides with you."

Melodramatic words, Dom thought, yet they were true. Everything, the ships, the concentration of fire power, all depended on them. The alert alarm cut through his thoughts, and he snapped to attention.

"Disconnect oxygen. Fall out when your name is called and proceed to the firing room in the order called. Toth . . ."

The names were spoken quickly, and the combatmen moved out. At the entrance to the firing room a suited man with a red-globed light checked the names on their chests against his roster to make sure they were in the correct order. Everything moved smoothly, easily, just like a drill, because the endless drills had been designed to train them for just this moment. The firing room was familiar, though they had never been there before, because their trainer had been an exact duplicate of it. The combatman ahead of Dom went to port, so he moved to starboard. The man preceding him was just climbing into a capsule, and Dom waited while the armorer helped him down into it and adjusted the armpit supports. Then it was his turn, and Dom slipped into the transparent plastic shell and settled against the seat as he seized the handgrips. The armorer pulled the supports hard up into his armpits, and he nodded when they seated right. A moment later, the man was gone, and he was alone in the semidarkness with the dim red glow shining on the top ring of the capsule that was just above his head. There was a sudden shudder, and he gripped hard, just as the capsule started forward.

As it moved, it tilted backwards until he was lying on his back, looking up through the metal rings that banded his plastic shell. His capsule was moved sideways, jerked to a stop, then moved again. Now the gun was visible, a half dozen capsules ahead of his, and he thought, as he always did during training, how like an ancient quick-firing cannon the gun was—a cannon that fired human beings. Every two seconds, the charging mechanism seized a capsule from one of the alternate feed belts, whipped it to the rear of the gun where it instantly vanished into the breech. Then another and another. The one ahead of Dom disappeared and he braced himself—and the mechanism suddenly and for no apparent reason halted.

There was a flicker of fear that something had gone wrong with the complex gun, before he realized that all of the first combatmen had been launched and that the computer was waiting a determined period of time for them to prepare the way for the bomb squad. His squad now, the men he would lead.

Waiting was harder than moving as he looked at the black mouth of the breech. The computer would be ticking away the seconds now, while at the same time tracking the target and keeping the ship aimed to the correct trajectory. Once he was in the gun, the magnetic field would seize the rings that banded his capsule, and the linear accelerator of the gun would draw him up the evacuated tube that penetrated the entire length of the great ship from stern to bow. Faster and faster the magnetic fields would pull him until he left the mouth of the gun at the correct speed and on the correct trajectory to . . .

His capsule was whipped up in a tight arc and shoved

into the darkness. Even as he gripped tight on the handholds, the pressure pads came up and hit him. He could not measure the time—he could not see and he could not breathe as the brutal acceleration pressed down on him. Hard, harder than anything he had ever experienced in training; he had that one thought, and then he was out of the gun.

In a single instant he went from acceleration to weightlessness, and he gripped hard so he would not float away from the capsule. There was a puff of vapor from the unheard explosions; he felt them through his feet, and the metal rings were blown in half, and the upper portion of the capsule shattered and hurled away. Now he was alone, weightless, holding to the grips that were fastened to the rocket unit beneath his feet. He looked about for the space battle that he knew was in progress and felt a slight disappointment that there was so little to see.

Something burned far off to his right, and there was a wavering in the brilliant points of the stars as some dark object occulted them and passed on. This was a battle of computers and instruments at great distances. There was very little for the unaided eye to see. The spaceships were black and swift and—for the most part—thousands of miles away. They were firing homing rockets and proximity shells, also just as swift and invisible. He knew that space around him was filled with signal jammers and false-signal generators, but none of this was visible. Even the target vessel toward which he was rushing was invisible.

For all that his limited senses could tell, he was alone in space, motionless, forgotten.

Something shuddered against the soles of his boots, and a jet of vapor shot out and vanished from the rocket unit. No, he was neither motionless nor forgotten. The combat computer was still tracking the target ship and had detected some minute variation from its predicted path. At the same time, the computer was following the progress of his trajectory, and it made the slight correction for this new data. Corrections must be going out at the same time to all the other combatmen in space, before and behind him. They were small and invisible—doubly invisible now that the metal rings had been shed. There was no more than an eighth of a pound of metal dispersed through the plastics and ceramics of a combatman's equipment. Radar could never pick them out from among all the interference. They should get through.

Jets blasted again, and Dom saw that the stars were turning above his head. Touchdown soon; the tiny radar in his rocket unit had detected a mass ahead and had directed that he be turned end for end. Once this was done he knew that the combat computer would cut free and turn control over to the tiny setdown computer that was part of his radar. His rockets blasted, strong now, punching the supports up against him, and he looked down past his feet at the growing dark shape that occulted the stars.

With a roar, loud in the silence, his headphones burst into life.

"Went, went—gone hungry. Went, went—gone hungry."

The silence grew again, but in it Dom no longer felt alone. The brief message had told him a lot.

Firstly, it was Sergeant Toth's voice; there was no mistaking that. Secondly, the mere act of breaking radio silence showed that they had engaged the enemy and that their presence was known. The code was a simple one that would be meaningless to anyone outside their company. Translated, it said that fighting was still going on but the advance squads were holding their own. They had captured the center section of the hull—always the best place to rendezvous since it was impossible to tell bow from stern in the darkness— and were holding it, awaiting the arrival of the bomb squad. The retrorockets flared hard and long, and the rocket unit crashed sharply into the black hull. Dom jumped free and rolled.

III

As he came out of the roll, he saw a suited figure looming above him, clearly outlined by the disk of the sun despite his black nonreflective armor. The top of the helmet was smooth. Even as he realized this, Dom was pulling the gropener from its holster.

A cloud of vapor sprang out, and the man vanished behind it. Dom was surprised, but he did not hesitate. Handguns, even recoilless ones like this that sent the burnt gas out to the sides, were a hazard in null-G space combat. Guns were not only difficult to aim but either had a recoil that would throw the user back out of position or the gas had to be vented sideways, when they would blind the user for vital moments. A fraction of a second was all a trained combatman needed.

As the gropener swung free, Dom thumbed the jet button lightly. The device was shaped like a short sword, but it had a vibrating saw blade where one sharpened edge should be, with small jets mounted opposite it in place of the outer edge. The jets drove the device forward, pulling him after it. As soon as it touched the other man's leg, he pushed the jets full on. As the vibrating ceramic blade speeded up, the force of the jets pressed it into the thin armor.

In less than a second, it had cut its way through and on into the flesh of the leg inside. Dom pressed the reverse jet to pull away as vapor gushed out, condensing to ice particles instantly, and his opponent writhed, clutched at his thigh—then went suddenly limp.

Dom's feet touched the hull, and the soles adhered. He realized that the entire action had taken place in the time it took him to straighten out from his roll and stand up. . . .

Don't think, act. Training. As soon as his feet adhered, he crouched and turned, looking about him. A heavy power ax sliced by just above his head, towing its wielder after it.

Act, don't think. His new opponent was on his left side, away from the gropener, and was already reversing the direction of his ax. A man has two hands. The drillger on his left thigh! Even as he remembered it, he had it in his hand, drill on and hilt-jet flaring. The foot-long, diamond-hard drill spun fiercely—its rotation cancelled by the counter-revolving weight in the hilt—while the jet drove it forward.

It went into the Edinburger's midriff, scarcely slowing as it tore a hole in the armor and plunged inside. As his opponent folded, Dom thumbed the reverse jet to push the drillger out. The power ax, still with momentum from the last blast of its jet, tore free of the dying man's hand and vanished into space.

There were no other enemies in sight. Dom tilted forward on one toe so that the surface film on the boot sole was switched from adhesive to neutral, then he stepped forward slowly. Walking like this took practice, but he had had that. Ahead was a group of dark figures lying prone on the hull, and he took the precaution of raising his hand to touch the horn on the top of his helmet so there would be no mistakes. This identification had been agreed upon just a few days ago and the plastic spikes glued on. The Edinburgers all had smooth-topped helmets.

Dom dived forward between the scattered forms and slid, face down. Before his body could rebound from the hull, he switched on his belly-sticker, and the surface film there held him flat. Secure for the moment among his own men, he thumbed the side of his helmet to change frequencies. There was now a jumble of noise through most of the frequencies, messages—both theirs and the enemy's—jamming, the false messages being broadcast by recorder units to cover the real exchange of information. There was scarcely any traffic on the bomb-squad frequency, and he waited for a clear spot. His men would have heard Toth's message, so they knew where to gather. Now he could bring them to him.

"Quasar, quasar, quasar," he called, then counted carefully for ten seconds before he switched on the blue bulb on his shoulder. He stood as he did this, let it burn for a single second, then dropped back to the hull before he could draw any fire. His men would be looking for the light and would assemble on it. One by one they began to crawl out of the darkness. He counted them as they appeared. A combatman, without the bulge of a bomb on his back, ran up and dived and slid, so that his helmet touched Dom's.

"How many, Corporal?" Toth's voice asked.

"One still missing but . . ."

"No buts. We move now. Set your charge and blow as soon as you have cover."

He was gone before Dom could answer. But he was right. They could not afford to wait for one man and risk the entire operation. Unless they moved soon, they would be trapped and killed up here. Individual combats were still going on about the hull, but it would not be long before the Edinburgers realized these were just holding actions and that the main force of attackers was gathered in strength. The bomb squad went swiftly and skillfully to work laying the ring of shaped charges.

The rear guards must have been called in, because the heavy weapons opened fire suddenly on all sides. These were .30-caliber high-velocity recoilless machine guns. Before firing, the gunners had traversed the hull, aiming for a grazing fire that was as close to the surface as possible. The gun computer remembered this and now fired along the selected pattern, aiming automatically. This was needed because, as soon as the firing began, clouds of gas jetted out, obscuring everything. Sergeant Toth appeared out of the smoke and shouted as his helmet touched Dom's.

"Haven't you blown it yet?"

"Ready now, get back."

"Make it fast. They're all down or dead now out there. But they will throw something heavy into this smoke soon, now that they have us pinpointed."

The bomb squad drew back, fell flat, and Dom pressed the igniter. Flames and gas exploded high, while the hull hammered up at them. Through the smoke rushed up a solid column of air, clouding and freezing into tiny crystals as it hit the vacuum. The ship was breached now, and they would keep it that way, blowing open the sealed compartments and bulkheads to let out the atmosphere. Dom and the Sergeant wriggled through the smoke together, to the edge of the wide, gaping hole that had been blasted in the ship's skin.

"Hotside, hotside!" the Sergeant shouted, and dived through the opening.

Dom pushed a way through the rush of men who were following the Sergeant and assembled his squad. He was still one man short. A weapons man with his machine gun on his back hurried by and leapt into the hole, with his ammunition carriers right behind him. The smoke cloud was growing because some of the guns were still firing, acting as a rear guard. It was getting hard to see the opening now. When Dom had estimated that half of the men had gone through, he led his own squad forward.

They pushed down into a darkened compartment, a storeroom of some kind, and saw a combatman at a hole about one hundred yards from them. "I'm glad you're here," he said as soon as Dom's helmet touched his. "We tried to the right first but there's too much resistance. Just holding them there."

Dom led his men in a floating run, the fastest movement possible in a null-G situation. The corridor was empty for the moment, dimly lit by the emergency bulbs. Holes had been blasted in the walls at regular intervals, to open the sealed compartments and empty them of air, as well as to destroy wiring and piping. As they passed one of the ragged-edged openings, spacesuited men erupted from it.

Dom dived under the thrust of a drillger, swinging his gropener out at the same time. It caught his attacker in the midriff, just as the man's other hand came up. The Edinburger folded and died, and a sharp pain lanced through Dom's leg. He looked down at the nipoff that was fastened to his calf and was slowly severing it.

The nipoff was an outmoded design for use against unarmored suits. It was killing him. The two curved blades were locked around his leg, and the tiny, geared-down motor was slowly closing them. Once started, the device could not be stopped.

It could be destroyed. Even as he realized this, he swung down his gropener and jammed it against the nipoff's handle. The pain intensified at the sideways pressure, and he almost blacked out. He attempted to ignore it. Vapor puffed out around the blades, and he triggered the compression ring on his thigh that sealed the leg from the rest of the suit. Then the gropener cut through the casing. There was a burst of sparks, and the motion of the closing of the blades stopped.

When Dom looked up, the brief battle was over and the counterattackers were dead. The rear guard had caught up and pushed over them. Helmutz must have accounted for more than one of them himself. He held his power ax high, fingers just touching the buttons in the haft so that the jets above the blade spurted alternately to swing the ax to and fro. There was blood on both blades.

IV

Dom switched on his radio; it was silent on all bands. The interior communication circuits of the ship were knocked out here, and the metal walls damped all radio signals.

"Report," he said. "How many did we lose?"

"You're hurt," Wing said, bending over him. "Want me to pull that thing off?"

"Leave it. The tips of the blades are almost touching, and you'd tear half my leg off. It's frozen in with the blood, and I can still get around. Lift me up."

The leg was getting numb now, with the blood supply cut off and the air replaced by vacuum. That was all for the best. He took the roll count.

"We've lost two men but we still have more than enough bombs for this job. Now let's move."

Sergeant Toth himself was waiting at the next corridor, where another hole had been blasted in the deck. He looked at Dom's leg but said nothing.

"How is it going?" Dom asked.

"Fair. We took some losses. We gave them more. Engineer says we are over the main hold now, so we are going straight down, pushing out men on each level to hold. Get going."

"And you?"

"I'll bring down the rear guard and pull the men from each level as we pass. You see that you have a way out for us when we all get down to you."

"You can count on that."

Dom floated out over the hole, then gave a strong kick with his good leg against the ceiling when he was lined up. He went down smoothly, and his squad followed. They passed one deck, two, then three. The openings had been nicely aligned for a straight drop. There was a flare of light and a burst of smoke ahead as another deck was blown through. Helmutz passed Dom, going faster, having pushed off harder with both legs. He was a full deck ahead when he plunged through the next opening, and the burst of high-velocity machine-gun fire almost cut him in two.

He folded in the middle, dead in the instant, the impact of the bullets driving him sideways and out of sight in the deck below.

Dom thumbed the jets on the gropener, and it pulled him aside before he followed the combatman.

"Bomb squad, disperse," he ordered. "Troops coming through." He switched to the combat frequency and looked up at the ragged column of men dropping down toward him.

"The deck below had been retaken. I am at the last occupied deck."

He waved his hand to indicate who was talking, and the stream of men began to jet their weapons and move on by him. "They're below me. The bullets came from this side." The combatmen pushed on without a word.

The metal flooring shook as another opening was blasted somewhere behind him. The continuous string of men moved by. A few seconds later a helmeted figure—with a horned helmet—appeared below and waved the all-clear. The drop continued.

On the bottom deck, the men were all jammed almost shoulder to shoulder, and more were arriving all the time.

"Bomb squad here, give me a report," Dom radioed. A combatman with a napboard slung at his waist pushed back out of the crowd.

"We reached the cargo hold—it's immense—but we're being pushed back. Just by weight of numbers. The Edinburgers are desperate. They are putting men through the MT screen in light pressure suits. Unarmored, almost unarmed. We kill them easily enough but they have pushed us out bodily. They're coming right from the invasion planet. Even when we kill them, the bodies block the way . . ."

"You the engineer?"

"Yes."

"Whereabouts in the hold is the MT screen?"

"It runs the length of the hold and is back against the far wall."

"Controls?"

"On the left side."

"Can you lead us over or around the hold so we can break in near the screen?"

The engineer took a single look at charts.

"Yes, around. Through the engine room. We can blast through close to the controls."

"Let's go then." Dom switched to combat frequency and waved his arm over his head. "All combatmen who can see me—this way. We're going to make a flank attack."

They moved down the long corridor as fast as they could, with the combatmen ranging out ahead of the bomb squad. There were sealed pressure doors at regular intervals, but these were bypassed by blasting through the bulkheads at the side. There was resistance and there were more dead as they advanced—dead from both sides. Then a group of men gathered ahead, and Dom floated up to the greatly depleted force of combatmen who had forced their way this far. A corporal touched his helmet to Dom's, pointing to a great sealed door at the corridor's end.

"The engine room is behind there. These walls are thick. Everyone off to one side, because we must use an octupled charge."

They dispersed, and the bulkheads heaved and buckled when the charge exploded. Dom, looking toward the corridor, saw a sheet of flame sear by, followed by a column of air that turned instantly to sparkling granules of ice. The engine room had still been pressurized.

There had been no warning, and most of the crewmen had not had their helmets sealed. They were violently and suddenly dead. The few survivors were killed quickly when they offered resistance with improvised weapons. Dom scarcely noticed this as he led his bomb squad after the engineer.

"That doorway is not on my charts," the engineer said, angrily, as though the spy who had stolen the information was at fault. "It must have been added after construction."

"Where does it go to?" Dom asked.

"The MT hold, no other place is possible."

Dom thought quickly. "I'm going to try and get to the MT controls without fighting. I need a volunteer to go with me. If we remove identification and wear Edinburger equipment we should be able to do it."

"I'll join you," the engineer said.

"No, you have a different job. I want a good combatman."

"Me," a man said, pushing through the others. "Pimenov, best in my squad. Ask anybody."

"Let's make this fast."

The disguise was simple. With the identifying spike knocked off their helmets and enemy equipment slung about them, they would pass any casual examination. A handful of grease obscured the names on their chests.

"Stay close behind and come fast when I knock the screen out," Dom told the others, then led the combatman through the door.

There was a narrow passageway between large tanks and another door at the far end. It was made of light metal but was blocked by a press of human bodies, spacesuited men who stirred and struggled but scarcely moved. The two combatmen pushed harder, and a sudden movement of the mob released the pressure; Dom fell forward, his helmet banging into that of the nearest man.

"What the devil you about?" the man said, twisting his head to look at Dom.

"More of them down there," Dom said, trying to roll his *r*'s the way the Edinburgers did.

"You're not one of us!" the man said and struggled to bring his weapon up.

Dom could not risk a fight here—yet the man had to be silenced. He was wearing a thin spacesuit. Dom could just reach the lightning prod, and he jerked it from its clip and jammed it against the Edinburger's side. The pair of needle-sharp spikes pierced suit and clothes and bit into his flesh, and when the hilt slammed against his body the circuit was closed. The handle of the lightning prod was filled with powerful capacitors that released their stored electricity in a single immense charge through the needles. The Edinburger writhed and died instantly.

They used his body to push a way into the crowd.

Dom had just enough sensation left in his injured leg to be aware when the clamped-on nipoff was twisted in his flesh by the men about them; he kept his thoughts from what it was doing to his leg.

V

Once the Edinburger soldiers were aware of the open door, they pulled it wide and fought their way through it. The combatmen would be waiting for them in the engine room. The sudden exodus relieved the pressure of the bodies for a moment, and Dom, with Pimenov struggling after him, pushed and worked his way toward the MT controls.

It was like trying to move in a dream. The dark hulk of the MT screen was no more than ten yards away, yet they couldn't seem to reach it. Soldiers sprang from the screen, pushing and crowding in, more and more, preventing any motion in that direction. The technicians stood at the controls, their helmet phones plugged into the board before them. Without gravity to push against, jammed into the crowd that floated at all levels in a fierce tangle of arms and legs, movement was almost impossible. Pimenov touched his helmet to Dom's.

"I'm going ahead to cut a path. Stay close behind me."

He broke contact before Dom could answer him, and let his power ax pull him forward into the press. Then he began to chop it back and forth in a short arc, almost hacking his way through the packed bodies. Men turned on him, but he did not stop, lashing out with his gropener as they tried to fight. Dom followed.

They were close to the MT controls before the combatman was buried under a crowd of stabbing, cursing Edinburgers. Pimenov had done his job, and he died doing it. Dom jetted his gropener and let it drag him forward until he slammed into the thick steel frame of the MT screen above the operators' heads. He slid the weapon along the frame, dragging himself headfirst through the press of suited bodies. There was a relatively clear space near the controls. He drifted down into it and let his drillger slide into the operator's back. The man writhed and died quickly. The other operator turned and took the weapon in his stomach. His face was just before Dom as his eyes widened and he screamed soundlessly with pain and fear. Dom could not escape the dead, horrified features as he struggled to drop the atomic bomb from his carrier. The murdered man stayed, pressed close against him all the time.

Now!

He cradled the bomb against his chest and, in a single swift motion, pulled out the arming pin, twisted the fuse to five seconds, and slammed down hard on the actuator. Then he reached up and switched the MT from *receive* to *send*.

The last soldiers erupted from the screen, and there was a growing gap behind them. Into this space and through the screen Dom threw the bomb.

After that, he kept the switch down and tried not to

think about what was happening among the men of the invasion army who were waiting before the MT screen on that distant planet.

Then he had to hold this position until the combatmen arrived. He sheltered behind the operator's corpse and used his drillger against the few Edinburgers who were close enough to realize that something had gone wrong. This was easy enough to do because, although they were soldiers, they were men from the invasion regular army and knew nothing about null-G combat. Very soon after this, there was a great stir, and the closest ones were thrust aside. An angry combatman blasted through, sweeping his power ax toward Dom's neck. Dom dodged the blow and switched his radio to combat frequency.

"Hold that! I'm Corporal Priego, bomb squad. Get in front of me and keep anyone else from making the same mistake."

The man was one of those who had taken the engine room. He recognized Dom now and nodded, turning his back to him and pressing against him. More combatmen stormed up to form an iron shield around the controls. The engineer pushed through between them, and Dom helped him reset the frequency on the MT screen.

After this, the battle became a slaughter and soon ended.

"Sendout!" Dom radioed as soon as the setting was made, then instructed the screen to transmit. He heard the words repeated over and over as the combatmen repeated the withdrawal signal so that everyone could hear it. Safety lay on the other side of the screen, now that it was tuned to Tycho Barracks on the Moon.

It was the Edinburgers, living, dead and wounded, who were sent through first. They were pushed back against the screen to make room for the combatmen who were streaming into the hold. The ones at the ends of the screen simply bounced against the hard surface and recoiled; the receiving screen at Tycho was far smaller than this great invasion screen. They were pushed along until they fell through, and combatmen took up positions to mark the limits of operating screen.

Dom was aware of someone in front of him, and he had to blink away the red film that was trying to cover his eyes.

"Wing," he said, finally recognizing the man. "How many others of the bomb squad made it?"

"None I know of, Dom. Just me."

No, don't think about the dead! Only the living counted now.

"All right. Leave your bomb here and get on through. One is all we really need." He tripped the release and pulled the bomb from Wing's rack before giving him a push toward the screen.

Dom had the bomb clamped to the controls when Sergeant Toth slammed up beside him and touched helmets.

"Almost done."

"Done now," Dom said, setting the fuse and pulling out the arming pin.

"Then get moving. I'll take it from here."

"No you don't. My job." He had to shake his head to make the haze go away but it still remained at the corners of his vision.

Toth didn't argue. "What's the setting?" he asked.

"Five and six. Five seconds after actuation the chemical bomb blows and knocks out the controls. One second later the atom bomb goes off."

"I'll stay around I think to watch the fun."

Time was acting strangely for Dom, speeding up and slowing down. Men were hurrying by, into the screen, first in a rush, then fewer and fewer. Toth was talking on the combat frequency, but Dom had switched the radio off because it hurt his head. The great chamber was empty now of all but the dead, with the automatic machine guns left firing at the entrances. One of them blew up as Toth touched helmets.

"They're all through. Let's go."

Dom had difficulty talking, so he nodded instead and hammered his fist down onto the actuator.

Men were coming toward them, but Toth had his arms around him, and full jets on his power ax were sliding them along the surface of the screen. And through.

When the brilliant lights of Tycho Barracks hit his eyes, Dom closed them, and this time the red haze came up, over him, all the way.

"How's the new leg?" Sergeant Toth asked. He slumped lazily in the chair beside the hospital bed.

"I can't feel a thing. Nerve channels blocked until it grows tight to the stump." Dom put aside the book he had been reading and wondered what Toth was doing here.

"I come around to see the wounded," the Sergeant said, answering the unasked question. "Two more besides you. Captain told me to."

"The Captain is as big a sadist as you are. Aren't we sick enough already?"

"Good joke." His expression did not change. "I'll tell the Captain. He'll like it. You going to buy out now?"

"Why not?" Dom wondered why the question made him angry. "I've had a combat mission, the medals, a good wound. More than enough points to get my discharge."

"Stay in. You're a good combatman when you stop thinking about it. There's not many of them. Make it a career."

"Like you, Sergeant? Make killing my life's work? Thank you, no. I intend to do something different, a little more constructive. Unlike you, I don't relish this whole dirty business, the killing, the outright plain murder. You like it." This sudden thought sent him sitting upright in the bed. "Maybe that's it. Wars, fighting, everything. It has nothing to do any more with territory rights or aggression or masculinity. I think that you people make wars because of the excitement of it, the thrill that nothing else can equal. You really *like* war."

Toth rose, stretched easily and turned to leave. He stopped at the door, frowning in thought.

"Maybe you're right, Corporal. I don't think about it much. Maybe I do like it." His face lifted in a cold tight smile. "But don't forget—*you like it too.*"

Dom went back to his book, resentful of the intrusion. His literature professor had sent it, along with a flattering note. He had heard about Dom on the broadcasts, and the entire school was proud, and so on. A book of poems by Milton, really good stuff.

> *No war, or battle's sound*
> *Was heard the world around.*

Yes, great stuff. But it hadn't been true in Milton's day and it still wasn't true. Did mankind really like war? They *must* like it or it wouldn't have lasted so long. This was an awful, criminal thought.

He too? Nonsense. He fought well, but he had trained himself. It would not be true that he actually liked all of that.

Dom tried to read again, but the page kept blurring before his eyes.

There are stories with serious messages, and there are stories which are just stories. Very occasionally there's a story that's just a story until the last few lines, whereupon the writer whangs you between the eyes with the message he's been preparing behind the scenes the whole time. Harry Harrison does that very difficult third thing more often than most writers.

Being a natural warrior—as I believe some people

are—says nothing about the warrior's intelligence, education, or interests. It's an aptitude, pure and simple, and the men who never learn they have the aptitude are probably luckier than the ones who know they do. I'm afraid that Mr. Harrison may be very well aware of that.

—DAD

Liberty Port

✪

David Drake

Commandant Horace Jolober had just lowered the saddle of his mobile chair, putting himself at the height of the Facilities Inspection Committee seated across the table, when the alarm hooted and Vicki cried from the window in the next room, "*Tanks! In the street!*"

The three Placidan bureaucrats flashed Jolober looks of anger and fear, but he had no time for them now even though they were his superiors. The stump of his left leg keyed the throttle of his chair. As the fans spun up, Jolober leaned and guided his miniature air-cushion vehicle out of the room faster than another man could have walked.

Faster than a man with legs could walk.

Vicki opened the door from the bedroom as Jolober swept past her toward the inside stairs. Her face was as calm as that of the statue which it resembled in its perfection, but Jolober knew that only the strongest emotion would have made her disobey his orders to stay in his private apartments while the inspection team was here. She was afraid that he was about to be killed.

A burst of gunfire in the street suggested she just might be correct.

"Chief!" called Jolober's mastoid implant in what he thought was the voice of Karnes, his executive officer. "I'm at the gate and the new arrivals, they're Hammer's, just came right through the wire! There's half a dozen tanks and they're shooting in the air!"

Could've been worse. Might yet be.

He slid onto the staircase, his stump boosting fan speed with reflexive skill. The stair treads were too narrow for Jolober's mobile chair to form an air cushion between the surface and the lip of its plenum chamber. Instead he balanced on thrust alone while the fans beneath him squealed, ramming the air hard enough to let him slope down above the staircase with the grace of a stooping hawk.

The hardware was built to handle the stress, but only flawless control kept the port commandant from up-ending and crashing down the treads in a fashion as dangerous as it would be humiliating.

Jolober was a powerful man who'd been tall besides until a tribarrel blew off both his legs above the knee. In his uniform of white cloth and lavish gold, he was dazzlingly obvious in any light. As he gunned his vehicle out into the street, the most intense light source was the rope of cyan bolts ripping skyward from the cupola of the leading tank.

The buildings on either side of the street enticed customers with displays to rival the sun, but the operators—each of them a gambler, brothel keeper, and saloon owner all in one—had their own warning systems. The lights were going out, leaving the plastic façades cold.

Lightless, the buildings faded to the appearance of the high concrete fortresses they were in fact. Repeated arches made the entrance of the China Doll, directly across the street from the commandant's offices, look spacious. The door itself was so narrow that only two men could pass it at a time, and no one could slip unnoticed past the array of sensors and guards that made sure none of those entering were armed.

Normally the facilities here at Paradise Port were open all day. Now an armored panel clanged down across the narrow door of the China Doll, its echoes merging with similar tocsins from the other buildings.

Much good that would do if the tanks opened up with their 20cm main guns. Even a tribarrel could blast holes in thumb-thick steel as easily as one had vaporized Jolober's knees and calves. . . .

He slid into the street, directly into the path of the lead tank. He would have liked to glance up toward the bedroom window for what he knew might be his last glimpse of Vicki, but he was afraid that he couldn't do that and still have the guts to do his duty.

For a long time after he lost his legs, the only thing which had kept Horace Jolober from suicide was the certainty that he had always done his duty. Not even Vicki could be allowed to take that from him.

The tanks were advancing at no more than a slow walk though their huge size gave them the appearance of speed. They were buttoned up—hatches down, crews hidden behind the curved surfaces of iridium armor that might just possibly turn a bolt from a gun as big as the one each tank carried in its turret.

Lesser weapons had left scars on the iridium. Where light powerguns had licked the armor—and even a tribarrelled automatic was light in comparison to a tank—the metal cooled again in a slope around the point where a little had been vaporized. High-velocity bullets made smaller, deeper craters plated with material from the projectile itself.

The turret of the leading tank bore a long gouge that began in a pattern of deep, radial scars. A shoulder-fired rocket had hit at a slight angle. The jet of white-hot gas spurting from the shaped-charge warhead had burned deep enough into even the refractory iridium that it would have penetrated the turret had it struck squarely.

If either the driver or the blower captain were riding with their heads out of the hatch when the missile detonated, shrapnel from the casing had decapitated them.

Jolober wondered if the present driver even saw him, a lone man in a street that should have been cleared by the threat of one hundred and seventy tons of armor howling down the middle of it.

An air-cushion jeep carrying a pintle-mounted needle stunner and two men in Port Patrol uniforms was driving alongside the lead tank, bucking and pitching in the current roaring from beneath the steel skirts of the tank's plenum chamber. While the driver fought to hold the light vehicle steady, the other patrolman bellowed through the jeep's loudspeakers. He might have been on the other side of the planet for all his chance of being heard over the sound of air sucked through intakes atop the tank's hull and then pumped beneath the skirts forcefully enough to balance the huge weight of steel and iridium.

Jolober grounded his mobile chair. He crooked his left ring finger so that the surgically redirected nerve impulse keyed the microphone implanted at the base of his jaw. "Gentlemen," he said, knowing that the base unit in the Port Office was relaying his words on the Slammers' general frequency. "You are violating the regulations which govern Paradise Port. Stop before somebody gets hurt."

The bow of the lead tank was ten meters away—and one meter less every second.

To the very end he thought they were going to hit him— by inadvertence, now, because the tank's steel skirt lifted in a desperate attempt to stop but the vehicle's mass overwhelmed the braking effect of its fans. Jolober knew that if he raised his chair from the pavement, the blast of air from the tank would knock him over and roll him along the concrete like a trash can in a windstorm—bruised but safe.

He would rather die than lose his dignity that way in front of Vicki.

The tank's bow slewed to the left, toward the China Doll. The skirt on that side touched the pavement with the sound of steel screaming and a fountain of sparks that sprayed across and over the building's high plastic façade.

The tank did not hit the China Doll, and it stopped short of Horace Jolober by less than the radius of its bow's curve.

The driver grounded his huge vehicle properly and cut the power to his fans. Dust scraped from the pavement, choking and chalky, swirled around Jolober and threw him into a paroxysm of coughing. He hadn't realized that he'd been holding his breath—until the danger passed and instinct filled his lungs.

The jeep pulled up beside Jolober, its fans kicking up still more dust, and the two patrolmen shouted words of concern and congratulation to their commandant. More men were appearing, patrolmen and others who had ducked into the narrow alleys between buildings when the tanks filled the street.

"Stecher," said Jolober to the sergeant in the patrol vehicle, "go back there—" he gestured toward the remainder of the column, hidden behind the armored bulk of the lead tank —"and help 'em get turned around. Get 'em back to the Refit Area where they belong."

"Sir, should I get the names?" Stecher asked.

The port commandant shook his head with certainty. "None of this happened," he told his subordinates. "I'll take care of it."

The jeep spun nimbly while Stecher spoke into his commo helmet, relaying Jolober's orders to the rest of the squad on street duty.

Metal rang again as the tank's two hatch covers slid

open. Jolober was too close to the hull to see the crewmen so he kicked his fans to life and backed, a few meters.

The mobile chair had been built to his design. Its only control was the throttle with a linkage which at high-thrust settings automatically transformed the plenum chamber to a nozzle. Steering and balance were matters of how the rider shifted his body weight. Jolober prided himself that he was just as nimble as he had been before.

And before he fell back into the trench on Primavera, half wrapped in the white flag, he'd waved to the oncoming tanks. The only conscious memory he retained of *that* moment was the sight of his right leg still balanced on the trench lip above him, silhouetted against the criss-crossing cyan bolts from the powerguns.

But Horace Jolober was just as much a man as he'd ever been. The way he got around proved it. And Vicki.

The driver staring out the bow hatch at him was a woman with thin features and just enough hair to show beneath her helmet. She looked scared, aware of what had just happened and aware also of just how bad it could've been.

Jolober could appreciate how she felt.

The man who lifted himself from the turret hatch was under thirty, angry, and—though Jolober couldn't remember the Slammers' collar pips precisely—a junior officer of some sort rather than a sergeant.

The dust had mostly settled by now, but vortices still spun above the muzzles of the tribarrel which the fellow had been firing skyward. "What're you doing, you bloody fool?" he shouted. "D'ye *want* to die?"

Not any more, thought Horace Jolober as he stared upward at the tanker. One of the port patrolmen had responded to the anger in the Slammer's voice by raising his needle stunner, but there was no need for that.

Jolober keyed his mike so that he didn't have to shout with the inevitable emotional loading. In a flat, certain voice, he said, "If you'll step down here, Lieutenant, we can discuss the situation like officers—which I am, and you will continue to be unless you insist on pushing things."

The tanker grimaced, then nodded his head and lifted himself the rest of the way out of the turret. "Right," he said. "Right. I . . ." His voice trailed off, but he wasn't going to say anything the port commandant hadn't heard before.

When you screw up real bad, you can either be afraid or you can flare out in anger and blame somebody else. Not because you don't know better, but because it's the only way to control your fear. It isn't pretty, but there's no pretty way to screw up bad.

The tanker dropped to the ground in front of Jolober and gave a sloppy salute. That was lack of practice, not deliberate insult, and his voice and eyes were firm as he said, "Sir. Acting Captain Tad Hoffritz reporting."

"Horace Jolober," the port commandant said. He raised his saddle to put his head at what used to be normal standing height, a few centimeters taller than Hoffritz. The Slammer's rank made it pretty clear why the disturbance had occurred. "Your boys?" Jolober asked, thumbing toward the tanks sheepishly reversing down the street under the guidance of white-uniformed patrolmen.

"Past three days they have been," Hoffritz agreed. His mouth scrunched again in an angry grimace and he said, "Look, I'm real sorry. I know how dumb that was. I just . . ."

Again, there wasn't anything new to say.

The tank's driver vaulted from her hatch with a suddenness which drew both men's attention. "Corporal Days," she said with a salute even more perfunctory than Hoffritz's had been. "Look, sir, *I* was drivin' and if there's a problem, it's my problem."

"Daisy—" began Captain Hoffritz.

"There's no problem, Corporal," Jolober said firmly. "Go back to your vehicle. We'll need to move it in a minute or two."

Another helmeted man had popped his head from the

turret—surprisingly, because this was a line tank, not a command vehicle with room for several soldiers in the fighting compartment. The driver looked at her captain, then met the worried eyes of the trooper still in the turret. She backed a pace but stayed within earshot.

"Six tanks out of seventeen," Jolober said calmly. Things *were* calm enough now that he was able to follow the crosstalk of his patrolmen, their voices stuttering at low level through the miniature speaker on his epaulet. "You've been seeing some action, then."

"Too bloody right," muttered Corporal Days.

Hoffritz rubbed the back of his neck, lowering his eyes, and said, "Well, running . . . There's four back at Refit deadlined we brought in on transporters, but—"

He looked squarely at Jolober. "But sure we had a tough time. That's why I'm CO and Chester's up there—" he nodded toward the man in the turret "—trying to work company commo without a proper command tank. And I guess I figured—"

Hoffritz might have stopped there, but the port commandant nodded him on.

"—I figured maybe it wouldn't hurt to wake up a few rear-echelon types when we came back here for refit. Sorry, sir."

"There's three other units, including a regiment of the Division Legere, on stand-down here at Paradise Port already, Captain," Jolober said. He nodded toward the soldiers in mottled fatigues who were beginning to reappear on the street. "Not rear-echelon troops, from what I've heard. And they need some relaxation just as badly as your men do."

"Yes, sir," Hoffritz agreed, blank-faced. "It was real dumb. I'll sign the report as soon as you make it out."

Jolober shrugged. "There won't be a report, Captain. Repairs to the gate'll go on your regiment's damage account and be deducted from Placida's payment next month." He smiled. "Along with any chairs or glasses you break in the casinos. Now, get your vehicle into the Refit Area where it belongs. And come back and have a good time in Paradise Port. That's what we're here for."

"*Thank* you, sir," said Hoffritz, and relief dropped his age by at least five years. He clasped Jolober's hand and, still holding it, asked, "You've seen service, too, haven't you, sir?"

"Fourteen years with Hampton's Legion," Jolober agreed, pleased that Hoffritz had managed not to stare at the stumps before asking the question.

"Hey, good outfit," the younger man said with enthusiasm. "We were with Hampton on Primavera, back, oh, three years ago?"

"Yes, I know," Jolober said. His face was still smiling, and the subject wasn't an emotional one any more. He felt no emotion at all . . . "One of your tanks shot—" his left hand gestured delicately at where his thighs ended "—these off on Primavera."

"Lord," Corporal Days said distinctly.

Captain Hoffritz looked as if he had been hit with a brick. Then his face regained its animation. "*No,* sir," he said. "You're mistaken. On Primavera, we were both working for the Federalists. Hampton was our infantry support."

Not the way General Hampton would have described the chain of command, thought Jolober. His smile became real again. He still felt pride in his old unit—and he could laugh at those outdated feelings in himself.

"Yes, that's right," he said aloud. "There'd been an error in transmitting map coordinates. When a company of these—" he nodded toward the great iridium monster, feeling sweat break out on his forehead and arms as he did so "—attacked my battalion, I jumped up to stop the shooting."

Jolober's smile paled to a frosty shadow of itself. "I was successful," he went on softly, "but not quite as soon as I would've liked."

"Oh, Lord and Martyrs," whispered Hoffritz. His face looked like that of a battle casualty.

"Tad, that was—" Corporal Days began.

"Shut it *off*, Daisy!" shouted the Slammers' commo man from the turret. Days' face blanked and she nodded.

"Sir, I—" Hoffritz said.

Jolober shook his head to silence the younger man. "In a war," he said, "a lot of people get in the way of rounds. I'm luckier than some. I'm still around to tell about it."

He spoke in the calm, pleasant voice he always used in explaining the—matter—to others. For the length of time he was speaking, he could generally convince even himself.

Clapping Hoffritz on the shoulder—the physical contact brought Jolober back to present reality, reminding him that the tanker was a young man and not a demon hidden behind armor and a tribarrel—the commandant said, "Go on, move your hardware and then see what Paradise Port can show you in the way of a good time."

"Oh, that I know already," said Hoffritz with a wicked, man-to-man smile of his own. "When we stood down here three months back, I met a girl named Beth. I'll bet she still remembers me, and the *Lord* knows I remember her."

"Girl?" Jolober repeated. The whole situation had so disoriented him that he let his surprise show.

"Well, you know," said the tanker. "A Doll, I guess. But believe me, Beth's woman enough for *me*."

"Or for anyone," the commandant agreed. "I know just what you mean."

Stecher had returned with the jeep. The street was emptied of all armor except Hoffritz's tank, and that was an object of curiosity rather than concern for the men spilling out the doors of the reopened brothels. Jolober waved toward the patrol vehicle and said, "My men'll guide you out of here, Captain Hoffritz. Enjoy your stay."

The tank driver was already scrambling back into her hatch. She had lowered her helmet shield, so the glimpse

Jolober got of her face was an unexpected, light-reflecting bubble.

Maybe Corporal Days had a problem with where the conversation had gone when the two officers started talking like two men. That was a pity, for her and probably for Captain Hoffritz as well. A tank was too small a container to hold emotional trouble among its crew.

But Horace Jolober had his own problems to occupy him as he slid toward his office at a walking pace. He had his meeting with the Facilities Inspection Committee, which wasn't going to go more smoothly because of the interruption.

A plump figure sauntering in the other direction tipped his beret to Jolober as they passed. "Ike," acknowledged the port commandant in a voice as neutral as a gun barrel that doesn't care in the least at whom it's pointed.

Red Ike could pass for human, until the rosy cast of his skin drew attention to the fact that his hands had only three fingers and a thumb. Jolober was surprised to see that Ike was walking across the street toward his own brothel, the China Doll, instead of being inside the building already. That could have meant anything, but the probability was that Red Ike had a tunnel to one of the buildings across the street to serve as a bolthole.

And since all the *real* problems at Paradise Port were a result of the alien who called himself Red Ike, Jolober could easily imagine why the fellow would want to have a bolthole.

Jolober had gone down the steps in a smooth undulation. He mounted them in a series of hops, covering two treads between pauses like a weary cricket climbing out of a well.

The chair's powerpack had more than enough charge left to swoop him up to the conference room. It was the man himself who lacked the mental energy now to balance himself on the column of driven air. He felt drained—the tribar-

rel, the tank . . . the memories of Primavera. If he'd decided
to, sure, but . . .

But maybe he was getting old.

The Facilities Inspection Committee—staff members,
actually, for three of the most powerful senators in the
Placidan legislature—waited for Jolober with doubtful
looks. Higgey and Wayne leaned against the conference
room window, watching Hoffritz's tank reverse sedately in
the street. The woman, Rodall, stood by the stairhead watching the port commandant's return.

"Why don't you have an elevator put in?" she asked.
"Or at least a ramp?" Between phrases, Rodall's full features
relaxed to the pout that was her normal expression.

Jolober paused beside her, noticing the whisper of air
from beneath his plenum chamber was causing her to twist
her feet away as if she had stepped into slime. "There aren't
elevators everywhere, Mistress," he said. "Most places,
there isn't even enough smooth surface to depend on ground
effect alone to get you more than forty meters."

He smiled and gestured toward the conference room's
window. Visible beyond the China Doll and the other buildings across the street was the reddish-brown expanse of the
surrounding landscape: ropes of lava on which only lichen
could grow, where a man had to hop and scramble from one
ridge to another.

The Placidan government had located Paradise Port in a
volcanic wasteland in order to isolate the mercenaries letting
off steam between battles with Armstrong, the other power
on the planet's sole continent. To a cripple in a chair which
depended on wheels or unaided ground effect, the twisting
lava would be as sure a barrier as sheer walls.

Jolober didn't say that so long as he could go anywhere
other men went, he could pretend he was still a man. If the
Placidan civilian could have understood that, she wouldn't
have asked why he didn't have ramps put in.

"Well, what *was* that?" demanded Higgey—thin, intense, and already half bald in his early thirties. "Was anyone killed?"

"Nothing serious, Master Higgey," Jolober said as he slid back to the table and lowered himself to his "seated" height. "And no, no one was killed or even injured."

Thank the Lord for his mercy.

"It *looked* serious, Commandant," said the third committee member—Wayne, half again Jolober's age and a retired colonel of the Placidan regular army. "I'm surprised you permit things like that to happen."

Higgey and Rodall were seating themselves. Jolober gestured toward the third chair on the curve of the round table opposite him and said, "Colonel, your, ah—opposite numbers in Armstrong tried to stop those tanks last week with a battalion of armored infantry. They got their butts kicked until they didn't *have* butts any more."

Wayne wasn't sitting down. His face flushed and his short white mustache bristled sharply against his upper lip.

Jolober shrugged and went on in a more conciliatory tone, "Look, sir, units aren't rotated back here unless they've had a hell of a rough time in the line. I've got fifty-six patrolmen with stunners to keep order . . . which we do, well enough for the people using Paradise Port. We aren't here to start a major battle of our own. Placida needs these mercenaries and needs them in fighting trim."

"That's a matter of opinion," said the retired officer with his lips pressed together, but at last he sat down.

The direction of sunrise is also a matter of opinion, Jolober thought. It's about as likely to change as Placida is to survive without the mercenaries who had undertaken the war her regular army was losing.

"I requested this meeting—" requested it with the senators themselves, but he hadn't expected them to agree "—in order to discuss just that, the fighting trim of the troops who undergo rest and refit here. So that Placida gets the most value of her, ah, payment."

The committee staff would do, if Jolober could get them to understand. Paradise Port was, after all, a wasteland with a village populated by soldiers who had spent all the recent past killing and watching their friends die. It wasn't the sort of place you'd pick for a senatorial junket.

Higgey leaned forward, clasping his hands on the table top, and said, "Commandant, I'm sure that those—" he waggled a finger disdainfully toward the window "—men out there would be in better physical condition after a week of milk and religious lectures than they will after the regime they choose for themselves. There are elements—"

Wayne nodded in stern agreement, his eyes on Mistress Rodall, whose set face refused to acknowledge either of her fellows while the subject was being discussed.

"—in the electorate and government who would like to try that method, but fortunately reality has kept the idea from being attempted."

Higgey paused, pleased with his forceful delivery and the way his eyes dominated those of the much bigger man across the table. "If you've suddenly got religion, Commandant Jolober," he concluded, "I suggest you resign your current position and join the ministry."

Jolober suppressed his smile. Higgey reminded him of a lap dog, too nervous to remain either still or silent, and too small to be other than ridiculous in its posturing. "My initial message was unclear, madam, gentlemen," he explained, looking around the table. "I'm not suggesting that Placida close the brothels that are part of the recreational facilities here."

His pause was not for effect, but because his mouth had suddenly gone very dry. But it was his duty to—

"I'm recommending that the Dolls be withdrawn from Paradise Port and that the facilities be staffed with human, ah, females."

Colonel Wayne stiffened and paled.

Wayne's anger was now mirrored in the expression on

Rodall's face. "Whores," she said. "So that those—*soldiers*—can disgrace and dehumanize real women for their fun."

"And kill them, one assumes," added Higgey with a touch of amusement. "I checked the records, Commandant. There've been seventeen Dolls killed during the months Paradise Port's been in operation. As it is, that's a simple damage assessment, but if they'd been human prostitutes—each one would have meant a manslaughter charge or even murder. People don't cease to have rights when they choose to sell their bodies, you know."

"When they're *forced* to sell their bodies, you mean," snapped Rodall. She glared at Higgey, who didn't mean anything of the sort.

"Scarcely to the benefit of your precious mercenaries," said Wayne in a distant voice. "Quite apart from the political difficulties it would cause for any senator who recommended the change."

"As a matter of fact," said Higgey, whose natural caution had tightened his visage again, "I thought you were going to use the record of violence here at Paradise Port as a reason for closing the facility. Though I'll admit that I couldn't imagine anybody selfless enough to do away with his own job."

No, you couldn't, you little weasel, thought Horace Jolober. But politicians have different responsibilities than soldiers, and politicians' flunkies have yet another set of needs and duties.

And none of them are saints. Surely no soldier who does his job is a saint.

"Master Higgey, you've precisely located the problem," Jolober said with a nod of approval. "The violence isn't a result of the soldiers, it's because of the Dolls. It isn't accidental, it's planned. And it's time to stop it."

"It's time for us to leave, you mean," said Higgey as he shoved his chair back. "Resigning still appears to be your best course, Commandant. Though I don't suppose the ministry is the right choice for a new career, after all."

"Master Higgey," Jolober said in the voice he would have used in an argument with a fellow officer, "I know very well that no one is irreplaceable—but *you* know that I am doing as good a job here as anybody you could hire to run Paradise Port. I'm asking you to listen for a few minutes to a proposal that will make the troops you pay incrementally better able to fight for you."

"We've come this far," said Rodall.

"There are no listening devices in my quarters," Jolober explained, unasked. "I doubt that any real-time commo link out of Paradise Port is free of interception."

He didn't add that time he spent away from *his* duties was more of a risk to Placida than pulling these three out of their offices and expensive lunches could be. The tanks roaring down the street should have proved that even to the committee staffers.

Jolober paused, pressing his fingertips to his eyebrows in a habitual trick to help him marshal his thoughts while the others stared at him. "Mistress, masters," he said calmly after a moment, "the intention was that Paradise Port and similar facilities be staffed by independent contractors from off-planet."

"Which is where they'll return as soon as the war's over," agreed Colonel Wayne with satisfaction. "Or as soon as they put a toe wrong, any one of them."

"The war's bad enough as it is," said Rodall. "Building up Placida's stock of *that* sort of person would make peace hideous as well."

"Yes, ma'am, I understand," said the port commandant. There were a lot of "that sort of person" in Placida just now, including all the mercenaries in the line—and Horace Jolober back here. "But what you have in Paradise Port isn't a group of entrepreneurs, it's a corporation—a monarchy, almost—subservient to an alien called Red Ike."

"Nonsense," said Wayne.

"We don't permit that," said Rodall.

"Red Ike owns a single unit here," said Higgey. "The China Doll. Which is all he can own by law, to prevent just the sort of situation you're describing."

"Red Ike provides all the Dolls," Jolober stated flatly. "Whoever owns them on paper, they're his. And *everything* here is his because he controls the Dolls."

"Well . . ." said Rodall. She was beginning to blush.

"There's no actual proof," Colonel Wayne said, shifting his eyes toward a corner of walls and ceiling. "Though I suppose the physical traits are indicative . . ."

"The government has decided it isn't in the best interests of Placida to pierce the corporate veil in this instance," said Higgey in a thin voice. "The androids in question are shipped here from a variety of off-planet suppliers."

The balding Placidan paused and added, with a tone of absolute finality. "If the question were mine to decide—which it isn't—I would recommend searching for a new port commandant rather than trying to prove the falsity of a state of affairs beneficial to us, to Placida."

"I think that really must be the final word on the subject, Commandant Jolober," Rodall agreed.

Jolober thought she sounded regretful, but the emotion was too faint for him to be sure. The three Placidans were getting up, and he had failed.

He'd failed even before the staff members arrived, because it was now quite obvious that they'd decided their course of action before the meeting. They—and their elected superiors—would rather have dismissed Jolober's arguments.

But if the arguments proved to be well founded, they would dismiss the port commandant, if necessary to end the discussion.

"I suppose I should be flattered," Jolober said as hydraulics lifted him in the saddle and pressure of his stump on the throttle let him rotate his chair away from the table. "That you came all this way to silence me instead of refusing me a meeting."

"You might recall," said Higgey, pausing at the doorway. His look was meant to be threatening, but the port commandant's bulk and dour anger cooled the Placidan's face as soon as their eyes met. "That is, we're in the middle of a war, and the definition of treason can be a little loose in such times. While you're not technically a Placidan citizen, Commandant, you—would be well advised to avoid activities which oppose the conduct of war as the government has determined to conduct it."

He stepped out of the conference room. Rodall had left ahead of him.

"Don't take it too hard, young man," said Colonel Wayne when he and Jolober were alone. "You mercenaries, you can do a lot of things the quick and easy way. It's different when you represent a government and need to consider political implications."

"I'd never understood there were negative implications, Colonel," Jolober said with the slow, careful enunciation which proved he was controlling himself rigidly, "in treating your employees fairly. Even the mercenary soldiers whom you employ."

Wayne's jaw lifted. "I beg your pardon, Commandant," he snapped. "I don't see anyone holding guns to the heads of poor innocents, forcing them to whore and gamble."

He strode to the door, his back parade-ground straight. At the door he turned precisely and delivered the broadside he had held to that point. "Besides, Commandant—if the Dolls are as dangerous to health and welfare as you say, why are you living with one yourself?"

Wayne didn't expect an answer, but what he saw in Horace Jolober's eyes suggested that his words might bring a physical reaction that he hadn't counted on. He skipped into the hall with a startled sound, banging the door behind him.

The door connecting the conference room to the port commandant's personal suite opened softly. Jolober did not look around.

Vicki put her long, slim arms around him from behind. Jolober spun, then cut power to his fans and settled his chair firmly onto the floor. He and Vicki clung to one another, legless man and Doll whose ruddy skin and beauty marked her as inhuman.

They were both crying.

Someone from Jolober's staff would poke his head into the conference room shortly to ask if the meeting was over and if the commandant wanted nonemergency calls routed through again.

The meeting was certainly over . . . but Horace Jolober had an emergency of his own. He swallowed, keyed his implant, and said brusquely, "I'm out of action till I tell you different. Unless it's another Class A flap."

The kid at the commo desk stuttered a "Yessir" that was a syllable longer than Jolober wanted to hear. Vicki straightened, wearing a bright smile beneath the tear streaks, but the big human gathered her to his chest again and brought up the power of his fans.

Together, like a man carrying a moderate-sized woman, the couple slid around the conference table to the door of the private suite. The chair's drive units were overbuilt because men are overbuilt, capable of putting out huge bursts of hysterical strength.

Drive fans and power packs don't have hormones, so Jolober had specified—and paid for—components that would handle double the hundred kilos of his own mass, the hundred kilos left after the tribarrel had chewed him. The only problem with carrying Vicki to bed was one of balance, and the Doll remained still in his arms.

Perfectly still, as she was perfect in all the things she did.

"I'm not trying to get rid of you, darling," Jolober said as he grounded his chair.

"It's all right," Vicki whispered. "I'll go now if you like. It's all right."

She placed her fingertips on Jolober's shoulders and lifted herself by those fulcrums off his lap and onto the bed, her toes curled beneath her buttocks. A human gymnast could have done as well—but no better.

"What I *want*," Jolober said forcefully as he lifted himself out of the saddle, using the chair's handgrips, "is to do my job. And when I've done it, I'll buy you from Red Ike for whatever price he chooses to ask."

He swung himself to the bed. His arms had always been long—and strong. Now he knew that he must look like a gorilla when he got on or off his chair . . . and when the third woman he was with after the amputation giggled at him, he began to consider suicide as an alterative to sex.

Then he took the job on Placida and met Vicki.

Her tears had dried, so both of them could pretend they hadn't poured out moments before. She smiled shyly and touched the high collar of her dress, drawing her fingertip down a centimeter and opening the garment by that amount.

Vicki wasn't Jolober's ideal of beauty—wasn't what he'd *thought* his ideal was, at any rate. Big blondes, he would have said. A woman as tall as he was, with hair the color of bleached straw hanging to the middle of her back.

Vicki scarcely came up to the top of Jolober's breastbone when he was standing—at standing height in his chair—and her hair was a black fluff that was as short as a soldier would cut it to fit comfortably under a helmet. She looked buxom, but her breasts were fairly flat against her broad, powerfully muscled chest.

Jolober put his index finger against hers on the collar and slid down the touch-sensitive strip that opened the fabric. Vicki's body was without blemish or pubic hair. She was

so firm that nothing sagged or flattened when her dress and
the supports of memory plastic woven into it dropped away.

She shrugged her arms out of the straps and let the garment spill as a pool of sparkling shadow on the counterpane
as she reached toward her lover.

Jolober, lying on his side, touched the collar of his uniform jacket.

"No need," Vicki said blocking his hand with one of
hers and opening his trouser fly with the other. "Come," she
added, rolling onto her back and drawing him toward her.

"But the—" Jolober murmured in surprise, leaning forward in obedience to her touch and demand. The metallic
braid and medals on his stiff-fronted tunic had sharp corners
to prod the Doll beneath him whether he wished or not.

"Come," she repeated. "This time."

Horace Jolober wasn't introspective enough to understand why his mistress wanted the rough punishment of his
uniform. He simply obeyed.

Vicki toyed with his garments after they had finished and
lay on the bed, their arms crossing. She had a trick of fold-
ing back her lower legs so that they vanished whenever she
sat or reclined in the port commandant's presence.

Her fingers tweaked the back of Jolober's waistband
and emerged with the hidden knife, the only weapon he carried.

"I'm at your mercy," he said, smiling. He mimed as
much of a hands-up posture as he could with his right elbow
supporting his torso on the mattress. "Have your way with
me."

In Vicki's hand, the knife was a harmless cylinder of
plastic—a weapon only to the extent that the butt of the
short tube could harden a punch. The knife was of memory
plastic whose normal state was a harmless block. No one
who took it away from Jolober in a struggle would find it of
any use as a weapon.

Only when squeezed after being cued by the pore pattern of Horace Jolober's right hand would it—

The plastic cylinder shrank in Vicki's hand, sprouting a double-edged 15cm blade.

"Via!" swore Jolober. Reflex betrayed him into thinking that he had legs. He jerked upright and started to topple off the bed because the weight of his calves and feet wasn't there to balance the motion.

Vicki caught him with both arms and drew him to her. The blade collapsed into the handle when she dropped it, so that it bounced as a harmless cylinder on the counterpane between them.

"My love, I'm *sorry*," the Doll blurted fearfully. "I didn't mean—"

"No, no," Jolober said, settled now on his thighs and buttocks so that he could hug Vicki fiercely. His eyes peered secretively over her shoulders, searching for the knife that had startled him so badly. "I was surprised that it . . . How *did* you get the blade to open, dearest? It's fine, it's nothing you did wrong, but I didn't expect that, is all."

They swung apart. The mattress was a firm one, but still a bad surface for this kind of conversation. The bedclothes rumpled beneath Jolober's heavy body and almost concealed the knife in a fold of cloth. He found it, raised it with his fingertips, and handed it to Vicki. "Please do that again," he said calmly. "Extend the blade."

Sweat was evaporating from the base of Jolober's spine, where the impermeable knife usually covered the skin.

Vicki took the weapon. She was so doubtful that her face showed no expression at all. Her fingers, short but perfectly formed, gripped the baton as if it were a knife hilt— and it became one. The blade formed with avalanche swiftness, darkly translucent and patterned with veins of stress. The plastic would not take a wire edge, but it could carve a roast or, with Jolober's strength behind it, ram twenty millimeters deep into hardwood.

"Like this?" Vicki said softly. "Just squeeze it and . . . ?"

Jolober put his hand over the Doll's and lifted the knife away between thumb and forefinger. When she loosed the hilt, the knife collapsed again into a short baton.

He squeezed—extended the blade—released it again—and slipped the knife back into its concealed sheath.

"You see, darling," Jolober said, "the plastic's been keyed to *my* body. Nobody else should be able to get the blade to form."

"I'd never use it against you," Vicki said. Her face was calm, and there was no defensiveness in her simple response.

Jolober smiled. "Of course, dearest; but there was a manufacturing flaw or you wouldn't be able to do that."

Vicki leaned over and kissed the port commandant's lips, then bent liquidly and kissed him again. "I told you," she said as she straightened with a grin, "I'm a part of you."

"And believe me," said Jolober, rolling onto his back to cinch up his short-legged trousers. "You're not a part of me I intend to lose."

He rocked upright and gripped the handles of his chair.

Vicki slipped off the bed and braced the little vehicle with a hand on the saddle and the edge of one foot on the skirt. The help wasn't necessary—the chair's weight anchored it satisfactorily, so long as Jolober mounted swiftly and smoothly. But it *was* helpful, and it was the sort of personal attention that was as important as sex in convincing Horace Jolober that someone really cared—*could* care—for him.

"You'll do your duty, though," Vicki said. "And I wouldn't want you not to."

Jolober laughed as he settled himself and switched on his fans. He felt enormous relief now that he had proved beyond doubt—he was sure of that—how much he loved

Vicki. He'd calmed her down, and that meant he was calm again, too.

"Sure I'll do my job," he said as he smiled at the Doll. "That doesn't mean you and *me*'ll have a problem. Wait and see."

Vicki smiled also, but she shook her head in what Jolober thought was amused resignation. Her hairless body was too perfect to be flesh, and the skin's red pigment gave the Doll the look of a statue in blushing marble.

"Via, but you're lovely," Jolober murmured as the realization struck him anew.

"Come back soon," she said easily.

"Soon as I can," the commandant agreed as he lifted his chair and turned toward the door. "But like you say, I've got a job to do."

If the government of Placida wouldn't give him the support he needed, by the Lord! he'd work through the mercenaries themselves.

Though his belly went cold and his stumps tingled as he realized he would again be approaching the tanks which had crippled him.

The street had the sharp edge which invariably marked it immediately after a unit rotated to Paradise Port out of combat. The troops weren't looking for sex or intoxicants— though most of them would have claimed they were.

They were looking for life. Paradise Port offered them things they thought equaled life, and the contrast between reality and hope led to anger and black despair. Only after a few days of stunning themselves with the offered pleasures did the soldiers on leave recognize another contrast: Paradise Port might not be all they'd hoped, but it was a lot better than the muck and ravening hell of combat.

Jolober slid down the street at a walking pace. Some of the soldiers on the pavement with him offered ragged salutes to the commandant's glittering uniform. He returned them

sharply, a habit he had ingrained in himself after he took
charge here.

Mercenary units didn't put much emphasis on saluting
and similar rear-echelon forms of discipline. An officer with
the reputation of being a tight-assed martinet in bivouac was
likely to get hit from behind the next time he led his troops
into combat.

There were regular armies on most planets—Colonel
Wayne was an example—to whom actual fighting was an
aberration. Economics or a simple desire for action led
many planetary soldiers into mercenary units . . . where the
old habits of saluting and snapping to attention surfaced
when the men were drunk and depressed.

Hampton's Legion hadn't been any more interested in
saluting than the Slammers were. Jolober had sharpened his
technique here because it helped a few of the men he served
feel more at home—when they were very far from home.

A patrol jeep passed, idling slowly through the pedes-
trians. Sergeant Stecher waved, somewhat uncertainly.

Jolober waved back, smiling toward his subordinate but
angry at himself. He keyed his implant and said "Central,
I'm back in business now, but I'm headed for the Refit Area
to see Captain van Zuyle. Let anything wait that can till I'm
back."

He should have cleared with his switchboard as soon as
he'd . . . calmed Vicki down. Here there'd been a crisis, and
as soon as it was over he'd disappeared. Must've made his
patrolmen very cursed nervous, and it was sheer sloppiness
that he'd let the situation go on beyond what it had to. It was
his job to make things simple for the people in Paradise Port,
both his staff and the port's clientele.

Maybe even for the owners of the brothel: but it was
going to have to be simple on Horace Jolober's terms.

At the gate, a tank was helping the crew repairing damage. The men wore khaki coveralls—Slammers rushed from
the Refit Area as soon as van Zuyle, the officer in charge

there, heard what had happened. The faster you hid the evidence of a problem, the easier it was to claim the problem had never existed.

And it was to everybody's advantage that problems never exist.

Paradise Port was surrounded with a high barrier of woven plastic to keep soldiers who were drunk out of their minds from crawling into the volcanic wasteland and hurting themselves. The fence was tougher than it looked—it looked as insubstantial as moonbeams—but it had never been intended to stop vehicles.

The gate to the bivouac areas outside Paradise Port had a sturdy framework and hung between posts of solid steel. The lead tank had been wide enough to snap both gateposts off at the ground. The gate, framework and webbing, was strewn in fragments for a hundred meters along the course it had been dragged between the pavement and the tank's skirt.

As Jolober approached, he felt his self-image shrink by comparison to surroundings which included a hundred-and-seventy-ton fighting vehicle. The tank was backed against one edge of the gateway.

With a huge *clang!* the vehicle set another steel post, blasting it home with the apparatus used in combat to punch explosive charges into deep bunkers. The ram vaporized osmium wire with a jolt of high voltage, transmitting the shock waves to the piston head through a column of fluid. It banged home the replacement post without difficulty, even though the "ground" was a sheet of volcanic rock.

The pavement rippled beneath Jolober, and the undamped harmonics of the quivering post were a scream that could be heard for kilometers. Jolober pretended it didn't affect him as he moved past the tank. He was praying that the driver was watching his side screens—or listening to the ground guide—as the tank trembled away from the task it had completed.

One of the Slammers' noncoms gestured reassuringly

toward Jolober. His lips moved as he talked into his commo helmet. The port commandant could hear nothing over the howl of the drive fans and prolonged grace notes from the vibrating post, but the tank halted where it was until he had moved past it.

A glance over his shoulder showed Jolober the tank backing into position to set the other post. It looked like a great tortoise, ancient and implacable, maneuvering to lay a clutch of eggs.

Paradise Port was for pleasure only. The barracks housing the soldiers and the sheds to store and repair their equipment were located outside the fenced perimeter. The buildings were prefabs extruded from a dun plastic less colorful than the ruddy lava fields on which they were set.

The bivouac site occupied by Hammer's line companies in rotation was unusual in that the large leveled area contained only four barracks buildings and a pair of broad repair sheds. Parked vehicles filled the remainder of the space.

At the entrance to the bivouac area waited a guard shack. The soldier who stepped from it wore body armor over her khakis. Her submachine gun was slung, but her tone was businesslike as she said, "Commandant Jolober? Captain van Zuyle's on his way to meet you right now."

Hold right here till you're invited in, Jolober translated mentally with a frown.

But he couldn't blame the Slammers' officer for wanting to assert his authority *here* over that of Horace Jolober, whose writ ran only to the perimeter of Paradise Port. Van Zuyle just wanted to prove that his troopers would be punished only with his assent—or by agreement reached with authorities higher than the port commandant.

There was a flagpole attached to a gable of one of the barracks. A tall officer strode from the door at that end and hopped into the driver's seat of the jeep parked there. Another khaki-clad soldier stuck her head out the door and called something, but the officer pretended not to hear. He spun his vehicle in an angry circle, rubbing its lowside skirts, and gunned it toward the entrance.

Jolober had met van Zuyle only once. The most memorable thing about the Slammers' officer was his anger—caused by fate, but directed at whatever was nearest to hand. He'd been heading a company of combat cars when the blower ahead of his took a direct hit.

Van Zuyle didn't have his face shield down because the shield made him and most troopers feel as though they'd stuck their heads in a bucket. And that dissociation which is mental rather than sensory, could get you killed in combat.

The shield would have darkened instantly to block the sleet of actinics from the exploding combat car. Without its protection . . . well, the surgeons could rebuild his face, with only a slight stiffness to betray the injuries. Van Zuyle could even see—by daylight or under strong illumination.

There just wasn't any way he'd ever be fit to lead a line unit again—and he was very angry about it.

Commandant Horace Jolober could understand how van Zuyle felt—better, perhaps, than anyone else on the planet could. It didn't make his own job easier, though.

"A pleasure to see you again, Commandant," van Zuyle lied brusquely as he skidded the jeep to a halt, passenger seat beside Jolober. "If you—"

Jolober smiled grimly as the Slammers' officer saw—and remembered—that the port commandant was legless and couldn't seat himself in a jeep on his air-cushion chair.

"No problem," said Jolober, gripping the jeep's side and the seat back. He lifted himself aboard the larger vehicle with an athletic twist that settled him facing front.

Of course, the maneuver was easier than it would have been if his legs were there to get in the way.

"Ah, your—" van Zuyle said, pointing toward the chair. Close up, Jolober could see a line of demarcation in his scalp. The implanted hair at the front had aged less than the gray-speckled portion which hadn't been replaced.

"No problem, Captain," Jolober repeated. He anchored his left arm around the driver's seat, gripped one of his chair's handles with the right hand, and jerked the chair into the bench seat in the rear of the open vehicle.

The jeep lurched: the air-cushion chair weighed almost as much as Jolober did without it, and he was a big man. "You learn tricks when you have to," he said evenly as he met the eyes of the Slammers' officer.

And your arms get very strong when they do a lot of the work your legs used to—but he didn't say that.

"My office?" van Zuyle asked sharply.

"Is that as busy as it looks?" Jolober replied, nodding toward the door where a soldier still waited impatiently for van Zuyle to return.

"Commandant, I've had a tank company come in shot to *hell,*" van Zuyle said in a voice that built toward fury. "Three vehicles are combat lossed and have to be stripped—*and* the other vehicles need more than routine maintenance—*and* half the personnel are on medic's release. Or dead. I'm trying to run a refit area with what's left, my staff of twenty-three, and the trainee replacements Central sent over who haven't ridden in a panzer, much less pulled maintenance on one. And you ask if I've got time to waste on you?"

"No, Captain, I didn't ask that," Jolober said with the threatening lack of emotion which came naturally to a man who had all his life been bigger and stronger than most of those around him. "Find a spot where we won't be disturbed, and we'll park there."

When the Slammers' officer frowned, Jolober added, "I'm not here about Captain Hoffritz, Captain."

"Yeah," sighed van Zuyle as he lifted the jeep and steered it sedately toward a niche formed between the iridium carcasses of a pair of tanks. "We're repairing things right now—" he thumbed in the direction of the gate "—and any other costs'll go on the damage chit; but I guess I owe you an apology besides."

"Life's a dangerous place," Jolober said easily. Van Zuyle wasn't stupid. He'd modified his behavior as soon as he was reminded of the incident an hour before—and the leverage it gave the port commandant if he wanted to push it.

Van Zuyle halted them in the gray shade that brought sweat to Jolober's forehead. The tanks smelled of hot metal because some of their vaporized armor had settled back onto the hulls as fine dust. Slight breezes shifted it to the nostrils of the men nearby, a memory of the blasts in which it had formed.

Plastics had burned also, leaving varied pungencies which could not conceal the odor of cooked human flesh.

The other smells of destruction were unpleasant. That last brought Jolober memories of his legs exploding in brilliant coruscance. His body tingled and sweated, and his mouth said to the Slammers' officer, "Your men are being cheated and misused every time they come to Paradise Port, Captain. For political reasons, my supervisors won't let me make the necessary changes. If the mercenary units serviced by Paradise Port unite and demand the changes, the government will be forced into the proper decision."

"Seems to me," said van Zuyle with his perfectly curved eyebrows narrowing, "that somebody could claim you were acting against your employers just now."

"Placida hired me to run a liberty port," said Jolober evenly. He was being accused of the worst crime a mercenary could commit: conduct that would allow his employers to forfeit his unit's bond and brand them forever as unemployable contract-breakers.

Jolober no longer was a mercenary in that sense; but he understood van Zuyle's idiom, and it was in that idiom that he continued, "Placida wants and needs the troops she hires to be sent back into action in the best shape possible. Her *survival* depends on it. If I let Red Ike run this place to his benefit and not to Placida's, then I'm not doing my job."

"All right," said van Zuyle. "What's Ike got on?"

A truck, swaying with its load of cheering troopers, pulled past on its way to the gate of Paradise Port. The man in the passenger's seat of the cab was Tad Hoffritz, his face a knife-edge of expectation.

"Sure, they need refit as bad as the hardware does," muttered van Zuyle as he watched the soldiers on leave with longing eyes. "Three days straight leave, half days after that when they've pulled their duty. But Via! I could use 'em here, especially with the tanks that're such a bitch if you're not used to crawling around in 'em."

His face hardened again. "Go on," he said, angry that Jolober knew how much he wanted to be one of the men on that truck instead of having to run a rear-echelon installation.

"Red Ike owns the Dolls like so many shots of liquor," Jolober said. He never wanted a combat job again—the thought terrified him, the noise and flash and the smell of his body burning. "He's using them to strip your men, everybody's men, in the shortest possible time," he continued in a voice out of a universe distant from his mind. "The games are honest—that's my job—but the men play when they're stoned, and they play with a Doll on their arm begging them to go on until they've got nothing left. How many of those boys—" he gestured to where the truck, now long past, had been "—are going to last three days?"

"We give 'em advances when they're tapped out," said van Zuyle with a different kind of frown. "Enough to last their half days—if they're getting their jobs done here. Works out pretty good."

"As a matter of fact," he went on, "the whole business works out pretty good. I never saw a soldier's dive without shills and B-girls. Don't guess you ever did either, Com-

mandant. Maybe they're better at it, the Dolls, but all that
means is that I get my labor force back quicker—and Hammer gets his tanks back in line with that much fewer problems."

"The Dolls—" Jolober began.

"The Dolls are clean," shouted van Zuyle in a voice like
edged steel. "They give full value for what you pay 'em.
And I've never had a Doll knife one of my guys—which is
a cursed sight better'n any place I been staffed with human
whores!"

"No," said Jolober, his strength a bulwark against the
Slammer's anger. "But you've had your men knife or stran-
gle Dolls, haven't you? All the units here've had incidents
of that sort. Do you think it's chance?"

Van Zuyle blinked. "I think it's a cost of doing business," he said, speaking mildly because the question had
surprised him.

"No," Jolober retorted. "It's a major profit center for
Red Ike. The Dolls don't just drop soldiers when they've
stripped them. They humiliate the men, taunt them . . . and
when one of these kids breaks and chokes the life out of the
bitch who's goading him, Red Ike pockets the damage assessment. And it comes out of money Placida would otherwise have paid Hammer's Slammers."

The Slammers' officer began to laugh. It was Jolober's
turn to blink in surprise.

"Sure," van Zuyle said, "androids like that cost a lot
more'n gateposts or a few meters of fencing, you bet."

"He's the only source," said Jolober tautly. "Nobody
knows where the Dolls come from—or where Ike does."

"Then nobody can argue the price isn't fair, can they?"
van Zuyle gibed. "And you know what, Commandant? Take
a look at this tank right here."

He pointed to one of the vehicles beside them. It was a
command tank, probably the one in which Hoffritz's prede-

cessor had ridden before it was hit by powerguns heavy enough to pierce its armor.

The first round, centered on the hull's broadside, had put the unit out of action and killed everyone aboard. The jet of energy had ignited everything flammable within the fighting compartment in an explosion which blew the hatches open. The enemy had hit the iridium carcass at least three times more, cratering the turret and holing the engine compartment.

"We couldn't replace this for the cost of twenty Dolls," van Zuyle continued. "And we're going to have to, you know, because she's a total loss. All I can do is strip her for salvage . . . and clean up as best I can for the crew, so we can say we had something to bury."

His too-pale, too-angry eyes glared at Jolober. "Don't talk to me about the cost of Dolls, Commandant. They're cheap at the price. I'll drive you back to the gate."

"You may not care about the dollar cost," said Jolober in a voice that thundered over the jeep's drive fans. "But what about the men you're sending back into the line thinking they've killed somebody they loved—or that they *should*'ve killed her?"

"Commandant, that's one I can't quantify," the Slammers' officer said. The fans' keeping lowered as the blades bit the air at a steeper angle and began to thrust the vehicle out of the bivouac area. "First time a trooper kills a human here, that I *can* quantify: we lose him. If there's a bigger problem and the Bonding Authority decides to call it mutiny, then we lost a lot more than that.

"And I tell you, buddy," van Zuyle added with a one-armed gesture toward the wrecked vehicles now behind them. "We've lost too fucking much already on this contract."

The jeep howled past the guard at the bivouac entrance. Wind noise formed a deliberate damper on Jolober's attempts to continue the discussion. "Will you forward my request to speak to Colonel Hammer?" he shouted. "I can't get through to him myself."

The tank had left the gate area. Men in khaki, watched by Jolober's staff in white uniforms, had almost completed their task of restringing the perimeter fence. Van Zuyle throttled back, permitting the jeep to glide to a graceful halt three meters short of the workmen.

"The Colonel's busy, Commandant," he said flatly. "And from now on, I hope you'll remember that *I* am, too."

Jolober lifted his chair from the back seat. "I'm going to win this, Captain," he said. "I'm going to do my job whether or not I get any support."

The smile he gave van Zuyle rekindled the respect in the tanker's pale eyes.

There were elements of four other mercenary units bivouacked outside Paradise Port at the moment. Jolober could have visited them in turn—to be received with more or less civility, and certainly no more support than the Slammers' officer had offered.

A demand for change by the mercenaries in Placidan service had to be just that: a demand by *all* the mercenaries. Hammer's Slammers were the highest-paid troops here, and by that standard—any other criterion would start a brawl— the premier unit. If the Slammers refused Jolober, none of the others would back him.

The trouble with reform is that in the short run, it causes more problems than continuing along the bad old ways. Troops in a combat zone, who know that each next instant may be their last, are more to be forgiven for short-term thinking than, say, politicians; but the pattern is part of the human condition.

Besides, nobody but Horace Jolober seemed to think there was anything to reform.

Jolober moved in a walking dream while his mind shuttled through causes and options. His data were interspersed with memories of Vicki smiling up at him from the bed and of his own severed leg toppling in blue-green silhouette. He shook his head gently to clear the images and found himself on the street outside the Port offices.

His stump throttled back the fans reflexively; but when Jolober's conscious mind made its decision, he turned away from the office building and headed for the garish façade of the China Doll across the way.

Rainbow pastels lifted slowly over the front of the building, the gradation so subtle that close up it was impossible to tell where one band ended and the next began. At random intervals of from thirty seconds to a minute, the gentle hues were replaced by glaring, super-saturated colors separated by dazzling blue-white lines.

None of the brothels in Paradise Port were sedately decorated, but the China Doll stood out against the competition.

As Jolober approached, a soldier was leaving and three more—one a woman—were in the queue to enter. A conveyor carried those wishing to exit, separated from one another by solid panels. The panels withdrew sideways into the wall as each client reached the street—but there was always another panel in place behind to prevent anyone from bolting into the building without being searched at the proper entrance.

All of the buildings in Paradise Port were designed the same way, with security as unobtrusive as it could be while remaining uncompromised. The entryways were three-meter funnels narrowing in a series of gaudy corbelled arches. Attendants—humans everywhere but in the China Doll—waited at the narrow end. They smiled as the customers passed—but anyone whom the detection devices in the archway said was armed was stopped right there.

The first two soldiers ahead of Jolober went through without incident. The third was a short man wearing lieutenant's pips and the uniform of Division Legere. His broad shoulders and chest narrowed to his waist as abruptly as those of a bulldog, and it was with a bulldog's fierce intransigence that he braced himself against the two attendants who had confronted him.

"I am Lieutenant Alexis Condorcet!" he announced as though he were saying "major general." "What do you mean by hindering me?"

The attendants in the China Doll were Droids, figures with smoothly masculine features and the same blushing complexion which set Red Ike and the Dolls apart from the humans with whom they mingled.

They were not male—Jolober had seen the total sexlessness of an android whose tights had ripped as he quelled a brawl. Their bodies and voices were indistinguishable from one another, and there could be no doubt that they were androids, artificial constructions whose existence proved that the Dolls could be artificial, too.

Though in his heart, Horace Jolober had never been willing to believe the Dolls were not truly alive. Not since Red Ike had introduced him to Vicki.

"Could you check the right-hand pocket of your blouse, Lieutenant Condorcet?" one of the Droids said.

"I'm not carrying a weapon!" Condorcet snapped. His hand hesitated, but it dived into the indicated pocket when an attendant started to reach toward it.

Jolober was ready to react, either by grabbing Condorcet's wrist from behind or by knocking him down with the chair. He didn't have time for any emotion, not even fear.

It was the same set of instincts that had thrown him to his feet for the last time, to wave off the attacking tanks.

Condorcet's hand came out with a roll of coins between two fingers. In a voice that slipped between injured and minatory he said, "Can't a man bring money into the Doll, then? Will you have me take my business elsewhere, then?"

"Your money's very welcome, sir," said the attendant who was reaching forward. His thumb and three fingers shifted in a sleight of hand; they reappeared holding a gold-striped China Doll chip worth easily twice the value of the rolled coins. "But let us hold these till you return. We'll be glad to give them back then without exchange."

The motion which left Condorcet holding the chip and transferred the roll to the attendant was also magically smooth.

The close-coupled soldier tensed for a moment as if he'd make an issue of it; but the Droids were as strong as they were polished, and there was no percentage in being humiliated.

"We'll see about that," said Condorcet loudly. He strutted past the attendants who parted for him like water before the blunt prow of a barge.

"Good afternoon, Port Commandant Jolober," said one of the Droids as they both bowed. "A pleasure to serve you again."

"A pleasure to feel wanted," said Jolober with an ironic nod of his own. He glided into the main hall of the China Doll.

The room's high ceiling was suffused with clear light which mimicked daytime outside. The hall buzzed with excited sounds even when the floor carried only a handful of customers. Jolober hadn't decided whether the space was designed to give multiple echo effects or if instead Red Ike augmented the hum with concealed sonic transponders.

Whatever it was, the technique made the blood of even the port commandant quicken when he stepped into the China Doll.

There were a score of gaming stations in the main hall, but they provided an almost infinite variety of ways to lose money. A roulette station could be collapsed into a skat table in less than a minute if a squad of drunken Frieslanders demanded it. The displaced roulette players could be accommodated at the next station over, where until then a Droid had been dealing desultory hands of fan-tan.

Whatever the game was, it was fair. Every hand, every throw, every pot was recorded and processed in the office of the port commandant. None of the facility owners doubted that a skewed result would be noticed at once by the computers, or that a result skewed in favor of the house would mean that Horace Jolober would weld their doors shut and ship all their staff off-planet.

Besides, they knew as Jolober did that honest games would get them most of the available money anyhow, so long as the Dolls were there to caress the winners to greater risks.

At the end of Paradise Port farthest from the gate were two establishments which specialized in the leftovers. They were staffed by human males, and their atmosphere was as brightly efficient as men could make it.

But no one whose psyche allowed a choice picked a human companion over a Doll.

The main hall was busy with drab uniforms, Droids neatly garbed in blue and white, and the stunningly gorgeous outfits of the Dolls. There was a regular movement of Dolls and uniforms toward the door on a room-width landing three steps up at the back of the hall. Generally the rooms beyond were occupied by couples, but much larger gatherings were possible if a soldier had money and the perceived need.

The curved doors of the elevator beside the front entrance opened even as Jolober turned to look at them. Red Ike stepped out with a smile and a Doll on either arm.

"Always a pleasure to see you, Commandant," Red Ike said in a tone as sincere as the Dolls were human. "Shana," he added to the red-haired Doll. "Susan—" he nodded toward the blond. "Meet Commandant Jolober, the man who keeps us all safe."

The redhead giggled and slipped from Ike's arm to Jolober's. The slim blond gave him a smile that would have been demure except for the fabric of her tank-top. It acted as a polarizing filter, so that when she swayed her bare torso flashed toward the port commandant.

"But come on upstairs, Commandant," Red Ike continued, stepping backwards into the elevator and motioning Jolober to follow him. "Unless your business is here—or in back?" He cocked an almost-human eyebrow toward the door in the rear while his face waited with a look of amused tolerance.

"We can go upstairs," said Jolober grimly. "It won't take long." His air cushion slid him forward. Spilling air tickled Shana's feet as she pranced along beside him; she giggled again.

There must be men who found that sort of girlish idiocy erotic or Red Ike wouldn't keep the Doll in his stock.

The elevator shaft was opaque and looked it from outside the car. The car's interior was a visiscreen fed by receptors on the shaft's exterior. On one side of the slowly rising car, Jolober could watch the games in the main hall as clearly as if he were hanging in the air. On the other, they lifted above the street with a perfect view of its traffic and the port offices even though a concrete wall and the shaft's iridium armor blocked the view in fact.

The elevator switch was a small plate which hung in the "air" that was really the side of the car. Red Ike had toggled it up. Down would have taken the car—probably much faster—to the tunnel beneath the street, the escape route which Jolober had suspected even before the smiling alien had used it this afternoon.

But there was a second unobtrusive control beside the first. The blond Doll leaned past Jolober with a smile and touched it.

The view of the street disappeared. Those in the car had a crystalline view of the activities in back of the China Doll as if no walls or ceilings separated the bedrooms. Jolober met—or thought he met—the eyes of Tad Hoffritz, straining upward beneath a black-haired Doll.

"*Via!*" Jolober swore and slapped the toggle hard enough to feel the solidity of the elevator car.

"Susan, Susan," Red Ike chided with a grin. "She will have her little joke, you see, Commandant."

The blond made a moue, then winked at Jolober.

Above the main hall was Red Ike's office, furnished in minimalist luxury. Jolober found nothing attractive in the sight of chair seats and a broad onyx desktop hanging in the air, but the decor did show off the view. Like the elevator, the office walls and ceiling were covered by passthrough visiscreens.

The russet wasteland, blotched but not relieved by patterns of lichen, looked even more dismal from twenty meters up than it did from Jolober's living quarters.

Though the view appeared to be panorama, there was no sign of where the owner himself lived. The back of the office was an interior wall, and the vista over the worms and pillows of lava was transmitted through not only the wall but the complex of rooms that was Red Ike's home.

On the roof beside the elevator tower was an aircar sheltered behind the concrete coping. Like the owners of all the other facilities comprising Paradise Port, Red Ike wanted the option of getting out fast, even if the elevator to his tunnel bolthole was blocked.

Horace Jolober had fantasies in which he watched the stocky humanoid scramble into his vehicle and accelerate away, vanishing forever as a fleck against the milky sky.

"I've been meaning to call on you for some time, Commandant," Red Ike said as he walked with quick little steps to his desk. "I thought perhaps you might like a replacement for Vicki. As you know, any little way in which I can make your task easier . . . ?"

Shana giggled. Susan smiled slowly and, turning at a precisely calculated angle, bared breasts that were much fuller than they appeared beneath her loose garment.

Jolober felt momentary desire, then fierce anger in reaction. His hands clenched on the chair handles, restraining his violent urge to hurl both Dolls into the invisible walls.

Red Ike sat behind the desktop. The thin shell of his chair rocked on invisible gimbals, tilting him to a comfortable angle that was not quite disrespectful of his visitor.

"Commandant," he said with none of the earlier hinted mockery, "you and I really ought to cooperate, you know. We need each other, and Placida needs us both."

"And the soldiers we're here for?" Jolober asked softly. "Do they need you, Ike?"

The Dolls had become as still as painted statues.

"You're an honorable man, Commandant," said the alien. "It disturbs you that the men don't find what they need in Paradise Port."

The chair eased more nearly upright. The intensity of Red Ike's stare reminded Jolober that he'd never seen the alien blink.

"But men like that—all of them now, and most of them for as long as they live . . . all they really need, Commandant, is a chance to die. I don't offer them that, it isn't my place. But I sell them everything they pay for, because I too am honorable."

"You don't know what honor is!" Jolober shouted, horrified at the thought—the nagging possibility—that what Red Ike said was true.

"I know what it is to keep my word, Commandant Jolober," the alien said as he rose from behind his desk with quiet dignity. "I promise you that if you cooperate with me, Paradise Port will continue to run to the full satisfaction of your employers.

"And I also promise," Red Ike went on unblinkingly, "that if you continue your mad vendetta, it will be the worse for you."

"Leave here," Jolober said. His mind achieved not calm, but a dynamic balance in which he understood everything—so long as he focused only on the result, not the reasons. "Leave Placida, leave human space, Ike. You push too hard. So far you've been lucky—it's only me pushing back, and I play by the official rules."

He leaned forward in his saddle, no longer angry. The desktop between them was a flawless black mirror. "But the mercs out there, they play by their own rules, and they're not going to like it when they figure out the game you're running on them. Get out while you can."

"Ladies," Red Ike said. "Please escort the commandant to the main hall. He no longer has any business here."

Jolober spent the next six hours on the street, visiting each of the establishments of Paradise Port. He drank little and spoke less, exchanging salutes when soldiers offered them and, with the same formality, the greetings of owners.

He didn't say much to Vicki later that night, when he returned by the alley staircase which led directly to his living quarters.

But he held her very close.

The sky was dark when Jolober snapped awake, though his bedroom window was painted by all the enticing colors of the façades across the street. He was fully alert and already into the short-legged trousers laid on the mobile chair beside the bed when Vicki stirred and asked, "Horace? What's the matter?"

"I don't—" Jolober began, and then the alarms sounded: the radio implanted in his mastoid, and the siren on the roof of the China Doll.

"Go ahead," he said to Central, thrusting his arms into the uniform tunic.

Vicki thumbed up the room lights but Jolober didn't need that, not to find the sleeves of a white garment with this much sky-glow. He'd stripped a jammed tribarrel once in pitch darkness, knowing that he and a dozen of his men were dead if he screwed up—and absolutely confident of the stream of cyan fire that ripped moments later from his gun muzzles.

"Somebody shot his way into the China Doll," said the voice. "He's holed up in the back."

The bone-conduction speaker hid the identity of the man on the other end of the radio link, but it wasn't the switchboard's artificial intelligence. Somebody on the street was cutting through directly, probably Stecher.

"Droids?" Jolober asked as he mounted his chair and powered up, breaking the charging circuit in which the vehicle rested overnight.

"Chief," said the mastoid, "we got a man down. Looks bad, and we can't get medics to him because the gun's covering the hallway. D'ye want me to—"

"*Wait!*" Jolober said as he bulled through the side door under power. Unlocking the main entrance—the entrance to the office of the port commandant—would take seconds that he knew he didn't have. "Hold what you got, I'm on the way."

The voice speaking through Jolober's jawbone was clearly audible despite wind noise and the scream of his chair as he leaped down the alley staircase in a single curving arc. "Ah, Chief? We're likely to have a, a crowd control problem if this don't get handled real quick."

"I'm on the way," Jolober repeated. He shot onto the street, still on direct thrust because ground effect wouldn't move him as fast as he needed to go.

The entrance of the China Doll was cordoned off, if four port patrolmen could be called a cordon. There were over a hundred soldiers in the street and more every moment that the siren—couldn't somebody cut it? Jolober didn't have time—continued to blare.

That wasn't what Stecher had meant by a "crowd control problem." The difficulty was in the way soldiers in the Division Legere's mottled uniforms were shouting—not so much as onlookers as a lynch mob.

Jolober dropped his chair onto its skirts—he needed the greater stability of ground effect. "Lemme through!" he snarled to the mass of uniformed backs which parted in a chorus of yelps when Jolober goosed his throttle. The skirt of his plenum chamber caught the soldiers just above the bootheels and toppled them to either side as the chair powered through.

One trooper spun with a raised fist and a curse in French. Jolober caught the man's wrist and flung him down almost absently. The men at the door relaxed visibly when their commandant appeared at their side.

Behind him, Jolober could hear off-duty patrolmen scrambling into the street from their barracks under the port offices. That would help, but—

"You, Major!" Jolober shouted, pointing at a Division Legere officer in the front of the crowd. The man was almost of a size with the commandant; fury had darkened his face several shades beyond swarthiness. "I'm deputizing you to keep order here until I've taken care of the problem inside."

He spun his chair again and drove through the doorway. The major was shouting to his back, "But the bastard's shot my—"

Two Droids were more or less where Jolober had expected them, one crumpled in the doorway and the other stretched full length a meter inside. The Droids were tough as well as strong. The second one had managed to grasp the man who shot him and be pulled a pace or two before another burst into the back of the Droid's skull had ended matters.

Stecher hadn't said the shooter had a submachine gun. That made the situation a little worse than it might have been, but it was so bad already that the increment was negligible.

Droids waited impassively at all the gaming stations, ready to do their jobs as soon as customers returned. They hadn't fled the way human croupiers would have—but nei-

ther did their programming say anything about dealing with
armed intruders.

The Dolls had disappeared. It was the first time Jolober
had been in the main hall when it was empty of their charm-
ing, enticing babble.

Stecher and two troopers in Slammers' khaki, and a pair
of technicians with a portable medicomp stood on opposite
sides of the archway leading into the back of the China Doll.
A second patrolman was huddled behind the three room-
wide steps leading up from the main hall.

Man down, Jolober thought, his guts ice.

The patrolman heard the chair and glanced back.
"*Duck!*" he screamed as Sergeant Stecher cried, "*Watch—*"

Jolober throttled up, bouncing to the left as a three-shot
burst snapped from the archway. It missed him by little
enough that his hair rose in response to the ionized track.

There *was* a man down, in the corridor leading back
from the archway. There was another man firing from a
room at the corridor's opposite end, and he'd just proved his
willingness to add the port commandant to the night's bag.

Jolober's chair leaped the steps to the broad landing
where Stecher crouched, but it was his massive arms that
braked his momentum against the wall. His tunic flapped
and he noticed for the first time that he hadn't sealed it before he left his quarters. "Report," he said bluntly to his
sergeant while running his thumb up the uniform's seam to
close it.

"Their officer's in there," Stecher said, bobbing his chin
to indicate the two Slammers kneeling beside him. The male
trooper was holding the female and trying to comfort her as
she blubbered.

To Jolober's surprise, he recognized both of them—the
commo tech and the driver of the tank which'd nearly run
him down that afternoon.

"He nutted, shot his way in to find a Doll," Stecher said
quickly. His eyes flicked from the commandant to the arch-

way, but he didn't shift far enough to look down the corridor. Congealed notches in the arch's plastic sheath indicated that he'd been lucky once already.

"Found her, found the guy she was with and put a burst into him as he tried to get away." Stecher thumbed toward the body invisible behind the shielding wall. "Guy from the Legere, an El-Tee named Condorcet."

"The bitch made him do it!" said the tank driver in a scream strangled by her own laced fingers.

"She's sedated," said the commo tech who held her.

In the perfect tones of Central's artificial intelligence, Jolober's implant said, "Major de Vigny of the Division Legere requests to see you. He is offering threats."

Letting de Vigny through would either take the pressure off the team outside or be the crack that made the dam fail. From the way Central put it, the dam wasn't going to hold much longer anyhow.

"Tell the cordon to pass him. But tell him keep his head down or he's that much more t'clean up t'morrow," Jolober replied with his mike keyed, making the best decision he could when none of 'em looked good.

"Tried knock-out gas but he's got filters," said Stecher. "Fast, too." He tapped the scarred jamb. "All the skin absortives're lethal, and I don't guess we'd get cleared t' use 'em anyhow?"

"Not while I'm in the chain of command," Jolober agreed grimly.

"She was with this pongo from the Legere," the driver was saying through her laced fingers. "Tad, he wanted her so much, so fucking *much,* like she was human or something . . ."

"The, ah, you know. Beth, the one he was planning to see," said the commo tech rapidly as he stroked the back of the driver—Corporal Days—Daisy. . . . "He tried to, you know, buy 'er from the Frog, but he wouldn't play. She got 'em, Beth did, to put all their leave allowance on a coin flip. She'd take all the money and go with the winner."

"The bitch," Daisy wailed. "The bitch the bitch the bitch . . ."

The Legere didn't promote amateurs to battalion command. The powerful major Jolober had seen outside rolled through the doorway, sized up the situation, and sprinted to the landing out of the shooter's line of sight.

Line of fire.

"Hoffritz, can you hear me?" Jolober called. "I'm the port commandant, remember?"

A single bolt from the submachine gun spattered plastic from the jamb and filled the air with fresher stenches.

The man sprawling in the corridor moaned.

"I've ordered up an assault team," said Major de Vigny with flat assurance as he stood up beside Jolober. "It was unexpected, but they should be here in a few minutes."

Everyone else in the room was crouching. There wasn't any need so long as you weren't in front of the corridor, but it was the instinctive response to knowing somebody was trying to shoot you.

"Cancel the order," said Jolober, locking eyes with the other officer.

"You aren't in charge when one of my men—" began the major, his face flushing almost black.

"The gate closes when the alarm goes off!" Jolober said in a voice that could have been heard over a tank's fans. "And I've ordered the air defense batteries," he lied, "to fire on anybody trying to crash through now. If you want to lead a mutiny against your employers, Major, now's the time to do it."

The two big men glared at one another without blinking. Then de Vigny said, "Blue Six to Blue Three," keying his epaulet mike with the code words. "Hold Team Alpha until further orders. Repeat, hold Alpha. Out."

"Hold Alpha," repeated the speaker woven into the epaulet's fabric.

"If Condorcet dies," de Vigny added calmly to the port commandant, "I will kill you myself, sir."

"Do you have cratering charges warehoused here?" Jolober asked with no emotion save the slight lilt of interrogation.

"What?" said de Vigny. "Yes, yes."

Jolober crooked his left ring finger so that Central would hear and relay his next words. "Tell the gate to pass two men from the Legere with a jeep and a cratering charge. Give them a patrol guide, and download the prints of the China Doll into his commo link so they can place the charge on the wall outside the room of the T of the back corridor."

De Vigny nodded crisply to indicate that he too understood the other. He began relaying it into his epaulet while Stecher drew and reholstered his needle stunner and Corporal Days mumbled.

"Has she tried?" Jolober asked, waving to the driver and praying that he wouldn't have to . . .

"He shot at 'er," the commo tech said, nodding sadly. "That's when she really lost it and medics had to calm her down."

No surprises there. Certainly no good ones.

"Captain Hoffritz, it's the port commandant again," Jolober called.

A bolt spat down the axis of the corridor.

"That's right, you bastard, *shoot!*" Jolober roared. "You blew my legs off on Primavera. Now finish the job and *prove* you're a fuck-up who's only good for killing his friends. Come on, I'll make it easy. I'll come out and let you take your time!"

"Chief—" said Stecher.

Jolober slid away from the shelter of the wall.

The corridor was the stem of a T, ten meters long. Halfway between Jolober and the cross corridor at the other end, capping the T, lay the wounded man. Lieutenant Condorcet was a tough little man to still be alive with the back of his tunic smoldering around the holes punched in him by three powergun bolts. The roll of coins he'd carried to add weight to his fist wouldn't have helped; but then, nothing much helped when the other guy had the only gun in the equation.

Like now.

The door of the room facing the corridor and Horace Jolober was ajar. Beyond the opening was darkness and a bubble of dull red: the iridium muzzle of Hoffritz's submachine gun, glowing with the heat of the destruction it had spit at others.

De Vigny cursed; Stecher was pleading or even calling an order. All Jolober could hear was the roar of the tank bearing down on him, so loud that the slapping bolts streaming toward him from its cupola were inaudible.

Jolober's chair slid him down the hall. His arms were twitching in physical memory of the time they'd waved a scrap of white cloth to halt the oncoming armor.

The door facing him opened. Tad Hoffritz's face was as hard and yellow as fresh bone. He leaned over the sight of his submachine gun. Jolober slowed, because if he kept on at a walking pace he would collide with Condorcet, and if he curved around the wounded man it might look as if he were dodging what couldn't be dodged.

He didn't want to look like a fool and a coward when he died.

Hoffritz threw down the weapon.

Jolober bounced to him, wrapping the Slammers' officer in both arms like a son. Stecher was shouting "Medics!" but the team with the medicomp had been in motion as soon as the powergun hit the floor. Behind all the battle was Major de Vigny's voice, remembering to stop the crew with the charge that might otherwise be set—and fired even though the need was over.

"I *loved* her," Hoffritz said to Jolober's big shoulder, begging someone to understand what he didn't understand himself. "I, I'd been drinking and I came back . . ."

With a submachine gun that shouldn't have made it into Paradise Port . . . but the detection loops hadn't been replaced in the hours since the tanks ripped them away; and anyhow, Hoffritz was an officer, a company commander.

He was also a young man having a bad time with what he thought was a woman. Older, calmer fellows than Hoffritz had killed because of that.

Jolober carried Hoffritz with him into the room where he'd been holed up. "Lights," the commandant ordered, and the room brightened.

Condorcet wasn't dead, not yet; but Beth, the Doll behind the trouble, surely was.

The couch was large and round. Though drumhead-thin, its structure could be varied to any degree of firmness the paying half of the couple desired. Beth lay in the center of it in a tangle of long black hair. Her tongue protruded from a blood-darkened face, and the prints of the grip that had strangled her were livid on her throat.

"She told me she loved *him*," Hoffritz mumbled. The commandant's embrace supported him, but it also kept Hoffritz from doing something silly, like trying to run.

"After what I'd done," the boy was saying, "she tells me she doesn't love me after all. She says I'm no good to her in bed, that I never gave her any pleasure at all. . . ."

"Just trying to maximize the claim for damages, son," Jolober said grimly. "It didn't mean anything real, just more dollars in Red Ike's pocket."

But Red Ike hadn't counted on Hoffritz shooting another merc. Too bad for Condorcet, too bad for the kid who shot him—

And just what Jolober needed to finish Red Ike on Placida.

"Let's go," Jolober said, guiding Hoffritz out of the

room stinking of death and the emotions that led to death. "We'll get you to a medic."

And a cell.

Condorcet had been removed from the corridor, leaving behind only a slime of vomit. Thank the Lord he'd fallen face down.

Stecher and his partner took the unresisting Hoffritz and wrapped him in motion restraints. The prisoner could walk and move normally, so long as he did it slowly. At a sudden movement, the gossamer webs would clamp him as tightly as a fly in a spiderweb.

The main hall was crowded, but the incipient violence facing the cordon outside had melted away. Judging from Major de Vigny's brusque, bellowed orders, the victim was in the hands of his medics and being shifted to the medicomp in Division Legere's bivouac area.

That was probably the best choice. Paradise Port had excellent medical facilities, but medics in combat units got to know their jobs and their diagnostic/healing computers better than anybody in the rear echelons.

"Commandant Jolober," said van Zuyle, the Slammers' bivouac commander, "I'm worried about my man here. Can I—"

"He's not your man any more, Captain," Jolober said with the weary chill of an avalanche starting to topple. "He's mine and the Placidan courts'—until I tell you different. We'll get him sedated and keep him from hurting himself, no problem."

Van Zuyle's face wore the expression of a man whipping himself to find a deity who doesn't respond. "Sir," he said, "I'm sorry if I—"

"You did the job they paid you t'do," Jolober said, shrugging away from the other man. He hadn't felt so weary since he'd awakened in the Legion's main hospital on Primavera: alive and utterly unwilling to believe that he could be after what happened.

"Outa the man's way," snarled one of the patrolmen, trying to wave a path through the crowd with her white-sleeved arms. "Let the commandant by!"

She yelped a curse at the big man who brushed through her gesture. "A moment, little one," he said—de Vigny, the Legere major.

"You kept the lid on good," Jolober said while part of his dazed mind wondered whose voice he was hearing. "Tomorrow I'll want to talk to you about what happened and how to keep from a repeat."

Anger darkened de Vigny's face. "I heard what happened," he said. "Condorcet was not the only human victim, it would seem."

"We'll talk," Jolober said. His chair was driving him toward the door, pushing aside anyone who didn't get out of the way. He didn't see them any more than he saw the air.

The street was a carnival of uniformed soldiers who suddenly had something to focus on that wasn't a memory of death—or a way to forget. There were dark undercurrents to the chatter, but the crowd was no longer a mob.

Jolober's uniform drew eyes, but the port commandant was too aloof and forbidding to be asked for details of what had really happened in the China Doll. In the center of the street, though—

"Good evening, Commandant," said Red Ike, strolling back toward the establishment he owned. "Without your courage, tonight's incident would have been even more unfortunate."

Human faces changed in the play of light washing them from the brothel fronts. Red Ike's did not. Colors overlay his features, but the lines did not modify as one shadow or highlight replaced another.

"It couldn't be more unfortunate for you, Ike," Jolober said to the bland alien while uniforms milled around them. "They'll pay you money, the mercs will. But they won't have you killing their men."

"I understand that the injured party is expected to pull through," Red Ike said emotionlessly. Jolober had the feeling that the alien's eyes were focused on his soul.

"I'm glad Condorcet'll live," Jolober said, too tired for triumph or subtlety. "But you're dead on Placida, Ike. It's just a matter of how long it takes me to wrap it up."

He broke past Red Ike, gliding toward the port offices and the light glowing from his room on the upper floor.

Red Ike didn't turn around, but Jolober thought he could feel the alien watching him nonetheless.

Even so, all Jolober cared about now was bed and a chance to reassure Vicki that everything was all right.

The alley between the office building and the Blue Parrot next door wasn't directly illuminated, but enough light spilled from the street to show Jolober the stairs.

He didn't see the two men waiting there until a third had closed the mouth of the alley behind him. Indonesian music began to blare from the China Doll.

Music on the exterior's a violation, thought the part of Jolober's mind that ran Paradise Port, but reflexes from his years as a combat officer noted the man behind him held a metal bar and that knives gleamed in the hands of the two by the stairs.

It made a hell of a fast trip back from the nightmare memories that had ruled Jolober's brain since he wakened.

Jolober's left stump urged the throttle as his torso shifted toward the alley mouth. The electronics reacted instantly but the mechanical links took a moment. Fans spun up, plenum chamber collapsed into a nozzle—

The attackers moved in on Jolober like the three wedges of a drill chuck. His chair launched him into the one with the club, a meter off the ground and rising with a hundred and eighty kilos of mass behind the impact.

At the last instant the attacker tried to duck away instead of swinging at Jolober, but he misjudged the speed of his intended victim. The center of the chair's frame, between the skirt and the saddle, batted the attacker's head toward the wall, dragging the fellow's body with it.

Jolober had a clear path to the street. The pair of knifemen thought he was headed that way and sprinted in a desperate attempt to catch a victim who moved faster than unaided humans could run.

They were in midstride, thinking of failure rather than defense, when Jolober pogoed at the alley mouth and came back at them like a cannonball.

But bigger and heavier.

One attacker stabbed at Jolober's chest and skidded the point on the battery compartment instead when the chair hopped. The frame slammed knife and man into the concrete wall from which they ricochetted to the ground, separate and equally motionless.

The third man ran away.

"Get 'em, boys!" Jolober bellowed as if he were launching his battalion instead of just himself in pursuit. The running man glanced over his shoulder and collided with the metal staircase. The noise was loud and unpleasant, even in comparison to the oriental music blaring from the China Doll.

Jolober bounced, cut his fan speed, and flared his output nozzle into a plenum chamber again. The chair twitched, then settled into ground effect.

Jolober's mind told him that he was seeing with a clarity and richness of color he couldn't have equalled by daylight, but he knew that if he really focused on an object it would blur into shadow. It was just his brain's way of letting him know that he was still alive.

Alive like he hadn't been in years.

Crooking his ring finger Jolober said, "I need a pickup on three men in the alley between us and the Blue Parrot."

"Three men in the alley between HQ and the Blue Parrot," the artificial intelligence paraphrased.

"They'll need a medic." One might need burial. "And I want them sweated under a psycomp—who sent 'em after me, the works."

Light flooded the alley as a team of patrolmen arrived. The point man extended a surface-luminescent area light powered from a backpack. The shadows thrown by the meter-diameter convexity were soft, but the illumination was the blaze of noon compared to that of moments before.

"Chief!" swallowed Stecher. "You all right? Chief!" He wasn't part of the team Central vectored to the alley, but word of mouth had brought him to the scene of the incident.

Jolober throttled up, clamped his skirts, and boosted himself to the fourth step where everyone could see him. The man who'd run into the stairs moaned as the sidedraft spat grit from the treads into his face.

"No problem," Jolober said. No problem they wouldn't be able to cure in a week or two. "I doubt these three know any more than that they got a call from outside Port to, ah, handle me . . . but get what they have, maybe we can cross-reference with some outgoing traffic."

From the China Doll; or just maybe from the Blue Parrot, where Ike fled when the shooting started. But probably not. Three thugs, nondescripts from off-planet who could've been working for any establishment in Paradise Port *except* the China Doll.

"Sir—" came Stecher's voice.

"It'll keep, Sergeant," Jolober interrupted. "Just now I've got a heavy date with a bed."

Vicki greeted him with a smile so bright that both of them could pretend there were no tears beneath it. The air was steamy with the bath she'd drawn for him.

He used to prefer showers, back when he'd had feet on which to stand. He could remember dancing on Quitly's Planet as the afternoon monsoon battered the gun carriages his platoon was guarding and washed the soap from his body.

But he didn't have Vicki then, either.

"Yeah," he said, hugging the Doll. "Good idea, a bath."

Instead of heading for the bathroom, he slid his chair to the cabinet within arm's reach of the bed and cut his fans. Bending over, he unlatched the battery compartment—the knifepoint hadn't even penetrated the casing—and removed the powerpack.

"I can—" Vicki offered hesitantly.

"S'okay, dearest," Jolober replied as he slid a fresh pack from the cabinet into place. His stump touched the throttle, spinning the fans to prove that he had good contact, then lifted the original pack into the cabinet and its charging harness.

"Just gave 'em a workout tonight and don't want t' be down on power tomorrow," he explained as he straightened. Vicki could have handled the weight of the batteries, he realized, though his mind kept telling him it was ludicrous to imagine the little woman shifting thirty-kilo packages with ease.

But she wasn't a woman.

"I worry when it's so dangerous," she said as she walked with him to the bathroom, their arms around one another's waist.

"Look, for Paradise Port, it was dangerous," Jolober said in a light appearance of candor as he handed Vicki his garments. "Compared to downtown in any capital city I've seen, it was pretty mild."

He lowered himself into the water, using the bars laid over the tub like a horizontal ladder. Vicki began to knead the great muscles of his shoulders, and Lord! but it felt good to relax after so long. . . .

"I'd miss you," she said.

"Not unless I went away," Jolober answered, leaning forward so that her fingers could work down his spine while the water lapped at them. "Which isn't going to happen any time soon."

He paused. The water's warmth unlocked more than his body. "Look," he said quietly, his chin touching the surface of the bath and his eyes still closed. "Red Ike's had it. He knows it, I know it. But I'm in a position to make things either easy or hard, and he knows that, too. We'll come to terms, he and I. And you're the—"

"Urgent from the gate," said Jolober's mastoid implant.

He crooked his finger, raising his head. "Put him through," he said.

Her through. "Sir," said Feldman's attenuated voice, "a courier's just landed with two men. They say they've got an oral message from Colonel Hammer, and they want me to alert you that they're coming. Over."

"I'll open the front door," Jolober said, lifting himself abruptly from the water, careful not to miskey the implant while his hands performed other tasks.

He wouldn't rouse the human staff. No need and if the message came by courier, it wasn't intended for other ears.

"Ah, sir," Feldman added unexpectedly. "One of them insists on keeping his sidearms. Over."

"Then he can insist on staying outside my perimeter!" Jolober snarled. Vicki had laid a towel on the saddle before he mounted and was now using another to silently dry his body. "You can detach two guards to escort 'em if they need their hands held, but *nobody* brings powerguns into Paradise Port."

"Roger, I'll tell them," Feldman agreed doubtfully. "Over and out."

"I have a fresh uniform out," said Vicki, stepping back so that Jolober could follow her into the bedroom, where the air was drier.

"That's three, today," Jolober said, grinning. "Well, I've done a lot more than I've managed any three other days.

"Via," he added more seriously. "It's more headway than I've made since they appointed me commandant."

Vicki smiled, but her eyes were so tired that Jolober's body trembled in response. His flesh remembered how much he had already been through today and yearned for the sleep to which the hot bath had disposed it.

Jolober lifted himself on his hands so that Vicki could raise and cinch his trousers. He could do it himself, but he was in a hurry, and . . . besides, just as she'd said, Vicki was a part of him in a real way.

"Cheer up, love," he said as he closed his tunic. "It isn't done yet, but it's sure getting that way."

"Good-bye, Horace," the Doll said as she kissed him.

"Keep the bed warm," Jolober called as he slid toward the door and the inner staircase. His head was tumbling with memories and images. For a change, they were all pleasant ones.

The port offices were easily identified at night because they *weren't* garishly illuminated like every other building in Paradise Port. Jolober had a small staff, and he didn't choose to waste it at desks. Outside of ordinary business hours, Central's artificial intelligence handled everything—by putting nonemergency requests on hold till morning, and by vectoring a uniformed patrol to the real business.

Anybody who insisted on personal service could get it by hammering at the Patrol entrance on the west side, opposite Jolober's private staircase. A patrolman would find the noisemaker a personal holding cell for the remainder of the night.

The front entrance was built like a vault door, not so much to prevent intrusion as to keep drunks from destroying the panel for reasons they'd be unable to remember sober. Jolober palmed the release for the separate bolting systems and had just begun to swing the door open in invitation when the two men in khaki uniforms, neither of them tall, strode up to the building.

"Blood and Martyrs!" Jolober said as he continued to back, not entirely because the door required it.

"You run a tight base here, Commandant," said Colonel Alois Hammer as he stepped into the waiting room. "Do you know my aide, Major Steuben?"

"By reputation only," said Jolober, nodding to Joachim Steuben with the formal correctness which that reputation enjoined. "Ah—with a little more information, I might have relaxed the prohibition on weapons."

Steuben closed the door behind them, moving the heavy panel with a control which belied the boyish delicacy of his face and frame. "If the colonel's satisfied with his security," Joachim said mildly, "then of course I am, too."

The eyes above his smile would willingly have watched Jolober drawn and quartered.

"You've had some problems with troops of mine today," said Hammer, seating himself on one of the chairs and rising again, almost as quickly as if he had continued to walk. His eyes touched Jolober and moved on in short hops that covered everything in the room like an animal checking a new environment.

"Only reported problems occurred," said Jolober, keeping the promise he'd made earlier in the day. He lighted the hologram projection tank on the counter to let it warm up. "There was an incident a few hours ago, yes."

The promise didn't matter to Tad Hoffritz, not after the shootings; but it mattered more than life to Horace Jolober that he keep the bargains he'd made.

"According to Captain van Zuyle's report," Hammer said as his eyes flickered over furniture and recesses dim under the partial lighting, "you're of the opinion the boy was set up."

"What you do with a gun," said Joachim Steuben softly

from the door against which he leaned, "is your own responsibility."

"As Joachim says," Hammer went on with a nod and no facial expression, "that doesn't affect how we'll deal with Captain Hoffritz when he's released from local custody. But it does affect how we act to prevent recurrences, doesn't it?"

"Load the file Ike One into the downstairs holo," said Jolober to Central.

He looked at Hammer, paused till their eyes met. "Sure, he was set up, just like half a dozen others in the past three months—only they were money assessments, no real problem.

"And the data prove," Jolober continued coolly, claiming what his data suggested but could *not* prove, "that it's going to get a lot worse than what happened tonight if Red Ike and his Dolls aren't shipped out fast."

The holotank sprang to life in a three-dimensional cross-hatching of orange lines. As abruptly, the lines shrank into words and columns of figures. "Red Ike and his Dolls— they were all his openly, then—first show up on Sparrowhome a little over five years standard ago, according to Bonding Authority records. Then—"

Jolober pointed toward the figures. Colonel Hammer put his smaller, equally firm, hand over the commandant's and said, "Wait. Just give me your assessment."

"Dolls have been imported as recreational support in seven conflicts," said Jolober as calmly as if his mind had not just shifted gears. He'd been a good combat commander for the same reason, for dealing with the situation that occurred rather than the one he'd planned for. "There's been rear-echelon trouble each time, and the riot on Ketelby caused the Bonding Authority to order the disbandment of a battalion of Guardforce O'Higgins."

"There was trouble over a woman," said Steuben unemotionally, reeling out the data he gathered because he was Hammer's adjutant as well as his bodyguard. "A fight be-

tween a ranger and an artilleryman led to a riot in which half
the nearest town was burned."

"Not a woman," corrected Jolober. "A Doll."

He tapped the surface of the holotank. "It's all here,
downloaded from Bonding Authority archives. You just
have to see what's happening so you know the questions to
ask."

"You can get me a line to the capital?" Hammer asked
as if he were discussing the weather. "I was in a hurry, and
I didn't bring along my usual commo."

Jolober lifted the visiplate folded into the surface of the
counter beside the tank and rotated it toward Hammer.

"I've always preferred nonhumans for recreation
areas," Hammer said idly as his finger played over the
plate's keypad. "Oh, the troops complain, but I've never
seen *that* hurt combat efficiency. Whereas real women gave
all sorts of problems."

"And real men," said Joachim Steuben, with a deadpan
expression that could have meant anything.

The visiplate beeped. "Main Switch," said a voice, tart
but not sleepy. "Go ahead."

"You have my authorization code," Hammer said to the
human operator on the other end of the connection. From
Jolober's flat angle to the plate, he couldn't make out the operator's features—only that he sat in a brightly illuminated
white cubicle. "Patch me through to the chairman of the Facilities Inspection Committee."

"Senator Dieter?" said the operator, professionally able
to keep the question short of being amazement.

"If he's the chairman," Hammer said. The words had
the angry undertone of a dynamite fuse burning.

"Yessir, she is," replied the operator with studied neu-
trality. "One moment please."

"I've been dealing with her chief aide," said Jolober
in a hasty whisper. "Guy named Higgey. His pager's
loaded—"

"Got you a long ways, didn't it, Commandant?" Hammer said with a gun-turret click of his head toward Jolober.

"Your pardon, sir," said Jolober, bracing reflexively to attention. He wasn't Hammer's subordinate, but they both served the same ideal—getting the job done. The ball was in Hammer's court just now, and he'd ask for support if he thought he needed it.

From across the waiting room, Joachim Steuben smiled at Jolober. That one had the same ideal, perhaps; but his terms of reference were something else again.

"The senator isn't at any of her registered work stations," the operator reported coolly.

"Son," said Hammer, leaning toward the visiplate, "you have a unique opportunity to lose the war for Placida. All you have to do is *not* get me through to the chairman."

"Yes, Colonel Hammer," the operator replied with an aplomb that made it clear why he held the job he did. "I've processed your authorization, and I'm running it through again on War Emergency Ord—"

The last syllable was clipped. The bright rectangle of screen dimmed gray. Jolober slid his chair in a short arc so that he could see the visiplate clearly past Hammer's shoulder.

"What is it?" demanded the woman in the dim light beyond. She was stocky, middle-aged, and rather attractive because of the force of personality she radiated even sleepless in a dressing gown.

"This is Colonel Alois Hammer," Hammer said. "Are you recording?"

"On *this* circuit?" the senator replied with a frosty smile. "Of course I am. So are at least three other agencies, whether I will or no."

Hammer blinked, startled to find himself on the wrong end of a silly question for a change.

"Senator," he went on without the hectoring edge that had been present since his arrival. "A contractor engaged by your government to provide services at Paradise Port has been causing problems. One of the Legere's down, in critical, and I'm short a company commander over the same incident."

"You've reported to the port commandant?" Senator Dieter said, her eyes unblinking as they passed over Jolober.

"The commandant reported to me because your staff stonewalled him," Hammer said flatly while Jolober felt his skin grow cold, even the tips of the toes he no longer had. "I want the contractor, a nonhuman called Red Ike, offplanet in seventy-two hours with all his chattels. That specifically includes his Dolls. We'll work—"

"That's too soon," said Dieter, her fingers tugging a lock of hair over one ear while her mind worked. "Even if—"

"Forty-*eight* hours, Senator," Hammer interrupted. "This is a violation of your bond. And I promise you, I'll have the support of all the other commanders of units contracted to Placidan service. Forty-eight hours, or we'll withdraw from combat and you won't have a front line."

"You *can't*—" Dieter began. Then all muscles froze, tongue and fingers among them, as her mind considered the implications of what the colonel had just told her.

"I have no concern over being able to win my case at the Bonding Authority hearing on Earth," Hammer continued softly. "But I'm quite certain that the present Placidan government won't be there to contest it."

Dieter smiled without humor. "Seventy-two hours," she said as if repeating the figure.

"I've shifted the Regiment across continents in less time, Senator," Hammer said.

"Yes," said Dieter calmly. "Well, there are political consequences to any action, and I'd rather explain myself to my constituents than to an army of occupation. I'll take care of it."

She broke the circuit.

"I wouldn't mind getting to know that lady," said Hammer, mostly to himself, as he folded the visiplate back into the counter.

"That takes care of your concerns, then?" he added sharply, looking up at Jolober.

"Yes, sir, it does," said Jolober, who had the feeling he had drifted into a plane where dreams could be happy.

"Ah, about Captain Hoffritz . . ." Hammer said. His eyes slipped, but he snapped them back to meet Jolober's despite the embarrassment of being about to ask a favor.

"He's not combat-fit right now, Colonel," Jolober said, warming as authority flooded back to fill his mind. "He'll do as well in our care for the next few days as he would in yours. After that, and assuming that no one wants to press charges—"

"Understood," said Hammer, nodding. "I'll deal with the victim and General Claire."

"—then some accommodation can probably be arranged with the courts."

"It's been a pleasure dealing with a professional of your caliber, Commandant," Hammer said as he shook Jolober's hand. He spoke without emphasis, but nobody meeting his cool blue eyes could have imagined that Hammer would have bothered to lie about it.

"It's started to rain," observed Major Steuben as he muscled the door open.

"It's permitted to," Hammer said. "We've been wet be—"

"A jeep to the front of the building," Jolober ordered with his ring finger crooked. He straightened and said, "Ah, Colonel? Unless you'd like to be picked up by one of your own vehicles?"

"Nobody knows I'm here," said Hammer from the doorway. "I don't want van Zuyle to think I'm second-guessing him—I'm not, I'm just handling the part that's mine to handle."

He paused before adding with an ironic smile, "In any case, we're four hours from exploiting the salient Hoffritz's company formed when they took the junction at Kettering."

A jeep with two patrolmen, stunners ready, scraped to a halt outside. The team was primed for a situation like the one in the alley less than an hour before.

"Taxi service only, boys," Jolober called to the patrolmen. "Carry these gentlemen to their courier ship, please."

The jeep was spinning away in the drizzle before Jolober had closed and locked the door again. It didn't occur to him that it mattered whether or not the troops bivouacked around Paradise Port knew immediately what Hammer had just arranged.

And it didn't occur to him, as he bounced his chair up the stairs calling, "Vicki! We've won!" that he should feel any emotion except joy.

"Vicki!" he repeated as he opened the bedroom door. They'd have to leave Placida unless he could get Vicki released from the blanket order on Dolls—but he hadn't expected to keep his job anyway, not after he went over the head of the whole Placidan government.

"Vi—"

She'd left a light on, one of the point sources in the ceiling. It was a shock, but not nearly as bad a shock as Jolober would have gotten if he'd slid onto the bed in the dark.

"Who?" his tongue asked while his mind couldn't think of anything to say, could only move his chair to the bedside and palm the hydraulics to lower him into a sitting position.

Her right hand and forearm were undamaged. She flexed her fingers and the keen plastic blade shot from her fist, then collapsed again into a baton. She let it roll onto the bedclothes.

"He couldn't force me to kill you," Vicki said. "He was very surprised, very. . . ."

Jolober thought she might be smiling, but he couldn't

be sure since she no longer had lips. The plastic edges of the knife Vicki took as she dressed him were not sharp enough for finesse, but she had not attempted surgical delicacy.

Vicki had destroyed herself from toes to her once-perfect face. All she had left was one eye with which to watch Jolober, and the parts of her body which she couldn't reach unaided. She had six ribs to a side, broader and flatter than those of a human's skeleton. After she laid open the ribs, she had dissected the skin and flesh of the left side farther.

Jolober had always assumed—when he let himself think about it—that her breasts were sponge implants. He'd been wrong. On the bedspread lay a wad of yellowish fat streaked with blood vessels. He didn't have a background that would tell him whether or not it was human normal, but it certainly was biological.

It was a tribute to Vicki's toughness that she had remained alive as long as she had.

Instinct turned Jolober's hand to the side so that he vomited away from the bed. He clasped Vicki's right hand with both of his, keeping his eyes closed so that he could imagine that everything was as it had been minutes before when he was triumphantly happy. His left wrist brushed the knife that should have remained an inert baton in any hands but his. He snatched up the weapon, feeling the blade flow out—

As it had when Vicki held it, turned it on herself.

"We are one, my Horace," she whispered, her hand squeezing his.

It was the last time she spoke, but Jolober couldn't be sure of that because his mind had shifted out of the present into a cosmos limited to the sense of touch: body-warm plastic in his left hand, and flesh cooling slowly in his right.

He sat in his separate cosmos for almost an hour, until the emergency call on his mastoid implant threw him back into an existence where his life had purpose.

"All units!" cried a voice on the panic push. "The—"

The blast of static which drowned the voice lasted only a fraction of a second before the implant's logic circuits shut the unit down to keep the white noise from driving Jolober mad. The implant would be disabled as long as the jamming continued—but jamming of this intensity would block even the most sophisticated equipment in the Slammers' tanks.

Which were probably carrying out the jamming.

Jolober's hand slipped the knife away without thinking—with fiery determination not to think—as his stump kicked the chair into life and he glided toward the alley stairs. He was still dressed, still mounted in his saddle, and that was as much as he was willing to know about his immediate surroundings.

The stairs rang. The thrust of his fans was a fitful gust on the metal treads each time he bounced on his way to the ground.

The voice could have been Feldman at the gate; she was the most likely source anyway. At the moment, Jolober had an emergency.

In a matter of minutes, it could be a disaster instead.

It was raining, a nasty drizzle which distorted the invitations capering on the building fronts. The street was empty except for a pair of patrol jeeps, bubbles in the night beneath canopies that would stop most of the droplets.

Even this weather shouldn't have kept soldiers from scurrying from one establishment to another, hoping to change their luck when they changed location. Overhanging façades ought to have been crowded with morose troopers, waiting for a lull—or someone drunk or angry enough to lead an exodus toward another empty destination.

The emptiness would have worried Jolober if he didn't have much better reasons for concern. The vehicles sliding down the street from the gate were unlighted, but there was no mistaking the roar of a tank.

Someone in the China Doll heard and understood the sound also, because the armored door squealed down across the archway even as Jolober's chair lifted him in that direction at high thrust.

He braked in a spray. The water-slicked pavement didn't affect his control, since the chair depended on thrust rather than friction—but being able to stop didn't give him any ideas about how he should proceed.

One of the patrol jeeps swung in front of the tank with a courage and panache which made Jolober proud of his men. The patrolman on the passenger side had ripped the canopy away to stand waving a yellow light-wand with furious determination.

The tank did not slow. It shifted direction just enough to strike the jeep a glancing blow instead of center-punching it. That didn't spare the vehicle; its light frame crumpled like tissue before it resisted enough to spin across the pavement at twice the velocity of the slowly advancing tank. The slight adjustment in angle did save the patrolmen, who were thrown clear instead of being ground between concrete and the steel skirts.

The tank's scarred turret made it identifiable in the light of the building fronts. Jolober crooked his finger and shouted, "Commandant to Corporal Days. For the *Lord's* sake, trooper, don't get your unit disbanded for mutiny! Colonel Hammer's already gotten Red Ike ordered off-planet!"

There was no burp from his mastoid as Central retransmitted the message a microsecond behind the original. Only then did Jolober recall that the Slammers had jammed his communications.

Not the Slammers alone. The two vehicles behind the tank were squat armored personnel carriers, each capable of hauling an infantry section with all its equipment. Nobody had bothered to paint out the fender markings of the Division Legere.

Rain stung Jolober's eyes as he hopped the last five meters to the sealed façade of the China Doll. Anything could

be covered, could be settled, except murder—and killing
Red Ike would be a murder of which the Bonding Authority
would have to take cognizance.

"Let me in!" Jolober shouted to the door. The armor
was so thick that it didn't ring when he pounded it. "Let
me—"

Normally the sound of a mortar firing was audible for a
kilometer, a hollow *shoomp!* like a firecracker going off in
an oil drum. Jolober hadn't heard the launch from beyond
the perimeter because of the nearby roar of drive fans.

When the round went off on the roof of the China Doll,
the charge streamed tendrils of white fire down as far as the
pavement, where they pocked the concrete. The snakepit
coruscance of blue sparks lighting the roof a moment later
was the battery pack of Red Ike's aircar shorting through the
new paths the mortar shell had burned in the car's circuitry.

The mercs were playing for keeps. They hadn't come to
destroy the China Doll and leave its owner to rebuild somewhere else.

The lead tank swung in the street with the cautious delicacy of an elephant wearing a hoopskirt. Its driving lights
blazed on, silhouetting the port commandant against the
steel door. Jolober held out his palm in prohibition, knowing
that if he could delay events even a minute, Red Ike would
escape through his tunnel.

Everything else within the China Doll was a chattel
which could be compensated with money.

There was a red flash and a roar from the stern of the
tank, then an explosion muffled by a meter of concrete and
volcanic rock. Buildings shuddered like sails in a squall; the
front of the port offices cracked as its fabric was placed
under a flexing strain that concrete was never meant to resist.

The rocket-assisted penetrators carried by the Slammers' tanks were intended to shatter bunkers of any thick-
ness imaginable in the field. Red Ike's bolthole was now a

long cavity filled with chunks and dust of the material intended to protect it.

The tanks had very good detection equipment, and combat troops live to become veterans by observing their surroundings. Quite clearly, the tunnel had not escaped notice when Tad Hoffritz led his company down the street to hoo-rah Paradise Port.

"Wait!" Jolober shouted, because there's always a chance until there's no chance at all.

"Get out of the way, Commandant!" boomed the tank's public address system, loudly enough to seem an echo of the penetrator's earth-shock.

"Colonel Hammer has—" Jolober shouted.

"We'd as soon not hurt you," the speakers roared as the turret squealed ten degrees on its gimbals. The main gun's bore was a 20cm tube aligned perfectly with Jolober's eyes.

They couldn't hear him; they wouldn't listen if they could; and anyway, the troopers involved in this weren't interested in contract law. They wanted justice, and to them that didn't mean a ticket off-planet for Red Ike.

The tribarrel in the tank's cupola fired a single shot. The bolt of directed energy struck the descending arch just in front of Jolober and gouged the plastic away in fire and black smoke. Bits of the covering continued to burn, and the underlying concrete added an odor of hot lime to the plastic and the ozone of the bolt's track through the air.

Jolober's miniature vehicle thrust him away in a flat arc, out of the door alcove and sideways in the street as a powergun fired from a port concealed in the China Doll's façade. The tank's main gun demolished the front wall with a single round.

The street echoed with the thunderclap of cold air filling the track seared through it by the energy bolt. The pistol shot an instant earlier could almost have been proleptic reflection, confused in memory with the sun-bright cyan glare of the tank cannon—and, by being confused, forgotten.

Horace Jolober understood the situation too well to mistake its events. The shot meant Red Ike was still in the China Doll, trapped there and desperate enough to issue his Droids lethal weapons that must have been difficult even for him to smuggle into Paradise Port.

Desperate and foolish, because the pistol bolt had only flicked dust from the tank's iridium turret. Jolober had warned Red Ike that combat troops played by a different rulebook. The message just hadn't been received until it was too late. . . .

Jolober swung into the three-meter alley beside the China Doll. There was neither an opening here nor ornamentation, just the blank concrete wall of a fortress.

Which wouldn't hold for thirty seconds if the combat team out front chose to assault it.

The tank had fired at the building front, not the door. The main gun could have blasted a hole in the armor, but that wouldn't have been a large enough entrance for the infantry now deploying behind the armored flanks of the APCs.

The concrete wall shattered like a bomb when it tried to absorb the point-blank energy of the 20cm gun. The cavity the shot left was big enough to pass a jeep with a careful driver. Infantrymen in battle armor, hunched over their weapons, dived into the China Doll. The interior lit with cyan flashes as they shot everything that moved.

The exterior lighting had gone out, but flames clawed their way up the thermoplastic façade. The fire threw a red light onto the street in which shadows of smoke capered like demons. Drips traced blazing lines through the air as they fell to spatter troops waiting their turn for a chance to kill.

The assault didn't require a full infantry platoon, but few operations have failed because the attackers had too many troops.

Jolober had seen the equivalent too often to doubt how

it was going to go this time. He didn't have long; very possibly he didn't have long enough.

Standing parallel to the sheer sidewall, Jolober ran his fans up full power, then clamped the plenum chamber into a tight nozzle and lifted. His left hand paddled against the wall three times. That gave him balance and the suggestion of added thrust to help his screaming fans carry out a task for which they hadn't been designed.

When his palm touched the coping, Jolober used the contact to center him, and rotated onto the flat roof of the China Doll.

Sparks spat peevishly from the corpse of the aircar. The vehicle's frame was a twisted wire sculpture from which most of the sheathing material had burned away, but occasionally the breeze brought oxygen to a scrap that was still combustible.

The penthouse that held Ike's office and living quarters was a squat box beyond the aircar. The mortar shell had detonated just as the alien started to run for his vehicle. He'd gotten back inside as the incendiary compound sprayed the roof, but bouncing fragments left black trails across the plush blue floor of the office.

The door was a section of wall broad enough to have passed the aircar. Red Ike hadn't bothered to close it when he fled to his elevator and the tunnel exit. Jolober, skimming again on ground effect, slid into the office shouting, "Ike! This—"

Red Ike burst from the elevator cage as the door rotated open. He had a pistol and eyes as wide as a madman's as he swung the weapon toward the hulking figure in his office.

Jolober reacted as the adrenaline pumping through his body had primed him to do. The arm with which he swatted at the pistol was long enough that his fingers touched the barrel, strong enough that the touch hurled the gun across the room despite Red Ike's deathgrip on the butt.

Red Ike screamed.

An explosion in the elevator shaft wedged the elevator doors as they began to close and burped orange flame against the far wall.

Jolober didn't know how the assault team proposed to get to the roof, but neither did he intend to wait around to learn. He wrapped both arms around the stocky alien and shouted, "Shut up and hold still if you want to get out of here alive!"

Red Ike froze, either because he understood the warning—or because at last he recognized Horace Jolober and panicked to realize that the port commandant had already disarmed him.

Jolober lifted the alien and turned his chair. It glided toward the door at gathering speed, logy with the double burden.

There was another blast from the office. The assault team had cleared the elevator shaft with a cratering charge whose directed blast sprayed the room with the bits and vapors that remained of the cage. Grenades would be next, then grappling hooks and more grenades just before—

Jolober kicked his throttle as he rounded the aircar. The fans snarled and the ride, still on ground effect, became greasy as the skirts lifted undesirably.

The office rocked in a series of dense white flashes. The room lights went out and a large piece of shrapnel, the fuze housing of a grenade, powdered a fist-sized mass of the concrete coping beside Jolober.

His chair's throttle had a gate. With the fans already at normal maximum, he sphinctered his skirts into a nozzle and kicked again at the throttle. He could smell the chair's circuits frying under the overload as it lifted Jolober and Red Ike to the coping—

But it did lift them, and after a meter's run along the narrow track to build speed, it launched them across the black, empty air of the alley.

Red Ike wailed. The only sound Horace Jolober made

was in his mind. He saw not a roof but the looming bow of a tank, and his fears shouted the word they hadn't been able to get out on Primavera either: "*No!*"

They cleared the coping of the other roof with a click, not a crash, and bounced as Jolober spilled air and cut thrust back to normal levels.

An explosion behind them lit the night red and blew chunks of Red Ike's office a hundred meters in the air.

Instead of trying to winkle out their quarry with gunfire, the assault team had lobbed a bunker-buster up the elevator shaft. The blast walloped Jolober even though distance and the pair of meter-high concrete copings protected his hunching form from dangerous fragments.

Nothing in the penthouse of the China Doll could have survived. It wasn't neat, but it saved lives where they counted—in the attacking force—and veteran soldiers have never put a high premium on finesse.

"You saved me," Red Ike said.

Jolober's ears were numb from the final explosion, but he could watch Red Ike's lips move in the flames lifting even higher from the front of the China Doll.

"I had to," Jolober said, marveling at how fully human the alien seemed. "Those men, they're line soldiers. They think that because there were so many of them involved, nobody can be punished."

Hatches rang shut on the armored personnel carriers. A noncom snarled an order to stragglers that could be heard even over the drive fans.

Red Ike started toward the undamaged aircar parked beside them on this roof. Jolober's left hand still held the alien's wrist. Ike paused as if to pretend his movement had never taken place. His face was emotionless.

"Numbers made it a mutiny," Jolober continued. Part of him wondered whether Red Ike could hear the words he was speaking in a soft voice, but he was unwilling to shout.

It would have been disrespectful.

Fierce wind rocked the flames as the armored vehicles, tank in the lead as before, lifted and began to howl their way out of Paradise Port.

"I'll take care of you," Red Ike said. "You'll have Vicki back in three weeks, I promise. Tailored to *you,* just like the other. You won't be able to tell the difference."

"There's no me to take care of any more," said Horace Jolober with no more emotion than a man tossing his uniform into a laundry hamper.

"You see," he added as he reached behind him, "if they'd killed you tonight, the Bonding Authority would have disbanded both units *whatever* the Placidans wanted. But me? Anything I do is my responsibility."

Red Ike began to scream in a voice that became progressively less human as the sound continued.

Horace Jolober was strong enough that he wouldn't have needed the knife despite the way his victim struggled.

But it seemed like a fitting monument for Vicki.

Betsy Mitchell, now Editor-in-Chief of Warner Aspect, once was Senior Editor of Baen Books and while there edited a number of volumes of original novellas, each around a single theme. I wrote Liberty Port *for one of these, and Betsy asked me to reprint it here when she commissioned* Dogs of War. *There's a story to the story, though.*

I usually didn't—and don't—get written contracts from Jim Baen, at least until well after I've been paid and the work delivered. Betsy was determined to do things right, however, and sent around a formal contract stating the terms and conditions on which I was writing the novella.

So far, so good; but there was a blank for the title of the piece. I called Betsy and told her I didn't have any idea what the title would be. I wouldn't even start thinking about it till I'd started work on the story itself, and that wasn't my next project. "Well, just put *something* down," Betsy said.

And I thought, "OK, honey . . . ," *and put in the title of a real work of necrophiliac pornography:* Screwing Bloody Dead Bodies.

"Eeou!" *Betsy recalls saying when the contract came back.*

In good time I wrote the story; but as I was doing the final pass—a little flaky, as I always am at that stage of a significant project—it occurred to me that circumstances had offered me an opportunity I'd hate myself for if I didn't seize. I thereupon wrote 500 words in normal submission form and laid those two pages on top the complete manuscript of Liberty Port. *The two pages were titled* "Screwing Bloody Dead Bodies," *and they involved a pair of soldiers at the scene of a massacre of civilians. One of them is having sexual congress with the corpses, and the other snatches disturbed blowflies from the air and eats them, claiming they taste like shrimp. I mailed off the combined manuscript and waited.*

Of course I wasn't there to watch what happened in NYC, but I'm told by Betsy and others that the scene went something like this: the receptionist tore open the envelope, pulled out the manuscript, and said, "Eeou! 'Screwing Bloody Dead Bodies'!"

Betsy walked over, saying, "Oh, he didn't really use that title, did he?" and started reading the manuscript. She says the next thing she thought* was that because Jim Baen and I are such good friends, she was going to have to publish the piece in an anthology with her name on the cover.

Page three of the manuscript revealed the truth, and everybody had a good laugh. Betsy's laughter may have been more restrained than mine was.

Before you ask, I didn't keep a copy of the dummy text,

---

*When she was next *capable* of thought . . . —Betsy Mitchell *and Betsy lost the original. This is a Drake manuscript that isn't going to make its way into anybody's archives. That's a good thing.*

But it was really *funny if you have the right sense of humor.*

—DAD

Straw

Gene Wolfe

Yes, I remember killing my first man very well; I was just seventeen. A flock of snow geese flew under us that day about noon. I remember looking over the side of the basket, and seeing them; and thinking that they looked like a pike-head. That was an omen, of course, but I did not pay any attention.

It was clear, fall weather—a trifle chilly. I remember that. It must have been about the mid-part of October. Good weather for the balloon. Clow would reach up every quarter hour or so with a few double handsful of straw for the brazier, and that was all it required. We cruised, usually, at about twice the height of a steeple.

You have never been in one? Well, that shows how things have changed. Before the Fire-wights came, there was hardly any fighting at all, and free swords had to travel all over the continent looking for what there was. A balloon was better than walking, believe me. Miles—he was our captain in those days—said that where there were three sol-

diers together, one was certain to put a shaft through a balloon; it was too big a target to resist, and that would show
you where the armies were.

No, we would not have been killed. You would have
had to slit the thing wide open before it would fall fast, and
a little hole like the business end of a pike would make
would just barely let you know it was there. The baskets do
not swing, either, as people think. Why should they? They
feel no wind—they are traveling with it. A man just seems
to hang there, when he is up in one of them, and the world
turns under him. He can hear everything—pigs and chick-
ens, and the squeak the windlass makes drawing water from
a well.

"Good flying weather," Clow said to me.

I nodded. Solemnly, I suppose.

"All the lift you want, in weather like this. The colder it
is, the better she pulls. The heat from the fire doesn't like the
chill, and tries to escape from it. That's what they say."

Blond Bracata spat over the side. "Nothing in our bel-
lies," she said, "that's what makes it lift. If we don't eat
today you won't have to light the fire tomorrow—I'll take
us up myself."

She was taller than any of us except Miles, and the
heaviest of us all; but Miles would not allow for size when
the food was passed out, so I suppose she was the hungriest
too.

Derek said: "We should have stretched one of that last
bunch over the fire. That would have fetched a pot of stew,
at the least."

Miles shook his head. "There were too many."

"They would have run like rabbits."

"And if they hadn't?"

"They had no armor."

Unexpectedly, Bracata came in for the captain. "They
had twenty-two men, and fourteen women. I counted them."

"The women wouldn't fight."

"I used to be one of them. I would have fought."

Clow's soft voice added, "Nearly any woman will fight if she can get behind you."

Bracata stared at him, not sure whether he was supporting her or not. She had her mitts on—she was as good with them as anyone I have ever seen—and I remember that I thought for an instant that she would go for Clow right there in the basket. We were packed in like fledglings in the nest, and fighting, it would have taken at least three of us to throw her out—by which time she would have killed us all, I suppose. But she was afraid of Clow. I found out why later. She respected Miles, I think, for his judgment and courage, without being afraid of him. She did not care much for Derek either way, and of course I was hardly there at all as far as she was concerned. But she was just a little frightened by Clow.

Clow was the only one I was not frightened by—but that is another story too.

"Give it more straw," Miles said.

"We're nearly out."

"We can't land in this forest."

Clow shook his head and added straw to the fire in the brazier—about half as much as he usually did. We were sinking toward what looked like a red and gold carpet.

"We got straw out of them anyway," I said, just to let the others know I was there.

"You can always get straw," Clow told me. He had drawn a throwing spike, and was feigning to clean his nails with it. "Even from swineherds, who you'd think wouldn't have it. They'll get it to be rid of us."

"Bracata's right," Miles said. He gave the impression that he had not heard Clow and me. "We have to have food today."

Derek snorted. "What if there are twenty?"

"We stretch one over the fire. Isn't that what you suggested? And if it takes fighting, we fight. But we have to eat today." He looked at me. "What did I tell you when you joined us, Jerr? High pay or nothing? This is the nothing. Want to quit?"

I said, "Not if you don't want me to."

Clow was scraping the last of the straw from the bag. It was hardly a handful. As he threw it in the brazier Bracata asked, "Are we going to set down in the trees?"

Clow shook his head and pointed. Away in the distance I could see a speck of white on a hill. It looked too far, but the wind was taking us there, and it grew and grew until we could see that it was a big house, all built of white brick, with gardens and outbuildings, and a road that ran up to the door. There are none like that left now, I suppose.

Landings are the most exciting part of traveling by balloon, and sometimes the most unpleasant. If you are lucky, the basket stays upright. We were not. Our basket snagged and tipped over and was dragged along by the envelope, which fought the wind and did not want to go down, cold though it was by then. If there had been fire in the brazier still, I suppose we would have set the meadow ablaze. As it was, we were tumbled about like toys. Bracata fell on top of me, as heavy as stone: and she had the claws of her mitts out, trying to dig them into the turf to stop herself, so that for a moment I thought I was going to be killed. Derek's pike had been charged, and the ratchet released in the confusion; the head went flying across the field, just missing a cow.

By the time I recovered my breath and got to my feet, Clow had the envelope under control and was treading it down. Miles was up too, straightening his hauberk and sword belt. "Look like a soldier," he called to me. "Where are your weapons?"

A pincer-mace and my pike were all I had, and the pincer-mace had fallen out of the basket. After five minutes of looking, I found it in the tall grass, and went over to help Clow fold the envelope.

When we were finished, we stuffed it in the basket and

put our pikes through the rings on each side so we could carry it. By that time we could see men on horseback coming down from the big house. Derek said, "We won't be able to stand against horsemen in this field."

For an instant I saw Miles smile. Then he looked very serious. "We'll have one of those fellows over a fire in half an hour."

Derek was counting, and so was I. Eight horsemen, with a cart following them. Several of the horsemen had lances, and I could see the sunlight winking on helmets and breastplates. Derek began pounding the butt of his pike on the ground to charge it.

I suggested to Clow that it might look more friendly if we picked up the balloon and went to meet the horsemen, but he shook his head. "Why bother?"

The first of them had reached the fence around the field. He was sitting a roan stallion that took it at a clean jump and came thundering up to us looking as big as a donjon on wheels.

"Greetings," Miles called. "If this be your land, lord, we give thanks for your hospitality. We'd not have intruded, but our conveyance has exhausted its fuel."

"You are welcome," the horseman called. He was as tall as Miles or taller, as well as I could judge, and as wide as Bracata. "Needs must, as they say, and no harm done." Three of the others had jumped their mounts over the fence behind him. The rest were taking down the rails so the cart could get through.

"Have you straw, lord?" Miles asked. I thought it would have been better if he had asked for food. "If we could have a few bundles of straw, we'd not trouble you more."

"None here," the horseman said, waving a mail-clad arm at the fields around us, "yet I feel sure my bailiff could find you some. Come up to the hall for a taste of meat and a glass of wine, and you can make your ascension from the terrace; the ladies would be delighted to see it, I'm certain. You're floating swords, I take it?"

"We are that," our captain affirmed, "but persons of good character nonetheless. We're called the Faithful Five—perhaps you've heard of us? High-hearted, fierce-fighting wind-warriors all, as it says on the balloon."

A younger man, who had reined up next to the one Miles called "lord," snorted. "If that boy is high-hearted, or a fierce fighter either, I'll eat his breeks."

Of course, I should not have done it. I have been too mettlesome all my life, and it has gotten me in more trouble than I could tell you of if I talked till sunset, though it has been good to me too—I would have spent my days following the plow, I suppose, if I had not knocked down Derek for what he called our goose. But you see how it was. Here I had been thinking of myself as a hard-bitten balloon soldier, and then to hear something like that. Anyway, I swung the pincer-mace overhand once I had a good grip on his stirrup. I had been afraid the extension spring was a bit weak, never having used one before, but it worked well; the pliers got him under the left arm and between the ear and the right shoulder, and would have cracked his neck for him properly if he had not been wearing a gorget. As it was, I jerked him off his horse pretty handily, and got out the little aniace that screwed into the mace handle. A couple of the other horsemen couched their lances, and Derek had a finger on the dog-catch of his pike; so all in all it looked as if there could be a proper fight, but "lord" (I learned afterwards that he was the Baron Ascolot) yelled at the young man I had pulled out of his saddle, and Miles yelled at me and grabbed my left wrist, and thus it all blew over.

When we had tripped the release and gotten the mace open and retracted again, Miles said: "He will be punished, lord. Leave him to me. It will be severe, I assure you."

"No, upon my oath," the baron declared. "It will teach my son to be less free with his tongue in the company of armed men. He has been raised at the hall, Captain, where everyone bends the knee to him. He must learn not to expect that of strangers."

The cart rolled up just then, drawn by two fine mules—either of them would have been worth my father's holding, I judged—and at the baron's urging we loaded our balloon into it and climbed in after it ourselves, sitting on the fabric. The horsemen galloped off, and the cart driver cracked his lash over the mules' backs.

"Quite a place," Miles remarked. He was looking up at the big house toward which we were making.

I whispered to Clow, "A palace, I should say," and Miles overheard me, and said: "It's a villa, Jerr—the unfortified country property of a gentleman. If there were a wall and a tower, it would be a castle, or at least a castellet."

There were gardens in front, very beautiful as I remember, and a fountain. The road looped up before the door, and we got out and trooped into the hall, while the baron's man—he was richer-dressed than anybody I had ever seen up till then, a fat man with white hair—sent two of the hostlers to watch our balloon while it was taken back to the stableyard.

Venison and beef were on the table, and even a pheasant with all his feathers put back; and the baron and his sons sat with us and drank some wine and ate a bit of bread each of hospitality's sake. Then the baron said, "Surely you don't fly in the dark, captain?"

"Not unless we must, lord."

"Then with the day drawing to a close, it's just as well for you that we've no straw. You can pass the night with us, and in the morning I'll send my bailiff to the village with the cart. You'll be able to ascend at mid-morning, when the ladies can have a clear view of you as you go up."

"No straw?" our captain asked.

"None, I fear, here. But they'll have aplenty in the village, never doubt it. They lay it in the road to silence the horses' hoofs when a woman's with child, as I've seen many a time. You'll have a cartload as a gift from me, if you can use that much." The baron smiled as he said that; he had a friendly face, round and red as an apple. "Now tell me," (he went on) "how it is to be a floating sword. I always find other men's trades of interest, and it seems to me you follow one of the most fascinating of all. For example, how do you gauge the charge you will make your employer?"

"We have two scales, lord," Miles began. I had heard all of that before, so I stopped listening. Bracata was next to me at table, so I had all I could do to get something to eat for myself, and I doubt I ever got a taste of the pheasant. By good luck, a couple of lasses—the baron's daughters—had come in, and one of them started curling a lock of Derek's hair around her finger, so that distracted him while he was helping himself to the venison, and Bracata put an arm around the other and warned her of Men. If it had not been for that I would not have had a thing; as it was, I stuffed myself on deer's meat until I had to loose my waistband. Flesh of any sort had been a rarity where I came from.

I had thought that the baron might give us beds in the house, but when we had eaten and drunk all we could hold, the white-haired fat man led us out a side door and over to a wattle-walled building full of bunks—I suppose it was kept for the extra laborers needed at harvest. It was not the palace bedroom I had been dreaming of; but it was cleaner than home, and there was a big fireplace down at one end with logs stacked ready by, so it was probably more comfortable for me than a bed in the big house itself would have been.

Clow took out a piece of cherry wood, and started carving a woman in it, and Bracata and Derek lay down to sleep. I made shift to talk to Miles, but he was full of thoughts, sitting on a bench near the hearth and chinking the purse (just like this one, it was) he had gotten from the baron; so I tried to sleep too. But I had had too much to eat to sleep so soon, and since it was still light out, I decided to walk around the villa and try to find somebody to chat with. The front looked too grand for me; I went to the back, thinking to make sure our balloon had suffered no hurt, and perhaps have another look at those mules.

There were three barns behind the house, built of stone up to the height of my waist, and wood above that, and white-washed. I walked into the nearest of them, not thinking about anything much besides my full belly until a big war horse with a white star on his forehead reached his head out of his stall and nuzzled at my cheek. I reached out and stroked his neck for him the way they like. He nickered, and I turned to have a better look at him. That was when I saw what was in his stall. He was standing on a span or more of the cleanest, yellowest straw I had ever seen. I looked up over my head then, and there was a loft full of it up there.

In a minute or so, I suppose it was, I was back in the building where we were to sleep, shaking Miles by the shoulder and telling him I had found all the straw anyone could ask for.

He did not seem to understand, at first. "Wagon loads of straw, Captain," I told him. "Why every horse in the place has as much to lay him on as would carry us a hundred leagues."

"All right," Miles told me.

"Captain—"

"There's no straw here, Jerr. Not for us. Now be a sensible lad and get some rest."

"But there is, Captain. I saw it. I can bring you back a helmetful."

"Come here, Jerr," he said, and got up and led me outside. I thought he was going to ask me to show him the straw; but instead of going back to where the barns were, he took me away from the house to the top of a grassy knoll. "Look out there, Jerr. Far off. What do you see?"

"Trees," I said. "There might be a river at the bottom of the valley; then more trees on the other side."

"Beyond that."

I looked to the horizon, where he seemed to be pointing. There were little threads of black smoke rising there, looking as thin as spider web at that distance.

"What do you see?"

"Smoke."

"That's straw burning, Jerr. House-thatch. That's why there's no straw here. Gold, but no straw, because a soldier gets straw only where he isn't welcome. They'll reach the river there by sundown, and I'm told it can be forded at this season. Now do you understand?"

They came that night at moonrise.

Not long after I sold my first Hammer story to Jim Baen, who published it in Galaxy, *I read* Straw, *Gene Wolfe's take on mercenary SF in the same magazine. I muttered, "I'll never be able to write this well."*

I was right about that.

—DAD

Tomb Tapper

✪

James Blish

The distant glare of the atomic explosion had already
faded from the sky as McDonough's car whirred away from
the blacked-out town of Port Jervis and turned north. He was
making fifty m.p.h. on U.S. Route 209 using no lights but
his parkers, and if a deer should bolt across the road ahead
of him he would never see it until the impact. It was hard
enough to see the road.

But he was thinking, not for the first time, of the old
joke about the man who tapped train wheels.

He had been doing it, so the story ran, for thirty years.
On every working day he would go up and down both sides
of every locomotive that pulled into the yards and hit the
wheels with a hammer; first the drivers, then the trucks.
Each time, he would cock his head, as though listening for
something in the sound. On the day of his retirement, he was
given a magnificent dinner, as befitted a man with long sen-
iority in the Brotherhood of Railway Trainmen—and some-

body stopped to ask him what he had been tapping for all those years.

He had cocked his head as though listening for something, but evidently nothing came. "I don't know," he said.

That's me, McDonough thought. I tap tombs, not trains. But what am I listening for?

The speedometer said he was close to the turnoff for the airport, and he pulled the dimmers on. There it was. There was at first nothing to be seen, as the headlights swept along the dirt road, but a wall of darkness deep as all night, faintly edged at the east by the low domed hills of the Neversink valley. Then another pair of lights snapped on behind him, on the main highway, and came jolting after McDonough's car, clear and sharp in the dust clouds he had raised.

He swung the car to a stop beside the airport fence and killed the lights; the other car followed. In the renewed blackness the faint traces of dawn on the hills were wiped out, as though the whole universe had been set back an hour. Then the yellow eye of a flashlight opened in the window of the other car and stared into his face.

He opened the door. "Martinson?" he said tentatively.

"Right here," the adjutant's voice said. The flashlight's oval spoor swung to the ground. "Anybody else with you?"

"No. You?"

"No. Go ahead and get your equipment out. I'll open up the shack."

The oval spot of light bobbed across the parking area and came to uneasy rest on the combination padlock which held the door of the operations shack secure. McDonough flipped the dome light of his car on long enough to locate the canvas sling which held the components of his electroencephalograph, and eased the sling out onto the sand.

He had just slammed the car door and taken up the burden when little chinks of light sprang into being in the blind windows of the shack. At the same time, cars came droning out onto the field from the opposite side, four of them, each with its wide-spaced unblinking slits of paired parking lights, and ranked themselves on either side of the landing strip. It would be dawn before long, but if the planes were ready to go before dawn, the cars could light the strip with their brights.

We're fast, McDonough thought, with brief pride. Even the Air Force thinks the Civil Air Patrol is just a bunch of amateurs, but we can put a mission in the air ahead of any other CAP squadron in this county. We can scramble.

He was getting his night vision back now, and a quick glance showed him that the wind sock was flowing straight out above the black, silent hangar against the pearly false dawn. Aloft, the stars were paling without any cloud-dimming, or even much twinkling. The wind was steady north up the valley; ideal flying weather.

Small lumpy figures were running across the field from the parked cars toward the shack. The squadron was scrambling.

"Mac!" Martinson shouted from inside the shack. "Where are you? Get your junk in here and get started!"

McDonough slipped inside the door, and swung his EEG components onto the chart table. Light was pouring into the briefing room from the tiny office, dazzling after the long darkness. In the briefing room the radio blinked a tiny red eye, but the squadron's communications officer hadn't yet arrived to answer it. In the office, Martinson's voice rumbled softly, urgently, and the phone gave him back thin unintelligible noises, like an unteachable parakeet.

Then, suddenly, the adjutant appeared at the office door and peered at McDonough. "What are you waiting for?" he said. "Get that mind reader of yours into the Cub on the double."

"What's wrong with the Aeronca? It's faster."

"Water in the gas; she ices up. We'll have to drain the tank. This is a hell of a time to argue." Martinson jerked open the squealing door which opened into the hangar, his hand groping for the light switch. McDonough followed him, supporting his sling with both hands, his elbows together. Nothing is quite so concentratedly heavy as an electronics chassis with a transformer mounted on it, and four of them make a back-wrenching load.

The adjutant was already hauling the servicing platform across the concrete floor to the cowling of the Piper Cub. "Get your stuff set," he said. "I'll fuel her up and check the oil."

"All right. Doesn't look like she needs much gas."

"Don't you ever stop talkin'? Let's move."

McDonough lowered his load to the cold floor beside the plane's cabin, feeling a brief flash of resentment. In daily life Martinson was a job printer who couldn't, and didn't, give orders to anybody, not even his wife. Well, those were usually the boys who let rank go to their heads, even in a volunteer outfit. He got to work.

Voices sounded from the shack, and then Andy Persons, the commanding officer, came bounding over the sill, followed by two sleepy-eyed cadets. "What's up?" he shouted. "That you, Martinson?"

"It's me. One of you cadets, pass me up that can. Andy, get the doors open, hey? There's a Russki bomber down north of us, somewhere near Howells. Part of a flight that was making a run on Schenectady."

"Did they get it?"

"No, they overshot, *way* over—took out Kingston instead. Stewart Field hit them just as they turned to regroup, and knocked this baby down on the first pass. We're supposed to—"

The rest of the adjutant's reply was lost in a growing, echoing roar, as though they were all standing underneath a vast trestle over which all the railroad trains in the world were crossing at once. The sixty-four-foot organ reeds of jets were being blown in the night zenith above the field—

another hunting pack, come from Stewart Field to avenge the hydrogen agony that had been Kingston.

His head still inside the plane's greenhouse, McDonough listened transfixed. Like most CAP officers, he was too old to be a jet pilot, his reflexes too slow, his eyesight too far over the line, his belly muscles too soft to take the five-gravity turns; but now and then he thought about what it might be like to ride one of those flying blowtorches, cruising at six hundred miles an hour before a thin black wake of kerosene fumes, or being followed along the ground at top speed by the double wave-front of the "supersonic bang." It was a noble notion, almost as fine as that of piloting the one-man Niagara of power that was a rocket fighter.

The noise grew until it seemed certain that the invisible jets were going to bullet directly through the hangar, and then dimmed gradually.

"The usual orders?" Persons shouted up from under the declining roar. "Find the plane, pump the live survivors, pick the corpses' brains? Who else is up?"

"Nobody," Martinson said, coming down from the ladder and hauling it clear of the plane. "Middletown squadron's deactivated; Montgomery hasn't got a plane; Newburgh hasn't got a field."

"Warwick has Group's L-16—"

"They snapped the undercarriage off it last week," Martinson said with gloomy satisfaction. "It's our baby, as usual. Mac, you got your ghoul-tools all set in there?"

"In a minute," McDonough said. He was already wearing the Walter goggles, pushed back up on his helmet, and the detector, amplifier, and power pack of the EEG were secure in their frames on the platform behind the Cub's rear seat. The "hair net"—the flexible network of electrodes which he would jam on the head of any dead man whose head had survived the bomber crash—was connected to them and hung in its clips under the seat, the leads strung to avoid fouling the plane's exposed control cables. Nothing remained to do now but to secure the frequency analyzer, which was the heaviest of the units and had to be bolted down just forward of the rear joystick so that its weight would not shift in flight. If the apparatus didn't have to be collimated after every flight, it could be left in the plane—but it did, and that was that.

"O.K.," he said, pulling his head out of the greenhouse. He was trembling slightly. These tomb-tapping expeditions were hard on the nerves. No matter how much training in the art of reading a dead mind you may have had, the actual experience is different, and cannot be duplicated from the long-stored corpses of the laboratory. The newly dead brain is an inferno, almost by definition.

"Good," Persons said. "Martinson, you'll pilot. Mac, keep on the air; we're going to refuel the Airoknocker and get it up by ten o'clock if we can. In any case we'll feed you any spottings we get from the Air Force as fast as they come in. Martinson, refuel at Montgomery if you have to; don't waste time coming back here. Got it?"

"Roger," Martinson said, scrambling into the front seat and buckling his safety belt. McDonough put his foot hastily into the stirrup and swung into the back seat.

"Cadets!" Persons said. "Pull chocks! Roll 'er!"

Characteristically, Persons himself did the heavy work of lifting and swinging the tail. The Cub bumped off the apron and out on the grass into the brightening morning.

"Switch off!" the cadet at the nose called. "Gas! Brakes!"

"Switch off, brakes," Martinson called back. "Mac, where to? Got any ideas?"

While McDonough thought about it, the cadet pulled the prop backwards through four turns. "Brakes! Contact!"

"Let's try up around the Otisville tunnel. If they were knocked down over Howells, they stood a good chance to wind up on the side of that mountain."

Martinson nodded and reached a gloved hand over his

head. "Contact!" he shouted, and turned the switch. The cadet swung the prop, and the engine barked and roared; at McDonough's left, the duplicate throttle slid forward slightly as the pilot "caught" the engine. McDonough buttoned up the cabin, and then the plane began to roll toward the far, dim edge of the grassy field.

The sky got brighter. They were off again; to tap on another man's tomb, and ask of the dim voice inside it what memories it had left unspoken when it had died.

The Civil Air Patrol is, and has been since 1941, an auxiliary of the United States Air Force, active in coastal patrol and in air-sea rescue work. By 1954—when its ranks totaled more than eighty thousand men and women, about fifteen thousand of them licensed pilots—the Air Force had nerved itself up to designating CAP as its Air Intelligence arm, with the job of locating downed enemy planes and radioing back information of military importance.

Aerial search is primarily the task of planes which can fly low and slow. Air Intelligence requires speed, since the kind of tactical information an enemy wreck may offer can grow cold within a few hours. The CAP's planes, most of them single-engine, private-flying models, had already been proven ideal aerial search instruments; the CAP's radio net, with its more than seventy-five hundred fixed, mobile and airborne stations, was more than fast enough to get information to wherever it was needed while it was still hot.

But the expected enemy, after all, was Russia; and how many civilians, even those who know how to fly, navigate, or operate a radio transmitter, could ask anyone an intelligent question in Russian, let alone understand the answer?

It was the astonishingly rapid development of electrical methods for probing the brain which provided the answer—in particular the development, in the late fifties, of flicker-stimulus aimed at the visual memory. Abruptly, EEG technicians no longer needed to use language at all to probe the brain for visual images, and read them; they did not even need to know how their apparatus worked, let alone the brain. A few moments of flicker into the subject's eyes, on a frequency chosen from a table, and the images would come swarming into the operator's toposcope goggles—the frequency chosen without the slightest basic knowledge of electrophysiology, as a woman choosing an ingredient from a cookbook is ignorant of—and indifferent to—the chemistry involved in the choice.

It was that engineering discovery which put tomb-tappers into the back seats of the CAP's putt-putts when the war finally began—for the images in the toposcope goggles did not stop when the brain died.

The world at dawn, as McDonough saw it from three thousand feet, was a world of long sculptured shadows, almost as motionless and three-dimensional as a lunar landscape near the daylight terminator. The air was very quiet, and the Cub droned as gently through the blue haze as any bee, gaining altitude above the field in a series of wide climbing turns. At the last turn the plane wheeled south over a farm owned by someone Martinson knew, a man already turning his acres from the seat of his tractor, and Martinson waggled the plane's wings at him and got back a wave like the quivering of an insect's antenna. It was all deceptively normal.

Then the horizon dipped below the Cub's nose again and Martinson was climbing out of the valley. A lake passed below them, spotted with islands, and with the brown barracks of Camp Cejwin, once a children's summer camp but now full of sleeping soldiers. Martinson continued south, skirting Port Jervis, until McDonough was able to pick up the main line of the Erie Railroad, going northeast toward Otisville and Howells. The mountain through which the Otisville tunnel ran was already visible as a smoky hulk to the far left of the dawn.

McDonough turned on the radio, which responded with

a rhythmical sputtering; the Cub's engine was not adequately shielded. In the background, the C.O.'s voice was calling them: "Huguenot to L-4. Huguenot to L-4."

"L-4 here. We read you, Andy. We're heading toward Otisville. Smooth as glass up here. Nothing to report yet."

"We read you weak but clear. We're dumping the gas in the Airoknocker *crackle* ground. We'll follow as fast as possible. No new AF spottings yet. If *crackle,* call us right away. Over."

"L-4 to Huguenot. Lost the last sentence, Andy. Cylinder static. Lost the last sentence. Please read it back."

"All right, Mac. If you see the bomber, *crackle* right away. Got it? If you see *crackle*, call us right away. Got it? Over."

"Got it, Andy. L-4 to Huguenot, over and out."

"Over and out."

The railroad embankment below them went around a wide arc and separated deceptively into two. One of the lines had been pulled up years back, but the marks of the long-ago stacked and burned ties still striped the gravel bed, and it would have been impossible for a stranger to tell from the air whether or not there were any rails running over those marks; terrain from the air can be deceptive unless you know what it is supposed to look like, rather than what it does look like. Martinson, however, knew as well as McDonough which of the two rail spurs was the discontinued one, and banked the Cub in a gentle climbing turn toward the mountain.

The rectangular acres wheeled slowly and solemnly below them, brindled with tiny cows as motionless as toys. After a while the deceptive spur line turned sharply east into a woolly green woods and never came out again. The mountain got larger, the morning ground haze rising up its nearer side, as though the whole forest were smoldering sullenly there.

Martinson turned his head and leaned it back to look out

of the corner of one eye at the back seat, but McDonough shook his head. There was no chance at all that the crashed bomber could be on this side of that heavy-shouldered mass of rock.

Martinson shrugged and eased the stick back. The plane bored up into the sky, past four thousand feet, past four thousand, five hundred. Lake Hawthorne passed under the Cub's fat little tires, an irregular sapphire set in the pommel of the mountain. The altimeter crept slowly past five thousand feet; Martinson was taking no chances on being caught in the downdraft on the other side of the hill. At six thousand, he edged the throttle back and leveled out, peering back through the plexiglas.

But there was no sign of any wreck on that side of the mountain, either.

Puzzled, McDonough forced up the top cabin flap on the right side, buttoned it into place against the buffeting slip-stream, and thrust his head out into the tearing gale. There was nothing to see on the ground. Straight down, the knife-edge brow of the cliff from which the railroad tracks emerged again drifted slowly away from the Cub's tail; just an inch farther on was the matchbox which was the Otisville siding shack. A sort of shaking of pepper around the matchbox meant people, a small crowd of them—though there was no train due until the Erie's No. 6, which didn't stop at Otisville anyhow.

He thumped Martinson on the shoulder. The adjutant tilted his head back and shouted, "What?"

"Bank right. Something going on around the Otisville station. Go down a bit."

The adjutant jerked out the carburetor-heat toggle and pulled back the throttle. The plane, idling, went into a long, whistling glide along the railroad right of way.

"Can't go too low here," he said. "If we get caught in the downdraft, we'll get slammed right into the mountain."

"I know that. Go on about four miles and make an airline approach back. Then you can climb into the draft. I want to see what's going on down there."

Martinson shrugged and opened the throttle again. The Cub clawed for altitude, then made a half-turn over Howells for the bogus landing run.

The plane went into normal glide and McDonough craned his neck. In a few moments he was able to see what had happened down below. The mountain from this side was steep and sharp; a wounded bomber couldn't possibly have hoped to clear it. At night, on the other hand, the mouth of the railroad tunnel was marked on all three sides, by the lights of the station on the left, the neon sign of the tavern which stood on the brow of the cliff on Otisville (POP. 3,000—HIGH AND HEALTHY) and on the right by the Erie's own signal standard. Radar would have shown the rest: the long regular path of the embankment leading directly into that cul-de-sac of lights, the beetling mass of contours which was the mountain. All these signs would mean "tunnel" in any language.

And the bomber pilot had taken the longest of all possible chances: to come down gliding along the right of way, in the hope of shooting his fuselage cleanly into that tunnel, leaving behind his wings with their dangerous engines and fuel tanks. It was absolutely insane, but that was what he had done.

And, miracle of miracles, he had made it. McDonough could see the wings now, buttered into two-dimensional profiles over the two pilasters of the tunnel. They had hit with such force that the fuel in them must have been vaporized instantly; at least, there was no sign of a fire. And no sign of a fuselage, either.

The bomber's body was inside the mountain, probably halfway or more down the tunnel's one-mile length. It was inconceivable that there could be anything intelligible left of it; but where one miracle has happened, two are possible.

No wonder the little Otisville station was peppered over with the specks of wondering people.

"L-4 to Huguenot. L-4 to Huguenot. Andy, are you there?"

"We read you, Mac. Go ahead."

"We've found your bomber. It's in the Otisville tunnel. Over."

"*Crackle* to L-4. You've lost your mind."

"That's where it is, all the same. We're going to try to make a landing. Send us a team as soon as you can. Out."

"Huguenot to L-4. Don't be a *crackle* idiot, Mac, you can't land there."

"Out," McDonough said. He pounded Martinson's shoulder and gestured urgently downward.

"You want to land?" Martinson said. "Why didn't you say so? We'll never get down on a shallow glide like this." He cleared the engine with a brief burp on the throttle, pulled the Cub up into a sharp stall, and slid off on one wing. The whole world began to spin giddily.

Martinson was losing altitude. McDonough closed his eyes and hung onto his back teeth.

Martinson's drastic piloting got them down to a rough landing, on the wheels, on the road leading to the Otisville station, slightly under a mile away from the mountain. They taxied the rest of the way. The crowd left the mouth of the tunnel to cluster around the airplane the moment it had come to a stop, but a few moments' questioning convinced McDonough that the Otisvilleans knew very little. Some of them had heard "a turrible noise" in the early morning, and with the first light had discovered the bright metal coating the sides of the tunnel. No, there hadn't been any smoke. No, nobody heard any sounds in the tunnel. You couldn't see the other end of it, though; something was blocking it.

"The signal's red on this side," McDonough said thoughtfully while he helped the adjutant tie the plane down. "You used to run the PBX board for the Erie in Port, didn't

you, Marty? If you were to phone the station master there,
maybe we could get him to throw a block on the other end
of the tunnel."

"If there's wreckage in there, the block will be on automatically."

"Sure. But we've got to go in there. I don't want the
Number Six piling in after us."

Martinson nodded, and went inside the railroad station.
McDonough looked around. There was, as usual, a motor-
ized hand truck parked off the tracks on the other side of the
embankment. Many willing hands helped him set it on the
right of way, and several huskies got the one-lung engine
started for him. Getting his own apparatus out of the plane
and onto the truck, however, was a job for which he refused
all aid. The stuff was just too delicate, for all its weight, to
be allowed in the hands of laymen—and never mind that
McDonough himself was almost as much of a layman in
neurophysiology as they were; he at least knew the colli-
mating tables and the cookbook.

"O.K.," Martinson said, rejoining them. "Tunnel's
blocked at both ends. I talked to Ralph at the dispatcher's;
he was steaming—says he's lost four trains already, and another due in from Buffalo in forty-four minutes. We cried a
little about it. Do we go now?"

"Right now."

Martinson drew his automatic and squatted down on the
front of the truck. The little car growled and crawled toward
the tunnel. The spectators murmured and shook their heads
knowingly.

Inside the tunnel it was as dark as always, and cold,
with a damp chill which struck through McDonough's flight
jacket and dungarees. The air was still, and in addition to its
musty smell it had a peculiar metallic stench. Thus far, however, there was none of the smell of fuel or of combustion
products which McDonough had expected. He found sud-

denly that he was trembling again, although he did not really believe that the EEG would be needed.

"Did you notice those wings?" Martinson said suddenly, just loud enough to be heard above the popping of the motor. The echoes distorted his voice almost beyond recognition.

"Notice them? What about them?"

"Too short to be bomber wings. Also, no engines."

McDonough swore silently. To have failed to notice a detail as gross as that was a sure sign that he was even more frightened than he had thought. "Anything else?"

"Well, I don't think they were aluminum; too tough. Titanium, maybe, or stainless steel. What have we got in here, anyhow? You *know* the Russkies couldn't get a fighter this far."

There was no arguing that. There was no answering the question, either—not yet.

McDonough unhooked the torch from his belt. Behind them, the white aperture of the tunnel's mouth looked no bigger than a nickel, and the twin bright lines of the rails looked forty miles long. Ahead, the flashlight revealed nothing but the slimy walls of the tunnel, coated with soot.

And then there was a fugitive bluish gleam. McDonough set the motor back down as far as it would go. The truck crawled painfully through the stifling blackness. The thudding of the engine was painful, as though his own heart were trying to move the heavy platform.

The gleam came closer. Nothing moved around it. It was metal, reflecting the light from his torch. Martinson lit his own and brought it into play.

The truck stopped, and there was absolute silence except for the ticking of water on the floor of the tunnel.

"It's a rocket," Martinson whispered. His torch roved over the ridiculously inadequate tail empennage facing them. It was badly crumpled. "In fair shape, considering. At the clip he was going, he must have slammed back and forth like an alarm clapper."

Cautiously they got off the truck and prowled around the gleaming, badly dented spindle. There were clean shears where the wings had been, but the stubs still remained, as though the metal itself had given to the impact before the joints could. That meant welded construction throughout, McDonough remembered vaguely. The vessel rested now roughly in the center of the tunnel, and the railroad tracks had spraddled under its weight. The fuselage bore no identifying marks, except for a red star at the nose; or rather, a red asterisk.

Martinson's torch lingered over the star for a moment, but the adjutant offered no comment. He went around the nose, McDonough trailing.

On the other side of the ship was the death wound; a small, ragged tear in the metal, not far forward of the tail. Some of the raw curls of metal were partially melted. Martinson touched one.

"Flak," he muttered. "Cut his fuel lines. Lucky he didn't blow up."

"How do we get in?" McDonough said nervously. "The cabin didn't even crack. And we can't crawl through that hole."

Martinson thought about it. Then he bent to the lesion in the ship's skin, took a deep breath, and bellowed at the top of his voice:

"*Hey* in there! Open up!"

It took a long time for the echoes to die away. McDonough was paralyzed with pure fright. Anyone of those distorted, ominous rebounding voices could have been an answer. Finally, however, the silence came back.

"So he's dead," Martinson said practically. "I'll bet even his footbones are broken, every one of 'em. Mac, stick your hair net in there and see if you can pick up anything."

"N-not a chance. I can't get anything unless the electrodes are actually t-touching the skull."

"Try it anyhow, and then we can get out of here and let the experts take over. I've about made up my mind it's a missile, anyhow. With this little damage, it could still go off."

McDonough had been repressing that notion since his first sight of the spindle. The attempt to save the fuselage intact, the piloting skill involved, and the obvious cabin windshield all argued against it; but even the bare possibility was somehow twice as terrifying, here under a mountain, as it would have been in the open. With so enormous a mass of rock pressing down on him, and the ravening energies of a sun perhaps waiting to break loose by his side—

No, no; it was a fighter, and the pilot might somehow still be alive. He almost ran to get the electrode net off the truck. He dangled it on its cable inside the flak tear, pulled the goggles over his eyes, and flicked the switch with his thumb.

The Walter goggles made the world inside the tunnel no darker than it actually was, but knowing that he would now be unable to see any gleam of light in the tunnel, should one appear from somewhere—say, in the ultimate glare of hydrogen fusion—increased the pressure of blackness on his brain. Back on the truck the frequency-analyzer began its regular, meaningless peeping, scanning the possible cortical output bands in order of likelihood: First the 0.5 to 3.5 cycles/second band, the delta wave, the last activity of the brain detectable before death; then the four to seven c.p.s. theta channel, the pleasure-scanning waves which went on even during sleep; the alpha rhythm, the visual scanner, at eight to thirteen c.p.s.; the beta rhythms at fourteen to thirty c.p.s. which mirror the tensions of conscious computation, not far below the level of real thought; the gamma band, where—

The goggles lit.

. . . And still the dazzling sky-blue sheep are grazing in the red field under the rainbow-billed and pea-green birds. . . .

McDonough snatched the goggles up with a gasp, and stared frantically into the blackness, now swimming with residual images in contrasting colors, melting gradually as the rods and cones in his retina gave up the energy they had absorbed from the scene in the goggles. Curiously, he knew at once where the voice had come from: it had been his mother's reading to him, on Christmas Eve, a story called "A Child's Christmas in Wales." He had not thought of it in well over two decades, but the scene in the toposcope goggles had called it forth irresistibly.

"What's the matter?" Martinson's voice said. "Get anything? Are you sick?"

"No," McDonough muttered. "Nothing."

"Then let's beat it. Do you make a noise like that over nothing every day? My Uncle Crosby did, but then, *he* had asthma."

Tentatively, McDonough lowered the goggles again. The scene came back, still in the same impossible colors, and almost completely without motion. Now that he was able to look at it again, however, he saw that the blue animals were not sheep; they were too large, and they had faces rather like those of kittens. Nor were the enormously slow-moving birds actually birds at all, except that they did seem to be flying—in unlikely straight lines, with slow, mathematically even flappings of unwinglike wings; there was something vegetable about them. The red field was only a dazzling blur, hazing the feet of the blue animals with the huge, innocent kittens' faces. As for the sky, it hardly seemed to be there at all; it was as white as paper.

"Come on," Martinson muttered, his voice edged with irritation. "What's the sense of staying in this hole any more? You bucking for pneumonia?"

"There's . . . something alive in there."

"Not a chance," Martinson said. His voice was noticeably more ragged. "You're dreaming. You said yourself you couldn't pick up—"

"I know what I'm doing," McDonough insisted, watching the scene in the goggles. "There's a live brain in there. Something nobody's ever hit before. It's powerful—no mind in the books ever put out a broadcast like this. It isn't human."

"All the more reason to call in the AF and quit. We can't get in there anyhow. What do you mean, it isn't human? It's a Red, that's all."

"No, it isn't," McDonough said evenly. Now that he thought he knew what they had found, he had stopped trembling. He was still terrified, but it was a different kind of terror: the fright of a man who has at last gotten a clear idea of what it is he is up against. "Human beings just don't broadcast like this. Especially not when they're near dying. And they don't remember huge blue sheep with cats' heads on them, or red grass, or a white sky. Not even if they come from the USSR. Whoever it is in there comes from some place else."

"You read too much. What about the star on the nose?"

McDonough drew a deep breath. "What about it?" he said steadily. "It isn't the insignia of the Red Air Force. I saw that it stopped you, too. No air force I ever heard of flies a red asterisk. It isn't a *cocarde* at all. It's just what it is."

"An asterisk?" Martinson said angrily.

"No, Marty, I think it's a star. A symbol for a *real* star. The AF's gone and knocked us down a spaceship." He pushed the goggles up and carefully withdrew the electrode net from the hole in the battered fuselage.

"And," he said carefully, "the pilot, whatever he is, is still alive—and thinking about home, wherever *that* is."

Though the Air Force had been duly notified by the radio net of McDonough's preposterous discovery, it took its own time about getting a technical crew over to Otisville. It had to, regardless of how much stock it took in the theory. The nearest source of advanced Air Force EEG equipment was just outside Newburgh, at Stewart Field, and it would have to be driven to Otisville by truck; no AF plane slow enough to duplicate Martinson's landing on the road could have handled the necessary payload.

For several hours, therefore, McDonough could do pretty much as he liked with his prize. After only a little urging, Martinson got the Erie dispatcher to send an oxyacetylene torch to the Port Jervis side of the tunnel, on board a Diesel camelback. Persons, who had subsequently arrived in the Aeronca, was all for trying it immediately in the tunnel, but McDonough was restrained by some dim memory of high school experiments with magnesium, a metal which looked very much like this. He persuaded the C.O. to try the torch on the smeared wings first.

The wings didn't burn. They carried the torch into the tunnel, and Persons got to work with it, enlarging the flak hole.

"Is that what-is-it still alive?" Persons asked, cutting steadily.

"I think so," McDonough said, his eyes averted from the tiny sun of the torch. "I've been sticking the electrodes in there about once every five minutes. I get essentially the same picture. But it's getting steadily weaker."

"D'you think we'll reach it before it dies?"

"I don't know. I'm not even sure I want to."

Persons thought that over, lifting the torch from the metal. Then he said, "You've got something there. Maybe I better try that gadget and see what I think."

"No," McDonough said. "It isn't tuned to you."

"Orders, Mac. Let me give it a try. Hand it over."

"It isn't that, Andy. I wouldn't buck you, you know that; you made this squadron. But it's dangerous. Do you want to have an epileptic fit? The chances are nine to five that you would."

"Oh," Persons said. "All right. It's your show." He resumed cutting.

After a while McDonough said, in a remote, emotionless voice: "That's enough. I think I can get through there now, as soon as it cools."

"Suppose there's no passage between the tail and the nose?" Martinson said. "More likely there's a firewall, and we'd never be able to cut through that."

"Probably," McDonough agreed. "We couldn't run the torch near the fuel tanks, anyhow, that's for sure."

"Then what good—"

"If these people think anything like we do, there's bound to be some kind of escape mechanism—something that blows the pilot's capsule free of the ship. I ought to be able to reach it."

"And fire it in *here?*" Persons said. "You'll smash the cabin against the tunnel roof. That'll kill the pilot for sure."

"Not if I disarm it. If I can get the charge out of it, all firing it will do is open the locking devices; then we can take the windshield off and get in. I'll pass the charge out back to you; handle it gently. Let me have your flashlight, Marty, mine's almost dead."

Silently, Martinson handed him the light. He hesitated a moment, listening to the water dripping in the background. Then, with a deep breath, he said, "Well. Here goes nothin'."

He clambered into the narrow opening.

The jungle of pipes, wires and pumps before him was utterly unfamiliar in detail, but familiar in principle. Human beings, given the job of setting up a rocket motor, set it up in this general way. McDonough probed with the light beam, looking for a passage large enough for him to wiggle through.

There didn't seem to be any such passage, but he squirmed his way forward regardless, forcing himself into any opening that presented itself, no matter how small and contorted it seemed. The feeling of entrapment was terrible. If he were to wind up in a cul-de-sac, he would never be able to worm himself backwards out of this jungle of piping . . .

He hit his head a sharp crack on a metal roof, and the metal resounded hollowly. A tank of some kind, empty, or nearly empty. Oxygen? No, unless the stuff had evaporated long ago; the skin of the tank was no colder than any of the other surfaces he had encountered. Propellant, perhaps, or compressed nitrogen—something like that.

Between the tank and what he took to be the inside of the hull, there was a low freeway, just high enough for him to squeeze through if he turned his head sideways. There were occasional supports and ganglions of wiring to be writhed around, but the going was a little better than it had been, back in the engine compartment. Then his head lifted into a slightly larger space, made of walls that curved gently against each other: the front of the tank, he guessed, opposed to the floor of the pilot's capsule and the belly of the hull. Between the capsule and the hull, up rather high, was the outside curve of a tube, large in diameter but very short; it was encrusted with motors, small pumps, and wiring.

An air lock? It certainly looked like one. If so, the trick with the escape mechanism might not have to be worked at all—if indeed the escape device existed.

Finding that he could raise his shoulders enough to rest on his elbows, he studied the wiring. The thickest of the cables emerged from the pilot's capsule; that should be the power line, ready to activate the whole business when the pilot hit the switch. If so, it could be shorted out—provided that there was still any juice in the batteries.

He managed to get the big nippers free of his belt, and dragged forward into a position where he could use them, with considerable straining. He closed their needlelike teeth around the cable and squeezed with all his might. The jaws closed slowly, and the cusps bit in.

There was a deep, surging hum, and all the pumps and

motors began to whirr and throb. From back the way he had come, he heard a very muffled distant shout of astonishment.

He hooked the nippers back into his belt and inched forward, raising his back until he was almost curled into a ball. By careful, small movements, as though he were being born, he managed to somersault painfully in the cramped, curved space, and get his head and shoulders back under the tank again, face up this time. He had to trail the flashlight, so that his progress backwards through the utter darkness was as blind as a mole's; but he made it, at long last.

The tunnel, once he had tumbled out into it again, seemed miraculously spacious—almost like flying.

"The damn door opened right up, all by itself," Martinson was chattering. "Scared me green. What'd you do—say 'Open sesame' or something?"

"Yeah," McDonough said. He rescued his electrode net from the hand truck and went forward to the gaping air lock. The door had blocked most of the rest of the tunnel, but it was open wide enough.

It wasn't much of an air lock. As he had seen from inside, it was too short to hold a man; probably it had only been intended to moderate the pressure drop between inside and outside, not prevent such a drop absolutely. Only the outer door had the proper bank-vault heaviness of a true air lock. The inner one, open, was now nothing but a narrow ring of serrated blades, machined to a Johannson-block finish so fine that they were airtight by virtue of molecular cohesion alone—a highly perfected iris diaphragm. McDonough wondered vaguely how the pinpoint hole in the center of the diaphragm was plugged when the iris was fully closed, but his layman's knowledge of engineering failed him entirely there; he could come up with nothing better than a vision of the pilot plugging that hole with a wad of well-chewed bubble gum.

He sniffed the damp, cold, still air. Nothing. If the pilot had breathed anything alien to Earth-normal air, it had already dissipated without trace in the organ pipe of the tunnel. He flashed his light inside the cabin.

The instruments were smashed beyond hope, except for a few at the sides of the capsule. The pilot has smashed them—or rather, his environment had.

Before him in the light of the torch was a heavy, transparent tank of iridescent greenish-brown fluid, with a small figure floating inside it. It had been the tank, which had broken free of its moorings, which had smashed up the rest of the compartment. The pilot was completely enclosed in what looked like an ordinary G-suit, inside the oil; flexible hoses connected to bottles on the ceiling fed him his atmosphere, whatever it was. The hoses hadn't broken, but something inside the G-suit had; a line of tiny bubbles was rising from somewhere near the pilot's neck.

He pressed the EEG electrode net against the tank and looked into the Walter goggles. The sheep with the kittens' faces were still there, somewhat changed in position; but almost all of the color had washed out of the scene. McDonough grunted involuntarily. There was now an atmosphere about the picture which hit him like a blow, a feeling of intense oppression, of intense distress . . .

"Marty," he said hoarsely. "Let's see if we can't cut into that tank from the bottom somehow." He backed down into the tunnel.

"Why? If he's got internal injuries—"

"The suit's been breached. It's filling with that oil from the bottom. If we don't drain the tank, he'll drown first."

"All right. Still think he's a man-from-Mars, Mac?"

"I don't know. It's too small to be a man, you can see that. And the memories aren't like human memories. That's all I know. Can we drill the tank some place?"

"Don't need to," Persons' echo-distorted voice said from inside the air lock. The reflections of his flashlight shifted in the opening like ghosts. "I just found a drain petcock. Roll up your trouser cuffs, gents."

But the oil didn't drain out of the ship. Evidently it went into storage somewhere inside the hull, to be pumped back into the pilot's cocoon when it was needed again.

It took a long time. The silence came flooding back into the tunnel.

"That oil-suspension trick is neat," Martinson whispered edgily. "Cushions him like a fish. He's got inertia still, but no mass—like a man in free fall."

McDonough fidgeted, but said nothing. He was trying to imagine what the multicolored vision of the pilot could mean. Something about it was nagging at him. It was wrong. Why would a still-conscious and gravely injured pilot be solely preoccupied with remembering the fields of home? Why wasn't he trying to save himself instead—as ingeniously as he had tried to save the ship? He still had electrical power, and in that litter of smashed apparatus which he alone could recognize, there must surely be expedients which still awaited his trial. But he had already given up, though he knew he was dying.

Or did he? The emotional aura suggested a knowledge of things desperately wrong, yet there was no real desperation, no frenzy, hardly any fear—almost as though the pilot did not know what death was, or, knowing it, was confident that it could not happen to him. The immensely powerful, dying mind inside the G-suit seemed curiously uncaring and passive, as though it awaited rescue with supreme confidence—so supreme that it could afford to drift, in an oil-suspended floating dream of home, nostalgic and unhappy, but not really afraid.

And yet it was dying!

"Almost empty," Andy Persons' quiet, garbled voice said into the tunnel.

Clenching his teeth, McDonough hitched himself into the air lock again and tried to tap the fading thoughts on a higher frequency. But there was simply nothing to hear or see, though with a brain so strong, there should have been, at as short a range as this. And it was peculiar, too, that the visual dream never changed. The flow of thoughts in a powerful human mind is bewilderingly rapid; it takes weeks of analysis by specialists before its essential pattern emerges. This mind, on the other hand, had been holding tenaciously to this one thought—complicated though it was—for a minimum of two hours. A truly subidiot performance—being broadcast with all the drive of a super genius.

Nothing in the cookbook provided McDonough with any precedent for it.

The suited figure was now slumped against the side of the empty tank, and the shades inside the toposcope goggles suddenly began to be distorted with regular, wrenching blurs: pain waves. A test at the level of the theta waves confirmed it; the unknown brain was responding to the pain with terrible knots of rage, real blasts of it, so strong and uncontrolled that McDonough could not endure them for more than a second. His hand was shaking so hard that he could hardly tune back to the gamma level again.

"We should have left the oil there," he whispered. "We've moved him too much. The internal injuries are going to kill him in a few minutes."

"We couldn't let him drown, you said so yourself," Persons said practically. "Look, there's a seam on this tank that looks like a torsion seal. If we break it, it ought to open up like a tired clam. Then we can get him out of here."

As he spoke, the empty tank parted into two shell-like halves. The pilot lay slumped and twisted at the bottom, like a doll, his suit glistening in the light of the C.O.'s torch.

"Help me. By the shoulders, real easy. That's it; lift. Easy, now."

Numbly, McDonough helped. It was true that the oil would have drowned the fragile, pitiful figure, but this was no help, either. The thing came up out of the cabin like a marionette with all its strings cut. Martinson cut the last of them: the flexible tubes which kept it connected to the ship. The three of them put it down, sprawling bonelessly.

. . . AND STILL THE DAZZLING SKY-BLUE SHEEP ARE GRAZING IN THE RED FIELD . . .

Just like that, McDonough saw it.

A coloring book!

That was what the scene was. That was why the colors were wrong, and the size referents. Of course the sheeplike animals did not look much like sheep, which the pilot could never have seen except in pictures. Of course the sheep's heads looked like the heads of kittens; everyone has seen kittens. Of course the brain was powerful out of all proportion to its survival drive and its knowledge of death; it was the brain of a genius, but a genius without experience. And of course, *this* way, the USSR could get a rocket fighter to the United States on a one-way trip.

The helmet fell off the body, and rolled off into the gutter which carried away the water condensing on the wall of the tunnel. Martinson gasped, and then began to swear in a low, grinding monotone. Andy Persons said nothing, but his light, as he played it on the pilot's head, shook with fury.

McDonough, his fantasy of space ships exploded, went back to the hand truck and kicked his tomb-tapping apparatus into small shards and bent pieces. His whole heart was a fuming caldron of pity and grief. He would never knock upon another tomb again.

The blond head on the floor of the tunnel, dreaming its waning dream of a colored paper field, was that of a little girl, barely eight years old.

Most military SF is about commanding officers, fighter pilots, or grunts. That's understandable: these are characters whose jobs lend themselves to dramatic scenes.

Most soldiers are none of those things: they're part of what's called the logistics tail, the nine or more people who are necessary to keep one combat soldier fed, armed, returned to health (or shipped home dead; that too), and thousands of other necessary supporting services.

Interrogators are a not-insignificant part of this huge service industry, but this is one of only two stories I know focusing on an interrogator's job. I wrote the other one: My Military Occupation Specialty was Enlisted Interrogator.

I thought about Tomb Tapper the afternoon my job was to interrogate a gutshot teenage girl as she died. I've thought about the story often since then.

And I've often thought of the girl as well.

—DAD

A Relic of War

✪

Keith Laumer

The old war machine sat in the village square, its impotent guns pointing aimlessly along the dusty street. Shoulder-high weeds grew rankly about it, poking up through the gaps in the two-yard-wide treads; vines crawled over the high, rust- and guano-streaked flanks. A row of tarnished enameled battle honors gleamed dully across the prow, reflecting the late sun.

A group of men lounged near the machine; they were dressed in heavy work clothes and boots; their hands were large and calloused, their faces weatherburned. They passed a jug from hand to hand, drinking deep. It was the end of a long workday and they were relaxed, good-humored.

"Hey, we're forgetting old Bobby," one said. He strolled over and sloshed a little of the raw whiskey over the soot-blackened muzzle of the blast cannon slanting sharply down from the forward turret. The other men laughed.

"How's it going, Bobby?" the man called.

Deep inside the machine there was a soft chirring sound.

"*Very well, thank you,*" a faint, whispery voice scraped from a grill below the turret.

"You keeping an eye on things, Bobby?" another man called.

"*All clear,*" the answer came: a bird-chirp from a dinosaur.

"Bobby, you ever get tired just setting here?"

"Hell, Bobby don't get tired," the man with the jug said. "He's got a job to do, old Bobby has."

"Hey, Bobby, what kind o'boy are you?" a plump, lazy-eyed man called.

"*I am a good boy,*" Bobby replied obediently.

"Sure Bobby's a good boy." The man with the jug reached up to pat the age-darkened curve of chromalloy above him. "Bobby's looking out for us."

Heads turned at a sound from across the square: the distant whine of a turbocar, approaching along the forest road.

"Huh! Ain't the day for the mail," a man said. They stood in silence, watching as a small, dusty cushion-car emerged from deep shadow into the yellow light of the street. It came slowly along to the plaza, swung left, pulled to a stop beside the boardwalk before a corrugated metal store front lettered BLAUVELT PROVISION COMPANY. The canopy popped open and a man stepped down. He was of medium height, dressed in a plain city-type black coverall. He studied the store front, the street, then turned to look across at the men. He came across toward them.

"Which of you men is Blauvelt?" he asked as he came up. His voice was unhurried, cool. His eyes flicked over the men.

A big, youngish man with a square face and sun-bleached hair lifted his chin.

"Right here," he said. "Who're you?"

"Crewe is the name. Disposal Officer, War Material

Commission." The newcomer looked up at the great machine looming over them. "Bolo *Stupendous,* Mark XXV," he said. He glanced at the men's faces, fixed on Blauvelt. "We had a report that there was a live Bolo out here. I wonder if you realize what you're playing with?"

"Hell, that's just Bobby," a man said.

"He's town mascot," someone else said.

"This machine could blow your town off the map," Crewe said. "And a good-sized piece of jungle along with it."

Blauvelt grinned; the squint lines around his eyes gave him a quizzical look.

"Don't go getting upset, Mr. Crewe," he said. "Bobby's harmless—"

"A Bolo's never harmless, Mr. Blauvelt. They're fighting machines, nothing else."

Blauvelt sauntered over and kicked at a corroded tread-plate. "Eighty-five years out in this jungle is kind of tough on machinery, Crewe. The sap and stuff from the trees eats chromalloy like it was sugar candy. The rains are acid, eat up equipment damn near as fast as we can ship it in here. Bobby can still talk a little, but that's about all."

"Certainly it's deteriorated; that's what makes it dangerous. Anything could trigger its battle reflex circuitry. Now, if you'll clear everyone out of the area, I'll take care of it."

"You move kind of fast for a man that just hit town," Blauvelt said, frowning. "Just what you got in mind doing?"

"I'm going to fire a pulse at it that will neutralize what's left of its computing center. Don't worry; there's no danger—"

"Hey," a man in the rear rank blurted. "That mean he can't talk any more?"

"That's right," Crewe said. "Also, he can't open fire on you."

"Not so fast, Crewe," Blauvelt said. "You're not messing with Bobby. We like him like he is." The other men were moving forward, forming up in a threatening circle around Crewe.

"Don't talk like a fool," Crewe said. "What do you think a salvo from a Continental Siege Unit would do to your town?"

Blauvelt chuckled and took a long cigar from his vest pocket. He sniffed it, called out: "All right, Bobby—fire one!"

There was a muted clatter, a sharp *click!* from deep inside the vast bulk of the machine. A tongue of pale flame licked from the cannon's soot-rimmed bore. The big man leaned quickly forward, puffed the cigar alight. The audience whooped with laughter.

"Bobby does what he's told, that's all," Blauvelt said. "And not much of that." He showed white teeth in a humorless smile.

Crewe flipped over the lapel of his jacket; a small, highly polished badge glinted there. "You know better than to interfere with a Concordiat officer," he said.

"Not so fast, Crewe," a dark-haired, narrow-faced fellow spoke up. "You're out of line. I heard about you Disposal men. Your job is locating old ammo dumps, abandoned equipment, stuff like that. Bobby's not abandoned. He's town property. Has been for near thirty years."

"Nonsense. This is battle equipment, the property of the Space Arm—"

Blauvelt was smiling lopsidedly. "Uh-uh. We've got salvage rights. No title, but we can make one up in a hurry. Official. I'm the Mayor here, and District Governor."

"This thing is a menace to every man, woman, and child in the settlement," Crewe snapped. "My job is to prevent tragedy—"

"Forget Bobby," Blauvelt cut in. He waved a hand at the jungle wall beyond the tilled fields. "There's a hundred million square miles of virgin territory out there," he said. "You

can do what you like out there. I'll even sell you provisions.
But just leave our mascot be, understand?"

Crewe looked at him, looked around at the other men.

"You're a fool," he said. "You're all fools." He turned
and walked away, stiff-backed.

In the room he had rented in the town's lone boardinghouse,
Crewe opened his baggage and took out a small, gray-plastic-
cased instrument. The three children of the landlord who
were watching from the latchless door edged closer.

"Gee, is that a real star radio?" the eldest, a skinny,
long-necked lad of twelve asked.

"No," Crewe said shortly. The boy blushed and hung
his head.

"It's a command transmitter," Crewe said, relenting.
"It's designed for talking to fighting machines, giving them
orders. They'll only respond to the special shaped-wave signal this puts out." He flicked a switch, and an indicator light
glowed on the side of the case.

"You mean like Bobby?" the boy asked.

"Like Bobby used to be." Crewe switched off the transmitter.

"Bobby's swell," another child said. "He tells us stories
about when he was in the war."

"He's got medals," the first boy said. "Were you in the
war, mister?"

"I'm not quite that old," Crewe said.

"Bobby's older'n grandad."

"You boys had better run along," Crewe said. "I have
to . . ." He broke off, cocked his head, listening. There were
shouts outside; someone was calling his name.

Crewe pushed through the boys and went quickly along
the hall, stepped through the door onto the boardwalk. He
felt rather than heard a slow, heavy thudding, a chorus of
shrill squeaks, a metallic groaning. A red-faced man was
running toward him from the square.

"It's Bobby!" he shouted. "He's moving! What'd you do to him, Crewe?"

Crewe brushed past the man, ran toward the plaza. The Bolo appeared at the end of the street, moving ponderously forward, trailing uprooted weeds and vines.

"He's headed straight for Spivac's warehouse!" someone yelled.

"Bobby! Stop there!" Blauvelt came into view, running in the machine's wake. The big machine rumbled onward, executed a half-left as Crewe reached the plaza, clearing the corner of a building by inches. It crushed a section of board-walk to splinters, advanced across a storage yard. A stack of rough-cut lumber toppled, spilled across the dusty ground. The Bolo trampled a board fence, headed out across a tilled field. Blauvelt whirled on Crewe.

"This is your doing! We never had trouble before—"

"Never mind that! Have you got a field car?"

"We—" Blauvelt checked himself. "What if we have?"

"I can stop it—but I have to be close. It will be into the jungle in another minute. My car can't navigate there."

"Let him go," a man said, breathing hard from his run. "He can't do no harm out there."

"Who'd of thought it?" another man said. "Setting there all them years—who'd of thought he could travel like that?"

"Your so-called mascot might have more surprises in store for you," Crewe snapped. "Get me a car, fast! This is an official requisition, Blauvelt!"

There was a silence, broken only by the distant crashing of timber as the Bolo moved into the edge of the forest. Hundred-foot trees leaned and went down before its advance.

"Let him go," Blauvelt said. "Like Stinzi says, he can't hurt anything."

"What if he turns back?"

"Hell," a man muttered. "Old Bobby wouldn't hurt us . . ."

"That car," Crewe snarled. "You're wasting valuable time."

Blauvelt frowned. "All right—but you don't make a move unless it looks like he's going to come back and hit the town. Clear?"

"Let's go."

Blauvelt led the way at a trot toward the town garage.

The Bolo's trail was a twenty-five-foot-wide swath cut through the virgin jungle; the tread-prints were pressed eighteen inches into the black loam, where it showed among the jumble of fallen branches.

"It's moving about twenty miles an hour, faster than we can go," Crewe said. "If it holds its present track, the curve will bring it back to your town in about five hours."

"He'll sheer off," Blauvelt said.

"Maybe. But we won't risk it. Pick up a heading of 270°, Blauvelt. We'll try an intercept by cutting across the circle."

Blauvelt complied wordlessly. The car moved ahead in the deep green gloom under the huge shaggy-barked trees. Oversized insects buzzed and thumped against the canopy. Small and medium lizards hopped, darted, flapped. Fern leaves as big as awnings scraped along the car as it clambered over loops and coils of tough root, leaving streaks of plant juice across the clear plastic. Once they grated against an exposed ridge of crumbling brown rock; flakes as big as saucers scaled off, exposing dull metal.

"Dorsal fin of a scout-boat," Crewe said. "That's what's left of what was supposed to be a corrosion resistant alloy."

They passed more evidences of a long-ago battle: the massive, shattered breech mechanism of a platform-mounted Hellbore, the gutted chassis of what might have been a bomb car, portions of a downed aircraft, fragments of shattered armor. Many of the relics were of Terran design, but often it was the curiously curved, spidery lines of a rusted Axorc microgun or implosion projector that poked through the greenery.

"It must have been a heavy action," Crewe said. "One of the ones toward the end that didn't get much notice at the time. There's stuff here I've never seen before, experimental types, I imagine, rushed in by the enemy for a last-ditch stand."

Blauvelt grunted.

"Contact in another minute or so," Crewe said.

As Blauvelt opened his mouth to reply, there was a blinding flash, a violent impact, and the jungle erupted in their faces.

The seat webbing was cutting into Crewe's ribs. His ears were filled with a high, steady ringing; there was a taste of brass in his mouth. His head throbbed in time with the thudding of his heart.

The car was on its side, the interior a jumble of loose objects, torn wiring, broken plastic. Blauvelt was half under him, groaning. He slid off him, saw that he was groggy but conscious.

"Changed your mind yet about your harmless pet?" he asked, wiping a trickle of blood from his right eye. "Let's get clear before he fires those empty guns again. Can you walk?"

Blauvelt mumbled, crawled out through the broken canopy. Crewe groped through debris for the command transmitter—

"Good God," Blauvelt croaked. Crewe twisted, saw the high, narrow, iodine-dark shape of the alien machine perched on jointed crawler-legs fifty feet away, framed by blast-scorched foliage. Its multiple-barreled micro-gun battery was aimed dead at the overturned car.

"Don't move a muscle," Crewe whispered. Sweat trickled down his face. An insect, like a stub-winged four-inch dragonfly, came and buzzed about them, moved on. Hot metal pinged, contracting. Instantly, the alien hunter-killer moved forward another six feet, depressing its gun muzzles.

"Run for it!" Blauvelt cried. He came to his feet in a scrabbling lunge; the enemy machine swung to track him . . .

A giant tree leaned, snapped, was tossed aside. The great green-streaked prow of the Bolo forged into view, interposing itself between the smaller machine and the men. It turned to face the enemy; fire flashed, reflecting against the surrounding trees; the ground jumped once, twice, to hard, racking shocks. Sound boomed dully in Crewe's blast-numbed ears. Bright sparks fountained above the Bolo as it advanced. Crewe felt the massive impact as the two fighting machines came together, he saw the Bolo hesitate, then forge ahead, rearing up, pushing the lighter machine aside, grinding over it, passing on, to leave a crumpled mass of wreckage in its wake.

"Did you see that, Crewe?" Blauvelt shouted in his ear. "Did you see what Bobby did? He walked right into its guns and smashed it flatter'n crockbrewed beer!"

The Bolo halted, turned ponderously, sat facing the men. Bright streaks of molten metal ran down its armored flanks, fell spattering and smoking into crushed greenery.

"He saved our necks," Blauvelt said. He staggered to his feet, picked his way past the Bolo to stare at the smoking ruins of the smashed adversary.

"*Unit Nine five four of the Line, reporting contact with hostile force,*" the mechanical voice of the Bolo spoke suddenly. "*Enemy unit destroyed. I have sustained extensive damage, but am still operational at nine point six percent base capability, awaiting further orders.*"

"Hey," Blauvelt said. "That doesn't sound like . . ."

"Now maybe you understand that this is a Bolo combat unit, not the village idiot," Crewe snapped. He picked his way across the churned-up ground, stood before the great machine.

"Mission accomplished, Unit Nine five four," he called. "Enemy forces neutralized. Close out Battle Reflex and revert to low alert status." He turned to Blauvelt.

"Let's go back to town," he said, "and tell them what their mascot just did."

Blauvelt stared up at the grim and ancient machine; his square, tanned face looked yellowish and drawn. "Let's do that," he said.

The ten-piece town band was drawn up in a double rank before the newly mown village square. The entire population of the settlement—some three hundred and forty-two men, women and children—were present, dressed in their best. Pennants fluttered from strung wires. The sun glistened from the armored sides of the newly-cleaned and polished Bolo. A vast bouquet of wild flowers poked from the no-longer-sooty muzzle of the Hellbore.

Crewe stepped forward.

"As a representative of the Concordiat government I've been asked to make this presentation," he said. "You people have seen fit to design a medal and award it to Unit Nine five four in appreciation for services rendered in defense of the community above and beyond the call of duty." He paused, looked across the faces of his audience.

"Many more elaborate honors have been awarded for a great deal less," he said. He turned to the machine; two men came forward, one with a stepladder, the other with a portable welding rig. Crewe climbed up, fixed the newly struck decoration in place beside the row of century-old battle honors. The technician quickly spotted it in position. The crowd cheered, then dispersed, chattering, to the picnic tables set up in the village street.

It was late twilight. The last of the sandwiches and stuffed eggs had been eaten, the last speeches declaimed, the last keg broached. Crewe sat with a few of the men in the town's lone public house.

"To Bobby," a man raised his glass.

"Correction," Crewe said. "To Unit Nine five four of the Line." The men laughed and drank.

"Well, time to go, I guess," a man said. The others chimed in, rose, clattering chairs. As the last of them left, Blauvelt came in. He sat down across from Crewe.

"You, ah, staying the night?" he asked.

"I thought I'd drive back," Crewe said. "My business here is finished."

"Is it?" Blauvelt said tensely.

Crewe looked at him, waiting.

"You know what you've got to do, Crewe."

"Do I?" Crewe took a sip from his glass.

"Damn it, have I got to spell it out? As long as that machine was just an oversized half-wit, it was all right. Kind of a monument to the war, and all. But now I've seen what it can do . . . Crewe, we can't have a live killer sitting in the middle of our town—never knowing when it might take a notion to start shooting again!"

"Finished?" Crewe asked.

"It's not that we're not grateful—"

"Get out," Crewe said.

"Now, look here, Crewe—"

"Get out. And keep everyone away from Bobby, understand?"

"Does that mean—?"

"I'll take care of it."

Blauvelt got to his feet. "Yeah," he said. "Sure."

After Blauvelt left, Crewe rose and dropped a bill on the table; he picked the command transmitter from the floor, went out into the street. Faint cries came from the far end of the town, where the crowd had gathered for fireworks. A yellow rocket arced up, burst in a spray of golden light, falling, fading . . .

Crewe walked toward the plaza. The Bolo loomed up, a vast, black shadow against the star-thick sky. Crewe stood before it, looking up at the already draggled pennants, the wilted nosegay drooping from the gun muzzle.

"Unit Nine five four, you know why I'm here?" he said softly.

"*I compute that my usefulness as an engine of war is ended,*" the soft rasping voice said.

"That's right," Crewe said. "I checked the area in a thousand-mile radius with sensitive instruments. There's no enemy machine left alive. The one you killed was the last."

"*It was true to its duty,*" the machine said.

"It was my fault," Crewe said. "It was designed to detect our command carrier and home on it. When I switched on my transmitter, it went into action. Naturally, you sensed that, and went to meet it."

The machine sat silent.

"You could still save yourself," Crewe said. "If you trampled me under and made for the jungle it might be centuries before . . ."

"*Before another man comes to do what must be done? Better that I cease now, at the hands of a friend.*"

"Good-bye, Bobby."

"*Correction: Unit Nine five four of the Line.*"

Crewe pressed the key. A sense of darkness fell across the machine.

At the edge of the square, Crewe looked back. He raised a hand in a ghostly salute; then he walked away along the dusty street, white in the light of the rising moon.

I once asked Keith whether his varied military service had included a tour in an armored unit. He assured me his only contact with tanks had been in basic training during WW II, when he was required to lie in a slit trench while a tank drove over him to demonstrate to the trainees that you had a better chance of surviving being overrun by tanks if you lay still than if you jumped out of your foxholes and became a target for their machine guns.

He got the feeling, the presence, of tanks very well, though. I note, however, that the three Bolo stories which I consider exceptionally better than the rest aren't really about tanks: they're about veterans who happen to be tanks.

—DAD

Basic Training

⭐

Mark L. Van Name

Week 1, Day 1

I knew I wasn't supposed to look anywhere but straight ahead, but I wanted to check down the road to my right, to see if Mom was still there. After she dropped me off everything happened so fast that I didn't even know if she had left yet or if she was still watching me. I sorta wanted her to watch me, but I sorta didn't, because she had started crying when the men yelled at me to get in line, and that had made me feel like crying and I knew I shouldn't cry. Daddy taught me that. Men don't cry. Now that he was gone I was supposed to be the man.

But I still wanted to see her, and Sergeant Minola sounded like he was yelling at some kid at the other end of the line, so I turned and looked.

She was gone. I couldn't even see her car, and that made me mad and it made me want to cry and I wished she was still there.

Then he was screaming in my ear, and it all happened

so fast that I couldn't tell what he said at first even though his voice was loud.

". . . some kind of hearing problem, Private?" He yelled louder. "Is my voice not clear enough for you?"

"No, sir!"

All of a sudden he was right in front of me, leaning into my face.

"Do I look like I sit around the office all day, playing pocket pool and having lunch at some air-conditioned officers' club?"

His face was the color of old cardboard and looked as hard as wood. The muscles in his neck and his arms stood out as he leaned over me, and I could not imagine him ever sitting around. "No, sir!"

"Then stop calling me sir! I work for a living, boy. You call me Sergeant! Do you understand me?"

"Yes, Sergeant."

"No wonder you have a hearing problem, Private. You don't talk loud enough to wake an ant sleeping on your lips." He stood up and backed away. "Now, do you understand me?"

I yelled as loud as I could, "Yes, Sergeant!" I was so scared my hands were shaking. The noon sun was so hot I was drenched with sweat, and I felt like I was going to throw up. I didn't want him to see any of it, I didn't want him to keep yelling at me, I didn't want to be there. It wasn't fair. None of the other boys I knew had to join, none of their fathers had died in this stupid war and made them have to become soldiers.

"What's your name, Private?"

"Larry, sir, uh, Sergeant."

"You don't get it, do you, boy?" He leaned again into my face. I could see the hairs in his nose and tiny scars like craters on his cheeks. "I don't give a rat's ass what your first name is. I don't care who you were or what you were back in that sorry excuse for a world that brought your sorry excuse for a recruit ass to me. What you are now is a private in my corps. Your first name is 'Private,' and your last name is something I'm only going to learn because I have to have some way to refer to your worthless self. Now, what is it, Private? What's your name?"

I wished he would stop yelling at me. It made it hard for me to talk, to think, even to stand there. I had to work my throat so I could talk. "Private Burger, Sergeant."

"Burger, huh? You some kind of cheap sandwich I'm gonna chew on, get sick, and spit out like those cheap rat burgers they sell across the bridge in Tampa? Is that what you are, boy?"

I didn't want to get mad, but he kept screaming at me and so I yelled back, "No, Sergeant!"

He nodded, stepped back, and walked to the center of the boys to my left. I could barely see him out of the corner of my eye.

"Let's get some things straight here," he said. "None of you like me, and I don't like you. I normally wouldn't cross the street to piss on worthless punks like you if you were on fire. But you are no longer just punks. You are part of my militia, and you are mine. You may have had mommies and daddies once, but now all you have is me and each other, and none of you is worth a damn without me. I am your world, the last thing you'll see before your miserable bodies fall asleep at night and the first thing you'll see when I drag you out of your bunks in the morning. Do you understand me?"

"Yes, Sergeant!" We all yelled, and the sound was so loud I almost jumped.

"I can't hear you!"

I took a deep breath and screamed as loud as I could. "Yes, Sergeant!" We didn't all finish at the same time, but it was close enough that the noise was amazing.

"My job is to train you to fight, and I will do that job. This war is the big one, and the heathens are playing for keeps. Winner takes all, and we will win because God is on our side. But the heathens are tough, don't mistake that. When I joined up ten years ago, we never would have taken kids your age, but now we're fighting here and in almost every town across America, and we can't afford to be picky. So I will teach you, and you will fight them and keep on fighting until we have killed them all for the glory of God and the corps. Do you understand?"

I didn't, but I knew the answer he wanted and I was sure not going to say anything else. "Yes, Sergeant!"

He took off his hat, tucked it under his left arm, and with his right pulled a cord from around his neck over his head. It was a necklace, a dark brown leather cord holding many smaller pieces of less dark leather. He held it in front of him as he walked back and forth in front of us.

"There is nothing pretty about killing, but there is also nothing magic. The heathens are men, the devil's men, but still men, and you can kill them as easily as they can kill you. And they will kill you. Unless you kill them first. Which I will train you to do." He stopped in front of the boy next to me, a black kid a little taller than I was. "Do you know what this is, Private?"

"No, Sergeant," the kid said.

"It's my ear collection, Private." He stuck it in the kid's face. "Right ears only, one ear for each heathen I killed, more than two dozen before I got called back from South America to teach worthless pukes like you."

I couldn't help myself. I turned my head for a better look. The ears didn't look like ears, more like shrunken leather Brussels sprouts, but as I looked closer I could see the folds and bends of an ear in some of them. I wanted to grab my own ears, make sure they were still there. I felt sicker and shakier and the air seemed heavy.

"Do you have a problem, Private Burger?"

I knew I shouldn't say anything, but I couldn't help myself and as soon as I started talking I couldn't stop. "It's

gross. I don't wanna see it. I don't wanna be here. I'm scared
and I wish you'd stop yelling at me . . ."

"Burger!" He was in my face, screaming, and I still
couldn't stop.

". . . and I don't know why my dad had to die and do
this to me and . . ."

"Burger!" He was even louder this time, but I couldn't
stop.

". . . I wish my mom were here and I wanna go home
and . . ."

He hit me in the stomach. I didn't see it coming, but one
minute I was screaming and the next I had no air and I was
falling down and holding my stomach. I kept trying to
breathe but somehow no air seemed to get in. The road was
hot and rough and scraped my cheek and my hands, but I
couldn't get up.

"You will not panic, Private Burger. You will not talk
unless I tell you to talk, and you will stop when I tell you to
stop. Do you understand, Private Burger?"

I nodded my head and squeaked out a "Yes, Sergeant,"
that I could barely hear. I hoped it was enough for him, because I didn't think I could be any louder.

"How old are you, Burger?"

My stomach felt like a hole in my body, and my throat
burned. I sucked in a little more air, enough to answer a bit
more loudly. "Ten, Sergeant."

"Well if you want to live to see eleven, Burger, you better learn these things, and you better learn 'em fast. Now get
up and stop dirtying my road."

Week 1, Day 4

My legs were shaking as I struggled to hold them together and six inches off the ground. The muscles in the tops
of my thighs and my stomach were on fire from the strain of

the leg lifts. The world narrowed into the pain in my legs, the sun blazing into my eyes, and the sound of Minola's voice. I could hear his boots clacking on the pavement, but I couldn't see him.

"Apart." His voice sounded distant, but clear.

Keeping my legs above the ground, I spread them as far as I could. Simply being able to move relieved the pain for a moment, but then it came back worse than before. I wanted to reach down and lift my legs with my hands, but the boot-print on my uniform sleeve and the dull ache in my left arm reminded me of the penalty for that particular cheat. I gritted my teeth, closed my eyes, and concentrated on blocking out the pain and keeping my legs up.

"Together."

I moved them back together, grateful again for the momentary movement. This was our tenth repetition, the last one. We always did ten. If I could hold out until Minola called the last movement, we'd be done. It was dinnertime, so I'd get to stand up, escape to the mess hall for half an hour, relax. All I had to do was finish this one.

"Down."

Yes! My stomach felt like it would cramp and I wanted to grab it, but I kept my hands under my head. My legs twitched and I sucked air, glad to be done. I was sure I could not have managed another.

"Up."

I couldn't believe it. We always did ten. I wanted to shout, but I clamped my jaw shut and only grunted as I lifted my legs. I heard a lot of other grunts and gasps, but no words; we had all learned.

"I know what you pukes are thinking," Minola said from somewhere closer but still behind me. "We did ten, so we should be done. It's not fair. Well, you're right; it's not fair. Tough shit. Sometimes you have to push a little harder. Now, apart."

Even spreading my legs brought no relief. The shaking

was worse, and I wasn't sure I could go on. I had counted on stopping, and now I had nothing left. I felt tears in the corners of my eyes, and I shook my head to make them fall out. I'd be damned if I would cry again in front of him. I might not be able to do these leg lifts, but I would not cry. That much, I could control.

"Together."

I couldn't do it. I tried, but my legs fell, and then Minola was staring down at me.

"Stand up, Burger!"

I stood to attention and faced him.

"Why did your legs fall, Burger?"

"Sergeant, I couldn't keep them up, Sergeant!"

"Bullshit. Look around you, boy. Do you see any other legs on the ground?"

I looked. Everyone was shaking, and some of their legs were almost touching the concrete, but all were above the ground. I couldn't believe I was the only one.

"That's right, Burger. They're doing it. You could have done it, but you gave up. You made up your mind you were done, and so you were." He stepped back. "Down! Fall in! Now!"

Everyone scrambled to line up in our usual formation. We dressed our ranks, left arms touching the guy to the left, right arms touching the guy in front, and then we snapped to attention.

Minola stood in front of us, arms crossed behind his back, the creases in his uniform, as always, so stiff they appeared to be carved from an unbelievably pure-green granite previously unknown in Florida. "It seems Burger decided to give up early on leg lifts. That means he didn't finish his exercises, so he needs to do a little more before dinner. And, as I keep trying to pound into your worthless skulls, you are supposed to be a team. If one of you doesn't finish, none of you have finished. So, you can all take a few minutes from your dinner break to double-time it down to the end of the compound and back."

Everyone groaned. I could feel them looking at me. We only had thirty minutes to eat, and this run would take ten of them. My fault, not theirs. Mine. I wanted to die. "Sergeant, request permission to speak, Sergeant!" I had to try.

For a second, I thought I saw him smile, but then it was gone. "Go ahead, Burger."

"Sergeant, this is my fault and the others should not have to run, Sergeant!"

He walked in front of me and bent into my face. "You don't get it, do you, boy? Listen to me. Read my lips. You are part of a team. If you fail, the team fails." He moved away, back in front of us. "If any of you fail, the team fails. You must be able to depend on one another absolutely, without doubt, because anything less will get you killed. Do you understand me?"

"Sergeant, yes, Sergeant!"

"Good. Left, face. Double-time, march!"

We ran in formation. I didn't see Minola in his usual spot to my left. Then, I heard his voice from behind us.

"The sooner you pukes finish this little run, the sooner you eat."

We trotted on. My legs felt like weights, but I was glad for the chance to be doing something. Maybe if I sat alone in the mess and stayed out of everyone's way, they'd forget me. Johnson and Gonzalez liked me, maybe they'd even sit with me. It wouldn't be so bad. All we had to do was make it to the storeroom at the other end of the complex, turn around, and run back. We did it many times each day. I wouldn't let them down this time. I could do this.

As we neared the storeroom and the point for our turn, I noticed a few of the bigger guys in front of me had slowed a bit. When I tried to slow, Johnson, the guy behind me, pushed me forward. I could barely keep running in the space between him and them. We started into the turn, and I felt a hand in my back and I stumbled and then I was on the ground and boots were kicking me. I covered my face and curled into a ball, trying to protect myself. I don't know how many people kicked me, but it was over fast and the platoon was moving on. My shoulders and neck and legs and stomach and ass hurt, and I tasted blood. The platoon was running away from me.

They were all I had left, and now I was losing them. Fuck that.

I got up and ran after them. I dusted my uniform as best I could as I ran. I didn't even try to run as Minola had taught us. I didn't care about my legs or my stomach or the blood in my mouth. I sprinted after them.

I caught them halfway back to Minola and fell into my position. No one spoke to me, and I didn't say anything.

When we were about to pass him, Minola called, "Platoon, halt!"

We stopped, everyone at attention and sucking air.

Minola looked at me but did not come closer.

"Burger."

"Sergeant, yes, Sergeant!"

"What happened to your uniform? You look even more like shit than usual."

No one moved, but I could feel them all watching me.

"Sergeant, I tripped and fell, Sergeant!"

"I see, Burger. What made you fall?"

"Sergeant, I was clumsy, Sergeant!"

He stared at me for a minute, then looked away. "Go clean up, then join the rest at mess. Everyone else, fall out. Back here in twenty minutes."

"Sergeant, yes, Sergeant!" we all shouted.

I ran through the group to the barracks. I figured if I changed fast I could still grab a bite. No one pushed me as I cut through.

Week 3, Day 5

The ceiling fans in the old warehouse bathed us in a slight breeze that was a wonderful relief from the unrelenting heat outside. The building smelled faintly of plastics and more strongly of sweat. We sat along the edges of a large square of faded blue workout mats. We were lined up in order of size, from Hughes, who at 16 and somewhere around six-four was a little bigger than Minola and everyone's pick as the guy most likely to be able to take the Sergeant, to Gonzalez, three seats to my right and a good couple of inches shorter than I was. Minola stood, shirtless, in the center of the mats and held aloft a gleaming bayonet.

"What is the spirit of the bayonet?" he asked.

"Sergeant, to kill, Sergeant!"

Minola granted us a rare full smile. "You've learned the words. I've let you hold the weapon. Now it's time to learn to use it." He walked along the border of the mats as he talked, now keeping the bayonet at our eye level. "This war is not like any movie you've seen. We're not charging up hills. We're not humping through a jungle. We're going from door to door, down streets, into buildings, fighting the enemy in our very own cities, cities their presence disgraces. Less than a mile away from the edge of this compound are heathen neighborhoods, perfectly good houses and streets infected with the devil's servants. Up to now, we've had to put up with them, because we haven't had the manpower to deal with them. Now we do: You. It's going to be your job to clean those neighborhoods. You won't have guns, because neither we nor the enemy in those houses have any ammo for the few guns we have. Ammo is too precious for untrained pukes fighting rear actions. We have to save it for those on the front lines. Which is why," he lifted the bayonet over his head, "you must become very good at both using your bayonet on others and defending against it your-self."

He put the bayonet in a bag at one edge of the mats and pulled out a black rubber replica. "So none of you darlings accidentally slices himself and messes up my nice mats, we'll practice with this rubber version. You attack, I'll defend. Who wants to start?"

Nobody spoke.

"Don't be shy, boys. This is your chance to hit me with something hard. Surely at least one of you babies has wanted to hit me."

Everyone had wanted that, and he knew it, but no one said a word. I sure wasn't going to volunteer. I had learned that lesson, and so had everyone else.

Minola laughed, a sound I rarely heard and one I was pretty sure I didn't like. "Okay, then, I'll pick. Hughes, on your feet, front and center."

"Sergeant, yes, Sergeant." Hughes went to the center of the mat and stood at attention in front of Minola.

"Relax, Hughes. When you're on this mat, you can stand any way you want. Take this weapon, and let me know when you're ready."

Hughes took the practice bayonet, backed away, and checked it out. He flipped it from hand to hand a few times, smiled, and settled into a half crouch.

Minola, in a similar but slightly wider stance, never looked away from him. His face was calm, his mouth slightly open. The muscles in his chest and stomach moved in and out in an unchanging, slow rhythm as he breathed.

"Sergeant, ready, Sergeant!"

"Then have at me, boy. Try to cut me."

Hughes, the bayonet in his right hand and that arm slightly bent, slowly edged toward Minola. He moved the bayonet from side to side in an arc about a foot and a half wide, no fast motions, everything under control. Never taking his eyes off Minola, he drew closer to the sergeant. He looked good to me, and I began to believe he might have a chance. Seeing Minola get hurt a little would be fine by me.

Minola didn't move. Nothing in his expression changed, and his breathing stayed the same.

Hughes thrust the bayonet slightly at Minola, not far, just a few inches.

Minola didn't react.

Hughes moved a little closer, and then suddenly he stabbed right at Minola's chest.

Minola wasn't there. He was to the side of where he had been, grabbing Hughes' arm, doing something with his feet, and then Hughes was on the ground and Minola was on top of him. Minola's knee pinned Hughes' back as he bent Hughes' arm backward until Hughes grunted in pain and dropped the bayonet. Still holding Hughes' arm with one hand, Minola picked up the bayonet with the other, dragged its sharper side across the back of Hughes' neck hard enough to leave a bright red line, then stood. Hughes rolled over and held his right arm with his left hand.

"Too obvious, Hughes, and too much weight on your front foot. You thought your size and a little experience with a knife would be enough—dumb. A move like that'll work only on someone with no training, and the heathens do train. Get back in your position. Who wants to be next?"

No one volunteered, so Minola ordered Langdon, a tall, wiry kid about fourteen with hair so blond his buzzed head looked bald from a distance, onto the mat. Langdon tried a different approach, dancing back and forth a lot and thrusting the bayonet at Minola's head each time he drew closer, but he lasted only a tiny bit longer and fared no better. On one lunge Minola seemed to fall, his leg shot out, and Langdon went down. Minola was on him instantly, taking the rubber bayonet and dragging it across Langdon's throat.

Two other guys also ended up with red throats, and then Minola called my name. I thought I was going to throw up as I walked to the center of the mat. I had been in a few short fights, but always with kids my size or only a little bigger, and never with a weapon. The bayonet felt foreign and I wanted to throw it away and run, but I knew that wouldn't work. I gripped it tightly, bent my legs, and hoped he wouldn't hurt me too much. I swung the bayonet lightly in his direction, hoping he'd maybe just take it away and I could finish without having to hit the mat or feel him drag the rubber blade across my throat.

He didn't move. Though he was staring at me, I couldn't sense any reaction in his eyes or his face. I wondered what he was seeing.

I swung the knife again, a little faster this time.

He slapped my face. I never saw the hand coming. "Is that all you can do, Burger? What a worthless baby you are."

He slapped my face again. "What are you waiting for, Burger? Your mommy to come save you?"

My face burned. I was having trouble breathing, and I shook my head. I wanted to hit him, hurt him.

He slapped me again, harder than before, stinging my face and snapping back my head. "Is this how your daddy died, Burger? Does being a worthless pussy of a mommy's boy run in your family?"

I couldn't stand it anymore. I yelled and charged him, the bayonet aimed right at his throat. I wanted to slice it open, shut him up, not have to take any more from him, kill him.

I was on my back on the mat before I knew what had happened. He was sitting on me, his knees pinning my arms, one arm over my mouth so I could barely breathe, the other pushing the bayonet into my throat. I was afraid he was really going to hurt me.

Without breathing hard, with no emotion in his voice, Minola said, "Anger can help you, but only if you control it. Burger got mad and lost control. I stayed in control." He dragged the bayonet across my throat, then got off me. "Now, he's dead, and I'm alive. Back to your position,

Burger." As Minola talked, he walked the perimeter of the mat, locking eyes briefly with each of the guys in the platoon. "You may think you're better than Burger, that you'd never get mad or lose control. You're not. Everyone loses it if the wrong thing happens to them. I can and will tell you never to get mad, to stay under control at all times. I can even teach you how best to maintain that control by focusing on your target and keeping your breathing easy.

"None of that training, though, will totally prepare you for what you will feel when the action is real, when the men you're hunting are also hunting you, when you either have to kill them or let them kill you. Only that experience will teach you those feelings, and once you've felt them—and you will, there is no way not to—you'll spend the rest of your life wishing you could get rid of them. But you won't be able to, and that's a cost you're gonna have to pay.

"Unless, of course, you die. Which is what this training has a chance of helping you avoid. When the craziness of combat hits you, this training and the other guys in your unit will be all that can keep you alive.

"I know you don't understand a fucking word I'm saying, but it's my job to tell you anyway. So we're going to do the only thing we can do that has any chance of helping: Practice. We're gonna practice until we get it automatic and right, until you learn how to attack and defend and stay in control while doing each.

"Johnson, you're up."

Week 5, Day 2

On my second day as the leader of Charlie squad, Minola assigned us to the obstacle course and left us alone there for an hour. We had a goal time of ten minutes flat. Our previous best was a little over ten and a half, but we'd logged that result last week, so I was sure we could hit the goal this time. After three tries, though, we were sucking wind, dirty, bruised, and still 15 seconds over. "We've gotta try again, guys," I said. "We've got less than half an hour to get rid of those fifteen seconds."

Langdon, the tallest of my squad members, said, "Bullshit. Tell Minola we made it, and let's catch some rest while we can. Right, guys?"

Gonzalez, who was having the worst time of the group, nodded in agreement. Peters and Johnson looked down, carefully not agreeing or disagreeing, waiting to see which way it would go. I knew Gonzalez would do the right thing if I pushed him, but Langdon could be a problem. Agreeing with him meant letting the team fail. Taking it to Minola would label me as a snitch. The only way out was to make it happen.

"Wrong, Langdon," I said. "If the Sergeant says we do it, we do it. We follow our orders."

"The only thing between us and those orders being done is you, dickhead," he said. He stretched to his full height and stared down at me. "If you could stop kissing up because Minola made you squad leader, you'd write ten minutes on the score sheet and leave us the fuck alone." He turned his back on me and started to walk away.

I was not going to let this happen, not on my watch. "Fall in!" I yelled.

The other three slowly lined up and stood to attention. Langdon stopped walking but did not join them. The others were watching me, though trying not to be obvious about it.

I walked slowly in front of Langdon and stood as close to him as I could without touching him. I craned my neck so I could look directly into his eyes. I silently counted to five and calmed my breathing as best I could. "Here's how it is, Langdon," I said, slowly and clearly, never looking away from him. "I'm squad leader. You may not like it. I don't know, and I don't give a shit. It's my job now to lead this squad, and it's your job to be part of it. This squad is a team, and you will not let this team down, and I will not dishonor it by lying." I wanted to yell, but I kept my voice level. "This squad is going to run this course until we do it in ten minutes. We can get it this next run, or the one after that, or ten runs later, but we will get it. We can all run it together, or we can carry your worthless unconscious ass on our backs while we run it. But we will do it. It's your call how."

Langdon stared at me for a few moments, then shook his head and joined the others in line. "Fuck it," he said as he snapped to attention, "let's run."

"I can't hear you!" I said.

"Let's run!" he shouted.

We took our marks, and on my command, we ran.

Week 7, Day 5

At 04:30, my squad crossed the Ninth Street DMZ about thirty yards below Twenty-Second Avenue, three quarters of a mile from the southeast edge of our compound. Cutting and tying back the razor wire took only a few minutes. No patrols were anywhere in sight. We hadn't hit the heathens in this part of St. Pete in months, and our recon teams knew they had become careless and rarely patrolled it in the early morning hours. We were due back by 05:15, almost an hour before their first patrol ever passed this area.

Once all five of us were through, we split into our teams and sprinted to the shadows on either side of Twenty-First Avenue. I took point and kept to the right side of the street, the side on which our target house sat. Gonzalez and Peters followed on the same side, with Langdon and Johnson staying parallel with them across the street. The other five squads in our platoon were doing their first forays at the same time in different spots around the city. If we all did our jobs well, by sunrise the heathens would find themselves down six key adults, and we'd all be back at the compound.

We were about a quarter of a mile due west from the home of our targets, a man named Sam Kaplan and his son, Tim. Kaplan ran a warehouse that was a major food and weapons depot for the heathens in this part of the city. Supplies were so tight that he was the only local with all the necessary access codes. Taking him out would mess them up for a couple days, enough time for more missions. Our briefing notes said he and his son left their house each morning about five so they could arrive well before any of their customers. Our job was to take them just outside their house and then get back home safely.

Only a few streetlights still burned in this area, and we had plenty of time to cover the quarter mile and secure our positions, so we never had to leave the darkness for more than a few seconds. Even so, we moved carefully from bush to tree to dead car to house corner, always staying spread out and in the shadows, checking for trouble at each stop. Never assume, Minola said. Take all the time the situation offers you. A few cats ran near us, and one even hissed, but no one seemed to notice. My heart was pounding and I could feel the sweat all over my upper body, but no lights came on, and no heathens attacked. Each time I stopped to check the area, I tried to take a slow, deep breath. The grass was a bit damp from an earlier rain, so the air was clear and fresh.

The only real dangers were the streets. Once we were over Ninth, we had to cross three more to reach our target. As point, I was the first to take each of them. I'd hold in the covering shadows on the near side until I had checked each house with a street view, then I'd dash across, grab the nearest cover, and check all the houses again. Only then would I wave over the others, who crossed all at once. Nothing fancy, everything by the numbers. When we were all safely over the last cross-street, I waved us down and counted off two minutes on my watch, making sure. Nothing stirred. No one followed. Time to get in position.

The target house was the third one down. I looped

around the rear of the nearest house and paused to make sure Langdon and Johnson had crossed safely. When they had, I made my way through backyards to the far side of the target. Gonzalez and Peters showed up a few seconds later. I doubled back to make sure Langdon and Johnson were in position on the other side. They were. By 04:44, one minute early, I was back in my position, and we were set to strike.

Conditions were pretty good for the assault. We had enough moonlight to see the targets, but not so much we would be obvious. One streetlight shone on the same side of the street a few houses down, but no other lights illuminated the block. Some lights were already on inside the small, one-story building, which was also good for us: harder for them to see out into the relative darkness.

I replayed the plan in my head, making sure I was missing nothing. It was simple and, Minola had said, intentionally overkill because it was our first mission. Langdon and Johnson were to take the two targets from behind, Langdon on the big one, Johnson on the smaller. They were to cover the targets' mouths to stop any noise and at the same time go for their throats. Gonzalez and Peters were to lag them by a step and attack from the front. Their targets were the hearts. Two hits per target within a second or two, and they should go down fast and quiet. I was coordinator and secondary backup. We would hit them as they turned down the sidewalk, get it all over in only a few seconds, and head back to the extraction point on our side of the DMZ.

Waiting was harder than it had been in the drills, harder than I had thought it would be. The night seemed louder, busier, the longer I leaned against the house's side. Crickets, frogs, odd animal rustlings, our own breathing—every noise seemed a possible warning to our targets. The house was insulated well enough that I couldn't hear any of the activity that had to be going on inside it, and that made me nervous. At the same time, that insulation was also protection, because they couldn't hear us. I kept my eyes on the front of the house and worked on calming myself, slowing my breathing. I flashed a thumbs-up to each of the teams, and both gave me the same.

Lights in the rear of the house snapped off right at 05:00. A few seconds later, the lights in the front went out, and the door opened. Two figures, one about six feet tall and the other about my size, stepped out. The larger turned back to the door and locked it. As they stepped out from under the slight overhang of the house's ceiling the light from the streetlight down the block gave me a brief glimpse of their faces. They looked tired but otherwise normal. If they knew we were there, they sure weren't showing it. The larger put his arm around the smaller, and they started walking.

When they turned right on the sidewalk, I twirled my finger in the go signal. Langdon and Johnson, bayonets drawn, darted from the other side of the house. The sound of their boots on the sidewalk was like shots going off, and for a second I wanted to run in fear that someone would hear, but then it was our turn to move and without thinking about doing it I was waving us forward. We charged, and I could see surprise come across the faces of the targets as we appeared from the side of the house. A second later, Langdon and Johnson were on them, Langdon taking the taller and Johnson the shorter. Each had his bayonet in his right hand and grabbed at the head of his target with his left.

Everything had felt slow, but now everything sped up and we moved without thinking, the training taking over. Langdon's hand closed on the man as Peters and I were still two steps from him, but the man spun away from Langdon's grip and avoided his bayonet. Langdon stumbled, and the man kicked him and then drew a knife, not as large as our bayonets but respectable. He waved the knife at Johnson, who let go of the boy to protect his forward arm. The boy also drew a knife as he ran for his father.

Then Gonzalez, Peters, and I reached them. Their backs were now to us, and before they could turn we were there.

Gonzalez went after the boy, Peters and I, the man. Peters caught him in the side, and as he turned I grabbed his hair, pulled down his head, and drew my knife across his throat. I felt it bite and catch for a second, then it came free smoothly. The man flailed as his blood spurted on Langdon, who was pulling his knife from somewhere in the man's chest. When I was clear, the man fell backward, right beside me.

I checked the others. Johnson and Gonzalez were straddling the boy, who was also down. Johnson was breathing hard and holding his left arm just above the elbow. A dark stain was spreading on his uniform. Gonzalez, his eyes looking wild in even this faint light, was cursing softly. He bent and began to cut the kid's ear.

"Tie off Johnson's arm, Gonzalez," I said.

He pulled the ear off with a slight tearing sound, then stood and showed it to us, his mouth open slightly, his breathing still ragged. Johnson was shaking but still standing.

"Johnson's arm, Gonzalez," I whispered. I grabbed his shoulder and shook it slightly. "Gonzalez."

He looked at me, and his eyes seemed to calm a bit. "Got it." He turned to Johnson, pulled an elastic bandage from his med kit, and started tying off the arm above the cut. The stain wasn't spreading, and Johnson's breathing was becoming regular, so I figured he was okay.

I took a look at Langdon. He was fine and motioned toward the man's head.

"You got the throat," he said. "Your kill, your ear."

Now I was having trouble breathing, and my arms were shaking slightly. I felt sick and hot and excited and scared and knew I had to regain control. We were alive, they were dead, and that's the best we could ask for. Langdon motioned again, then Gonzalez finished and he and Johnson stood and faced me.

"Ready," they said.

They were watching me, awaiting the word. We were exposed in the light on the sidewalk, and we couldn't afford to be there long.

I bent and drew my blade across the man's right ear. I had to saw back and forth twice, and then the sharp blade cut it cleanly free. It was damp and small in my hand. I held it up to the others, a tiny trophy dark in the gray morning, and they smiled. I was smiling, too.

I stuffed the ear in my pocket, wiped the knife on the shirt of the dead man, and gave the signal to head out.

When Mark was ten years old, his mother Nancy (a really wonderful person) enrolled Mark in Young Marines to provide him with male role models. In this she was successful.

Basic Training *is generally autobiographical with two particularly notable exceptions: his unit didn't kill anybody, though they put a couple older guys in the hospital; and in the fictional version, he leaves out the part where the DI put a boot on his head and rubbed his face in his vomit.*

I should perhaps add that Nancy had no idea of what Mark learned in Young Marines until she read this story.

—DAD

Witch War

✪

Richard Matheson

Seven pretty little girls sitting in a row. Outside, night, pouring rain—war weather. Inside, toasty warm. Seven overralled little girls chatting. Plaque on the wall saying: P.G. CENTER.

Sky clearing its throat with thunder, picking and dropping lint lightning from immeasurable shoulders. Rain hushing the world, bowing the trees, pocking earth. Square building, low, with one wall plastic.

Inside, the buzzing talk of seven pretty little girls.

"So I says to him—'Don't give me *that,* Mr. High and Mighty.' So he says, 'Oh yeah?' And I says, 'Yeah!' "

"Honest, will I ever be glad when this thing's over. I saw the cutest hat on my last furlough. Oh, *what* I wouldn't give to wear it!"

"You too? Don't I *know* it! You just can't get your hair right. Not in *this* weather. Why don't they let us get rid of it?"

"*Men!* They make me sick."

Seven gestures, seven postures, seven laughters ringing thin beneath thunder. Teeth showing in girl giggles. Hands tireless, painting pictures in the air.

P.G. Center. Girls. Seven of them. Pretty. Not one over sixteen. Curls. Pigtails. Bangs. Pouting little lips—smiling, frowning, shaping emotion on emotion. Sparkling young eyes—glittering, twinkling, narrowing, cold or warm.

Seven healthy young bodies restive on wooden chairs. Smooth adolescent limbs. Girls—pretty girls—seven of them.

An Army of ugly shapeless men, stumbling in mud, struggling along pitch-black muddy road.

Rain a torrent. Buckets of it thrown on each exhausted man. Sucking sound of great boots sinking into oozy yellow-brown mud, pulling loose. Mud dripping from heels and soles.

Plodding men—hundreds of them—soaked, miserable, depleted. Young men bent over like old men. Jaws hanging loosely, mouths gasping at black wet air, tongues lolling, sunken eyes looking at nothing, betraying nothing.

Rest.

Men sink down in the mud, fall on their packs. Heads thrown back, mouths open, rain splashing on yellow teeth. Hands immobile—scrawny heaps of flesh and bone. Legs without motion—khaki lengths of worm-eaten wood. Hundreds of useless limbs fixed to hundreds of useless trunks.

In back, ahead, beside rumble trucks and tanks and tiny cars. Thick tires splattering mud. Fat treads sinking, tearing at mucky slime. Rain drumming wet fingers on metal and canvas.

Lightning flashbulbs without pictures. Momentary burst of light. The face of war seen for a second—made of rusty guns and turning wheels and faces staring.

Blackness. A night hand blotting out the brief storm glow. Windblown rain flitting over fields and roads, drenching trees and trucks. Rivulets of bubbly rain tearing scars from the earth. Thunder, lightning.

A whistle. Dead men resurrected. Boots in sucking mud again—deeper, closer, nearer. Approach to a city that bars the way to a city that bars the way to a . . .

An officer sat in the communication room of the P.G. Center. He peered at the operator, who sat hunched over the control board, phones over his ears, writing down a message.

The officer watched the operator. They are coming, he thought. Cold, wet, and afraid they are marching at us. He shivered and shut his eyes.

He opened them quickly. Visions fill his darkened pupils—of curling smoke, flaming men, unimaginable horrors that shape themselves without word or pictures.

"Sir," said the operator, "from advance observation post. Enemy forces sighted."

The officer got up, walked over to the operator and took the message. He read it, face blank, mouth parenthesized. "Yes," he said.

He turned on his heel and went to the door. He opened it and went into the next room. The seven girls stopped talking. Silence breathed on the walls.

The officer stood with his back to the plastic window. "Enemies," he said. "Two miles away. Right in front of you."

He turned and pointed out the window. "Right out there. Two miles away. Any questions?"

A girl giggled.

"Any vehicles?" another asked.

"Yes. Five trucks, five small command cars, two tanks."

"That's too easy," laughed the girl, slender fingers fussing with her hair.

"That's all," said the officer. He started from the room. "Go to it," he added and, under his breath. "Monsters!"

He left.

"Oh, me," sighed one of the girls, "Here we go again."

"What a bore," said another. She opened her delicate mouth and plucked out chewing gum. She put it under her chair seat.

"At least it stopped raining," said a redhead, tying her shoelaces.

The seven girls looked around at each other. *Are you ready?* said their eyes. *I'm ready, I suppose.* They adjusted themselves on the chairs with girlish grunts and sighs. They hooked their feet around the legs of their chairs. All gum was placed in storage. Mouths were tightened into prudish fixity. The pretty little girls made ready for the game.

Finally they were silent on their chairs. One of them took a deep breath. So did another. They all tensed their milky flesh and clasped fragile fingers together. One quickly scratched her head to get it over with. Another sneezed prettily.

"Now," said a girl on the right end of the row.

Seven pairs of beady eyes shut. Seven innocent little minds began to picture, to visualize, to transport.

Lips rolled into thin gashes, faces drained of color, bodies shivered passionately. Their fingers twitching with concentration, seven pretty little girls fought a war.

The men were coming over the rise of a hill when the attack came. The leading men, feet poised for the next step, burst into flame.

There was no time to scream. Their rifles slapped down into the muck, their eyes were lost in fire. They stumbled a few steps and fell, hissing and charred, into the soft mud.

Men yelled. The ranks broke. They began to throw up their weapons and fire at the night. More troops puffed incandescently, flared up, were dead.

"Spread out!" screamed an officer as his gesturing fingers sprouted flame and his face went up in licking yellow heat.

The men looked everywhere. Their dumb terrified eyes searched for an enemy. They fired into the fields and woods. They shot each other. They broke into flopping runs over the mud.

A truck was enveloped in fire. Its driver leaped out, a two-legged torch. The truck went bumping over the road, turned, wove crazily over the field, crashed into a tree, exploded and was eaten up in blazing light. Black shadows flitted in and out of the aura of light around the flames. Screams rent the night.

Man after man burst into flame, fell crashing on his face in the mud. Spots of searing light lashed the wet darkness— screams—running coals, spluttering, glowing, dying—incendiary ranks—trucks cremated—tanks blowing up.

A little blonde, her body tense with repressed excitement. Her lips twitch, a giggle hovers in her throat. Her nostrils dilate. She shudders in giddy fright. She imagines, imagines . . .

A soldier runs headlong across a field, screaming, his eye insane with horror. A gigantic boulder rushes at him from the black sky.

His body is driven into the earth, mangled. From the rock edge, fingertips protrude.

The boulder lifts from the ground, crashes down again, a shapeless trip hammer. A flaming truck is flattened. The boulder flies again to the black sky.

A pretty brunette, her face a feverish mask. Wild thoughts tumble through her virginal brain. Her scalp grows taut with ecstatic fear. Her lips draw back from clenching teeth. A gasp of terror hisses from her lips. She imagines, imagines . . .

A soldier falls to his knees. His head jerks back. In the light of burning comrades, he stares dumbly at the white-foamed wave that towers over him.

It crashes down, sweeps his body over the muddy earth, fills his lungs with salt water. The tidal wave roars over the field, drowns a hundred flaming men, tosses their corpses in the air with thundering whitecaps.

Suddenly the water stops, flies into a million pieces, and disintegrates.

A lovely little redhead, hands drawn under her chin in tight bloodless fists. Her lips tremble, a throb of delight expands her chest. Her white throat contracts, she gulps in a breath of air. Her nose wrinkles with dreadful joy. She imagines, imagines . . .

A running soldier collides with a lion. He cannot see in the darkness. His hands strike wildly at the shaggy mane. He clubs with his rifle butt.

A scream. His face is torn off with one blow of thick claws. A jungle roar billows in the night.

A red-eyed elephant tramples wildly through the mud, picking up men in its thick trunk, hurling them through the air, mashing them under driving black columns.

Wolves bound from the darkness, spring, tear at throats. Gorillas scream and bounce in the mud, leap at falling soldiers.

A rhinoceros, leather skin glowing in the light of living torches, crashes into a burning tank, wheels, thunders into blackness, is gone.

Fangs—claws—ripping teeth—shrieks—trumpeting—roars. The sky rains snakes.

Silence. Vast brooding silence. Not a breeze, not a drip of rain, not a grumble of distant thunder. The battle is ended.

Grey morning mist rolls over the burned, the torn, the drowned, the crushed, the poisoned, the sprawling dead.

Motionless trucks—silent tanks, wisps of oily smoke still rising from their shattered hulks. Great death covering the field. Another battle in another war.

Victory—everyone is dead.

The girls stretched languidly. They extended their arms and rotated their round shoulders. Pink lips grew wide in pretty little yawns. They looked at each other and tittered in embarrassment. Some of them blushed. A few looked guilty.

Then they all laughed out loud. They opened more gum-packs, drew compacts from pockets, spoke intimately with schoolgirl whispers, with late-night dormitory whispers.

Muted giggles rose up flutteringly in the warm room.

"Aren't we awful?" one of them said, powdering her pert nose.

Later they all went downstairs and had breakfast.

The first time I watched the autopsy of a murder victim, I was struck by the fact that while the staff removed the brain, they were discussing Carolina's chances in the forthcoming basketball season; and then I thought about Witch War. *This too is a part of the truth about war.*

—DAD

Transstar

✪

Raymond E. Banks

he small group of Earth colonists stood on a hill, tense and expectant, as their leader advanced. He walked slowly away from the huddled mob, holding up his gun. You could hear the mother weep.

I stood at ease to one side, as was proper. I knew what would happen, because I was from Transstar. We have been taught to understand the inevitable.

The child came running out of the woods. I noted that they were not the woods of Earth, though they were brown. Nor was the grass the grass of Earth, though it was green.

The child cried, "Mother!" The leader raised his gun and shot it.

Even though I understood that the child was no longer a "him" and had become an "it" since falling into the hands of the aliens, I felt a tremor underneath my conditioning. In Transstar you are taught that the conditioning is a sheath, pliable but breakable; you do not put all faith in it.

Now the important thing was the reaction of the small group of Earth colonists.

They had seen the heartbreaking inevitable. They knew with the logic of their minds that the boy had to die. On this planet there were two races, two kinds of life: the eaber and the Earthmen. The eaber would lure a child away if they could and see to its infection, returning it to the Earth colony.

It was a good trick the first time or two, and for the love of their children three thousand lives had been lost, two starting colonies wiped out. This third colony had to succeed. I suspected that was why Transstar sent me here.

The leader turned sadly towards his colonists. A man advanced: "A burial! It is safe to bury!"

"It is not safe to bury," said the leader.

The man raised his arm. The leader hesitated and lost both his leadership and his life, because the half-maddened parent shot him in the chest . . .

Rackrill came to my Transstar ship. "You stood there," he said, eyes accusing. "You sit here now. You let the eaber do these things to us—yet you're from Transstar, representing the incredible power of the Sol system. Why?"

"Transstar was formed to handle star-sized situations," I replied. "So far this colony is meeting only the problems of a local situation."

"Local situation!" He laughed bitterly. "I'm the third mayor in three weeks."

"There'll be no more children lost to the eaber," I said.

"That's for certain sure," he said, "but Transstar might lose one of its representatives if it doesn't help us in our fight against the eaber. Our colony is sickened to watch you with your magnificent starship and your empire of power, standing by while we suffer."

"I am sorry."

He raised his hands and stepped toward me, but an orange light hummed from the walls. He looked surprised. He dropped his hands.

"Now that you've properly cursed me, tell me the real reason for your visit, Mr. Mayor," I said, flicking the protective button off.

He eased into his chair wearily. It was a great planet to take the starch out of the leaders.

"We had a visit from the eaber." He went on talking eagerly. The eaber had picked this planet, Point Everready, as an advance planet-city for their own culture. They would kill the Earth colony if it didn't leave. Rackrill had told them about Transstar, about me. That I represented the total war capacity of the solar system. That I was in instantaneous touch with Transstar Prime, near Mars, and that behind me stood a million space ships and countless prime fighting men with weapons of power and vigor that could pulverize the eaber to dust. That I was there to see that the Earth colony survived.

"This is only partly true," I said. "I am here to see *whether* an Earth colony can survive."

Anyway, Rackrill had gotten the eaber stirred up. They were coming to see me. Okay?

"I am Transstar," I said. "I can only observe, not interfere."

He got mad again, but there was really no more to say. He left, going from the marvelous machinery of my ship back to the crudeness of the village. I felt sorry for him and his people and wished I could reassure him.

I could not.

Yet somewhere back at Transstar Prime there was more than ordinary interest in Point Everready. I wondered, as every Transstar agent must, how far Transstar would go on this project. Few Transstar men have ordered Condition Prime Total Red. Condition Prime Total Red is the complete amassing and release of our total war-making capacity directed at one enemy in one place at one time. You don't get a CPTR more than once in decades; men in Transstar have served a lifetime and never directed one.

This is good, because CPTR is devastating in cost, machines, and men. It is the most jealously guarded prerogative of the Transstar system, which is in itself merely a check-and-report to keep track of all Earth colonies spread out among the stars.

I looked at my condition panel. It glowed an off-white on the neat starship wall. Condition white, nothing unusual; the same color I had stared at for five years as a full agent and fifteen years before that as both associate and assistant, learning the Transstar operation.

I thought about the dead boy, sleeping now on the grasses of Everready, as I made my daily report, pricking a card with three simple marks, feeding it to the transmitter which reported back to Prime. It seemed unfair, even with all my years of Transstar conditioning, that a boy would only deserve three pinpricks in a daily report. The human race had not been standing behind him.

It probably would not stand behind this colony.

For that matter, though I had the safety of this rather expensive starship, the human race would probably not stand behind *me,* if the eaber turned out to be tough aliens. Many an agent has died in local or regional situations.

I drank a cup of tea, but the warm drink didn't help. Somehow these last years I had become more emotional. It was hard to be a Transstar agent—for, by the time you learned how, you were too knowing in the ways of space to keep that prep school enthusiasm. I remembered the men who had lived and the men who had died as I drank my tea and felt sad.

Toward midnight the colonists sent scout ships up, as ordered by Rackrill. They were met by an equal number of eaber scout ships.

The patrol fight was dull, with drones being chopped

off by both sides. Nothing decisive. The eaber were good. I wondered if they also had a Transstar somewhere back at their home planet, a totality of force that might match Condition Prime Total Red, and result in a stand-off fight. This had never happened in history. Someday we might even find somebody better than CPTR.

At that instant expansion to the stars would stop, I knew.

Whatever I thought about the eaber at long distance, I'd have a chance to learn more. A couple of them were now approaching my ship.

They were sentient life. They were neither monsters nor particularly Earthlike. It was this balance of like-unlike that gave me the beginnings of a shudder under my conditioning.

The reddish one advanced into my cabin. "Euben," he said. He made a motion of turning with his hands, tapered fingers spread. A surge of sickness tickled in me, rushed up to a nerve agony. I just had time to relax and let the raping power of his ray, or whatever it was, knock me out into a welcome darkness. A nonconditioned man would have screamed and writhed on the floor, fighting the overpowering darkness. I rushed with it, gave in to it.

Presently there was a gentle bird-twitter. I sat up; Euben's power turned off. He laughed down at me.

"Some Earth-power, some potency," he said, gesturing at my control panel. I had, indeed, pushed my orange safety button, which should have frozen him immobile as it had Rackrill. It had no effect on him or his friend.

I tried to get up but was as weak and shaking as an old man. So I sat there.

"You are the protector to the Earthians," he said.

"No, Euben. I am merely here to observe."

"You'll observe them made extinct, Watcher," he said. "This is the perimeter of eaber. We want this planet ourselves."

"That remains to be seen," I said, finally rising stiffly and plopping into my chair. I turned off the useless orange button.

Euben roamed his eyes around the ship. "Better than your colony has. You are special."

"I am special," I said.

"They say you represent great power," he said.

"That is true."

"We have waited a long time to see this power," said Euben. "We have exterminated two of your colonies, and have not seen it."

"If this is all of eaber, it isn't very large," I said. "This planet could hardly hold a hundred thousand."

"I said we were perimeter. Behind us, thousands of planets. Trillions of eaber. There is nothing like us in the universe."

"We've heard that before."

This time he brought up two hands, to begin his twirling. I reacted with a hypnosis block, which shunted off all my natural functions for a micro-second (with the help of the plate I was standing on). The pain was much less. He merely brought me to my knees.

"Ah, you are not totally feeble," he said. "Still I make you bow to me with the twisting of my bare hands in the air."

"Yes. But Earthmen do not greet new races with tricks and talk like two small boys bragging about how tough their older brothers are," I said. "I am not here to brag tough. I am here to observe."

"If you don't like what you observe?"

"Perhaps we will do something about it. Perhaps not."

He threw back his head and laughed. "You will die, die, die," he said. "Watch this." He nudged the other eaber who stepped forward and brought something out of his robe.

It was a boned, dehydrated human.

The thing—evidently a human survivor of an earlier

colony—had the floppy, mindless manner of a puppy dog, mewling and whimpering on its long chain. Euben snapped his fingers. The former human ki-yied and scampered back under its owner's robe.

"Cute," said Euben. "De-skeletoned Earthmen bring a good price in the pet-shops of eaber, so you are not a total loss in the universe."

There came a sudden scream and convulsion from the eaber's robe. The eaber jumped back. The tragic, deboned human fell to the floor dead, spending a thin, too-bright red ebb of blood.

"Eh—how did you do that?" asked Euben, stepping back a little.

"I am Transstar," I said. "Certain things we do not permit with our life-form. I urge you not to continue this practice."

"So—" said Euben toeing at the dead man. "And he was so cute, too. Ah, well. There are more out there."

I controlled my voice and did not look down. "Can you establish your need for this planet?" I asked.

"Yes. We are eaber; that is enough anywhere in space."

I stepped to a wall chart and made a gesture. "This planet also falls along our perimeter. We occupy this space—so. We have well utilized the solar and alpha planet systems, and it is time that we move out once more. This planet is but one of a thousand Earth colonies moving out to new space."

Euben shook his head. "What a ridiculous civilization! All space in this arc is eaber. We close the door, so—"

He made a fast gesture with his hand that tore inside of me, like a hot knife, scraping the bottom of my lungs. I was pretty much riding on my conditioning now. I was sickened, angry with Euben and his race. But it was slightly different from dealing with an Earth neighbor you dislike. Bravery and caution! Always bravery—and caution.

"So you block us here," I said. "Perhaps we will go elsewhere for a hundred or a thousand years. It's no use to fight over space. There are millions of planets."

"Do you truly believe so?" smiled Euben. "Naive! The eaber do not like unknown life-forms prowling the universe. We will come to solar and alpha, as you call them, and put you on a chain like that one dead on the floor."

"We might resist that," I said.

"How?" said Euben, bringing a black box out from under his robe.

I have had my share of black boxes in my Transstar years. Before it was barely in sight, I had retreated to my all-purpose closet. He laughed, peering at me through the observation window and trying the various rays and whatnot in his weapon. Nothing much happened for a while—heat, radiation, gas, sonic vibrations, the standard stuff. Pretty soon I knew he could take me; but it would take him about three days. Fair enough.

The eaber was tough, but not unbeatable—at least on what he had shown me.

He put away his black box. I stepped through the door. Decontamination worked all right, but the heat-reducer was wheezing like an asthma victim in a grain field.

"So. You are junior good," said Euben. He turned and left the ship, whistling in a very Earthian way, not bothering to look back.

The other eaber remained. I offered him a cup of tea, which he drank greedily. He had something that looked a little like a serpent's tongue which he ran quickly over the control board panels. He sniff-tasted the instruments, the furnishings, the modest weapons and communications equipment I had. Then he stepped back.

"You will not survive eaber," he said. He left, not bothering to step over the deboned Earthman.

I picked up the soft, cooling mass and set it on the TV cradle. I didn't call through channels. I slapped the Transstar

Central button and let them have a look at the creature on the plate.

Hennessy was on the monitor at Transstar Prime, near Mars. He gasped. "That's not good," he said. "Just a minute."

I sank into the chair and made more tea with shaking hands. The screen above me lighted and I was staring at Twelve. Thirteen is as high as you get in Transstar. "You've bought it," he said. "In your arc you have the only mind-contact with the eaber. Elsewhere they've only made patrol war."

"Anybody solved them?" I asked.

"Yes and no," said Twelve Jackson slowly. "They can hit us with a freeze-burn system they've got. Explodes you. We can reach them with most of our conventionals, but they don't die easily. Range and depth of their civilization, unknown."

I told him about their trillion—according to Euben. Then I asked, "What's my condition?"

Jackson hesitated and I saw his hands twiddle over his buttons. "Condition orange," he said, taking me off white. Power reached through space. In seventy-five seconds I could feel the sudden, subtle shift in the ship's power fields, as they built up.

"Don't get excited," he said. "I've got a dozen oranges on the board."

"What about the colony here?" I asked.

"A colony is a local situation," said Jackson. "Unfortunately, if we squandered our life-power every time a few colonists died, we'd still be confined to the moon. They colonize of their own free will."

I touched the dead Earthman.

"Yeah," he said. "Nobody knew about that. It'll get your planet plenty of free space in the TV casts. We'll get a little blubbering from the League for Space Safety."

"It makes me want to blubber a little myself," I said.

Twelve Jackson gave me a long, hard look. "Stay Transstar or get out," he said.

I gave him the rest of my report-interview on the tape and tried to get some sleep. The eaber came over the colony about midnight and bombed it a little, and I groaned awake.

It must have been a half hour later that I heard a scratching on the ship's window. It was Rackrill, peering in at me.

When I joined him in the soft spring night he was excited.

"I've got something to show your high-falutin boys back at Mars," he said. "A real something."

We went in silence to his headquarters through the sweet night grasses of Everready. It was truly a planet of richness and beauty in a natural sense, and I thought again of the contrast of the poisoned boy and the monstrosities of human pets that the eaber had created under this moon, in their eaber cities, on this fine world.

My mood was shattered the instant we stepped into Rackrill's combination mayor's home and administration center. The Colony Correspondent had arrived.

There are simply too many Earth colonies for the space news services to cover them all. So they assign a Colony correspondent to cover the whole arc, and you always find them where the most trouble is.

This one was a woman. She was of the young, peppy breed of females that start out life as a tomboy and remain in trouble all of their lives because they like to take chances. I was doubly disturbed. First, because it meant that wildly distorted stories would soon be muddying things back in solar and alpha; second, because this cute lady reminded me of my own Alicia, who had been a Transstar agent along with me, back a seeming thousand years ago when I was merely a Four. She had the same snapping black eyes, the same statuesque figure, the same light-humored air.

"Well, so Transstar is really here!" she said. "Hey, Chief, how about a Transstar quote?"

"Young lady, I am not Chief," I said drily. "My name is Webster, and I hold the Transstar rank of Seven, and you well know that all Transstar quotes must come from Transstar Prime."

"Those fossilized, dehumanized old men on Mars," she said. "Never mind. I'll find my own stories."

"Not here you won't," said Rackrill, with authority's natural fear of the tapes. "It's past midnight. Go to bed. Tomorrow my tape man will give you a tour."

She stuck out her tongue. "I've had the tour. They're all alike, full of lies and grease, signifying nothing. Only thing I ever learned on an official tour was how to defend myself against the passes of the tape men."

But she allowed herself to be pushed out. I guess it was the near-tragic urgency of our manner.

Rackrill led me into an inner room. On the bed rested a woman, but there was a strangeness to her. She was ancient in her skin, yet something about her bones told you she was hardly thirty. Her flesh was blue-splotched, the eyes animal-bright. Rackrill gestured at her; she whimpered and squirmed in her bed.

I laid a hand on his arm. "The eaber can hypnotize and make a hand gesture that tears you apart inside," I said. "Don't hold up your hands in front of her."

"We got her story," said Rackrill, low-voiced. "She's been a prisoner of the eaber for over a year. From Colony Two, I guess. The eaber used her for—breeding."

He led me to a smaller cot, where a blanket covered a figure. For a fleeting second I didn't want him to pull back the blanket. He pulled it back.

The creature on the bed was dead, shot with a Colony bullet. You could tell that it was a boy about three feet long. There was Earthman in him and eaber. The head and arms were Earthian, the rest eaber. It was shocking to see the hard-muscled, dwarf body under that placid, almost handsome head.

"Barely five months," whispered the hag on the bed. "Forced insemination. Always the hands twisting—always the pain."

"A friendly scientific experiment," said Rackrill. "They want drones for the slag jobs in their cities. Jobs eaber won't do. They've produced a hundred or so of those idiots from captive women colonists. Force-fed and raised—this one is barely five months old, yet look at his size!"

I said nothing, busy with taking my tape, holding on to my objectivity through a force of will and my conditioning.

Rackrill opened the dead mouth. It was an exaggerated eaber tongue, black and reptile shaped. "No speech, therefore no intellect. Nor does it have mind speech like true eaber. It begs for food and does crude tasks to get it. I showed it to the men. One of them shot it. Nobody blamed him. Tomorrow we're going out and take these rats, and rescue those poor women that are still over there. Does your highness condescend to ask for a little Transstar help?"

"Transstar won't like this life-form meddling," I said. "This is the second time."

Rackrill slumped into a chair, looking at the woman who whispered some private incantation against the evils she had come to know.

"I've got two thousand colonists, five hundred ships," he said. "With or without your help, we're going out tomorrow and take them."

"They've got a few more ships, Rackrill."

He appeared not to hear. He sat there staring at the woman while I gathered up the eaber drone's body to take back to my ship.

"For God's sake, get Transstar," he said, as I left, and it was a prayer.

Shortly before noon next day, Rackrill was back at my

ship. He pointed to the sky over the colony, where his small fighting ships were rising. "What did your bosses say?" he asked.

"They said," I replied, "that Transstar has to look after the safety of the whole human race, and cannot match colonists man for man. There are safe places in alpha and solar to live—men are not obligated to seek danger. However, they are disturbed about the drone. I am to give an official protest and warning to Euben the eaber, which I have done."

"Is that *all!*"

I closed my eyes. "They also demoted me one rank, from a Seven to a Six, for having left my ship unattended in the middle of last night. During the time we examined the drone, a bumptious Colony correspondent sneaked in to my ship and taped an eaber monstrosity I had on the TV plate. She flung her sensationalism to the planets and nations of alpha and solar. To put it mildly, this has rocked the galaxy, which is fine with our Colony Correspondent. She gets paid according to the number of TV stations that play her tape."

"The universe should know!" cried Rackrill.

"The universe has always known," I said. "Every history book tells of worse things in almost every Middlesex village and town. Transstar is not in show business or in policy making. It observes and objectively attends to the broad general welfare of the Earthian universe."

Rackrill's voice was hoarse. "I have one empty ship," he said bitterly. "I lack a pilot. Will Transstar at least do me the favor of helping to fill that?"

"It will," I said, reaching for my combat slacks.

This was a wild, foolish mission, and I knew it. But I wanted to get as close as I could to eaber-land, which I had only observed at a distance. And I wanted to do something about the affronts to my system.

Sometimes it's good to fire a killing ray, even if it doesn't mean much.

We passed over three middle-sized eaber cities, the queerest cities I'd ever seen.

"Practically all landing fields," said a feminine voice in my ear. I looked to my left. The Colony Correspondent was riding a patrol ship on my right. I thanked her for achieving my embarrassment.

"Oh, that's all right, Doc," she said. "You're official-dom. Natural enemy. You'll get in your licks."

"I'd rather take mine in kicks. And I know where I'd like to plant my foot," I said.

I got a brash laugh. Foolish girl! Women do not have to be aggressive. There's the kind that makes a fetish of rushing in where brave men hesitate. On their maimed and dead persons the news tapes fatten and flourish.

Rackrill's group thought they were fighting the battle of the eon. They were trying to land at the most advanced city, where the captive Earthwomen were thought to be. The action was good. I was gloriously bashed around and managed to shoot down my eaber ship. It wasn't a difficult action for a Transstar-trained man. I was more interested in observing that the eaber had out an equal patrol of five hundred to oppose us. But, with all the noise and banging that a thousand-ship fight makes, I could observe that there were easily ten or fifteen thousand more eaber military ships on the ground we ranged over.

So the cities were not colonies. They were military bases for a large operation.

More interesting than the ships at hand were the extremely large areas being cleared and laid out for additional ship concentrations. I estimated that they could eventually base over a hundred thousand ships.

That would interest Transstar immensely.

Rackrill broke off the action when he had a mere hundred ships left. We limped back to the colony without being able to land in eaber territory. In fact, I doubted if the eaber chiefs regarded this as more than a quiet afternoon's patrol action. With their layout I couldn't blame them.

We almost missed the colony and had to sweep back once more. Yes, there was my Transstar ship, glowing orangely on the ground. But what a changed ground! It was brown and bare, a desert as far as the horizon.

During Rackrill's attack a secret eaber counterattack had swept the colony's transport ships, its buildings, and Rackrill's fifteen hundred colonists into oblivion.

In times of shock men do drastic—or foolish—things. Rackrill's group of survivors began to bring down the cooking equipment and bedding from their ships, preparing a camp for the night on the blighted cemetery of their colony, dazed and tearful.

"Ada, Ada," Rackrill moaned softly, his thick fingers picking at a gleaming aluminum pot. "Ada gone, Johnny gone—"

I noticed that Martha Stoner, the tape girl, had at last lost some of her high gloss. She stared at the scene, stunned. I could almost calibrate the change in her, from a high-spirited girl to a shocked and understanding woman.

I couldn't hold back comment. "Now you see the frontier," I said to her. "Now you've got a real tape that all the stations can use." She shook her head dumbly. "Go home, Rackrill," I advised the benumbed leader. "Take your men and go home."

He turned on me with teeth bared and lip trembling. "You—and that Transstar fraud. You let this happen! Tell your piddling button-pushers we will never go home!"

The words rang bravely on the scorched ground, while an eaber patrol, high up, gently wafted over us on an observation mission.

I shook my head. "At least go off in the forest where you have some protection—and some wood for your fires!"

I turned to go. A clod of soil struck my back, then a small stone.

"Go, Transstar filth, go!" They were all picking up the chant now.

"I'll file a tape all right!" cried Martha. "I can still get through to the world. The people will act, even if Transstar won't."

I didn't want to run.

I swear, this was my worst moment, because I had seen this distress many times. I understood their monumental shock. But if I did not run I could be seriously disabled by their attack. At any moment one might pull a gun. My job was to remain in good health so I could observe.

So I ran toward my ship.

They followed in a ragged company, shouting, cursing, and at last pulling guns. I barely escaped into the orange-hued safety of the Transstar ship before the rays flew. The colonists danced and pranced around the ship, shooting at it and beating on it, like nothing so much as forest natives attacking an interloper. I understood and discreetly closed the portholes.

"Order them home," I begged Twelve Jackson. "They are doomed here."

"We don't have the power," said Jackson. "We can only help them home if they want to go."

I rang up Euben on the eaber channel which I used for official communications—so far, mostly for protests. Euben made his innocent, bird-twitter laugh. "Thank you for your protest about the colony extinction," he said. "This keeps my clerks busy. Your colony may leave at any time. In fact, I recommend this. We will need all the space on this planet very soon."

Three days passed.

I found the remnant of Rackrill's tattered colony in a sort of forest stockade. They were stiff with me, embarrassed about the stoning incident. They were ghost men, and a few women, going through the motions of building crude houses and planting their food.

Martha was an exception.

"They will stay," she said proudly, her eyes glowing. "They will be buttressed by the great crusade our space tapes have started. First the story of the miserable pet-human, then the eaber drone thing, then the mass attack on the unguarded colony. Back home men are leaving their jobs, pouring their savings into fighting ships. Institutions are subscribing money. Governments are amassing new fighters. We've got the backing of all the thinking men in solar and alpha!"

"It is too late in civilization for an emotion-powered, unorganized mass movement to succeed," I said. "Only Transstar is properly equipped for space war."

"Even Transstar men are quitting to join us!" she cried.

"Possibly a few at the lower levels. Not the agents."

"No—not the dehumanized agents! Nor the feeble old men of Transstar Prime who stole their power from the government of men, who drool over buttons they never dare push!"

"The eaber do this to provoke us," I said, "to show our power at their command, at their site of battle, at a time they control. That's why Transstar Prime won't be sucked into the trap."

"They want to fight us. The time is now!" she said.

"The time is not yet," I said.

I went back to my lonely ship, haunted by the faces of Rackrill and his men as they glowed on my report tapes. I hunted the news broadcasts of solar and alpha and watched the revulsion and convulsion of men back home—the enormous waste of the emotional jag. I saw ships starting from Earth to reach us, ill-prepared even to reach the Moon, hurling across space vastnesses to become derelicts. I saw men throwing their pocket money at passing paraders of the anti-eaber crusade, normal shipping woefully hampered by the ridiculous items being sent to Rackrill's defenders. Government leaders, sensing the temper of the voters, threw their weight at Transstar Prime, calling for action. They got nowhere. Transstar resists temporary popular politics just as it does local situations.

"You certainly can't call this a local situation!" I told Twelve Jackson.

He sighed. "No, not any more. But the principle is missing. Everybody's mad, but the eaber haven't yet posed a major threat to the human race."

"They've got a couple hundred thousand fighting ships at our perimeter," I said.

"They haven't invaded territory we call our own. All the fighting is in no man's land. We're trained to determine a real danger from a false one, and so far they don't seem to be a real danger."

"It can get late fast," I said.

"Are you ready to ask for Condition Prime Total Red?"

There was a silence while I tried to separate my sympathetic feelings from the intelligence of the military situation. "No, sir," I said.

"Thirteen Mayberry agrees with you," said Twelve, looking over his shoulder, and then I saw the shadow of a sleeve of the top man. Transstar's Prime Prime, as the agents half-jokingly called him.

At least the desiccated old men near Mars were getting more interested.

On the day the first Earth-crusade task force arrived, both Martha and Rackrill came to the ship.

"You know it's the end of Transstar," Martha told me. She was more subdued and serious, but she still had the high-school glow of mysticism in her eyes. "The people have been sold out for the last time."

"No one's been sold out," I said. "We are in a painful

contact with a race that is both powerful and primitive. They can't be reasoned with, yet we can't blow them up until, at least, they give evidence that they intend to blow us up. So far it's only a border incident, as they used to be called in one-world days."

"We aren't waiting," said Martha. "Five thousand ships! The first wave of the anti-eaber crusade will attack soon."

Martha put me so much in mind of Alicia—the way she held her head, the way she moved her hands. Once both Alicia and I had been at a point of resigning from Transstar and leading normal lives. But something in the blood and bone had made our marriage to Transstar stronger—until she was killed on a mission, and it was forever too late for me to quit. I was aware that I was too loyal to the organization, which was, after all, merely another society of men.

Yet, right now, I found myself questioning Prime's judgment.

Certainly they could have given me power to negotiate for the colony with Euben. Certainly there were some potent weapons, short of total war, which we could have used on these vain primitives as easily as the ones they used on us. Nor need I have been brought to my knees in front of Euben.

Yet my orders were to observe—report—take no action.

We went aloft to watch the Earthmen's attack. Both Martha and Rackrill were set for an initial penetration to the first eaber city. As the massive fleet from Earth wheeled in from space and went directly to the attack, they cheered like students in a rooting section. I cautioned them that five thousand ships, strained from a long flight from alpha, could hardly upset the eaber.

"It's only the first group!" cried Martha. "This is only the glorious beginning!"

The eaber took no chances. They lofted fifteen thousand ships and pulled the Earthmen into a box.

It took them about four hours to defeat the Earth attack.

When the four hours passed, only about three hundred of the Earth fleet remained to sink to the oblivion of Rackrill's colony and lick their wounds.

"No matter," said Martha as we landed. "There will be more tomorrow and the day after that and after that. We'll blacken the skies with ships."

But she went quickly, avoiding my eyes.

"You'll always have sanctuary on my ship," I told Rackrill as he went.

"Your ship!" he snorted. "After today I'd rather trust my own stockade when Euben comes around. Incidentally, he has been kidnaping my work parties. Tell him we don't like that. Tell him we've been able to catch a few eaber, and when we do we cut them into four equal parts while they're still alive."

"Please don't," I said.

Euben came along as I was having my evening tea. "Ah, my scholarly friend with the glasses and the tea-drinking, the big words and the scoldings. I must thank you for keeping at least a part of our fleet in practice. A rather nice patrol action today, Webster. Is that your Transstar?"

"No. I ask you now what your intentions are as to this planet and our future relations," I said, aware that Transstar Prime, through this ship, had been watching the long day's affairs.

Euben had brought his friend with him. They both lolled at their ease in my cabin.

"It has been hard to determine," said Euben. "We have finally decided that, rather than waste rays killing off all Earthmen, we shall simply turn them into eaber. An inferior eaber, but still eaber. We have taken a few samples from Rackrill's post as prototypes."

"This is forbidden!" I snapped.

"You will declare war?" asked Euben eagerly. I thought his eagerness had grown.

"We don't know whom we deal with," I said. "You may be only a patrol captain, with a small command."

"I could also be commander-in-chief of all the eaber in space," said Euben. "Which I happen to be."

He said it too offhandedly for it to be a lie, although I suspected he was really deputy commander to the silent eaber who stood behind him.

"Then I formally demand that you cease and desist all harassments, mutilations, and hostilities against humans," I said.

Euben looked at me a long time. Then he held out what could reasonably be called an arm, which his companion grasped.

My ship seemed to whirl about me. It was no such thing. Instead I was suspended upside down in the air over my desk, and Euben and the other left the ship. "Farewell, brave-foolish," called Euben mockingly. "Next time I come it is to collect you for eaberization!"

His laugh was proud and full of confidence.

When I finally managed to right myself and get back behind my desk, I called Transstar Prime and got Twelve Jackson. I feared I saw a flick of amusement in his eyes. "They are determined now for war," I said. "How do we stand?"

"You continue to observe," said Jackson. "Point Everready is not necessary to Earth. And you have not convinced us that a battle needs to be fought."

I had not convinced them. But what did *I*—a mere agent—have to do with it?

I rang off and closed the ship, in sorrow and anger. I had been aloof from the situation, to the point where Euben had stood me on my head and threatened to capture me bodily.

I put on my combat slacks and broke out my weapons. Transstar could remain uninvolved, but I wasn't going to sit at my desk, be stood on my ear, and blithely be turned into an eaber all for the glory of the organization.

I rode over to Rackrill's stockade full of cold purpose.

I was no rugged primitive colonist. I was a trained agent, with quite a few good weapons and considerable experience in hostilities, especially against alien life-forms. Euben would have no easy time taking me.

I found Rackrill in more trouble. "Look," he fumed, pointing to a dead eaber at the wall of the stockade. "We shot this fellow. Look closely."

It was easy to see that it was one of his own colonists, upon whom extensive biology had been used to turn him into something eaberlike.

"It's going to happen to us all," shuddered Martha. "The crusade has collapsed. There'll be no more Earth ships. Distances are too great—governments are too busy with their home affairs. We have been outlawed in all major planets."

I stared at the white-faced colonial leaders in distaste.

"For God's sake, quit sniveling and feeling sorry for yourselves," I said. "We're going to fight these beasts and do it right. First, I want an antenna. I can draw power from my ship that the eaber can't crack. Second, I want to fight an eaber-type war. Get your colonists together for indoctrination. These eaber have primitive mind-reading abilities; I want to start training our men to set up mind guards against that. Last, we're going to dig some tunnels in this ground and blow the eaber into orbit. They don't like things underground. They have no defense for it. So let's get organized!"

"Thank God!" cried Martha. "Transstar is coming in at last."

"No," I said. "Just Charles Webster."

We fought the eaber for twenty days.

They couldn't penetrate the power wall I set up with the help of the ship, using Transstar power. They couldn't waylay our work parties in the woods after I taught them how to use mind-blocks which were meaningless to the eaber.

We got our tunnel through and blew up one third of an

eaber city with one of my strontium 90 pills. We were also able to capture a few eaber patrol ships and send them right back, with fair-sized atomic blasts. The rest we manned and used against the eaber. They were totally confused with being attacked by their own ships. It wasn't enough to destroy a twentieth of their operation. But it kept them busy.

I was never once outside my combat slacks.

I got little sleep. I lived for the present moment, working hand and shoulder with Rackrill's men. When disaster came, it came all at once.

I led a night patrol to place the next strontium 90 pill overland—tunneling was too slow. I caught an eaber freeze-ray that shattered my leg. In the confusion we lost Martha to the eaber, which I only learned when I'd been carried back to the stockade.

When dawn broke, Rackrill shook me out of a dazed sleep.

"Look," he said.

"Ten thousand ships to destroy two dozen men," I laughed. "It's all right, Alicia."

Rackrill slapped my face. "Better come out of it, Webster. Can we stand an attack like that?"

I gulped a wake-up pill and brought myself alert. "No, we cannot. This is our day for extinction. Our only decision now is to pick the time and place of our going. Let's get over to the Transstar ship as fast as possible."

"I'm not leaving Point Everready," growled Rackrill.

"Nor am I," I said. "Let's move, man."

It was a sticky hour getting back to my ship. By that time our stockade, power block and all, had been pulverized to dust behind us by the attacking weight of the eaber ships.

"Take me up, Rackrill," I said as we reached the bottom of the ship. "I can't climb any more."

He pointed up dumbly. The fox faces of Euben and his eternal companion grinned down at us. I shifted out a gun and took off the safety. "Take me up, Rackrill."

It was almost ceremonial as Rackrill and the bare half-dozen who had made it through gathered about me in the cabin. I eased painfully into my chair. Euben saw my leg and grinned. "Looks like an amputation before we can make you a useful eaber," he said.

My bullet skipped across his shoulder. "Stand over by that wall, you," I said. "You, Euben! I'm talking to you."

"You cannot order me," he said, but he moved back sprightly enough. "I humor you, you see," he said. "Your stockade is gone. You have nothing but this ship. I have decided to have it gently blasted into space as worthless junk."

He gestured out of the window, where his ships were making passes now. My Transstar ship shuddered. "We can bounce it off the planet like a harmless rubber ball," he said. He gestured in back of me. "I have also returned your woman, of whom you think so much. She is worthless to become an eaber."

I turned and saw the thin shape of what had once been Martha, huddled on my navigator's bench. It was obvious that they had treated her roughly. From the trickle of blood at her mouth, she was badly hemorrhaged. She could not live.

I stared down at her. It was hard to tell if she still recognized me. She opened her mouth slightly, and I saw the black familiar shape of the eaber reptile tongue.

I turned away, light-headed with sorrow and anger.

I jabbed a button and looked up at the tall TV. It wasn't Twelve Jackson. It was Thirteen Mayberry, Mr. Prime himself.

"What are you staring at, you old goat?" I cried, a little hysterically. "Sore because I took action to save my own hide?"

"No, you young fool. I was just wondering how long you'd permit this minor outrage to go on."

"It ends now!" I said. "Listen, Prime, I have Earth people here who demand sanctuary of Transstar."

"You have it," he said. "We will up that ship, son. No power in the universe will keep it on the ground."

"The eaber are upping it quite nicely, thanks," I said. "But we don't want it upped!"

I had to stop talking while the thudding blows of the gentle eaber rays buffeted the ship.

"Not upped?" asked Mayberry.

"No, sir, not upped. We're staying! We hold the ground that this Transstar ship rests on, in the name of Earth. It isn't much, only about fifty feet long and twenty-five wide, but it's Earth territory. No race or force may deprive us of our real estate."

"You tell him!" cried Rackrill.

I turned to Euben. "Now, friend," I said, "just ease this ship back to our ground. It's Earth ground. We intend to hold it!"

"Your leg wound has made you mad," said Euben, with a shrug. "We have decided that you are not even worthy to be eaber pets."

"Last warning, Euben! You've got yourself a Transstar situation."

Euben didn't hesitate.

He turned his hands in the air. I rolled in pain, but I kept seated. When I could see again from the pain, I looked up. Mayberry and Jackson and Hennessy and the forty-one division commanders of Transstar were blazing from the wall. The TV looked like a Christmas tree.

"Transstar orders this ship down and that ground preserved in the name of Earth-alpha!" said Mayberry shortly to Euben.

Euben looked at the old man and shook his head. "Madmen," he said. "I spit on you." He spit on the screen at Mayberry. He had learned Earth insults well.

"My condition is Prime Total Red," I told Mayberry.

He leaned forward and closed the seldom-closed circuit at Transstar Prime.

"Your condition is Prime Total Red, and your ship is now command post for all Earth-alpha star power."

I leaned over and tapped a button. We left Point Everready in the beautiful swoop that only a Transstar ship could perform. I held us high in the atmosphere over the planet and looked sadly down. It had been a beautiful planet.

I hit another button and looked up at the forty-one division commanders of Transstar. "Your orders are to destroy the eaber," I said.

I sat back. For a few seconds it was deathly silent, while Euben sputtered and fussed about his quick ride up over the planet. Then there was the faintest whisper of—something—back and out and behind us.

"Brace yourselves, folks," I told the Earthmen. "It's going to be loud and crowded around here!"

Euben jabbered at some kind of communicator he held in his hands. His partner likewise gabbled.

"We have a hundred and fifty thousand ships," he told me. "We'll tear you to shreds!"

I kicked a chair over at him. "Sit down. You're going to want to sit in a minute."

"Something's wrong with the ship!" cried Rackrill. "It's heavy and dead!"

"We're drawing most of the broadcast power this side of Mars," I said. "In a minute you'll be glad we have that protection!"

Transstar came then. The fast patrols whisked out of black space and leaped into our atmosphere like gleaming fish, fired a rocking blast of weaponry, and were gone to rendezvous, reform, and pass again. They were like nothing the eaber had ever seen. They were made for a star-go like this, a burst of light, a dazzle, and a thunder that came and came and came. Behind them came the light patrols and then the medium patrols and then the heavy patrols and then the fast light shock ships and then the medium shock ships and then the heavy shocks, wave upon wave upon wave.

Even wrapped in our thick blanket of power we were stunned.

The planet came alight like a pearl below us. The air was jammed with sound shocks, the dazzle was like a spreading, thickening bomb of light that transfixed the eyeballs even through the dark screens I had set up.

"This is early stuff," I told Euben conversationally. "They just do a little holding till the important ships arrive. Patrols and first shocks—the usual things, you know."

Euben's mouth was open. He took time to swallow before he screamed orders to his ships below.

The patrols and shocks were suddenly past firing range. For a moment you could see the planet through the haze. Its shore lines and rivers had sickened and wavered. The eaber ships, which had been a blanket, were a tattered rag.

Hennessy, the headquarters jokester, couldn't resist a comment that probably earned him a fine. "Here comes the cavalry," he said over the TV.

And they came.

It was good professional stuff, geared to star action. Now we had the regulars. They came in waves of ten thousand, which was a wee bit impressive, I thought. There were the ground regulars, the medium regulars, and the high regulars, each division with thirty categories, each category with its subdivisions of missiles, rockets, and drones. The atmosphere screamed at us. The density of the light assumed sun proportions, and our poor little ship was like a chip on an angry ocean. Rackrill had his mouth wide open. He was yelling to relieve his tension at the awesome sight; the others were lost in the overwhelming cataclysm of it. I had seen it in movies.

I poured myself a cup of tea.

"These are just the on-call regulars," I told Euben. "Of course, you realize that in a Prime Red we're getting total mobilization. We'll get slightly less than a million ships in the first hour. The rest will come later."

Euben had stopped shouting orders. He stared at me. He said something that I couldn't hear. The pounding went on for fifteen minutes; then the planet cleared. There weren't any shore lines or rivers any more. There weren't very many eaber ships.

"Stop it," he said.

I shook my head. "Sorry. A Prime Red can't be stopped easily. Once the momentum starts it has to run its course. Get set now. Here come your specials."

As the specials started to arrive, I taunted the division commanders. "Transstar is getting rusty. You've hardly nicked the planet. Can't your boys shoot properly any more?"

They came in fat and sleek. Far off they waddled and wallowed, like a bunch of old ladies hitting a bargain counter. But suddenly they were serious, close up, and I had to close the portholes against the awesome roar and light of their work. You name the ray, bullet, bomb, gas—it was there.

A half hour later the din eased off and we looked. A large fragment of seared rock floated in space. The entire eaber fleet had long ago disappeared. So had everything else except that radioactive rock.

The last wave was the massive attack unit, very slow and lumbering compared to the others, but packed with power. The first five thousand took eager bites of the rock— and there was nothing left for the other twenty-five thousand. There was nothing left at all of Point Everready except some haze hanging below us in space. But it was too late to stop the attack.

To one side of us the returning waves began to streak by—the patrols, fast, light, medium, and heavy, the shocks, first, second, and third, the regulars in their streaming divisions and then the specials. Meanwhile, closer by, the second wave was coming in, first patrols and first shocks, darting a few shots to keep their hand in, at the floating dust patches.

Euben looked out and saw ships to his left and to his right and behind him and below him and above him and in all positions in between. It was such a heavy concentration that the stars were blocked out and, though no atmosphere existed for a nonexistent planet, we were a planet of moving ships, ourselves creating a gravity and a stinking jet-flame atmosphere. It was a moving dream of hell, enough to make your mind crack open with the motion of it. It was the phantom action of a near-million starships—and another million on the way.

This was the total war capacity delivered to order.

What it cost in disruption and money and waste was incredible to contemplate. But that was Prime Total Red— everything we had. And it wasn't at all pointless.

"The eaber surrender," said Euben.

He stood respectfully now, his commander behind him. I guess he was thinking of the remaining eaber colonies on other planets, as there was nothing left to surrender here.

I handed him a rag. "You may now wipe the spit off my TV plate receiver," I said. He did it with alacrity.

"We will go elsewhere," said Euben's companion. "After all, space is big. There is plenty of room for two great races."

"One great race," I said.

"Of course," he said affably. "May we have our lives spared?"

"We want you to have them—so you can take the word home."

The action outside had stilled. I opened the ports and began to move slowly toward another planet where the eaber had dwellings, as requested by the shaken Euben. Rackrill patted my shoulder. "Boy, that Transstar!" he exulted.

"It's quite a lot," I admitted. I painfully inched over to the stricken Martha and squeezed her hand. I thought she squeezed back. I thought I saw a flicker of joy at our success—but there was so much eaber and so much death in her eyes it was hard to know. I had to leave her then, for the medics came aboard for her.

I began to glide down on the new planet to discharge Euben and the other eaber. "Look," I said gesturing over my shoulder. Behind us the Transstar fleet followed docilely, the mass and weight of them, guns racked and quiet, the great beast behind my tiny patrol dot.

"We'll stay around a few days in case you want to argue some more," I told Euben.

He shook his head. "That will not be necessary, my good friend. We are not stupid. In the future you'll see very little of the eaber."

The ship settled. I opened the door and put down the ladder and Euben's companion descended, then Euben. "I am sorry—" he began.

But I thought of Martha and the dead boy who had died on Everready and the pet human and the drone eaber and the others who had suffered and died to make this creature sorry. So I planted my good foot on his rear. He crashed into his master and they both fell in the mud at the bottom of the ladder. They got up, mud-splattered, and ran like the wind toward eaberdom, capes flying out behind them.

Rackrill laughed. It was the first relaxed laugh I'd heard in all that assignment. It pulled things back to normal.

I turned back to my blazing board and hit a button. "Condition White," I said, "and don't kid me that you got up all these starships on seventy-five seconds' notice. They left

Earth-alpha weeks ago. You knew from the first we were in for a Condition Prime Total Red with the eaber."

The old man grinned. "It's the agents who louse us up. We were afraid you'd observe so long that you'd start the action on an orange and build a whole new tradition—Ten."

Ten! I remembered then that anybody who ordered a CPTR was automatically up for Ten rank and sent to a nice, soft job at Prime.

"Save me a wide, plump chair at the TV console at Prime," I said. "Get me a desk-sized teapot, and a soft cushion for a bum leg."

I turned the ship around and started to lead the massive fleet home.

I stared at the far-flung stars of space as I drank my tea, eyes blurred a little with tears. I was an organization man. The organization was all I had, or would ever have. It didn't seem enough. Even the playing of the Transstar victory song left me depressed.

Then suddenly the light broke.

A Transstar agent is both the most and the least important of men. He is a fireman who puts out fires—a hero, but a shadow. A master sometimes, but mostly a servant. I winked at Mayberry on the screen. They saw I knew and winked back. They had finally lost a pompous, Transstar-impressed agent and gained a useful career man.

They were satisfied.

So was I.

A war is expensive: it absorbs a great deal of a society's available resources. Though governments usually phrase the decision for war in terms of right and wrong, the real equation boils down to a question of whether the society (or at least the decisionmaker) will be better off as a result of war than as a result of peace on the available terms. This is obvious to anyone who knows history, but it's such a hard truth that Transstar *is one of very few stories to address the situation.*

If I had written Transstar, *the conclusion would have been different. I wanted to ask Ray Banks whether the tone was his or a change by H.L. Gold, an editor famous for rewriting stories . . . but Banks died two years before I located him. I don't regret not knowing the answer to that question nearly as much as I regret not having been able to tell Banks how much his story moved me, when I first read it as a teenager and every time I've reread it since.*

—DAD

Time Piece

★

Joe Haldeman

They say you've got a fifty-fifty chance every time you go out. That makes it one chance in eight that you'll live to see your third furlough; the one I'm on now.

Somehow the odds don't keep people from trying to join. Even though not one in a thousand gets through the years of training and examination, there's no shortage of cannon fodder. And that's what we are. The most expensive, best trained cannon fodder in the history of warfare. Human history, anyhow; who can speak for the enemy?

I don't even call them snails anymore. And the thought of them doesn't trigger that instant flash of revulsion, hate, kill-fever—the psyconditioning wore off years ago, and they didn't renew it. They've stopped doing it to new recruits; no percentage in berserkers. I was a wild one the first couple of trips, though.

Strange world I've come back to. Gets strangers every time, of course. Even sitting here in a bogus twenty-first century bar, where everyone speaks Basic and there's real wood on the walls and peaceful holograms instead of plug-ins and music made by men . . .

But it leaks through. I don't pay by card, let alone by coin. The credit register monitors my alpha waves and communicates with the bank every time I order a drink. And, in case I've become addicted to more modern vices, there's a feelie matrix (modified to look like an old-fashioned visi-phone booth) where I can have my brain stimulated directly. Thanks but no, thanks—always get this picture of dirty hands inside my skull, kneading, rubbing. Like when you get too close to the enemy and they open a hole in your mind and you go spinning down and down and never reach the bottom till you die. I almost got too close last time.

We were on a three-man reconnaissance patrol, bound for a hellish little planet circling the red giant Antares. Now red giant stars don't form planets in the natural course of things, so we had ignored Antares; we control most of the space around it, so why waste time in idle exploration? But the enemy had detected this little planet—God knows how—and about ten years after they landed there, we monitored their presence (gravity waves from the ships' braking) and my team was assigned the reconnaissance. Three men against many, many of the enemy—but we weren't supposed to fight if we could help it; just take a look around, record what we saw, and leave a message beacon on our way back, about a light-year out from Antares. Theoretically, the troopship following us by a month will pick up the information and use it to put together a battle plan. Actually, three more recon patrols precede the troop ship at one-week intervals; insurance against the high probability that any one patrol will be caught and destroyed. As the first team in, we have a pretty good chance of success, but the ones to follow would be in trouble if we didn't get back out. We'd be past caring, of course: the enemy doesn't take prisoners.

We came out of lightspeed close to Antares, so the bulk

of the star would mask our braking disturbance, and inserted the ship in a hyperbolic orbit that would get us to the planet—Anomaly, we were calling it—in about twenty hours.

"Anomaly must be tropical over most of its surface," Fred Sykes, nominally the navigator, was talking to himself and at the two of us while he analyzed the observational data rolling out of the ship's computer. "No axial tilt to speak of. Looks like they've got a big outpost near the equator, lots of electromagnetic noise there. Figures . . . the goddamn snails like it hot. We requisitioned hot-weather gear, didn't we, Pancho?"

Pancho, that's me. "No, Fred, all we got's parkas and snowshoes." My full name is Francisco Jesus Mario Juan-José Hugo de Naranja, and I outrank Fred, so he should at least call me Francisco. But I've never pressed the point. Pancho it is. Fred looked up from his figure and the rookie, Paul Spiegel, almost dropped the pistol he was cleaning.

"But why . . ." Paul was staring. "We knew the planet was probably Earthlike if the enemy wanted it. Are we gonna have to go tromping around in spacesuits?"

"No, Paul, our esteemed leader and supply clerk is being sarcastic again." He turned back to his computer. "Explain, Pancho."

"No, that's all right," Paul reddened a bit and also went back to his job. "I remember you complaining about having to take the standard survival issue."

"Well, I was right then and I'm doubly right now. We've *got* parkas back there, and snowshoes, and a complete terranorm environment recirculator, and everything else we could possibly need to walk around in comfort on every planet known to man—*Dios!* That issue masses over a metric ton, more than a giga-watt laser. A laser we could use, but crampons and pith helmets and elephant guns . . ."

Paul looked up again. "Elephant guns?" He was kind of a freak about weapons.

"Yeah."

"That's a gun that shoots elephants?"

"Right. An elephant gun shoots elephants."

"Is that some new kind of ammunition?"

I sighed, I really sighed. You'd think I'd get used to this after twelve years—or four hundred—in the service. "No, kid, elephants were animals, big gray wrinkled animals with horns. You used an elephant gun to shoot *at* them.

"When I was a kid in Rioplex, back in the twenty-first, we had an elephant in the zoo; used to go down in the summer and feed him synthos through the bars. He had a long nose like a fat tail, he ate with that."

"What planet were they from?"

It went on like that for a while. It was Paul's first trip out, and he hadn't yet gotten used to the idea that most of his compatriots were genuine antiques, preserved by the natural process of relativity. At lightspeed you age imperceptibly, while the universe's calendar adds a year for every light-year you travel. Seems like cheating. But it catches up with you eventually.

We hit the atmosphere of Anomaly at an oblique angle and came in passive, like a natural meteor, until we got to a position where we were reasonably safe from detection (just above the south polar sea), then blasted briefly to slow down and splash. Then we spent a few hours in slow flight at sea level, sneaking up on their settlement.

It appeared to be the only enemy camp on the whole planet, which was typical. Strange for a spacefaring, aggressive race to be so incurious about planetary environments, but they always seemed to settle in one place and simply expand radially. And they do expand; their reproduction rate makes rabbits look sick. Starting from one colony, they can fill a world in two hundred years. After that, they control their population by infantiphage and stellar migration.

We landed about a hundred kilometers from the edge of their colony, around local midnight. While we were outside setting up the espionage monitors, the ship camouflaged itself to match the surrounding jungle optically, thermally, magnetically, etc.—We were careful not to get too far from the ship; it can be a bit hard to find even when you know where to look.

The monitors were to be fed information from flea-sized flying robots, each with a special purpose, and it would take several hours for them to wing into the city. We posted a one-man guard, one-hour shifts; the other two inside the ship until the monitors started clicking. But they never started.

Being senior, I took the first watch. A spooky hour, the jungle making dark little noises all around, but nothing happened. Then Fred stood the next hour, while I put on the deepsleep helmet. Figured I'd need the sleep—once data started coming in, I'd have to be alert for about forty hours. We could all sleep for a week once we got off Anomaly and hit lightspeed.

Getting yanked out of deepsleep is like an ice-water douche to the brain. The black nothing dissolved and there was Fred a foot away from my face, yelling my name over and over. As soon as he saw my eyes open, he ran for the open lock, priming his laser on the way (definitely against regulations, could hole the hull that way; I started to say something but couldn't form the words). Anyhow, what were we doing in free fall? And how could Fred run across the deck like that while we were in free fall?

Then my mind started coming back into focus and I could analyze the sinking, spinning sensation—not free-fall vertigo at all, but what we used to call snail-fever. The enemy was very near. Crackling combat sounds drifted in from outdoors.

I sat up on the cot and tried to sort everything out and get going. After long seconds my arms and legs got the idea, I struggled up and staggered to the weapons cabinet. Both the lasers were gone, and the only heavy weapon left was a grenade launcher. I lifted it from the rack and made my way to the lock.

Had I been thinking straight, I would've just sealed the lock and blasted—the presence in my mind was so strong that I should have known there were too many of the enemy, too close, for us to stand and fight. But no one can think while their brain is being curdled that way. I fought the urge to just let go and fall down that hole in my mind, and slid along the wall to the airlock. By the time I got there my teeth were chattering uncontrollably and my face was wet with tears.

Looking out, I saw a smoldering gray lump that must have been Paul, and Fred screaming like a madman, fanning the laser on full over a 180-degree arc. There couldn't have been anything alive in front of him; the jungle was a lurid curtain of fire, but a bolt lanced in from behind and Fred dissolved in a pink spray of blood and flesh.

I saw them then, moving fast for snails, shambling in over thick brush toward the ship. Through the swirling fog in my brain I realized that all they could see was the light pouring through the open lock, and me silhouetted in front. I tried to raise the launcher but couldn't—there were too many, less than a hundred meters away, and the inky whirlpool in my mind just got bigger and bigger and I could feel myself slipping into it.

The first bolt missed me; hit the ship and it shuddered, ringing like a huge cathedral bell. The second one didn't miss, taking off my left hand just above the wrist, roasting what remained of my left arm. In a spastic lurch I jerked up the launcher and yanked the trigger, holding it down while dozens of micro-ton grenades popped out and danced their blinding way up to and across the enemy's ragged line. Dazzled blind, I stepped back and stumbled over the med-robot, which had smelled blood and was eager to do its duty. On top of the machine was a switch that some clown had labeled EMERGENCY EXIT; I slapped it, and as the lock clanged shut the atomic engines muttered—growled—screamed into life and a ten-gravity hand slid me across the blood-slick deck and slammed me back against the rear-wall padding. I felt ribs crack and something in my neck snapped. As the world squeezed away, I knew I was a dead man but it was better to die in a bed of pain than to just fall and fall.

I woke up to the less-than-tender ministrations of the med-robot, who had bound the stump of my left arm and was wrapping my chest in plastiseal. My body from forehead to shins ached from radiation burns, earned by facing the grenades' bursts, and the nonexistent hand seemed to writhe in painful, impossible contortions. But numbing anesthetic kept the pain at a bearable distance, and there was an empty space in my mind where the snail-fever had been, and the gentle hum told me we were at lightspeed; things could have been one flaming hell of a lot worse. Fred and Paul were gone but that just moved them from the small roster of live friends to the long list of dead ones.

A warning light on the control panel was blinking stroboscopically. We were getting near the hole—excuse me, "relativistic discontinuity"—and the computer had to know where I wanted to go. You go in one hole at light-speed and you'll come out of some other hole; *which* hole you pop out of depends on your angle of approach. Since they say that only about one percent of the holes are charted, if you go in at any old angle you're liable to wind up in Podunk, on the other side of the galaxy, with no ticket back.

I just let the light blink, though. If it doesn't get any response from the crew, the ship programs itself automatically to go to Heaven, the hospital world, which was fine with me. They cure what ails you and then set you loose with a compatible soldier of the opposite sex, for an extended vacation on that beautiful world. Someone once told me there were over a hundred worlds named Hell, but there's only one Heaven. Clean and pretty from the tropical seas to the

Northern pine forests. Like Earth used to be, before we strangled it.

A bell had been ringing all the time I'd been conscious, but I didn't notice it until it stopped. That meant that the information capsule had been jettisoned, for what little it was worth. Planetary information, very few espionage-type data; just a tape of the battle. Be rough for the next recon patrol.

I fell asleep knowing I'd wake up on the other side of the hole, bound for Heaven.

I pick up my drink—an old-fashioned old-fashioned—with my new left hand and the glass should feel right, slick but slightly tacky with the cold-water sweat, fine ridges molded into the plastic. But there's something missing, hard to describe, a memory stored in your fingertips that a new growth has to learn all over again. It's a strange feeling, but in a way seems to fit with this crazy Earth, where I sit in my alcoholic time capsule and, if I squint with my mind, can almost believe I'm back in the twenty-first.

I pay for the nostalgia—wood and natural food, human bartender and waitress who are also linguists, it all comes dear—but I can afford it, if anyone can. Compound interest, of course. Over four centuries have passed Earth since I first went off to the war, and my salary's been deposited at the Chase Manhattan Credit Union ever since. They're glad to do it; when I die, they keep the interest and the principal reverts to the government. Heirs? I had one illegitimate son (conceived on my first furlough) and when I last saw his gravestone, the words on it had washed away to barely legible dimples.

But I'm still a young man (at lightspeed you age imperceptibly while the universe winds down outside) and the time you spend going from hole to hole is almost incalculably small. I've spent most of the past half millennium at lightspeed, the rest of the time usually convalescing from battle. My records show that I've logged a trifle under one year in actual combat. Not bad for 438 years' pay. Since I first lifted off I've aged twelve years by my biological calendar. Complicated, isn't it—next month I'll be thirty, 456 years after my date of birth.

But one week before my birthday I've got to decide whether to try my luck for a fourth trip out or just collect my money and retire. No choice, really. I've got to go back.

It's something they didn't emphasize when I joined up, back in 2088—maybe it wasn't so obvious back then, the war only decades old—but they can't hide it nowadays. Too many old vets wandering around, like animated museum pieces.

I could cash in my chips and live in luxury for another hundred years. But it would get mighty lonely. Can't talk to anybody on Earth but other vets and people who've gone to the trouble to learn Basic.

Everyone in space speaks Basic. You can't lift off until you've become fluent. Otherwise, how could you take orders from a fellow who should have been food for worms centuries before your grandfather was born? Especially since language melted down into one Language.

I'm tone-deaf. Can't speak or understand Language, where one word has ten or fifteen different meanings, depending on pitch. To me it sounds like puppydogs yapping. Same words over and over; no sense.

Of course, when I first lived on earth, there were all sorts of languages, not just one Language. I spoke Spanish (still do when I can find some other old codger who remembers) and learned English—that was before they called it Basic—in military training. Learned it damned well, too. If I weren't tone-deaf I'd crack Language and maybe I'd settle down.

Maybe not. The people are so strange, and it's not just the Language. Mindplugs and homosex and voluntary suicide. Walking around with nothing on but paint and powder. We had Fullerdomes when I was a kid; but you didn't *have* to live under one. Now if you take a walk out in the country for a breath of fresh air, you'll drop over dead before you can exhale.

My mind keeps dragging me back to Heaven. I'd retire in a minute if I could spend my remaining century there. Can't, of course; only soldiers allowed in space. And the only way a soldier gets to Heaven is the hard way.

I've been there three times; once more and I'll set a record. That's motivation of a sort, I suppose. Also, in the unlikely event that I should live another five years, I'll get a commission, and a desk job if I live through my term as a field officer. Doesn't happen too often—but there aren't too many desk jobs that people can handle better than cyborgs.

That's another alternative. If my body gets too garbaged for regeneration, and they can save enough of my brain, I could spend the rest of eternity hooked up to a computer, as a cyborg. The only one I've ever talked to seemed to be happy.

I once had an African partner named N'gai. He taught me how to play O'wari, a game older than Monopoly or even chess. We sat in this very bar (or the identical one that was in its place two hundred years ago) and he tried to impress on my non-Zen-oriented mind just how significant this game was to men in our position.

You start out with forty-eight smooth little pebbles, four in each one of the twelve depressions that make up the game board. Then you take turns, scooping the pebbles out of one hole and distributing them one at a time in holes to the left. If you dropped your last pebble in a hole where your opponent had only one or two, why, you got to take those pebbles off the board. Sounds exciting, doesn't it?

But N'gai sat there in a cloud of bhang-smoke and mumbled about the game and how it was just like the big game we were playing, and every time he took a pebble off the board, he called it by name. And some of the names I didn't know, but a lot of them were on my long list.

And he talked about how we were like the pieces in this simple game; how some went off the board after the first couple of moves, and some hopped from place to place all through the game and came out unscathed, and some just sat in one place all the time until they got zapped from out of nowhere. . . .

After a while I started hitting the bhang myself, and we abandoned the metaphor in a spirit of mutual intoxication.

And I've been thinking about that night for six years, or two hundred, and I think that N'gai—his soul find Buddha—was wrong. The game isn't all that complex.

Because in O'wari, either person can win.

The snails populate ten planets for every one we destroy.

Solitaire, anyone?

Due to oddities in the way LBJ and his henchman Robert McNamara conducted US foreign policy, Joe Haldeman and I both spent our twenty-fifth birthdays in Viet Nam. Mine wasn't a lot of fun, and his was much worse than that.

Joe returned to become one of the most justly honored SF writers of his generation. I've always been amazed at the way Joe in Time Piece *tells a very different story from the one you start out thinking you're going to read.*

—DAD

Clash by Night

✪

Henry Kuttner & C.L. Moore

Introduction

A half mile beneath the shallow Venusian Sea the black impervium dome that protects Montana Keep rests frowningly on the bottom. Within the Keep is carnival, for the Montanans celebrate the four-hundred-year anniversary of Earthman's landing on Venus. Under the great dome that houses the city all is light and color and gaiety. Masked men and women, bright in celoflex and silks, wander through the broad streets, laughing, drinking the strong native wines of Venus. The sea bottom has been combed, like the hydroponic tanks, for rare delicacies to grace the tables of the nobles.

Through the festival grim shadows stalk, men whose faces mark them unmistakably as members of a Free Company. Their finery cannot disguise that stamp, hard-won through years of battle. Under the domino masks their mouths are hard and harsh. Unlike the undersea dwellers, their skins are burned black with the ultraviolet rays that filter through the cloud layer of Venus. They are skeletons at the feast. They are respected but resented. They are Free Companions—

We are on Venus, nine hundred years ago, beneath the Sea of Shoals, not much north of the equator. But there is a wide range in time and space. All over the cloud planet the underwater Keeps are dotted, and life will not change for many centuries. Looking back, as we do now, from the civilized days of the Thirty-fourth Century, it is too easy to regard the men of the Keeps as savages, groping, stupid and brutal. The Free Companies have long since vanished. The islands and continents of Venus have been tamed, and there is no war.

But in periods of transition, of desperate rivalry, there is always war. The Keeps fought among themselves, each striving to draw the fangs of the others by depriving them of their reserves of korium, the power source of the day. Students of that era find pleasure in sifting the legends and winnowing out the basic social and geopolitical truths. It is fairly well known that only one factor saved the Keeps from annihilating one another—the gentlemen's agreement that left war to the warriors, and allowed the undersea cities to develop their science and social cultures. That particular compromise was, perhaps, inevitable. And it caused the organization of the Free Companies, the roving bands of mercenaries, highly trained for their duties, who hired themselves out to fight for whatever Keeps were attacked or wished to attack.

Ap Towrn, in his monumental "Cycle of Venus," tells the saga through symbolic legends. Many historians have recorded the sober truth, which, unfortunately, seems often Mars-dry. But it is not generally realized that the Free Companions were almost directly responsible for our present high culture. War, because of them, was not permitted to usurp the place of peace-time social and scientific work. Fighting was highly specialized, and, because of technical advances, manpower was no longer important. Each band of Free Companions numbered a few thousand, seldom more.

It was a strange, lonely life they must have led, shut out from the normal life of the Keeps. They were vestigian but necessary, like the fangs of the marsupians who eventually evolved into Homo sapiens. But without those warriors, the Keeps would have been plunged completely into total war, with fatally destructive results.

Harsh, gallant, indomitable, serving the god of battles so that it might be destroyed—working toward their own obliteration—the Free Companies roar down the pages of history, the banner of Mars streaming above them in the misty air of Venus. They were doomed as Tyrannosaurus Rex was doomed, and they fought on as he did, serving, in their strange way, the shape of Minerva that stood behind Mars.

Now they are gone. We can learn much by studying the place they held in the Undersea Period. For, because of them, civilization rose again to the heights it had once reached on Earth, and far beyond.

"These lords shall light the mystery
Of mastery or victory,
And these ride high in history,
But these shall not return."

The Free Companions hold their place in interplanetary literature. They are a legend now, archaic and strange. For they were fighters, and war has gone with unification. But we can understand them a little more than could the people of the Keeps.

This story, built on legends and fact, is about a typical warrior of the period—Captain Brian Scott of Doone's Free Companions. He may never have existed—

I.

O, it's Tommy this, an' Tommy that, an' "Tommy, go away";
But it's "Thank you, Mr. Atkins," when the band begins to
   play,

The band begins to play, my boys, the band begins to play—
O, it's "Thank you, Mr. Atkins," when the band begins to
play.

—R. Kipling circa 1900

Scott drank stinging uisqueplus and glowered across the smoky tavern. He was a hard, stocky man, with thick gray-shot brown hair and the scar of an old wound crinkling his chin. He was thirty-odd, looking like the veteran he was, and he had sense enough to wear a plain suit of blue celoflex, rather than the garish silks and rainbow fabrics that were all around him.

Outside, through the transparent walls, a laughing throng was carried to and fro along the movable ways. But in the tavern it was silent, except for the low voice of a harpman as he chanted some old ballad, accompanying himself on his complicated instrument. The song came to an end. There was scattering applause, and, from the hot-box overhead the blaring music of an orchestra burst out. Instantly the restraint was gone. In the booths and at the bar men and women began to laugh and talk with casual unrestraint. Couples were dancing now.

The girl beside Scott, a slim, tan-skinned figure with glossy black ringlets cascading to her shoulders, turned inquiring eyes to him.

"Want to, Brian?"

Scott's mouth twisted in a wry grimace. "Suppose so, Jeana. Eh?" He rose, and she came gracefully into his arms. Brian did not dance too well, but what he lacked in practice he made up in integration. Jeana's heartshaped face, with its high cheekbones and vividly crimson lips, lifted to him.

"Forget Bienne. He's just trying to ride you."

Scott glanced toward a distant booth, where two girls sat with a man—Commander Fredric Bienne of the Doones. He was a gaunt, tall, bitter-faced man, his regular features twisted into a perpetual sneer, his eyes somber under heavy dark brows. He was pointing, now, toward the couple on the floor.

"I know," Scott said. "He's doing it, too. Well, the hell with him. So I'm a captain now and he's still a commander. That's tough. Next time he'll obey orders and not send his ship out of the line, trying to ram."

"That was it, eh?" Jeana asked. "I wasn't sure. There's plenty of talk."

"There always is. Oh, Bienne's hated me for years. I reciprocate. We simply don't get on together. Never did. Every time I got a promotion, he chewed his nails. Figured he had a longer service record than I had and deserved to move up faster. But he's too much of an individualist—at the wrong times."

"He's drinking a lot," Jeana said.

"Let him. Three months we've been in Montana Keep. The boys get tired of inaction—being treated like this." Scott nodded toward the door, where a Free Companion was arguing with the keeper. "No noncoms allowed in here. Well, the devil with it."

They could not hear the conversation above the hubbub, but its importance was evident. Presently the soldier shrugged, his mouth forming a curse, and departed. A fat man in scarlet silks shouted encouragement.

"—want any . . . Companions here!"

Scott saw Commander Bienne, his eyes half closed, get up and walk toward the fat man's booth. His shoulder moved in an imperceptible shrug. The hell with civilians, anyhow. Serve the lug right if Bienne smashed his greasy face. And that seemed the probable outcome. For the fat man was accompanied by a girl, and obviously wasn't going to back down, though Bienne, standing too close to him, was saying something insulting, apparently.

The auxiliary hot-box snapped some quick syllables, lost in the general tumult. But Scott's trained ear caught the words. He nodded to Jeana, made a significant clicking noise with his tongue, and said, "This is it."

She, too, had heard. She let Scott go. He headed toward the fat man's booth just in time to see the beginning of a brawl. The civilian, red as a turkey cock, had struck out suddenly, landing purely by accident on Bienne's gaunt cheek. The commander, grinning tightly, stepped back a pace, his fist clenching. Scott caught the other's arm.

"Hold it, commander."

Bienne swung around, glaring. "What business is it of yours? Let—"

The fat man, seeing his opponent's attention distracted, acquired more courage and came in swinging. Scott reached past Bienne, planted his open hand in the civilian's face, and pushed hard. The fat man almost fell backward on his table.

As he rebounded, he saw a gun in Scott's hand. The captain said curtly, "'Tend to your knitting, mister."

The civilian licked his lips, hesitated, and sat down. Under his breath he muttered something about too-damn-cocky Free Companions.

Bienne was trying to break free, ready to swing on the captain. Scott holstered his gun. "Orders," he told the other, jerking his head toward the hot-box. "Get it?"

"—mobilization. Doonemen report to headquarters. Captain Scott to Administration. Immediate mobilization—"

"Oh," Bienne said, though he still scowled. "O.K. I'll take over. There was time for me to take a crack at that louse, though."

"You know what instant mobilization means," Scott grunted. "We may have to leave at an instant's notice. Orders, commander."

Bienne saluted halfheartedly and turned away. Scott went back to his own booth. Jeana had already gathered her purse and gloves and was applying lip juice.

She met his eyes calmly enough.

"I'll be at the apartment, Brian. Luck."

He kissed her briefly; conscious of a surging excitement at the prospect of a new venture. Jeana understood his emotion. She gave him a quick, wry smile, touched his hair lightly, and rose. They went out into the gay tumult of the ways.

Perfumed wind blew into Scott's face. He wrinkled his nose disgustedly. During carnival seasons the Keeps were less pleasant to the Free Companions than otherwise; they felt more keenly the gulf that lay between them and the undersea dwellers. Scott pushed his way through the crowd and took Jeana across the ways to the center fast-speed strip. They found seats.

At a clover-leaf intersection Scott left the girl, heading toward Administration, the cluster of taller buildings in the city's center. The technical and political headquarters were centered here, except for the laboratories, which were in the suburbs near the base of the Dome. There were a few small test-domes a mile or so distant from the city, but these were used only for more precarious experiments. Glancing up, Scott was reminded of the catastrophe that had unified science into something like a freemasonry. Above him, hanging without gravity over a central plaza, was the globe of the Earth, half shrouded by the folds of a black plastic pall. In every Keep on Venus there was a similar ever-present reminder of the lost mother planet.

Scott's gaze went up farther, to the Dome, as though he could penetrate the impervium and the mile-deep layer of water and the clouded atmosphere to the white star that hung in space, one quarter as brilliant as the Sun. A star—all that remained of Earth, since atomic power had been unleashed there two centuries ago. The scourge had spread like flame, melting continents and leveling mountains. In the libraries there were wire-tape pictorial records of the Holocaust. A religious cult—Men of the New Judgment—had sprung up, and advocated the complete destruction of science; followers of that dogma still existed here and there. But the cult's teeth had been drawn when technicians unified, outlawing experiments with atomic power forever, making use of that force punishable by death, and permitting no one to join their society without taking the Minervan Oath.

"—to work for the ultimate good of mankind . . . taking all precaution against harming humanity and science . . . requiring permission from those in authority before undertaking any experiment involving peril to the race . . . remembering always the extent of the trust placed in us and remembering forever the death of the mother planet through misuse of knowledge—"

The Earth. A strange sort of world it must have been, Scott thought. Sunlight, for one thing, unfiltered by the cloud layer. In the old days, there had been few unexplored areas left on Earth. But here on Venus, where the continents had not yet been conquered—there was no need, of course, since everything necessary to life could be produced under the Domes—here on Venus, there was still a frontier. In the Keeps, a highly specialized social culture. Above the surface, a primeval world, where only the Free Companions had their fortresses and navies—the navies for fighting, the forts to house the technicians who provided the latter-day sinews of war, science instead of money. The Keeps tolerated visits from the Free Companions, but would not offer them headquarters, so violent the feeling, so sharp the schism, in the public mind, between war and cultural progress.

Under Scott's feet the sliding way turned into an escalator, carrying him into the Administration Building. He stepped to another way which took him to a lift, and, a moment or two later, was facing the door-curtain bearing the face of President Dane Crosby of Montana Keep.

Crosby's voice said, "Come in, Captain," and Scott brushed through the curtain, finding himself in a medium-

sized room with muraled walls and a great window over-
looking the city. Crosby, a white-haired, thin figure in blue
silks, was at his desk. He looked like a tired old clerk out of
Dickens, Scott thought suddenly, entirely undistinguished
and ordinary. Yet Crosby was one of the greatest sociopoliticians on Venus.

Cinc Rhys, leader of Doone's Free Companions, was
sitting in a relaxer, the apparent antithesis of Crosby. All the
moisture in Rhys' body seemed to have been sucked out of
him years ago by ultraviolet actinic, leaving a mummy of
brown leather and whipcord sinew. There was no softness in
the man. His smile was a grimace. Muscles lay like wire
under the swarthy cheeks.

Scott saluted. Rhys waved him to a relaxer. The look of
subdued eagerness in the cinc's eyes was significant—an
eagle poising himself, smelling blood. Crosby sensed that,
and a wry grin showed on his pale face.

"Every man to his trade," he remarked, semi-ironically.
"I suppose I'd be bored stiff if I had too long a vacation. But
you'll have quite a battle on your hands this time, Cinc
Rhys."

Scott's stocky body tensed automatically. Rhys glanced
at him.

"Virginia Keep is attacking, Captain. They've hired the
Helldivers—Flynn's outfit."

There was a pause. Both Free Companions were anxious to
discuss the angles, but unwilling to do so in the presence of
a civilian, even the president of Montana Keep. Crosby rose.

"The money settlement's satisfactory, then?"

Rhys nodded. "Yes, that's all right. I expect the battle
will take place in a couple of days. In the neighborhood of
Venus Deep, at a rough guess."

"Good. I've a favor to ask, so if you'll excuse me for a
few minutes, I'll—" He left the sentence unfinished and

went out through the door-curtain. Rhys offered Scott a cigarette.

"You get the implications, captain—the Helldivers?"

"Yes, sir. Thanks. We can't do it alone."

"Right. We're short on manpower and armament both. And the Helldivers recently merged with O'Brien's Legion, after O'Brien was killed in that polar scrap. They're a strong outfit, plenty strong. Then they've got their specialty—submarine attack. I'd say we'll have to use H-plan 7."

Scott closed his eyes, remembering the files. Each Free Company kept up-to-date plans of attack suited to the merits of every other Company of Venus. Frequently revised as new advances were made, as groups merged, and as the balance of power changed on each side, the plans were so detailed that they could be carried into action at literally a moment's notice. H-plan 7, Scott recalled, involved enlisting the aid of the Mob, a small but well-organized band of Free Companions led by Cinc Tom Mendez.

"Right," Scott said. "Can you get him?"

"I think so. We haven't agreed yet on the bonus. I've been telaudioing him on a tight beam, but he keeps putting me off—waiting till the last moment, when he can dictate his own terms."

"What's he asking, sir?"

"Fifty thousand cash and a fifty percent cut on the loot."

"I'd say thirty percent would be about right."

Rhys nodded. "I've offered him thirty-five. I may send you to his fort—carte blanche. We can get another Company, but Mendez has got beautiful sub-detectors—which would come in handy against the Helldivers. Maybe I can settle things by audio. If not, you'll have to fly over to Mendez and buy his services, at less than fifty per if you can."

Scott rubbed the old scar on his chin with a calloused forefinger. "Meantime Commander Bienne's in charge of mobilization. When—"

"I telaudioed our fort. Air transports are on the way now."

"It'll be quite a scrap," Scott said, and the eyes of the two men met in perfect understanding. Rhys chuckled dryly.

"And good profits. Virginia Keep has a big supply of korium . . . dunno how much, but plenty."

"What started the fracas this time?"

"The usual thing, I suppose," Rhys said disinterestedly. "Imperialism. Somebody in Virginia Keep worked out a new plan for annexing the rest of the Keeps. Same as usual."

They stood up as the door-curtain swung back, admitting President Crosby, another man, and a girl. The man looked young, his boyish face not yet toughened under actinic burn. The girl was lovely in the manner of a plastic figurine, lit from within by vibrant life. Her blond hair was cropped in the prevalent mode, and her eyes, Scott saw, were an unusual shade of green. She was more than merely pretty—she was instantly exciting.

Crosby said, "My niece, Ilene Kane—and my nephew, Norman Kane." He performed introductions, and they found seats.

"What about drinks?" Ilene suggested. "This is rather revolting formal. The fight hasn't started yet, after all."

Crosby shook his head at her. "You weren't invited here anyway. Don't try to turn this into a party—there isn't too much time, under the circumstances."

"O.K.," Ilene murmured. "I can wait." She eyed Scott interestedly.

Norman Kane broke in. "I'd like to join Doone's Free Companions, sir. I've already applied, but now that there's a battle coming up, I hate to wait till my application's approved. So I thought—"

Crosby looked at Cinc Rhys. "A personal favor, but the decision's up to you. My nephew's a misfit—a romanticist.

Never liked the life of a Keep. A year ago he went off and joined Starling's outfit."

Rhys raised an eyebrow. "That gang? It's not a recommendation, Kane. They're not even classed as Free Companions. More like a band of guerrillas, and entirely without ethics. There've even been rumors they're messing around with atomic power."

Crosby looked startled. "I hadn't heard that."

"It's no more than a rumor. If it's ever proved, the Free Companions—all of them—will get together and smash Starling in a hurry."

Norman Kane looked slightly uncomfortable. "I suppose I was rather a fool. But I wanted to get in the fighting game, and Starling's group appealed to me—"

The cinc made a sound in his throat. "They would. Swashbuckling romantics, with no idea of what war means. They've not more than a dozen technicians. And they've no discipline—it's like a pirate outfit. War today, Kane, isn't won by romantic animals dashing at forlorn hopes. The modern soldier is a tactician who knows how to think, integrate, and obey. If you join our Company, you'll have to forget what you learned with Starling."

"Will you take me, sir?"

"I think it would be unwise. You need the training course."

"I've had experience—"

Crosby said, "It would be a favor, Cinc Rhys, if you'd skip the red tape. I'd appreciate it. Since my nephew wants to be a soldier, I'd much prefer to see him with the Doones."

Rhys shrugged. "Very well. Captain Scott will give you your orders, Kane. Remember that discipline is vitally important with us."

The boy tried to force back a delighted grin. "Thank you, sir."

"Captain—"

*   *   *

Scott rose and nodded to Kane. They went out together. In the anteroom was a telaudio set, and Scott called the Doone's local headquarters in Montana Keep. An integrator answered, his face looking inquiringly from the screen.

"Captain Scott calling, subject induction."

"Yes, sir. Ready to record."

Scott drew Kane forward. "Photosnap this man. He'll report to headquarters immediately. Name, Norman Kane. Enlist him without training course—special orders from Cinc Rhys."

"Acknowledged, sir."

Scott broke the connection. Kane couldn't quite repress his grin.

"All right," the captain grunted, a sympathetic gleam in his eyes. "That fixes it. They'll put you in my command. What's your specialty."

"Flitterboats, sir."

"Good. One more thing. Don't forget what Cinc Rhys said, Kane. Discipline is damned important, and you may not have realized that yet. This isn't a cloak-and-sword war. There are no Charges of Light Brigades. No grandstand plays—that stuff went out with the Crusades. Just obey orders, and you'll have no trouble. Good luck."

"Thank you, sir," Kane saluted and strode out with a perceptible swagger. Scott grinned. The kid would have *that* knocked out of him pretty soon.

A voice at his side made him turn quickly, Ilene Kane was standing there, slim and lovely in her celoflex gown.

"You seem pretty human after all, Captain," she said. "I heard what you told Norman."

Scott shrugged. "I did that for his own good—and the good of the Company. One man off the beam can cause plenty trouble, Mistress Kane."

"I envy Norman," she said. "It must be a fascinating life you lead. I'd like it—for a while. Not for long. I'm one of the useless offshoots of this civilization, not much good for anything. So I've perfected one talent."

"What's that?"

"Oh, hedonism, I suppose you'd call it. I enjoy myself. It's not often too boring. But I'm a bit bored now. I'd like to talk to you, captain."

"Well, I'm listening," Scott said.

Ilene Kane made a small grimace. "Wrong semantic term. I'd like to get inside of you psychologically. But painlessly. Dinner and dancing. Can do?"

"There's no time," Scott told her. "We may get our orders any moment." He wasn't sure he wanted to go out with this girl of the Keeps, though there was definitely a subtle fascination for him, an appeal he could not analyze. She typified the most pleasurable part of a world he did not know. The other facets of that world could not impinge on him; geopolitics or nonmilitary science held no appeal, were too alien. But all worlds touch at one point—pleasure. Scott could understand the relaxations of the undersea groups, as he could not understand or feel sympathy for their work or their social impulses.

Cinc Rhys came through the door-curtain, his eyes narrowed. "I've some telaudioing to do, Captain," he said. Scott knew what implications the words held: the incipient bargain with Cinc Mendez. He nodded.

"Yes, sir. Shall I report to headquarters?"

Rhys' harsh face seemed to relax suddenly as he looked from Ilene to Scott. "You're free till dawn. I won't need you till then, but report to me at six a.m. No doubt you've a few details to clean up."

"Very well, sir," Scott watched Rhys go out. The cinc had meant Jeana, of course. But Ilene did not know that.

"So?" she asked. "Do I get a turn-down? You might buy me a drink, anyway."

There was plenty of time. Scott said, "It'll be a pleasure," and Ilene linked her arm with his. They took the drop-per to ground-level.

As they came out on one of the ways, Ilene turned her head and caught Scott's glance. "I forgot something, Captain. You may have, a previous engagement. I didn't realize—"

"There's nothing," he said. "Nothing important."

It was true; he felt a mild gratitude toward Jeana at the realization. His relationship with her was the peculiar one rendered advisable by his career. Free-marriage was the word for it; Jeana was neither his wife nor his mistress, but something midway between. The Free Companions had no firmly grounded foundation for social life; in the Keeps they were visitors, and in their coastal forts they were—well, soldiers. One would no more bring a woman to a fort than aboard a ship of the line. So the women of the Free Companions lived in the Keeps, moving from one to another as their men did; and because of the ever-present shadow of death, ties were purposely left loose. Jeana and Scott had been free-married for five years now. Neither made demands on the other. No one expected fidelity of a Free Companion. Soldiers lived under such iron disciplines that when they were released, during the brief peacetimes, the pendulum often swung far in the opposite direction.

To Scott, Ilene Kane was a key that might unlock the doors of the Keep—doors that opened to a world of which he was not a part, and which he could not quite understand.

II.

I, a stranger and afraid
In a world I never made.

                                                        —*Housman*

There were nuances, Scott found, which he had never known existed. A hedonist like Ilene devoted her life to such nuances; they were her career. Such minor matters as making the powerful, insipid Moonflower Cocktails more palatable by filtering them through lime-soaked sugar held between the teeth. Scott was a uisqueplus man, having the average soldier's contempt for what he termed hydroponic drinks, but the cocktails Ilene suggested were quite as effective as acrid, burning amber uisqueplus. She taught him, that night, such tricks as pausing between glasses to sniff lightly at happy-gas, to mingle sensual excitement with mental by trying the amusement rides designed to give one the violent physical intoxication of breathless speed. Nuances all, which only a girl with Ilene's background could know. She was not representative of Keep life. As she had said, she was an offshoot, a casual and useless flower on the great vine that struck up inexorably to the skies, its strength in its tough, reaching tendrils—scientists and technicians and sociopoliticians. She was doomed in her own way, as Scott was in his. The undersea folk served Minerva; Scott served Mars; and Ilene served Aphrodite—not purely the sexual goddess, but the patron of arts and pleasure. Between Scott and Ilene was the difference between Wagner and Strauss; the difference between crashing chords and tinkling arpeggios. In both was a muted bittersweet sadness, seldom realized by either. But that undertone was brought out by their contact. The sense of dim hopelessness in each responded to the other.

It was carnival, but neither Ilene nor Scott wore masks. Their faces were masks enough, and both had been trained to reserve, though in different ways. Scott's hard mouth kept its tight grimness even when he smiled. And Ilene's smiles came so often that they were meaningless.

Through her, Scott was able to understand more of the undersea life than he had ever done before. She was for him a catalyst. A tacit understanding grew between them, not needing words. Both realized that, in the course of progress, they would eventually die out. Mankind tolerated them because that was necessary for a little time. Each responded differently. Scott served Mars; he served actively; and the girl, who was passive, was attracted by the antithesis.

Scott's drunkenness struck physically deep. He did not show it. His stiff silver-brown hair was not disarranged, and his hard, burned face was impassive as ever. But when his brown eyes met Ilene's green ones a spark of—something— met between them.

Color and light and sound. They began to form a pattern now, were not quite meaningless to Scott. They were, long past midnight, sitting in an Olympus, which was a private cosmos. The walls of the room in which they were seemed nonexistent. The gusty tides of gray, faintly luminous clouds seemed to drive chaotically past them, and, dimly, they could hear the muffled screaming of an artificial wind. They had the isolation of the gods.

And the Earth was without form, and void; and darkness was upon the face of the deep—That was, of course, the theory of the Olympus rooms. No one existed, no world existed, outside of the chamber; values automatically shifted, and inhibitions seemed absurd.

Scott relaxed on a translucent cushion like a cloud. Beside him, Ilene lifted the bit of a happy-gas tube to his nostrils. He shook his head.

"Not now, Ilene."

She let the tube slide back into its reel. "Nor I. Too much of anything is unsatisfactory, Brian. There should always be something untasted, some anticipation left—You have that. I haven't."

"How?"

"Pleasures—well, there's a limit. There's a limit to human endurance. And eventually I build up a resistance psychically, as I do physically, to everything. With you, there's always the last adventure. You never know when death will come. You can't plan. Plans are dull; it's the unexpected that's important."

Scott shook his head slightly. "Death isn't important either. It's an automatic cancellation of values. Or, rather—" He hesitated, seeking words. "In this life you can plan, you can work out values, because they're all based on certain conditions. On—let's say—arithmetic. Death is a change to a different plane of conditions, quite unknown. Arithmetical rules don't apply as such to geometry."

"You think death has its rules?"

"It may be a lack of rules, Ilene. One lives realizing that life is subject to death; civilization is based on that. That's why civilization concentrates on the race instead of the individual. Social self-preservation."

She looked at him gravely. "I didn't think a Free Companion could theorize that way."

Scott closed his eyes, relaxing. "The Keeps know nothing about Free Companions. They don't want to. We're men. Intelligent men. Our technicians are as great as the scientists under the Domes."

"But they work for war."

"War's necessary," Scott said. "Now, anyway."

"How did you get into it? Should I ask?"

He laughed a little at that. "Oh, I've no dark secrets in my past. I'm not a runaway murderer. One—drifts. I was born in Australia Keep. My father was a tech, but my grandfather had been a soldier. I guess it was in my blood. I tried various trades and professions. Meaningless. I wanted something that . . . hell, I don't know. Something, maybe, that needs all of a man. Fighting does. It's like a religion. Those cultists—Men of the New Judgment—they're fanatics, but you can see that their religion is the only thing that matters to them."

"Bearded, dirty men with twisted minds, though."

"It happens to be a religion based on false premises.

There are others, appealing to different types. But religion was too passive for me, in these days."

Ilene examined his harsh face. "You'd have preferred the church militant—the Knights of Malta, fighting Saracens."

"I suppose. I had no values. Anyhow, I'm a fighter."

"Just how important is it to you? The Free Companions?"

Scott opened his eyes and grinned at the girl. He looked unexpectedly boyish.

"Damn little, really. It has emotional appeal. Intellectually, I know that it's a huge fake. Always has been. As absurd as the Men of the New Judgment. Fighting's doomed. So we've no real purpose. I suppose most of us know there's no future for the Free Companions. In a few hundred years—well!"

"And still you go on. Why? It isn't money."

"No. There is a . . . a drunkenness to it. The ancient Norsemen had their berserker madness. We have something similar. To a Dooneman, his group is father, mother, child, and God Almighty. He fights the other Free Companions when he's paid to do so, but he doesn't hate the others. They serve the same toppling idol. And it *is* toppling, Ilene. Each battle we win or lose brings us closer to the end. We fight to protect the culture that eventually will wipe us out. The Keeps—when they finally unify, will they need a military arm? I can see the trend. If war was an essential part of civilization, each Keep would maintain its own military. But they shut us out—a necessary evil. If they would end war now!" Scott's fist unconsciously clenched. "So many men would find happier places in Venus—undersea. But as long as the Free Companions exist, there'll be new recruits."

Ilene sipped her cocktail, watching the gray chaos of clouds flow like a tide around them. In the dimly luminous light

Scott's face seemed like dark stone, flecks of brightness showing in his eyes. She touched his hand gently.

"You're a soldier, Brian. You wouldn't change."

His laugh was intensely bitter. "Like hell I wouldn't, Mistress Ilene Kane! Do you think fighting's just pulling a trigger? I'm a military strategist. That took ten years. Harder cramming than I'd have had in a Keep Tech-Institute. I have to know everything about war from trajectories to mass psychology. This is the greatest science the System has ever known, and the most useless. Because war will die in a few centuries at most. Ilene—you've never seen a Free Company's fort. It's science, marvelous science, aimed at military ends only. We have our psych-specialists. We have our engineers, who plan everything from ordnance to the frictional quotient on flitterboats. We have the foundries and mills. Each fortress is a city made for war, as the Keeps are made for social progress."

"As complicated as that?"

"Beautifully complicated and beautifully useless. There are so many of us who realize that. Oh, we fight—it's a poison. We worship the Company—that is an emotional poison. But we live only during wartime. It's an incomplete life. Men in the Keeps have full lives; they have their work, and their relaxations are geared to fit them. We don't fit."

"Not all the undersea races," Ilene said. "There's always the fringe that doesn't fit. At least you have a *raison d'être*. You're a soldier. I can't make a lifework out of pleasure. But there's nothing else for me."

Scott's fingers tightened on hers. "You're the product of a civilization, at least. I'm left out."

"With you, Brian, it might be better. For a while. I don't think it would last for long."

"It might."

"You think so now. It's quite a horrible thing, feeling yourself a shadow."

"I know."

"I want you, Brian," Ilene said, turning to face him. "I want you to come to Montana Keep and stay here. Until our experiment fails. I think it'll fail presently. But, perhaps, not for some time. I need your strength. I can show you how to get the most out of this sort of life—how to enter into it. True hedonism. You can give me—companionship perhaps. For me the companionship of hedonists who know nothing else isn't enough."

Scott was silent. Ilene watched him for a while.

"Is war so important?" she asked at last.

"No," he said, "it isn't at all. It's a balloon. And it's empty, I know that. Honor of the regiment!" Scott laughed. "I'm not hesitating, really. I've been shut out for a long time. A social unit shouldn't be founded on an obviously doomed fallacy. Men and women are important, nothing else, I suppose."

"Men and women—or the race?"

"Not the race," he said with abrupt violence. "Damn the race! It's done nothing for me. I can fit myself into a new life. Not necessarily hedonism. I'm an expert in several lines; I have to be. I can find work in Montana Keep."

"If you like. I've never tried. I'm more of a fatalist, I suppose. But . . . what about it, Brian?"

Her eyes were almost luminous, like shining emeralds, in the ghostly light.

"Yes," Scott said. "I'll come back. To stay."

Ilene said, "Come back? Why not stay now?"

"Because I'm a complete fool, I guess. I'm a key man, and Cinc Rhys needs me just now."

"Is it Rhys or the Company?"

Scott smiled crookedly. "Not the Company. It's just a job I have to do. When I think how many years I've been slaving, pretending absurdities were important, knowing that I was bowing to a straw dummy— *No!* I want your life—the sort of life I didn't know could exist in the Keeps. I'll be back, Ilene. It's something more important than love.

Separately we're halves. Together we may be a complete whole."

She didn't answer. Her eyes were steady on Scott's. He kissed her.

Before morning bell he was back in the apartment. Jeana had already packed the necessary light equipment. She was asleep, her dark hair cascading over the pillow, and Scott did not waken her. Quietly he shaved, showered, and dressed. A heavy, waiting silence seemed to fill the city like a cup brimmed with stillness.

As he emerged from the bathroom, buttoning his tunic, he saw the table had been let down and two places set at it. Jeana came in, wearing a cool morning frock. She set cups down and poured coffee.

"Morning, soldier," she said. "You've time for this, haven't you?"

"Uh-huh." Scott kissed her, a bit hesitantly. Up till this moment, the breaking with Jeana had seemed easy enough. She would raise no objections. That was the chief reason for free-marriage. However—

She was sitting in the relaxer, sweeting the coffee, opening a fresh celopack of cigarettes. "Hung over?"

"No. I vitamized. Feel pretty good." Most bars had a vitamizing chamber to nullify the effects of too much stimulant. Scott was, in fact, feeling fresh and keenly alert. He was wondering how to broach the subject of Ilene to Jeana.

She saved him the trouble.

"If it's a girl, Brian, just take it easy. No use doing anything till this war's over. How long will it take?"

"Oh, not long. A week at most. One battle may settle it, you know. The girl—"

"She's not a Keep girl."

"Yes."

Jeana looked up, startled. "You're crazy."

"I started to tell you," Scott said impatiently. "It isn't just—her. I'm sick of the Doones. I'm going to quit."

"Hm-m-m. Like that?"

"Like that."

Jeana shook her head. "Keep women aren't tough."

"They don't need to be. Their men aren't soldiers."

"Have it your own way. I'll wait till you get back. Maybe I've got a hunch. You see, Brian, we've been together for five years. We fit. Not because of anything like philosophy or psychology—it's a lot more personal. It's just us. As man and woman, we get along comfortably. There's love, too. Those close emotional feelings are more important, really, than the long view. You can get excited about futures, but you can't live them."

Scott shrugged. "Could be I'm starting to forget about futures. Concentrating on Brian Scott."

"More coffee . . . there. Well, for five years now I've gone with you from Keep to Keep, waiting every time you went off to war, wondering if you'd come back, knowing that I was just a part of your life, but—I sometimes thought—the most important part. Soldiering's seventy-five percent. I'm the other quarter. I think you need that quarter—you need the whole thing, in that proportion, actually. You could find another woman, but she'd have to be willing to take twenty-five percent."

Scott didn't answer. Jeana blew smoke through her nostrils.

"O.K., Brian. I'll wait."

"It isn't the girl so much. She happens to fit into the pattern of what I want. You—"

"I'd never be able to fit that pattern," Jeana said softly. "The Free Companions need women who are willing to be soldiers' wives. Free-wives, if you like. Chiefly it's a matter of not being too demanding. But there are other things. No, Brian. Even if you wanted that, I couldn't make myself over into one of the Keep people. It wouldn't be me. I wouldn't respect myself, living a life that'd be false to me; and you wouldn't like me that way either. I couldn't and wouldn't change. I'll have to stay as I am. A soldier's wife. As long as you're a Dooneman, you'll need me. But if *you* change—" She didn't finish.

Scott lit a cigarette, scowling. "It's hard to know, exactly."

"I may not understand you, but I don't ask questions and I don't try to change you. As long as you want that, you can have it from me. I've nothing else to offer you. It's enough for a Free Companion. It's not enough—or too much—for a Keep-dweller."

"I'll miss you," he said.

"That'll depend, too. I'll miss you." Under the table her fingers writhed together, but her face did not change. "It's getting late. Here, let me check your chronometer." Jeana leaned across the table, lifted Scott's wrist, and compared his watch with the central-time clock on the wall. "O.K. On your way, soldier."

Scott stood up, tightening his belt. He bent to kiss Jeana, and, though she began to turn her face away, after a moment she raised her lips to his.

They didn't speak. Scott went out quickly, and the girl sat motionless, the cigarette smoldering out unheeded between her fingers. Somehow it did not matter so much, now, that Brian was leaving her for another woman and another life. As always, the one thing of real importance was that he was going into danger.

Guard him from harm, she thought, not knowing that she was praying. *Guard him from harm!*

And now there would be silence, and waiting. That, at least, had not changed. Her eyes turned to the clock.

Already the minutes were longer.

III

'E's the kind of a giddy harumfrodite—soldier an' sailor too!

—*Kipling*

Commander Bienne was superintending the embarkation of the last Doonemen when Scott arrived at headquarters. He saluted the captain briskly, apparently untired by his night's work of handling the transportation routine.

"All checked, sir."

Scott nodded. "Good. Is Cinc Rhys here?"

"He just arrived." Bienne nodded toward a door-curtain. As Scott moved away, the other followed.

"What's up, commander?"

Bienne pitched his voice low. "Bronson's laid up with endemic fever." He forgot to say "sir." "He was to handle the left wing of the fleet. I'd appreciate that job."

"I'll see if I can do it."

Bienne's lips tightened, but he said nothing more. He turned back to his men, and Scott went on into the cinc's office. Rhys was at the telaudio. He looked up, his eyes narrowed.

"Morning, Captain. I've just heard from Mendez."

"Yes, sir?"

"He's still holding out for a fifty percent cut on the korium ransom from Virginia Keep. You'll have to see him. Try and get the Mob for less than fifty if you can. Telaudio me from Mendez's fort."

"Check, sir."

"Another thing. Bronson's in sick bay."

"I heard that. If I may suggest Commander Bienne to take his place at left-wing command—"

But Cinc Rhys raised his hand. "Not this time. We can't afford individualism. The commander tried to play a lone hand in the last war. You know we can't risk it till he's back in line—thinking of the Doones instead of Fredric Bienne."

"He's a good man, sir. A fine strategist."

"But not yet a good integrating factor. Perhaps next time. Put Commander Geer on the left wing. Keep Bienne with you. He needs discipline. And—take a flitterboat to Mendez."

"Not a plane?"

"One of the technicians just finished a new tight-beam camouflager for communications. I'm having it installed immediately on all our planes and gliders. Use the boat; it isn't far to the Mob's fort—that long peninsula on the coast of Southern Hell."

Even on the charts that continent was named Hell—for obvious reasons. Heat was only one of them. And, even with the best equipment, a party exploring the jungle there would soon find itself suffering the tortures of the damned. On the land of Venus, flora and fauna combined diabolically to make the place uninhabitable to Earthmen. Many of the plants even exhaled poisonous gases. Only the protected coastal forts of the Free Companies could exist—and that was because they *were* forts.

Cinc Rhys frowned at Scott. "We'll use H-plan 7 if we can get the Mob. Otherwise we'll have to fall back on another outfit, and I don't want to do that. The Helldivers have too many subs, and we haven't enough detectors. So do your damndest."

Scott saluted. "I'll do that, sir." Rhys waved him away, and he went out into the next room, finding Commander Bienne alone. The officer turned an inquiring look toward him.

"Sorry," Scott said. "Geer gets the left-wing command this time."

Bienne's sour face turned dark red. "I'm sorry I didn't take a crack at you before mobilization," he said. "You hate competition, don't you?"

Scott's nostrils flared. "If it had been up to me, you'd have got that command, Bienne."

"Sure. I'll bet. All right, Captain. Where's my bunk? A flitterboat?"

"You'll be on right wing, with me. Control ship *Flintlock*."

"With you. Under you, you mean," Bienne said tightly. His eyes were blazing. "Yeah."

Scott's dark cheeks were flushed, too. "Orders, commander," he snapped. "Get me a flitterboat pilot. I'm going topside."

Without a word Bienne turned to the telaudio. Scott, a tight, furious knot in his stomach, stamped out of headquarters, trying to fight down his anger. Bienne was a jackass. A lot he cared about the Doones—

Scott caught himself and grinned sheepishly. Well, he cared little about the Doones himself. But while he was in the Company, discipline was important—integration with the smoothly running fighting machine. No place for individualism. One thing he and Bienne had in common; neither had any sentiment about the Company.

He took a lift to the ceiling of the Dome. Beneath him Montana Keep dropped away, shrinking to doll size. Somewhere down there, he thought, was Ilene. He'd be back. Perhaps this war would be a short one—not that they were ever much longer than a week, except in unusual cases where a Company developed new strategies.

He was conducted through an air lock into a bubble, a tough, transparent sphere with a central vertical core through which the cable ran. Except for Scott, the bubble was empty. After a moment it started up with a slight jar. Gradually the water outside the curving walls changed from black to deep green, and thence to translucent chartreuse. Sea creatures were visible, but they were nothing new to Scott; he scarcely saw them.

The bubble broke surface. Since air pressure had been constant, there was no possibility of the bends, and Scott opened the panel and stepped out on one of the buoyant floats that dotted the water above Montana Keep. A few sightseers crowded into the chamber he had left, and presently it was drawn down, out of sight.

In the distance Free Companions were embarking from a larger float to an air ferry. Scott glanced up with a weather eye. No storm, he saw, though the low ceiling was, as usual, torn and twisted into boiling currents by the winds. He remembered, suddenly, that the battle would probably take place over Venus Deep. That would make it somewhat harder for the gliders—there would be few of the thermals found, for instance, above the Sea of Shallows here.

A flitterboat, low, fast, and beautifully maneuverable, shot in toward the quay. The pilot flipped back the overhead shell and saluted Scott. It was Norman Kane, looking ship-shape in his tight-fitting gray uniform, and apparently ready to grin at the slightest provocation.

Scott jumped lightly down into the craft and seated himself beside the pilot. Kane drew the transparent shell back over them. He looked at Scott.

"Orders, Captain?"

"Know where the Mob's fort is? Good. Head there. Fast."

Kane shot the flitterboat out from the float with a curtain of v-shaped spray rising from the bow. Drawing little water, maneuverable, incredibly fast, these tiny craft were invaluable in naval battle. It was difficult to hit one, they moved so fast. They had no armor to slow them down. They carried high-explosive bullets fired from small-caliber guns, and were, as a rule, two-man craft. They complemented the heavier ordnance of the battlewagons and destroyers.

Scott handed Kane a cigarette. The boy hesitated.

"We're not under fire," the captain chuckled. "Discipline clamps down during a battle, but it's O.K. for you to have a smoke with me. Here!" He lit the white tube for Kane.

"Thanks, sir. I guess I'm a bit—over-anxious?"

"Well, war has its rules. Not many, but they mustn't be broken." Both men were silent for a while, watching the blank gray surface of the ocean ahead. A transport plane passed them, flying low.

"Is Ilene Kane your sister?" Scott asked presently.

Kane nodded. "Yes, sir."

"Thought so. If she'd been a man, I imagine she'd have been a Free Companion."

The boy shrugged. "Oh, I don't know. She doesn't have the— I don't know. She'd consider it too much effort. She doesn't like discipline."

"Do you?"

"It's fighting that's important to me. Sir." That was an afterthought. "Winning, really."

"You can lose a battle even though you win it," Scott said rather somberly.

"Well, I'd rather be a Free Companion than do anything else I know of. Not that I've had much experience—"

"You've had experience of war with Starling's outfit, but you probably learned some dangerous stuff at the same time. War isn't swashbuckling piracy these days. If the Doones tried to win battles by that sort of thing, there'd be no more Doones in a week or so."

"But—" Kane hesitated. "Isn't that sort of thing rather necessary? Taking blind chances, I mean—"

"There are desperate chances," Scott told him, "but there are no blind chances in war—not to a good soldier. When I was green in the service, I ran a cruiser out of the line to ram. I was demoted, for a very good reason. The enemy ship I rammed wasn't as important to the enemy as our cruiser was to us. If I'd stayed on course, I'd have helped sink three or four ships instead of disabling one and putting my cruiser out of action. It's the great god integration we worship, Kane. It's much more important now than it ever was on Earth, because the military has consolidated. Army, navy, air, undersea—they're all part of one organization now. I suppose the only important change was in the air."

"Gliders, you mean? I knew powered planes couldn't be used in battle."

"Not in the atmosphere of Venus," Scott agreed. "Once powered planes get up in the cloud strata, they're fighting crosscurrents and pockets so much they've got no time to do accurate firing. If they're armored, they're slow. If they're light, detectors can spot them and antiaircraft can smash them. Unpowered gliders are valuable not for bombing but for directing attacks. They get into the clouds, stay hidden, and use infrared telecameras which are broadcast on a tight beam back to the control ships. They're the eyes of the fleet. They can tell us— *White water ahead, Kane! Swerve!*"

The pilot had already seen the ominous boiling froth foaming out in front of the bow. Instinctively he swung the flitterboat in a wrenching turn. The craft heeled sidewise, throwing its occupants almost out of their seats.

"Sea beast?" Scott asked, and answered his own question. "No, not with those spouts. It's volcanic. And it's spreading fast."

"I can circle it, sir," Kane suggested.

Scott shook his head. "Too dangerous. Backtrack."

Obediently the boy sent the flitterboat racing out of the area of danger. Scott had been right about the extent of the danger; the boiling turmoil was widening almost faster than the tiny ship could flee. Suddenly the line of white water caught up with them. The flitterboat jounced like a chip, the wheel being nearly torn from Kane's grip. Scott reached over and helped steady it. Even with two men handling the wheel, there was a possibility that it might wrench itself free. Steam rose in veils beyond the transparent shell. The water had turned a scummy brown under the froth.

Kane jammed on the power. The flitterboat sprang forward like a ricocheting bullet, dancing over the surface of the seething waves. Once they plunged head-on into a swell, and a screaming of outraged metal vibrated through the craft. Kane, tight-lipped, instantly slammed in the auxiliary, cutting out the smashed motor unit. Then, unexpectedly, they were in clear water, cutting back toward Montana Keep.

Scott grinned. "Nice handling. Lucky you didn't try to circle. We'd never have made it."

"Yes, sir." Kane took a deep breath. His eyes were bright with excitement.

"Circle now. Here." He thrust a lighted cigarette between the boy's lips. "You'll be a good Dooneman, Kane. Your reactions are good and fast."

"Thanks, sir."

Scott smoked silently for a while. He glanced toward the north, but, with the poor visibility, he could not make out the towering range of volcanic peaks that were the backbone of Southern Hell. Venus was a comparatively young planet, the internal fires still bursting forth unexpectedly. Which was why no forts were ever built on islands—they had an unhappy habit of disappearing without warning!

The flitterboat rode hard, at this speed, despite the insulating system of springs and shock absorbers. After a ride in one of these "spankers"—the irreverent name the soldiers had for them—a man needed arnica if not a chiropractor. Scott shifted his weight on the soft air cushions under him, which felt like cement.

Under his breath he hummed:

> *"It ain't the 'eavy 'aulin' that 'urts the 'orses' 'oofs,*
> *It's the 'ammer, 'ammer, 'ammer on the 'ard 'ighway!"*

*   *   *

The flitterboat scooted on, surrounded by monotonous sea and cloud, till finally the rampart of the coast grew before the bow, bursting suddenly from the fog-veiled horizon. Scott glanced at his chronometer and sighed with relief. They had made good time, in spite of the slight delay caused by the subsea volcano.

The fortress of the Mob was a huge metal and stone castle on the tip of the peninsula. The narrow strip that separated it from the mainland had been cleared, and the pockmarks of shell craters showed where guns had driven back onslaughts from the jungle—the reptilian, ferocious giants of Venus, partially intelligent but absolutely untractable because of the gulf that existed between their methods of thinking and the culture of mankind. Overtures had been made often enough; but it had been found that the reptile-folk were better left alone. They would not parley. They were blindly bestial savages, with whom it was impossible to make truce. They stayed in the jungle, emerging only to hurl furious attacks at the forts—attacks doomed to failure, since fang and talon were matched against lead-jacketed bullet and high explosive.

As the flitterboat shot in to a jetty, Scott kept his eyes straight ahead—it was not considered good form for a Free Companion to seem too curious when visiting the fort of another Company. Several men were on the quay, apparently waiting for him. They saluted as Scott stepped out of the boat.

He gave his name and rank. A corporal stepped forward.

"Cinc Mendez is expecting you, sir. Cinc Rhys telaudioed an hour or so back. If you'll come this way—"

"All right, Corporal. My pilot—"

"He'll be taken care of, sir. A rubdown and a drink, perhaps, after a spanker ride."

Scott nodded and followed the other into the bastion that thrust out from the overhanging wall of the fort. The sea gate was open, and he walked swiftly through the courtyard in the corporal's wake, passing a door-curtain, mounting an escalator, and finding himself, presently, before another curtain that bore the face of Cinc Mendez, plump, hoglike, and bald as a bullet.

Entering, he saw Mendez himself at the head of a long table, where nearly a dozen officers of the Mob were also seated. In person Mendez was somewhat more prepossessing than in effigy. He looked like a boar rather than a pig—a fighter, not a gourmand. His sharp black eyes seemed to drive into Scott with the impact of a physical blow.

He stood up, his officers following suit. "Sit down, Captain. There's a place at the foot of the table. No reflections on rank, but I prefer to be face to face with the man I'm dealing with. But first—you just arrived? If you'd like a quick rubdown, we'll be glad to wait."

Scott took his place. "Thank you, no, Cinc Mendez. I'd prefer not to lose time."

"Then we'll waste none on introductions. However, you can probably stand a drink." He spoke to the orderly at the door, and presently a filled glass stood at Scott's elbow.

His quick gaze ran along the rows of faces. Good soldiers, he thought—tough, well trained, and experienced. They had been under fire. A small outfit, the Mob, but a powerful one.

Cinc Mendez sipped his own drink. "To business. The Doonemen wish to hire our help in fighting the Helldivers. Virginia Keep has bought the services of the Helldivers to attack Montana Keep." He enumerated on stubby fingers. "You offer us fifty thousand cash and thirty-five percent of the korium ransom. So?"

"That's correct."

"We ask fifty percent."

"It's high. The Doones have superior manpower and equipment."

"To us, not to the Helldivers. Besides, the percentage is

contingent. If we should lose, we get only the cash payment."

Scott nodded. "That's correct, but the only real danger from the Helldivers is their submarine corps. The Doones have plenty of surface and air equipment. We might lick the Helldivers without you."

"I don't think so." Mendez shook his bald head. "They have some new underwater torpedoes that make hash out of heavy armor plate. But *we* have new sub-detectors. We can blast the Helldivers' subs for you before they get within torpedo range."

Scott said bluntly, "You've been stalling, Cinc Mendez. We're not that bad off. If we can't get you, we'll find another outfit."

"With sub-detectors?"

"Yardley's Company is good at undersea work."

A major near the head of the table spoke up. "That's true, sir. They have suicide subs—not too dependable, but they have them."

Cinc Mendez wiped his bald head with his palms in a slow circular motion. "Hm-m-m. Well, Captain, I don't know. Yardley's Company isn't as good as ours for this job."

"All right," Scott said, "I've *carte blanche*. We don't know how much korium Virginia Keep has in her vaults. How would this proposition strike you: the Mob gets fifty percent of the korium ransom up to a quarter of a million; thirty-five percent above that."

"Forty-five."

"Forty, above a quarter of a million; forty-five below that sum."

"Gentlemen?" Cinc Mendez asked, looking down the table. "Your vote?"

There were several ayes, and a scattering of nays. Mendez shrugged.

"Then I have the deciding vote. Very well. We get forty-five percent of the Virginia Keep ransom up to a quarter of a million; forty percent on any amount above that. Agreed. We'll drink to it."

Orderlies served drinks. As Mendez rose, the others followed his example. The cinc nodded to Scott.

"Will you propose a toast, Captain?"

"With pleasure. Nelson's toast, then—a willing foe and sea room!"

They drank to that, as Free Companions had always drunk that toast on the eve of battle. As they seated themselves once more, Mendez said, "Major Matson, please telaudio Cinc Rhys and arrange details. We must know his plans."

"Yes, sir."

Mendez glanced at Scott. "Now how else may I serve you?"

"Nothing else. I'll get back to our fort. Details can be worked out on the telaudio, on tight beam."

"If you're going back in that flitterboat," Mendez said sardonically, "I strongly advise a rubdown. There's time to spare, now we've come to an agreement."

Scott hesitated. "Very well. I'm . . . uh . . . starting to ache." He stood up. "Oh, one thing I forgot. We've heard rumors that Starling's outfit is using atomic power."

Mendez's mouth twisted into a grimace of distaste. "Hadn't heard that. Know anything about it, gentlemen?"

Heads were shaken. One officer said, "I've heard a little talk about it, but only talk, so far."

Mendez said, "After this war, we'll investigate further. If there's truth in the story, we'll join you, of course, in mopping up the Starlings. No court-martial is necessary for *that* crime!"

"Thanks. I'll get in touch with other Companies and see what they've heard. Now, if you'll excuse me—"

He saluted and went out, exultation flaming within him. The bargain had been a good one—for the Doonemen badly needed the Mob's help against the Helldivers. Cinc Rhys would be satisfied with the arrangement.

An orderly took him to the baths, where a rubdown relaxed his aching muscles. Presently he was on the quay again, climbing into the flitterboat. A glance behind him showed that the gears of war were beginning to grind. There was little he could see, but men were moving about through the courtyard with purposeful strides, to the shops, to administration, to the laboratories. The battlewagons were anchored down the coast, Scott knew, in a protected bay, but they would soon move out to their rendezvous with the Doones.

Kane, at the controls of the flitterboat, said, "They repaired the auxiliary unit for us, sir."

"Courtesies of the trade." Scott lifted a friendly hand to the men on the quay as the boat slid toward open water. "The Doone fort, now. Know it?"

"Yes, sir. Are . . . are the Mob fighting with us, if I may ask?"

"They are. And they're a grand lot of fighters. You're going to see action, Kane. When you hear battle stations next, it's going to mean one of the sweetest scraps that happened on Venus. Push down that throttle—we're in a hurry!"

The flitterboat raced southwest at top speed, its course marked by the flying V of spray.

"One last fight," Scott thought to himself. "I'm glad it's going to be a good one."

IV

We eat and drink our own damnation.
—The Book of Common Prayer

The motor failed when they were about eight miles from the Doone fort.

It was a catastrophe rather than merely a failure. The overstrained and overheated engine, running at top speed, blew back. The previous accident, at the subsea volcano, had brought out hidden flaws in the alloy which the Mob's repair men had failed to detect, when they replaced the smashed single unit. Sheer luck had the flitterboat poised on a swell when the crack-up happened. The engine blew out and down, ripping the bow to shreds. Had they been bow-deep, the blast would have been unfortunate for Scott and the pilot—more so than it was.

They were perhaps a half mile from the shore. Scott was deafened by the explosion and simultaneously saw the horizon swinging in a drunken swoop. The boat turned turtle, the shell smacking into water with a loud cracking sound. But the plastic held. Both men were tangled together on what had been their ceiling, sliding forward as the flitterboat began to sink bow first. Steam sizzled from the ruined engine.

Kane managed to touch one of the emergency buttons. The shell was, of course, jammed, but a few of the segments slid aside, admitting a gush of acrid sea water. For a moment they struggled there, fighting the crosscurrents till the air had been displaced. Scott, peering through cloudy green gloom, saw Kane's dark shadow twist and kick out through a gap. He followed.

Beneath him the black bulk of the boat dropped slowly and was gone. His head broke surface, and he gasped for breath, shaking droplets from his lashes and glancing around. Where was Kane?

The boy appeared, his helmet gone, sleek hair plastered to his forehead. Scott caught his eye and pulled the trigger on his life vest, the inflatable undergarment which was always worn under the blouse on sea duty. As chemicals mixed, light gas rushed into the vest, lifting Scott higher in the water. He felt the collar cushion inflate against the back of his head—the skull-fitting pillow that allowed ship-wrecked men to float and rest without danger of drowning in their sleep. But he had no need for this now.

Kane, he saw, had triggered his own life vest. Scott hurled himself up, searching for signs of life. There weren't any. The gray-green sea lay desolate to the misty horizon. A half mile away was a mottled chartreuse wall that marked the jungle. Above and beyond that dim sulphurous red lit the clouds.

Scott got out his leaf-bladed smatchet, gesturing for Kane to do the same. The boy did not seem worried. No doubt this was merely an exciting adventure for him, Scott thought wryly. Oh, well.

Gripping the smatchet between his teeth, the captain began to swim shoreward. Kane kept at his side. Once Scott warned his companion to stillness and bent forward, burying his face in the water and peering down at a great dim shadow that coiled away and was gone—a sea snake, but, luckily, not hungry. The oceans of Venus were perilous with teeming, ferocious life. Precautions were fairly useless. When a man was once in the water, it was up to him to get out of it as rapidly as possible.

Scott touched a small cylinder attached to his belt and felt bubbles rushing against his palm. He was slightly relieved. When he had inflated the vest, this tube of compressed gas had automatically begun to release, sending out a foul-smelling vapor that permeated the water for some distance around. The principle was that of the skunk adjusted to the environment of the squid, and dangerous undersea life was supposed to be driven away by the Mellison tubes; but it didn't work with carrion eaters like the snakes. Scott averted his nose. The gadgets were named Mellison tubes, but the men called them Stinkers, a far more appropriate term.

Tides on Venus are unpredictable. The clouded planet

has no moon, but it is closer to the Sun than Earth. As a rule the tides are mild, except during volcanic activity, when tidal waves sweep the shores. Scott, keeping a weather eye out for danger, rode the waves in toward the beach, searching the strip of dull blackness for signs of life.

Nothing.

He scrambled out at last, shaking himself like a dog, and instantly changed the clip in his automatic for high explosive. The weapon, of course, was watertight—a necessity on Venus. As Kane sat down with a grunt and deflated his vest, Scott stood eying the wall of jungle thirty feet away. It stopped there abruptly, for nothing could grow on blacksand.

The rush and whisper of the waves made the only sound. Most of the trees were lianalike, eking out a precarious existence, as the saying went, by taking in each other's washing. The moment one of them showed signs of solidity, it was immediately assailed by parasitic vines flinging themselves madly upward to reach the filtered sunlight of Venus. The leaves did not begin for thirty feet above the ground; they made a regular roof up there, lying like crazy shingles, and would have shut out all light had they not been of light translucent green. Whitish tendrils crawled like reaching serpents from tree to tree, tentacles of vegetable octopi. There were two types of Venusian fauna: the giants who could crash through the forest, and the supple, small grounddwellers—insects and reptiles mostly—who depended on poison sacs for self-protection. Neither kind was pleasant company.

There were flying creatures, too, but these lived in the upper strata, among the leaves. And there were ambiguous horrors that lived in the deep mud and the stagnant pools under the forest, but no one knew much about these.

"Well," Scott said, "that's that."

Kane nodded. "I guess I should have checked the motors."

"You wouldn't have found anything. Latent flaws—it would have taken black night to bring 'em out. Just one of those things. Keep your gas mask handy, now. If we get anywhere near poison flowers and the wind's blowing this way, we're apt to keel over like that." Scott opened a waterproof wallet and took out a strip of sensitized litmus, which he clipped to his wrist. "If this turns blue, that means gas, even if we don't smell it."

"Yes, sir. What now?"

"We-el—the boat's gone. We can't telaudio for help." Scott fingered the blade of his smatchet and slipped it into the belt sheath. "We head for the fort. Eight miles. Two hours, if we can stick to the beach and if we don't run into trouble. More than that if Signal Rock's ahead of us, because we'll have to detour inland in that case." He drew out a collapsible single-lenser telescope and looked southwest along the shore. "Uh-huh. We detour."

A breath of sickening sweetness gusted down from the jungle roof. From above, Scott knew, the forest looked surprisingly lovely. It always reminded him of an antique candlewick spread he had once bought Jeana—immense rainbow flowers scattered over a background of pale green. Even among the flora competition was keen; the plants vied in producing colors and scents that would attract the winged carriers of pollen.

There would always be frontiers, Scott thought. But they might remain unconquered for a long time, here on Venus. The Keeps were enough for the undersea folk; they were self-sustaining. And the Free Companions had no need to carve out empires on the continents. They were fighters, not agrarians. Land hunger was no longer a part of the race. It might come again, but not in the time of the Keeps.

The jungles of Venus held secrets he would never know. Men can conquer lands from the air, but they cannot hold them by that method. It would take a long, slow period of encroachment, during which the forest and all it represented would be driven back, step by painful step—and that belonged to a day to come, a time Scott would not know. The savage world would be tamed. But not now—not yet.

At the moment it was untamed and very dangerous. Scott stripped off his tunic and wrung water from it. His clothing would not dry in this saturated air, despite the winds. His trousers clung to him stickily, clammy coldness in their folds.

"Ready, Kane?"

"Yes, sir."

"Then let's go."

They went southwest, along the beach, at a steady, easy lope that devoured miles. Speed and alertness were necessary in equal proportion. From time to time Scott scanned the sea with his telescope, hoping to sight a vessel. He saw nothing. The ships would be in harbor, readying for the battle; and planes would be grounded for installation of the new telaudio device Cinc Rhys had mentioned.

Signal Rock loomed ahead, an outthrust crag with eroded, unscalable sides towering two hundred feet and more. The black strip of sand ended there. From the rock there was a straight drop into deep water, cut up by a turmoil of currents. It was impossible to take the sea detour; there was nothing else for it but to swerve inland, a dangerous but inevitable course. Scott postponed the plunge as long as possible, till the scarp of Signal Rock, jet black with leprous silvery patches on its surface, barred the way. With a quizzical look at Kane he turned sharply to his right and headed for the jungle.

"Half a mile of forest equals a hundred miles of beach hiking," he remarked.

"That bad, sir? I've never tackled it."

"Nobody does, unless they have to. Keep your eyes open and your gun ready. Don't wade through water, even when you can see bottom. There are some little devils that are pretty nearly transparent—vampire fish. If a few of those fasten on you, you'll need a transfusion in less than a minute. I wish the volcanoes would kick up a racket. The beasties generally lie low when that happens."

Under a tree Scott stopped, seeking a straight, long limb. It took a while to find a suitable one, in that tangle of coiling lianas, but finally he succeeded, using his smatchet blade to hack himself a light five-foot pole. Kane at his heels, he moved on into the gathering gloom.

"We may be stalked," he told the boy. "Don't forget to guard the rear."

The sand had given place to sticky whitish mud that plastered the men to their calves before a few moments had passed. A patina of slickness seemed to overlay the ground. The grass was colored so much like the mud itself that it was practically invisible, except by its added slipperiness. Scott slowly advanced keeping close to the wall of rock on his left where the tangle was not so thick. Nevertheless he had to use the smatchet more than once to cut a passage through vines.

He stopped, raising his hand, and the squelch of Kane's feet in the mud paused. Silently Scott pointed. Ahead of them in the cliff base, was the mouth of a burrow.

The captain bent down, found a small stone, and threw it toward the den. He waited, one hand lightly on his gun, ready to see something flash out of that burrow and race toward them. In the utter silence a new sound made itself heard—tiny goblin drums, erratic and resonant in a faraway fashion. Water, dropping from leaf to leaf, in the soaked jungle ceiling above them. *Tink, tink, tink-tink, tink, tink-tink*—

"O.K.," Scott said quietly. "Watch it, though." He went on, gun drawn, till they were level with the mouth of the burrow. "Turn, Kane. Keep your eye on it till I tell you to stop." He gripped the boy's arm and guided him, holstering his own weapon. The pole, till now held between biceps and body, slipped into his hand. He used it to probe the slick sur-

face of the mud ahead. Sinkhole and quicksands were fre-
quent, and so were traps, camouflaged pits built by mud-
wolves—which, of course, were not wolves, and belonged
to no known genus. On Venus, the fauna had more subdivisions than on old Earth, and lines of demarcation were more
subtle.

"All right now."

Kane, sighing with relief, turned his face forward again.
"What was it?"

"You never know what may come out of those holes,"
Scott told him. "They come fast, and they're usually poisonous. So you can't take chances with the critters. Slow down
here. I don't like the looks of that patch ahead."

Clearings were unusual in the forest. There was one
here, twenty feet wide, slightly saucer-shaped. Scott gin-
gerly extended the pole and probed. A faint ripple shook the
white mud, and almost before it had appeared the captain
had unholstered his pistol and was blasting shot after shot at
the movement.

"Shoot, Kane!" he snapped. "Quick! Shoot at it!"

Kane obeyed, though he had to guess at his target. Mud
geysered up, suddenly crimson-stained. Scott, still firing,
gripped the boy's arm and ran him back at a breakneck pace.

The echoes died. Once more the distant elfin drums
whispered through the green gloom.

"We got it," Scott said, after a pause.

"We did?" the other asked blankly. "What—"

"Mud-wolf, I think. The only way to kill those things is
to get 'em before they get out of the mud. They're fast and
they die hard. However—" He warily went forward. There
was nothing to see. The mud had collapsed into a deeper
saucer, but the holes blasted by the high-x bullets had filled
in. Here and there were traces of thready crimson.

"Never a dull moment," Scott remarked. His crooked
grin eased the tension. Kane chuckled and followed the captain's example in replacing his half-used clip with a full one.

*   *   *

The narrow spine of Signal Rock extended inland for a quarter mile before it became scalable. They reached that point finally, helping each other climb, and finding themselves, at the summit, still well below the leafy ceiling of the trees. The black surface of the rock was painfully hot, stinging their palms as they climbed, and even striking through their shoe soles.

"Halfway point, Captain?"

"Yeah. But don't let that cheer you. It doesn't get any better till we hit the beach again. We'll probably need some fever shots when we reach the fort, just in case. Oh-oh. Mask, Kane, quick." Scott lifted his arm. On his wrist the band of litmus had turned blue.

With trained accuracy they donned the respirators. Scott felt a faint stinging on his exposed skin, but that wasn't serious. Still, it would be painful later. He beckoned to Kane, slid down the face of the rock, used the pole to test the mud below, and jumped lightly. He dropped in the sticky whiteness and rolled over hastily, plastering himself from head to foot. Kane did the same. Mud wouldn't neutralize the poison flowers' gas, but it would absorb most of it before it reached the skin.

Scott headed toward the beach, a grotesque figure. Mud dripped on the eye plate, and he scrubbed it away with a handful of white grass. He used the pole constantly to test the footing ahead.

Nevertheless the mud betrayed him. The pole broke through suddenly, and as Scott automatically threw his weight back, the ground fell away under his feet. He had time for a crazy feeling of relief that this was quicksand, not a mud-wolf's den, and then the clinging, treacherous stuff had sucked him down knee-deep. He fell back, keeping his grip on the pole and swinging the other end in an arc toward Kane.

The boy seized it in both hands and threw himself flat.

His foot hooked over an exposed root. Scott, craning his neck at a painfully awkward angle and trying to see through the mud-smeared vision plates, kept a rattrap grip on his end of the pole, hoping its slickness would not slip through his fingers.

He was drawn down farther, and then Kane's anchorage began to help. The boy tried to pull the pole toward him, hand over hand. Scott shook his head. He was a good deal stronger than Kane, and the latter would need all his strength to keep a tight grip on the pole.

Something stirred in the shadows behind Kane. Scott instinctively let go with one hand, and, with the other, got out his gun. It had a sealed mechanism, so the mud hadn't harmed the firing, and the muzzle had a one-way trap. He fired at the movement behind Kane, heard a muffled tumult, and waited till it had died. The boy, after a startled look behind him, had not stirred.

After that, rescue was comparatively easy. Scott simply climbed along the pole, spreading his weight over the surface of the quicksand. The really tough part was pulling his legs free of that deadly grip. Scott had to rest for five minutes after that.

But he got out. That was the important thing.

Kane pointed inquiringly into the bushes where the creature had been shot, but Scott shook his head. The nature of the beast wasn't a question worth deciding, as long as it was apparently *hors de combat*. Readjusting his mask, Scott turned toward the beach, circling the quicksand, and Kane kept at his heels.

Their luck had changed. They reached the shore with no further difficulty and collapsed on the black sand to rest. Presently Scott used a litmus, saw that the gas had dissipated, and removed his mask. He took a deep breath.

"Thanks, Kane," he said. "You can take a dip now if you want to wash off that mud. But stay close inshore. No, don't strip. There's no time."

The mud clung like glue and the black sand scratched like pumice. Still, Scott felt a good deal cleaner after a few minutes in the surf, while Kane stayed on guard. Slightly refreshed, they resumed the march.

An hour later a convoy plane, testing, sighted them, telaudioed the fort, and a flitterboat came racing out to pick them up. What Scott appreciated most of all was the stiff shot of uisqueplus the pilot gave him.

Yeah. It was a dog's life, all right!

He passed the flask to Kane.

Presently the fort loomed ahead, guarding Doone Harbor. Large as the landlocked bay was, it could scarcely accommodate the fleet. Scott watched the activity visible with an approving eye. The flitterboat rounded the sea wall, built for protection against tidal waves, and shot toward a jetty. Its almost inaudible motor died; the shell swung back.

Scott got out, beckoning to an orderly.

"Yes, sir?"

"See that this soldier gets what he needs. We've been in the jungle."

The man didn't whistle sympathetically, but his mouth pursed. He saluted and helped Kane climb out of the flitterboat. As Scott hurried along the quay, he could hear an outburst of friendly profanity from the men on the dock, gathering around Kane.

He nodded imperceptibly. The boy would make a good Free Companion—always granted that he could stand the gaff under fire. That was the acid test. Discipline was tightened then to the snapping point. If it snapped—well, the human factor always remained a variable, in spite of all the psychologists could do.

He went directly to his quarters, switching on the telaudio to call Cinc Rhys. The cinc's seamed, leathery face resolved itself on the screen.

"Captain Scott reporting for duty, sir."

Rhys looked at him sharply. "What happened?"

"Flitterboat crack-up. Had to make it in here on foot."

The cinc called on his God in a mild voice. "Glad you made it. Any accident?"

"No, sir. The pilot's unharmed, too. I'm ready to take over, after I've cleaned up."

"Better take a rejuvenation—you probably need it. Everything's going like clockwork. You did a good job with Mendez—a better bargain than I'd hoped for. I've been talking with him on the telaudio, integrating our forces. We'll go into that later, though. Clean up and then make general inspection."

"Check, sir."

Rhys clicked off. Scott turned to face his orderly.

"Hello, Briggs. Help me off with these duds. You'll probably have to cut 'em off."

"Glad to see you back, sir. I don't think it'll be necessary to cut—" Blunt fingers flew deftly over zippers and clasps. "You were in the jungle?"

Scott grinned wryly. "Do I look as if I'd been gliding?"

"Not all the way, sir—no."

Briggs was like an old bulldog—one of those men who proved the truth of the saying: "Old soldiers never die; they only fade away." Briggs could have been pensioned off ten years ago, but he hadn't wanted that. There was always a place for old soldiers in the Free Companies, even those who were unskilled. Some became technicians; others military instructors; the rest, orderlies. The forts were their homes. Had they retired to one of the Keeps, they would have died for lack of interests.

Briggs, now—he had never risen above the ranks, and knew nothing of military strategy, ordnance, or anything except plain fighting. But he had been a Dooneman for forty years, twenty-five of them on active service. He was sixty-odd now, his squat figure slightly stooped like an elderly bear, his ugly face masked with scar tissue.

"All right. Start the shower, will you?"

Briggs stumped off, and Scott, stripped of his filthy, sodden garments, followed. He luxuriated under the stinging spray, first hot soapy water, then alcomix, and after that plain water, first hot, then cold. That was the last task he had to do himself. Briggs took over, as Scott relaxed on the slab, dropping lotion into the captain's burning eyes, giving him a deft but murderous rubdown, combining osteopathic and chiropractic treatment, adjusting revitalizing lamps, and measuring a hypo shot to nullify fatigue toxins. When the orderly was finished, Scott was ready to resume his duties with a clear brain and a refreshed body.

Briggs appeared with fresh clothing. "I'll have the old uniform cleaned, sir. No use throwing it away."

"You can't clean that," Scott remarked, slipping into a singlet. "Not after I rolled in mud. But suit yourself. I won't be needing it for long."

The orderly's fingers, buttoning Scott's tunic, stopped briefly and then resumed their motion. "Is that so, sir?"

"Yeah. I'm taking out discharge papers."

"Another Company, sir?"

"Don't get on your high horse," Scott told the orderly. "It's not that. What would you do if it were? Court-martial me yourself and shoot me at sunrise?"

"No, sir. Begging your pardon, sir, I'd just think you were crazy."

"Why I stand you only the Lord knows," Scott remarked. "You're too damn independent. There's no room for new ideas in that plastic skull of yours. You're the quintessence of dogmatism."

Briggs nodded. "Probably, sir. When a man's lived by one set of rules for as long as I have, and those rules work out, I suppose he might get dogmatic."

"Forty years for you—about twelve for me."

"You came up fast, Captain. You'll be cinc here yet."

"That's what you think."

"You're next in line after Cinc Rhys."

"But I'll be out of the Doones," Scott pointed out. "Keep that under your belt, Briggs."

The orderly grunted. "Can't see it, sir. If you don't join another Company, where'll you go?"

"Ever heard of the Keeps?"

Briggs permitted himself a respectful snort. "Sure. They're fine for a binge, but—"

"I'm going to live in one. Montana Keep."

"The Keeps were built with men and machines. I helped at the building of Doone fort. Blood's mixed with the plastic here. We had to hold back the jungle while the technicians were working. Eight months, sir, and never a day passed without some sort of attack. And attacks always meant casualties then. We had only breastworks. The ships laid down a barrage, but barrages aren't impassable. That was a fight, Captain."

Scott thrust out a leg so that Briggs could lace his boots. "And a damn good one. I know." He looked down at the orderly's baldish, brown head where white hairs straggled.

"You know, but you weren't there, Captain. I was. First we dynamited. We cleared a half circle where we could dig in behind breastworks. Behind us were the techs, throwing up a plastic wall as fast as they could. The guns were brought in on barges. Lying offshore were the battlewagons. We could hear the shells go whistling over our heads—it sounded pretty good, because we knew things were O.K. as long as the barrage kept up. But it couldn't be kept up day and night. The jungle broke through. For months the smell of blood hung here, and that drew the enemy."

"But you held them off."

"Sure, we did. Addison Doone was cinc then—he'd formed the Company years before, but we hadn't a fort. Doone fought with us. Saved my life once, in fact. Anyhow—we got the fort built, or rather the techs did. I won't forget the kick I got out of it when the first big gun blasted off from the wall behind us. There was a lot to do after that, but when that shell was fired, we knew we'd done the job."

Scott nodded. "You feel a proprietary interest in the fort, I guess."

Briggs looked puzzled. "The fort? Why, that doesn't mean much, Captain. There are lots of forts. It's something more than that; I don't quite know what it is. It's seeing the fleet out there—breaking in the rookies—giving the old toasts at mess—knowing that—" He stopped at a loss.

Scott's lips twisted wryly.

"You don't really know, do you, Briggs?"

"Know what, sir?"

"Why you stay here. Why you can't believe I'd quit."

Briggs gave a little shrug. "Well,—it's the Doones," he said. "That's all, Captain. It's just that."

"And what the devil will it matter, in a few hundred years?"

"I suppose it won't. No, sir. But it isn't our business to think about that. We're Doonemen, that's all."

Scott didn't answer. He could easily have pointed out the fallacy of Briggs' argument, but what was the use? He stood up, the orderly whisking invisible dust off his tunic.

"All set, sir. Shipshape."

"Check, Briggs. Well, I've one more scrap, anyhow. I'll bring you back a souvenir, eh?"

The orderly saluted, grinning. Scott went out, feeling good. Inwardly he was chuckling rather sardonically at the false values he was supposed to take seriously. Of course many men had died when Doone fort had been built. But did that, in itself, make a tradition? What good was the fort? In a few centuries it would have outlived its usefulness. Then it would be a relic of the past. Civilization moved on, and, these days, civilization merely tolerated the military.

So—what was the use? Sentiment needed a valid reason for its existence. The Free Companions fought, bitterly, doggedly, with insane valor, in order to destroy themselves. The ancient motives for war had vanished.

What was the use? All over Venus the lights of the great forts were going out—and, this time, they would never be lit again—not in a thousand lifetimes!

V

And we are here as on a darkling plain
Swept with confused alarms of struggle and flight,
Where ignorant armies clash by night.
                              —Arnold circa 1870

The fort was a completely self-contained unit, military rather than social. There was no need for any agrarian development, since a state of complete siege never existed. Food could be brought in from the Keeps by water and air.

But military production was important, and, in the life of the fort, the techs played an important part, from the experimental physicist to the spot welder. There were always replacements to be made, for, in battle, there were always casualties. And it was necessary to keep the weapons up-to-date, continually striving to perfect new ones. But strategy and armament were of equal importance. An outnumbered fleet had been known to conquer a stronger one by the use of practical psychology.

Scott found Commander Bienne at the docks, watching the launching of a new sub. Apparently Bienne hadn't yet got over his anger, for he turned a scowling, somber face to the captain as he saluted.

"Hello, commander," Scott said. "I'm making inspection. Are you free?"

Bienne nodded. "There's not much to do."

"Well—routine. We got that sub finished just in time, eh?"

"Yes." Bienne couldn't repress his pleasure at sight of the trim, sleek vessel beginning to slide down the ways. Scott, too, felt his pulses heighten as the sub slipped into the water, raising a mighty splash, and then settling down to a smooth, steady riding on the waves. He looked out to where the great battlewagons stood at anchor, twelve of them, gray-green monsters of plated metal. Each of them carried launching equipment for gliders, but the collapsible aircraft were stowed away out of sight as yet. Smaller destroyers lay like lean-flanked wolves among the battleships. There were two fast carriers, loaded with gliders and flitterboats. There were torpedo boats and one low-riding monitor, impregnable, powerfully armed, but slow. Only a direct hit could disable a monitor, but the behemoths had their disadvantages. The battle was usually over before they lumbered into sight. Like all monitors, this one—the *Armageddon*—was constructed on the principle of a razorback hog, covered, except for the firing ports, by a tureen-shaped shield, strongly braced from within. The *Armageddon* was divided into groups of compartments and had several auxiliary engines, so that, unlike the legendary *Rover*, when a monitor died, it did *not* die all over. It was, in effect, a dinosaur. You could blow off the monster's head, and it would continue to fight with talons and lashing tail. Its heavy guns made up in mobility for the giant's unwieldiness—but the trouble was to get the monitor into battle. It was painfully slow.

Scott scowled. "We're fighting over Venus Deep, eh?"

"Yes," Bienne nodded. "That still goes. The Helldivers are already heading toward Montana Keep, and we'll intercept them over the Deep."

"When's zero hour?"

"Midnight tonight."

Scott closed his eyes, visualizing their course on a mental chart. Not so good. When battle was joined near island groups, it was sometimes possible for a monitor to slip up under cover of the islets, but that trick wouldn't work now.

Too bad—for the Helldivers were a strong outfit, more so since their recent merger with O'Brien's Legion. Even with the Mob to help, the outcome of the scrap would be anyone's guess. The *Armageddon* might be the decisive factor.

"I wonder—" Scott said. "No. It'd be impossible."

"What?"

"Camouflaging the *Armageddon*. If the Helldivers see the monitor coming, they'll lead the fight away from it, faster than that tub can follow. I was thinking we might get her into the battle without the enemy realizing it."

"She's camouflaged now."

"Paint, that's all. She can be spotted. I had some screwy idea about disguising her as an island or a dead whale."

"She's too big for a whale and floating islands look a bit suspicious."

"Yeah. But if we *could* slip the *Armageddon* in without scaring off the enemy—Hm-m-m. Monitors have a habit of turning turtle, don't they?"

"Right. They're top-heavy. But a monitor can't fight upside down. It's not such a bright idea, Captain." Briefly Bienne's sunken eyes gleamed with sneering mockery. Scott grunted and turned away.

"All right. Let's take a look around."

The fleet was shipshape. Scott went to the shops. He learned that several new hulls were under way, but would not be completed by zero hour. With Bienne, he continued to the laboratory offices. Nothing new. No slip-ups; no surprises. The machine was running smoothly.

By the time inspection was completed, Scott had an idea. He told Bienne to carry on and went to find Cinc Rhys. The cinc was in his office, just clicking off the telaudio as Scott appeared.

"That was Mendez," Rhys said. "The Mob's meeting our fleet a hundred miles off the coast. They'll be under our orders, of course. A good man, Mendez, but I don't entirely trust him."

"You're not thinking of a double cross, sir?"

Cinc Rhys made disparaging noises. "Brutus is an honorable man. No, he'll stick to his bargain. But I wouldn't cut cards with Mendez. As a Free Companion, he's trustworthy. Personally— Well, how do things look?"

"Very good, sir. I've an idea about the *Armageddon*."

"I wish I had," Rhys said frankly. "We can't get that damned scow into the battle in any way I can figure out. The Helldivers will see it coming, and lead the fight away."

"I'm thinking of camouflage."

"A monitor's a monitor. It's unmistakable. You can't make it look like anything else."

"With one exception, sir. You can make it look like a disabled monitor."

Rhys sat back, giving Scott a startled glance. "That's interesting. Go on."

"Look here, sir." The captain used a stylo to sketch the outline of a monitor on a convenient pad. "Above the surface, the *Armageddon*'s dome-shaped. Below, it's a bit different, chiefly because of the keel. Why can't we put a fake superstructure on the monitor—build a false keel on it, so it'll seem capsized?"

"It's possible."

"Everybody knows a monitor's weak spot—that it turns turtle under fire sometimes. If the Helldivers saw an apparently capsized *Armageddon* drifting toward them, they'd naturally figure the tub was disabled."

"It's crazy," Rhys said. "One of those crazy ideas that might work." He used the local telaudio to issue crisp orders. "Got it? Good. Get the *Armageddon* under way as soon as the equipment's aboard. Alterations will be made at sea. We can't waste time. If we had them made in the yards, she'd never catch up with the fleet."

The cinc broke the connection, his seamed, leathery face twisting into a grin. "I hope it works. We'll see."

He snapped his fingers. "Almost forgot. President Crosby's nephew—Kane?—he was with you when you cracked up, wasn't he? I've been wondering whether I should have waived training for him. How did he show up in the jungle?"

"Quite well," Scott said. "I had my eye on him. He'll make a good soldier."

Rhys looked keenly at the captain. "What about discipline? I felt that was his weak spot."

"I've no complaint to make."

"So. Well, maybe. Starling's outfit is bad training for anyone—especially a raw kid. Speaking of Starling, did Cinc Mendez know anything about his using atomic power?"

"No, sir. If Starling's doing that, he's keeping it plenty quiet."

"We'll investigate after the battle. Can't afford that sort of thing—we don't want another holocaust. It was bad enough to lose Earth. It decimated the race. If it happened again, it'd wipe the race out."

"I don't think there's much danger of that. On Earth, it was the big atomic-power stations that got out of control. At worst, Starling can't have more than hand weapons."

"True. You can't blow up a world with those. But you know the law—no atomic power on Venus."

Scott nodded.

"Well, that's all." Rhys waved him away. "Clear weather."

Which, on this perpetually clouded world, had a tinge of irony.

After mess Scott returned to his quarters, for a smoke and a brief rest. He waved away Briggs' suggestion of a rubdown and sent the orderly to the commissary for fresh tobacco.

"Be sure to get Twenty Star," he cautioned. "I don't want that green hydroponic cabbage."

"I know the brand, sir." Briggs looked hurt and departed. Scott settled back in his relaxer, sighing.

Zero hour at twelve. The last zero hour he'd ever know. All through the day he had been conscious that he was fulfilling his duties for the last time.

His mind went back to Montana Keep. He was living again those other-worldly moments in the cloud-wrapped Olympus with Ilene. Curiously, he found it difficult to visualize the girl's features. Perhaps she was a symbol—her appearance did not matter. Yet she was very lovely.

In a different way from Jeana. Scott glanced at Jeana's picture on the desk, three-dimensional and tinted after life. By pressing a button on the frame, he could have given it sound and motion. He leaned forward and touched the tiny stud. In the depths of the picture the figure of Jeana stirred, smiling. The red lips parted.

Her voice, though soft, was quite natural.

"Hello, Brian," the recording said. "Wish I were with you now. Here's a present, darling." The image blew him a kiss, and then faded back to immobility.

Scott sighed again. Jeana was a comfortable sort of person. But— Oh, hell! She wasn't willing to change. Very likely she couldn't. Ilene perhaps was equally dogmatic, but she represented the life of the Keeps—and that was what Scott wanted now.

It was an artificial life Ilene lived, but she was honest about it. She knew its values were false. At least she didn't pretend, like the Free Companions, that there were ideals worth dying for. Scott remembered Briggs. The fact that men had been killed during the building of Doone fort meant a lot to the old orderly. He never asked himself—why? Why had they died? Why was Doone fort built in the first place? For war. And war was doomed.

One had to believe in an ideal before devoting one's life

to it. One had to feel he was helping the ideal to survive—watering the plant with his blood so eventually it would come to flower. The red flower of Mars had long since blown. How did that old poem go?

> One thing is certain, and the rest is lies;
> The flower that once has blown forever dies.

It was true. But the Free Companions blindly pretended that the flower was still in blazing scarlet bloom, refusing to admit that even the roots were withered and useless, scarcely able now to suck up the blood sacrificed to its hopeless thirst.

New flowers bloomed; new buds opened. But in the Keeps, not in the great doomed forts. It was the winter cycle, and, as the last season's blossoms faded, the buds of the next stirred into life. Life questing and intolerant. Life that fed on the rotting petals of the rose of war.

But the pretense went on, in the coastal forts that guarded the Keeps. Scott made a grimace of distaste. Blind, stupid folly! He was a man first, not a soldier. And man is essentially a hedonist, whether he identifies himself with the race or not.

Scott could not. He was not part of the undersea culture, and he could never be. But he could lose himself in the hedonistic backwash of the Keeps, the froth that always overlies any social unit. With Ilene, he could, at least, seek happiness, without the bitter self-mockery he had known for so long. Mockery at his own emotional weaknesses in which he did not believe.

Ilene was honest. She knew she was damned, because unluckily she had intelligence.

So—Scott thought—they would make a good pair.

Scott looked up as Commander Bienne came into the room. Bienne's sour, mahogany face was flushed deep red under the bronze. His lids were heavy over angry eyes. He swung the door-curtain shut after him and stood rocking on his heels, glowering at Scott.

He called Scott something unprintable.

The captain rose, an icy knot of fury in his stomach. Very softly he said, "You're drunk, Bienne. Get out. Get back to your quarters."

"Sure—you little tinhorn soldier. You like to give orders, don't you? You like to chisel, too. The way you chiseled me out of that left-wing command today. I'm pretty sick of it, Captain Brian Scott."

"Don't be a damned fool! I don't like you personally any more than you like me, but that's got nothing to do with the Company. I recommended you for that command."

"You lie," Bienne said, swaying. "And I hate your guts."

Scott went pale, the scar on his cheek flaming red. Bienne came forward. He wasn't too drunk to coordinate. His fist lashed out suddenly and connected agonizingly with Scott's molar.

The captain's reach was less than Bienne's. He ducked inside of the next swing and carefully smashed a blow home on the point of the other's jaw. Bienne was driven back, crashing against the wall and sliding down in a limp heap, his head lolling forward.

Scott, rubbing his knuckles, looked down, considering. Presently he knelt and made a quick examination. A knockout, that was all.

Oh, well.

Briggs appeared, showing no surprise at sight of Bienne's motionless body. The perfect orderly walked across to the table and began to refill the humidor with the tobacco he had brought.

Scott almost chuckled.

"Briggs."

"Yes, sir?"

"Commander Bienne's had a slight accident. He— slipped. Hit his chin on something. He's a bit tight, too. Fix him up, will you?"

"With pleasure, sir." Briggs hoisted Bienne's body across his brawny shoulders.

"Zero hour's at twelve. The commander must be aboard the *Flintlock* by then. And sober. Can do?"

"Certainly, sir," Briggs said, and went out.

Scott returned to his chair, filling his pipe. He should have confined Bienne to his quarters, of course. But—well, this was a personal matter. One could afford to stretch a point, especially since Bienne was a valuable man to have aboard during action. Scott vaguely hoped the commander would get his thick head blown off.

After a time he tapped the dottle from his pipe and went off for a final inspection.

At midnight the fleet hoisted anchor.

By dawn the Doones were nearing the Venus Deep.

The ships of the Mob had already joined them, seven battleships, and assorted cruisers, destroyers, and one carrier. No monitor. The Mob didn't own one—it had capsized two months before, and was still undergoing repairs.

The combined fleets sailed in crescent formation, the left wing, commanded by Scott, composed of his own ship, the *Flintlock*, and the *Arquebus*, the *Arrow*, and the *Misericordia*, all Doone battlewagons. There were two Mob ships with him, the *Navaho* and the *Zuni*, the latter commanded by Cinc Mendez. Scott had one carrier with him, the other being at right wing. Besides these, there were the lighter craft.

In the center were the battleships *Arbalest*, *Lance*, *Gatling*, and *Mace*, as well as three of Mendez's. Cinc Rhys was aboard the *Lance*, controlling operations. The camouflaged monitor *Armageddon* was puffing away valiantly far behind, well out of sight in the mists.

Scott was in his control room, surrounded by teleaudio screens and switchboards. Six operators were perched on stools before the controls, ready to jump to action when orders came through their earphones. In the din of battle spoken commands often went unheard, which was why Scott wore a hush-mike strapped to his chest.

His eyes roved over the semicircle of screens before him.

"Any report from the gliders yet?"

"No, sir."

"Get me air-spotting command."

One of the screens flamed to life; a face snapped into view on it.

"Report."

"Nothing yet, Captain. Wait." There was a distant thunder. "Detectors clamped on a teleaudio tight-beam directly overhead."

"Enemy glider in the clouds?"

"Apparently. It's out of the focus now."

"Try to relocate it."

A lot of good that would do. Motored planes could easily be detected overhead, but a glider was another matter. The only way to spot one was by clamping a detector focus directly on the glider's teleaudio beam—worse than a needle in a haystack. Luckily the crates didn't carry bombs.

"Report coming in, sir. One of our gliders."

Another screen showed a face. "Pilot reporting, sir. Located enemy."

"Good. Switch in the teleaudio, infra. What sector?"

"V. D. eight hundred seven northwest twenty-one."

Scott said into his hush-mike, "Get Cinc Rhys and Commander Geer on tight-beam. And Cinc Mendez."

Three more screens lit up, showing the faces of the three officers.

"Cut in the pilot."

Somewhere over Venus Deep the glider pilot was arc-ing his plane through the cloud-layer, the automatic telaudio-camera, lensed to infrared, penetrating the murk and revealing the ocean below. On the screen ships showed, driving forward in battle formation.

Scott recognized and enumerated them mentally. The *Orion*, the *Sirius,* the *Vega,* the *Polaris*—uh-huh. Lighter ships. Plenty of them. The scanner swept on.

Cinc Rhys said, "We're outnumbered badly. Cinc Mendez, are your sub-detectors in operation?"

"They are. Nothing yet."

"We'll join battle in half an hour, I judge. We've located them, and they've no doubt located us."

"Check."

The screens blanked out. Scott settled back, alertly at ease. Nothing to do now but wait, keeping ready for the unexpected. The *Orion* and the *Vega* were the Helldivers' biggest battleships, larger than anything in the line of the Doones—or the Mob. Cinc Flynn was no doubt aboard the *Orion.* The Helldivers owned a monitor, but it had not showed on the infrared aerial scanner. Probably the behemoth wouldn't even show up in time for the battle.

But even without the monitor, the Helldivers had an overwhelming surface display. Moreover, their undersea fleet was an important factor. The sub-detectors of Cinc Mendez might—probably would—cut down the odds. But possibly not enough.

The *Armageddon,* Scott thought, might be the point of decision, the ultimate argument. And, as yet, the camouflaged monitor was lumbering through the waves far in the wake of the Doones.

Commander Bienne appeared on a screen. He had frozen into a disciplined, trained robot, personal animosities forgotten for the time. Active duty did that to a man.

Scott expected nothing different, however, and his

voice was completely impersonal as he acknowledged Bienne's call.

"The flitterboats are ready to go, Captain."

"Send them out in fifteen minutes. Relay to left wing, all ships carrying flitters."

"Check."

For a while there was silence. A booming explosion brought Scott to instant alertness. He glanced up at the screens.

A new face appeared. "Helldivers opening up. Testing for range. They must have gliders overhead. We can't spot 'em."

"Get the men under cover. Send up a test barrage. Prepare for return fire. Contact our pilots over the Helldivers."

It was beginning now—the incessant, racking thunder that would continue till the last shot was fired. Scott cut in to Cinc Rhys as the latter signaled.

"Reporting, sir."

"Harry the enemy. We can't do much yet. Change to R-8 formation."

Cinc Mendez said, "We've got three enemy subs. Our detectors are tuned up to high pitch."

"Limit the range so our subs will be outside the sphere of influence."

"Already did that. The enemy's using magnetic depth charges, laying an undersea barrage as they advance."

"I'll talk to the sub command." Rhys cut off. Scott listened to the increasing fury of explosions. He could not yet hear the distinctive *clap-clap* of heat rays, but the quarters were not yet close enough for those undependable, though powerful, weapons. It took time for a heat ray to warm up, and during that period a well-aimed bullet could smash the projector lens.

"Casualty, sir. Direct hit aboard destroyer *Bayonet*."

"Extent of damage?"

"Not disabled. Complete report later."

After a while a glider pilot came in on the beam.

"Shell landed on the *Polaris,* sir."

"Use the scanner."

It showed the Helldivers' battlewagon, part of the superstructure carried away, but obviously still in fighting trim. Scott nodded. Both sides were getting the range now. The hazy clouds still hid each fleet from the other, but they were nearing.

The sound of artillery increased. Problems of trajectory were increased by the violent winds of Venus, but accurate aiming was possible. Scott nodded grimly as a crash shook the *Flintlock.*

They were getting it now. Here, in the brain of the ship, he was as close to the battle as any member of a firing crew. The screens were his eyes.

They had the advantage of being able to use infrared, so that Scott, buried here, could see more than he could have on deck, with his naked eye. Something loomed out of the murk and Scott's breath stopped before he recognized the lines of the Doone battlewagon *Misericordia.* She was off course. The captain used his hush-mike to snap a quick reprimand.

Flitterboats were going out now, speedy hornets that would harry the enemy fleet. In one of them, Scott remembered, was Norman Kane. He thought of Ilene and thrust the thought back, out of his mind. No time for that now.

Battle stations allowed no time for wool gathering.

The distant vanguard of the Helldivers came into sight on the screens. Cinc Mendez called.

"Eleven more subs. One got through. Seems to be near the *Flintlock.* Drop depth bombs."

Scott nodded and obeyed. Shuddering concussions shook the ship. Presently a report came in: fuel slick to starboard.

Good. A few well-placed torpedoes could do a lot of damage.

The *Flintlock* heeled incessantly under the action of the heavy guns. Heat rays were lancing out. The big ships could not easily avoid the searing blasts that could melt solid metal, but the flitterboats, dancing around like angry insects, sent a rain of bullets at the projectors. But even that took integration. The rays themselves were invisible, and could only be traced from their targets. The camera crews were working overtime, snapping shots of the enemy ships, tracing the rays' points of origin, and telaudioing the information to the flitterboats.

"Helldivers' *Rigel* out of action."

On the screen the big destroyer swung around, bow pointing forward. She was going to ram. Scott snapped orders. The *Flintlock* went hard over, guns pouring death into the doomed *Rigel*.

The ships passed, so close that men on the *Flintlock*'s decks could see the destroyer lurching through the haze. Scott judged her course and tried desperately to get Mendez. There was a delay.

"QM—QM—emergency! Get the *Zuni*!"

"Here she answers, sir."

Scott snapped, "Change course. QM. Destroyer *Rigel* bearing down on you."

"Check." The screen blanked. Scott used a scanner. He groaned at the sight. The *Zuni* was swinging fast, but the *Rigel* was too close—too damned close.

She rammed.

Scott said, "Hell." That put the *Zuni* out of action. He reported to Cinc Rhys.

"All right, Captain. Continue R-8 formation."

Mendez appeared on a screen. "Captain Scott. We're disabled. I'm coming aboard. Have to direct sub-strafing operations. Can you give me a control board?"

"Yes, sir. Land at Port Sector 7."

*   *   *

Hidden in the mist, the fleets swept on in parallel courses, the big battlewagons keeping steady formation, pouring heat rays and shells across the gap. The lighter ships strayed out of line at times, but the flitterboats swarmed like midges, dog-fighting when they were not harrying the larger craft. Gliders were useless now, at such close quarters.

The thunder crashed and boomed. Shudders rocked the *Flintlock*.

"Hit on Helldivers' *Orion.* Hit on *Sirius.*"

"Hit on Mob ship *Apache.*"

"Four more enemy subs destroyed."

"Doone sub X-*16* fails to report."

"Helldivers' *Polaris* seems disabled."

"Send out auxiliary flitterboats, units nine and twenty."

Cinc Mendez came in, breathing hard. Scott waved him to an auxiliary control unit seat.

"Hit on *Lance.* Wait a minute. Cinc Rhys a casualty, sir."

Scott froze. "Details."

"One moment— Dead, sir."

"Very well," Scott said after a moment. "I'm assuming command. Pass it along."

He caught a sidelong glance from Mendez. When a Company's cinc was killed, one of two things happened— promotion of a new cinc, or a merger with another Company. In this case Scott was required, by his rank, to assume temporarily the fleet's command. Later, at the Doone fort, there would be a meeting and a final decision.

He scarcely thought of that now. Rhys dead! Tough, unemotional old Rhys, killed in action. Rhys had a free-wife in some Keep, Scott remembered. The Company would pension her. Scott had never seen the woman. Oddly, he wondered what she was like. The question had never occurred to him before.

The screens were flashing. Double duty now—or triple. Scott forgot everything else in directing the battle.

It was like first-stage anesthesia—it was difficult to judge time. It might have been an hour or six since the battle had started. Or less than an hour, for that matter.

"Destroyer disabled. Cruiser disabled. Three enemy subs out of action—"

It went on, endlessly. At the auxiliaries Mendez was directing sub-strafing operations. Where in hell's the *Armageddon,* Scott thought? The fight would be over before that overgrown tortoise arrived.

Abruptly a screen flashed QM. The lean, beak-nosed face of Cinc Flynn of the Helldivers showed.

"Calling Doone command."

"Acknowledging," Scott said. "Captain Scott, emergency command."

Why was Flynn calling? Enemy fleets in action never communicated, except to surrender.

Flynn said curtly, "You're using atomic power, Captain. Explanation, please."

Mendez jerked around. Scott felt a tight band around his stomach.

"Done without my knowledge or approval, of course, Cinc Flynn. My apologies. Details?"

"One of your flitterboats fired an atomic-powered pistol at the *Orion.*"

"Damage?"

"One seven-unit gun disabled."

"One of ours, of the same caliber, will be taken out of action immediately. Further details, sir?"

"Use your scanner, Captain, on Sector Mobile 18 south *Orion.* Your apology is accepted. The incident will be erased from our records."

Flynn clicked off. Scott used the scanner, catching a Doone flitterboat in its focus. He used the enlarger.

The little boat was fleeing from enemy fire, racing back

toward the Doone fleet, heading directly toward the *Flint-lock*, Scott saw. Through the transparent shell he saw the bombardier slumped motionless, his head blown half off. The pilot, still gripping an atomic-fire pistol in one hand, was Norman Kane. Blood streaked his boyish, strained face.

So Starling's outfit did have atomic power, then. Kane must have smuggled the weapon out with him when he left. And, in the excitement of battle, he had used it against the enemy.

Scott said coldly, "Gun crews starboard. Flitterboat Z-19-4. Blast it."

Almost immediately a shell burst near the little craft. On the screen Kane looked up, startled by his own side firing upon him. Comprehension showed on his face. He swung the flitterboat off course, zigzagging, trying desperately to dodge the barrage.

Scott watched, his lips grimly tight. The flitterboat exploded in a rain of spray and debris.

Automatic court-martial.

After the battle, the Companies would band together and smash Starling's outfit.

Meantime, this was action. Scott returned to his screens, erasing the incident from his mind.

Very gradually, the balance of power was increasing with the Helldivers. Both sides were losing ships, put out of action rather than sunk, and Scott thought more and more often of the monitor *Armageddon*. She could turn the battle now. But she was still far astern.

Scott never felt the explosion that wrecked the control room. His senses blacked out without warning.

He could not have been unconscious for long. When he opened his eyes, he stared up at a shambles. He seemed to be the only man left alive. But it could not have been a direct hit, or he would not have survived either.

He was lying on his back, pinned down by a heavy

crossbeam. But no bones were broken. Blind, incredible luck had helped him there. The brunt of the damage had been borne by the operators. They were dead, Scott saw at a glance.

He tried to crawl out from under the beam, but that was impossible. In the thunder of battle his voice could not be heard.

There was a movement across the room, halfway to the door. Cinc Mendez stumbled up and stared around, blinking. Red smeared his plump cheeks.

He saw Scott and stood, rocking back and forth, staring. Then he put his hand on the butt of his pistol.

Scott could very easily read the other's mind. If the Doone captain died now, the chances were that Mendez could merge with the Doones and assume control. The politico-military balance lay that way.

If Scott lived, it was probable that he would be elected cinc.

It was, therefore, decidedly to Mendez's advantage to kill the prisoned man.

A shadow crossed the doorway. Mendez, his back to the newcomer, did not see Commander Bienne halt on the threshold, scowling at the tableau. Scott knew that Bienne understood the situation as well as he himself did. The commander realized that in a very few moments Mendez would draw his gun and fire.

Scott waited. The cinc's fingers tightened on his gun belt.

Bienne, grinning crookedly, said, "I thought that shell had finished you, sir. Guess it's hard to kill a Dooneman."

Mendez took his hand off the gun, instantly regaining his poise. He turned to Bienne.

"I'm glad you're here, commander. It'll probably take both of us to move that beam."

"Shall we try, sir?"

Between the two of them, they managed to shift the

weight off Scott's torso. Briefly the latter's eyes met Bienne's. There was still no friendliness in them, but there was a look of wry self-mockery.

Bienne hadn't saved Scott's life, exactly. It was, rather, a question of being a Dooneman. For Bienne was, first of all, a soldier, and a member of the Free Company.

Scott tested his limbs; they worked.

"How long was I out, commander?"

"Ten minutes, sir. The *Armageddon*'s in sight."

"Good. Are the Helldivers veering off?"

Bienne shook his head. "So far they're not suspicious."

Scott grunted and made his way to the door, the others at his heels. Mendez said, "We'll need another control ship."

"All right. The *Arquebus*. Commander, take over here. Cinc Mendez—"

A flitterboat took them to the *Arquebus,* which was still in good fighting trim. The monitor *Armageddon,* Scott saw, was rolling helplessly in the trough of the waves. In accordance with the battle plan, the Doone ships were leading the Helldivers toward the apparently capsized giant. The technicians had done a good job; the false keel looked shockingly convincing.

Aboard the *Arquebus,* Scott took over, giving Mendez the auxiliary control for his sub-strafers. The cinc beamed at Scott over his shoulder.

"Wait till that monitor opens up, Captain."

"Yeah . . . we're in bad shape, though."

Neither man mentioned the incident that was in both their minds. It was tacitly forgotten—the only thing to do now.

Guns were still bellowing. The Helldivers were pouring their fire into the Doone formation, and they were winning. Scott scowled at the screens. If he waited too long, it would be just too bad.

Presently he put a beam on the *Armageddon.* She was

in a beautiful position now, midway between two of the Helldivers' largest battleships.

"Unmask. Open fire."

Firing ports opened on the monitor. The sea titan's huge guns snouted into view. Almost simultaneously they blasted, the thunder drowning out the noise of the lighter guns.

"All Doone ships attack," Scott said. "Plan R-7."

This was it. *This was it!*

The Doones raced in to the kill. Blasting, bellowing, shouting, the guns tried to make themselves heard above the roaring of the monitor. They could not succeed, but that savage, invincible onslaught won the battle.

It was nearly impossible to maneuver a monitor into battle formation, but, once that was accomplished, the only thing that could stop the monster was atomic power.

But the Helldivers fought on, trying strategic formation. They could not succeed. The big battlewagons could not get out of range of the *Armageddon*'s guns. And that meant—

Cinc Flynn's face showed on the screen.

"Capitulation, sir. Cease firing."

Scott gave orders. The roar of the guns died into humming, incredible silence.

"You gave us a great battle, cinc."

"Thanks. So did you. Your strategy with the monitor was excellent."

So—that was that. Scott felt something go limp inside of him. Flynn's routine words were meaningless; Scott was drained of the vital excitement that had kept him going till now.

The rest was pure formula.

Token depth charges would be dropped over Virginia Keep. They would not harm the Dome, but they were the rule. There would be the ransom, paid always by the Keep which backed the losing side. A supply of korium, or its negotiable equivalent. The Doone treasury would be swelled. Part of the money would go into replacements and new keels. The life of the forts would go on.

Alone at the rail of the *Arquebus,* heading for Virginia Keep, Scott watched slow darkness change the clouds from pearl to gray, and then to invisibility. He was alone in the night. The wash of waves came up to him softly as the *Arquebus* rushed to her destination, three hundred miles away.

Warm yellow lights gleamed from ports behind him, but he did not turn. This, he thought, was like the cloud-wrapped Olympus in Montana Keep, where he had promised Ilene—many things.

Yet there was a difference. In an Olympus a man was like god, shut away completely from the living world. Here, in the unbroken dark, there was no sense of alienage. Nothing could be seen—Venus has no moon, and the clouds hid the stars. And the seas are not phosphorescent.

Beneath these waters stand the Keeps, Scott thought. They hold the future. Such battles as were fought today are fought so that the Keeps may not be destroyed.

And men will sacrifice. Men have always sacrificed, for a social organization or a military unit. Man must create his own ideal. "If there had been no God, man would have created Him."

Bienne had sacrificed today, in a queer, twisted way of loyalty to his fetish. Yet Bienne still hated him, Scott knew.

The Doones meant nothing. Their idea was a false one. Yet, because men were faithful to that ideal, civilization would rise again from the guarded Keeps. A civilization that would forget its doomed guardians, the watchers of the seas of Venus, the Free Companions yelling their mad, futile battle cry as they drove on—as this ship was driving—into a night that would have no dawn.

Ilene.

Jeana.

It was no such simple choice. It was, in fact, no real choice at all. For Scott knew, very definitely, that he could never, as long as he lived, believe wholeheartedly in the Free Companions. Always a sardonic devil deep within him would be laughing in bitter self-mockery.

The whisper of the waves drifted up.

It wasn't sensible. It was sentimental, crazy, stupid, slopping thinking.

But Scott knew, now, that he wasn't going back to Ilene.

He was a fool.

But he was a soldier.

When Kuttner and Moore wrote Clash by Night, *they created a sub-genre of SF about mercenaries based on the condottieri of Quattrocento Italy. Hammer's Slammers and my career as a professional writer stem more or less directly from the fact I read this story when I was thirteen. Gordy Dickson, Jerry Pournelle, and I suspect many other writers could say something similar.*

—DAD

About the Authors

Raymond Banks was known for intricate, well-plotted science fiction stories that appeared in a variety of science fiction magazines, including *The Magazine of Fantasy & Science Fiction* and *Galaxy*, during the 1950s and 60s. Some of his notable stories are "The Short Ones," "The Littlest People," and "The City that Loves You."

James Blish (1921–1975) spent his career writing stories about certain aspects of science fiction, psychic powers, miniature humans, and antigravity, for example, and then expanded those stories into longer pieces with the broader scope of a novel. The finished pieces *The Seedling Stars*, *A Case of Conscience*, and *Jack of Eagles* are prime examples of how his novels grew from short stories. He also produced excellent television novelizations, most notably the *Star Trek* logs 1–12 and the classic novel *Spock Must Die!*

David Drake writes, "I was born in 1945, got my undergraduate degree at the University of Iowa, and was in the middle of Duke Law School when I was drafted and sent to Viet Nam. I came back, finished law school, and became for eight years Assistant Town Attorney for the Town of Chapel Hill. I'd never thought of being a writer, but I've always loved to tell stories. I'd sold a few stories before I was drafted. After I came back to the World I started writing seriously—as therapy, I now believe, though at the time I loudly told myself that I was fine, perfectly normal. (Thank goodness the way I was then *isn't* normal, at least for human beings.) The Hammer's Slammers series, of which this is an example, resulted from that focus on writing after my return."

Joe Haldeman's first science fiction novel, *The Forever War*, won both the Hugo and Nebula Awards when it was published in 1974. Since then, he has returned to the theme of future war several times, most notably in his trilogy *Worlds*, *Worlds Apart*, and *Worlds Enough and Time*, about a future Earth facing nuclear extinction, and *Forever Peace*, a further exploration of the dehumanizing potential of armed conflict. Other novels include *Mindbridge*, *All My Sins Remembered*, and his alternate world opus *The Hemingway Hoax*, expanded from his Nebula Award–winning novella of the same name. His powerful non-science fiction writing includes *War Year*, drawn from experiences during his tour of duty in Viet Nam, and *1968*, a portrait of America in the Viet Nam era.

Harry Harrison has turned out many multi-layered science fiction novels that examine the evolution of war, bureaucracy, and society while masquerading as comedic space opera adventures. His series characters include interstellar thief, con man, and troubleshooter "Slippery Jim" DiGriz, from the *Stainless Steel Rat* series, hapless soldier Bill in the *Bill the Galactic Hero* novels, and numerous others. He is also a renowned editor, having worked with such luminaries in the field as John W. Campbell, Brian Aldiss, and Bruce McAllister. He has also edited his own anthologies, including the acclaimed *Nova* series.

Henry Kuttner (1914–1958) was primarily known for his work in science fiction, but occasionally turned out a witty dark fantasy or horror story like "Masquerade." The best of his short fiction can be found in the collection *A Gnome There Was*, *No Boundaries*, and *Return to Otherness*. He cut his teeth writing for *Weird Tales*, but his inventiveness and explorations of themes such as the robots, wonder children and madmen from the future soon had him contributing to many of the most popular magazines of the Pulp era. Working with his wife and writing partner C.L. Moore, he revisited the setting of "Clash by Night" in their excellent novel *Fury*.

Keith Laumer (1925–1993) was best known for his series of stories and novels about the interstellar diplomat Jaime Retief, but he had written all types of science fiction in his career, from razor-sharp military fiction in his *Bolo* series to alternate reality fiction in his Imperium novels. His experience in the U.S. Army and Air Force served him well in extrapolating what the military of the future might be like. His diplomatic Retief stories were also grounded in real life experience from his tour of duty as a Foreign Service Vice-Consul in Rangoon.

Richard Matheson is one of the most respected dark fantasy and horror writers of the past forty years. His novel *I Am Legend* is considered one of the seminal vampire novels of the 20th century, a classic tale of the last man on an Earth that is populated entirely by the undead. His books *The Shrinking Man* and *Hell House* also broke new ground in the horror field. His work has been adapted for television as well, most notably as several episodes of original *Twilight*

Zone series, and also made into several recent motion pictures, including *What Dreams May Come* and *The Haunting*.

C.L. Moore (1911–1987) never gained the critical or popular acclaim she deserved as one of the earliest female science fiction writers. She was often an uncredited coauthor with Henry Kuttner, combining on books that crossed the boundary between science fiction and fantasy such as *Valley of the Flame* and *Well of the Worlds*. However, the short fiction she wrote alone deserves recognition on its own merits of strong character development and psychological motivation of those characters. The two stories she's best known for are her first published tale "Shambleau," which introduced her hero Northwest Smith, and "Vintage Season" which details a group of tourists from the future watching the past unobserved, the latter considered a classic tale of speculative fiction.

David Drake writes, "Mark L. Van Name, born in 1955, is Executive Vice President and General Manager, eTesting Labs Inc., a Ziff Davis Media company. He's a geek, which isn't uncommon today, and he's highly literate; which has never been common. The combination is close to unique; it made Mark one of the top computer journalists in the world before he moved into upper management. He's sold over a thousand computer-related articles, a couple dozen essays, and nine SF stories. For reasons that may become evident in this story, Mark is one of my closest friends. If we were either of us different people, that would scare the hell out of us."

As a small boy, Gene Wolfe used to hide behind the candy case in the Richmond Pharmacy to read the pulps—and in a sense, he says, he has never come out. His wife, Rosemary tries to keep him out of mischief . . . still unaware—they've been together for more than 40 years—that he is it. He's written "No Planets Strike," which was nominated for a Hugo, plus a couple of hundred other stories. Also some books, he says with grand understatement, including *Operation Ares*, *The Fifth Head of Cerberus* and *Shadow & Claw*. The most recent is *Exodus From The Long Sun* . . . part of *The Book Of The Long Sun*, a tetrology.

VISIT WARNER ASPECT ONLINE!

THE WARNER ASPECT HOMEPAGE

You'll find us at: www.twbookmark.com then by clicking on Science Fiction and Fantasy.

NEW AND UPCOMING TITLES

Each month we feature our new titles and reader favorites.

AUTHOR INFO

Author bios, bibliographies and links to personal websites.

CONTESTS AND OTHER FUN STUFF

Advance galley giveaways, autographed copies, and more.

THE ASPECT BUZZ

What's new, hot and upcoming from Warner Aspect: awards news, bestsellers, movie tie-in information . . .